KNAVE OF SANDS

For Michael

TO SAERJA

WRAVELLIAN

QUORMANTH

BELLGARD

THE MOUNTAIN PASS

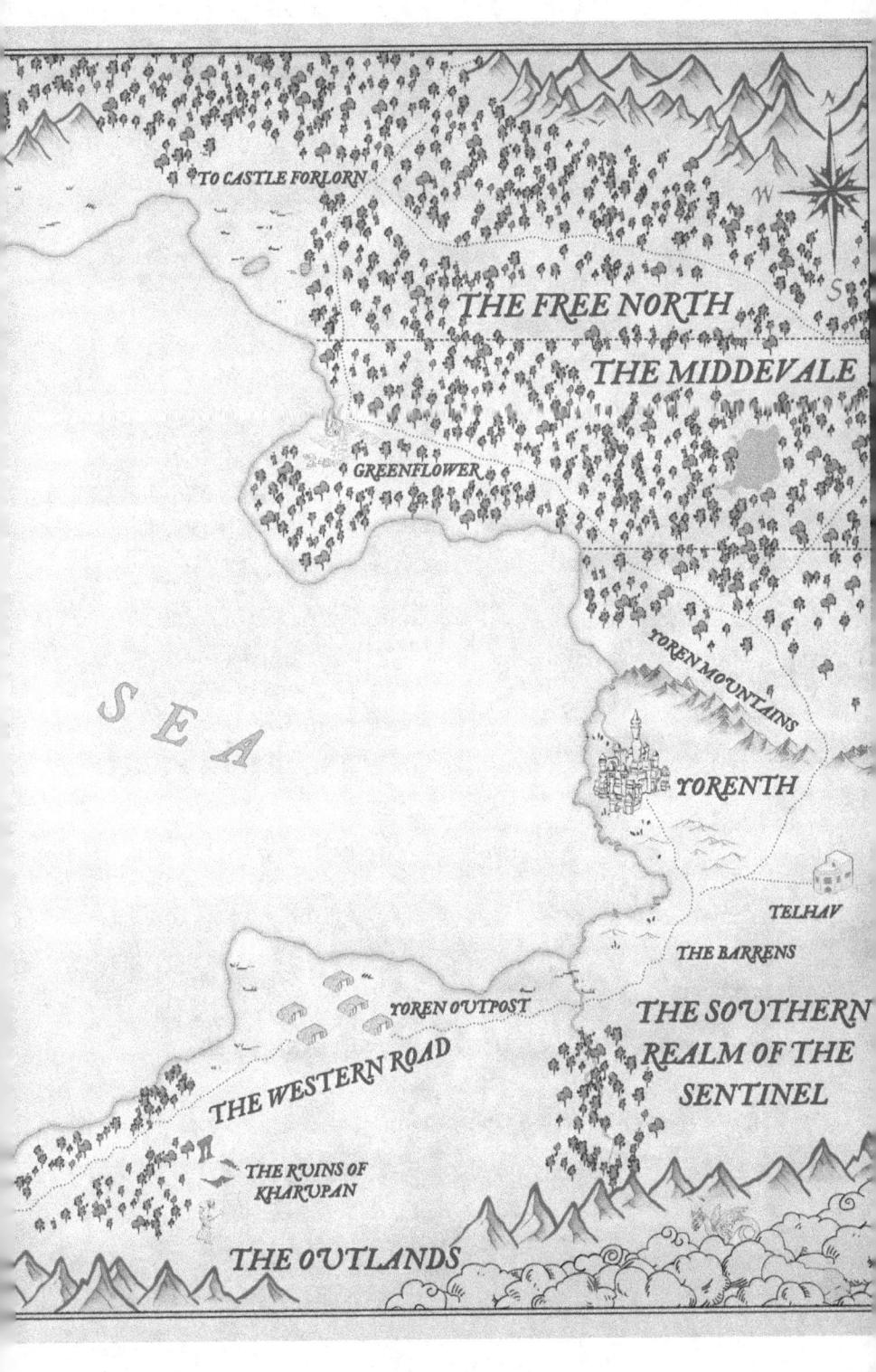

1

KYR

A SMUGGLER'S moon was rising over the spire-toothed sky of Yorenth, a blackbird casting its watchful eye upon a pair like any other, who had set out that evening on portentous dealings.

The usual din of the glassworks—roaring fires and pounding forge hammers, endless metallic grinding and the occasional shattering—had only picked up as night fell and the malaise of the day's heat faded.

The pair walked against the crowd headed to the heart of the Sledge for the Threydas night market like two poison eels, the woman of the pair glancing jealously back at passersby.

'Kyr,' the man drawled, focusing her.

'Sylas,' she singsonged back.

Errands were always a source of distractions for Kyr. As they walked, she'd been remembering night markets past, but it could be as simple as stopping to admire a cat she passed on the street or imagining the details of someone's life by the worn lines of their face, before realizing she'd walked all the way back to the Knaves' Keep, lost in a dream.

Kyr liked to daydream.

'We're here,' Sylas said gruffly, stopping before a nondescript green door and adjusting the long, brown, woolen cloak he always wore. 'Remember, you're here to observe.'

Kyr rolled her eyes. 'I know, I know. I won't embarrass you, myself, or by extension, the guild,' she said, saluting half-heartedly.

Sylas chuckled, muttering under his breath, 'Lady guide us.' She never knew what he meant by that.

Clearing his throat, Sylas gripped the tarnished brass handle and swept the door open with such force it swung around and hit the wall behind it.

Kyr peered over his shoulder into the dimly-lit, haze-filled room—ostensibly where the trade union met during the day—and saw a man with his back to them, sitting at a long wooden table littered with official-looking papers and illuminated by a lone tallow candle.

The man turned in one swift movement, pulling a pipe from his mouth, and smiled. There was something Kyr didn't like about the expression, but that wasn't uncommon in her line of work. He was exceedingly tall, even more so than she or Sylas, and thin, with scant, greasy blond hair lying across his scalp.

'Ah, Sylas,' the man said, rising to his feet.

'Cyregoth,' Sylas replied, striding across the room to clasp forearms with him.

Cyregoth's almost-yellow eyes flicked to Kyr. 'And I see you've brought a companion.' The smile that still tugged at the edges of his mouth was unreadable.

'Hm?' Sylas turned. 'Oh, yes. That's my Kyr. She's become quite useful to me over the years. My weighted die.' He smirked. 'One day, maybe, I'll be sending her in my stead, eh?'

'Not too soon, though? I hope?' Cyregoth replied, uncannily soft. Still he watched her.

'No, no. You're not rid of me yet.' Sylas whisked off his cloak and sat down, already looking over some of the papers spread out before him.

Cyregoth finally looked away, *thank the Spirits*, his expression turning vaguely sour as he looked down at Sylas. 'Good,' he said pointedly, rounding the table to sit at its head. 'I have the information you asked for.'

Sylas nodded, wiry forearms flexing as he flicked through documents. Kyr stayed by the door.

'My employer confirms there has been a disruption in the flow of alchemical compounds to Yorenth, and thus, the counting house.'

'This has something to do with those blights in the countryside, doesn't it?' Sylas pulled another paper toward him, licking its edge and turning it over. 'This is the customs manifest?'

'It is.' Cyregoth scratched his chin. 'Yes, the blights have completely altered the properties of several of the known ingredients used in the locks' alchemy.'

'Third month in a row there's been no shipments of filcher's bane,' Sylas mused.

Cyregoth nodded. 'This, of course, means that the potions used to access the locks can no longer be produced. I heard they had to use the last of their stores just to get them off.' He paused, before letting out a satisfied sigh. 'Yes, the alchemical locks used to secure the most sensitive vaults in the counting house have been rendered completely ineffective.'

Kyr raised her brows. The counting house had always been an impossible ambition of the guild's. The potions needed to bypass the locks were unique to each one, the recipe known only to the royal alchemist and high-ranking members of the Guild of Bankers.

Cyregoth continued. 'The locks have been replaced with mundane ones as of last Tyrdas. There could be a spattering of spelled locks, but everything perfectly pickable.' He gestured dismissively with a hand.

'This is good work, Cyregoth. *Very* good!'

Cyregoth's lips formed more of a flat line than a smile. His hand reached into his dark-colored tunic and withdrew a folded piece of parchment. 'Then I trust we have an arrangement?'

Sylas took it. 'That we do.'

'My employer will be pleased.' Cyregoth stood, and he and Sylas shook hands again.

Kyr, still by the door, crossed her arms.

Cyregoth looked her over. 'Goodbye, Kyr. Maybe we'll meet again one day?'

'Maybe,' she said. *Not.*

As soon as they were back out into the cool night air, Sylas put a hand on Kyr's back, huddling close to her. 'That was just the good news we needed. You know, I even think Cyregoth liked you. He never likes anyone.' Kyr winced, but Sylas was grinning. 'I bring you, Kyr—not Vasha, not Fenrow—*you*, because you're the one I trust. The future of the guild, hm?' His hardened eyes studied her reaction. 'Your natural proclivities make you the obvious heir.'

Kyr looked at him sideways. 'You sound like you've had one too many.'

He laughed heartily and looked away, but as soon as his head was turned, Kyr smiled. It wasn't the first time he'd made such a comment. Kyr knew not to press further, and to accept it for the compliment it was.

The two headed back toward the Knaves' Keep, this time in the direction of the market, glass fires lighting their way. The mining district, called the Sledge by those who lived and worked there, was home to the Knaves' Keep, thanks to their generous contributions to the nobleman Araman Thay, whose family owned many of the sand mines there.

Kyr watched her mentor out of the corner of her eye as they

walked. He was pleased. The Keep would be lively with preparations and reveling this night.

Food stalls began to line the narrow streets even before they reached the square, and Kyr breathed in deep the scent of salted fish, roasting nuts, and pungent fermented eggs.

High above, the blackbird circled.

———

Sylas had spent weeks meticulously planning the heist ahead of the Yorenth counting house undergoing repairs.

'The bricklayers, that's you,' he said, giving each guild member a pointed look, 'are set to arrive at midday to work on repairs to the foundation in the undercroft of the west tower. Now, that's where the vaults are . . .'

Sylas was always exacting when it came to how he wanted things done, always going over the particulars of the plan with them again and again until Kyr thought she'd hear his gravelly voice in her sleep. She watched his eyes, like black marbles hidden behind strands of greasy, dark brown hair, greedily sweeping over the diagram of the west tower laid out before them. Sylas's chambers were a sacred place in the Knaves' Keep, its walls covered in years of coded messages scrawled in guild symbols, every surface littered with stolen artifacts. Few were ever allowed to see it, and Kyr always felt a sense of pride whenever Sylas called for her there.

He'd found her—tow-headed and badly sunburnt—huddled amongst stray dogs in the shade of a glass forge. It had been one of those sunny, idle days of her childhood, indelible in her memory. She'd made a promise to him that day that if he took her in, she would be one of his best.

'Big talk coming from a . . . what, you can't be more than eight years old, can you?' he said, eyeing her. He was young then, with *thicker hair and a long beard that Kyr soon learned she liked to play with.*

'I'm seven,' she answered, straightening. In truth, she had no idea how old she was, but seven sounded like a good number. A lucky one.

He smiled, a gold tooth glinting at the back of his mouth. 'Alright, pup.'

She made a second promise of her own that day, that she would never find herself dirty, flea-bitten, and living off rodents and scarabs again.

With her steady hand, it turned out she had a knack for opening doors to places she wasn't supposed to go and pilfering even the most impenetrable coffers. Over the years, she'd made herself quite useful.

Around the table now stood Kyr and three others, quite a crowd compared to how she preferred to work. Fenrow, their light-footed scout, could disarm any pesky warning devices against theft or trespassing, and otherwise watch their backs. Vasha, their fixer, was there if they needed to talk or, Spirits forbid, bribe their way out of any troublesome situations with the guards. Then there was Grym, their strongarm, and Kyr, their master picklock.

Sylas unceremoniously dropped a heap of oatmeal-colored laborer's clothing on the table.

'We have to wear *this*?' Vasha fretted, his mouth quirked up in faint disgust as he held the bulky tunic out before him. 'It does nothing to compliment my resplendent eyes, and it's going to wash Kyr out.'

Kyr stuck her tongue out at him, but then her lips curled into a smirk, betraying her amusement at Vasha's teasing.

Sylas gave them an exasperated look, like a parent tired of his children's petty squabbles. 'Just put the damn threads on.'

It was easy enough getting in the door of the counting house thanks to those 'damn threads.' The city guard—a distracted pair of Sun's Own stood at the entrance, sweating under their capes and heavy armor and crushing scarabs beneath their boots for entertainment—took one look at them and waved them through. With it not being a market day, the ordinarily bustling main hall was much sleepier than usual, and yet, somehow everyone was distracted. Tellers idly checked their ledgers, guards were absorbed in bored conversation, accountholders were in a hurry. One man rushed past with several goats on a lead.

They passed under a magnificent stained-glass ceiling, bars of aqua and gold light falling over them. Kyr wondered what it might be like to be in this place as someone other than a vagabond, to be wearing the sabatons of a knight instead of these worn, cracked leather boots coming apart at the seams. She'd found herself wondering about other lives more than usual lately. Maybe it was boredom. Maybe she was getting too old for this.

She hung on the thought as they carried on down an unremarkable, far less ornate hall toward the west tower.

It's almost too easy. Where's the thrill?

The counting house's private guards posted at the entrance to the west tower at least made somewhat of an effort at their duties, confirming there were indeed supposed to be bricklayers working that day, then let them continue on their way after some tedious flirting with the ever-charming Vasha.

'An' there's four of you . . .' said the guard, a tall, powerfully built Valeman, looking up from a ledger to give each of them a bored glance. 'Right, you're on the schedule. Won't be causing any trouble for us now, will you?' he joked, not bothering to hide his gaze that fixed on Vasha and traveled along his body, all bronze skin and nimble muscle.

Vasha returned a dazzling smile. 'I should hope not. Bricklaying is terribly boring work. I'm sure we could find much more interesting things to discuss.'

'I'm sure we could,' the guard replied, smirking and leaning on his spear.

'Now, imagine if I hadn't been wearing this,' Vasha said, as soon as they were out of earshot, gesturing to his tunic. He gave Kyr a wink.

It was a wonder he was such a good thief when he broke one of the Knaves' Keep's primary tenets—always be unmemorable in all your interactions—so often and with such gleeful amusement.

As they reached the inner courtyard within the tower's hexagonal structure, a nobleman clad in an orange, embroidered cloak with a large, feathered cap glided past them, sneering at Vasha and Kyr's giggling.

'All the money in the world for all that dye, just to wear *that*?' It only made the giggling worse.

Kyr stopped along the courtyard's edge and leaned out through one of the archways. A Sentinel kestrel, the piebald twin to the brown knave or all-black rook, was perched high above on the roof tiles.

Good luck, then. She took a deep breath as they came to the door the diagram had indicated. Mundane as any other they had passed.

Beside her, Vasha began idly whistling. The door was already unlocked, just as Sylas said, to allow laborers into the undercroft. Kyr opened it and stepped across the threshold, revealing a cramped spiral staircase leading down to underground vaults.

Six, they've gotten careless over the years.

The counting house had always been too great a target, and clearly the Sun's Own thought so too. Now, though, with faulty locks and the Crown's focus fractured by rumors of weather-changing blights and Queen Attiqah's madness, their carelessness would be a crucial mistake, and just the stroke of luck her crew needed.

Fenrow spotted several poorly hidden warning devices, a surprisingly rudimentary system of ropes, pulleys, and bells, which were easy enough to avoid.

'This is what Sylas spent all this time preparing us for?' Fenrow scoffed. Still, he cut the main line to the undercroft anyway.

'Got to keep our noses to the grindstone, I guess,' Grym replied.

Fenrow laughed bitterly. 'I guess.'

Kyr thought it strange too, though she supposed there wasn't much else to be done by way of security. The preparations, getting in, that had been the hard part, and that was over.

She'd heard stories of the advanced magic-fueled technology of the First Age, but that was all long lost to the firestorms that heralded the Second Age—*if* you believed the Crown historian's accounts.

As they reached the bottom of the spiraling stone staircase, rows and rows of old business ledgers and dust-coated small, locked chests filled shelves along the length of the wall, likely containing trinkets and heirlooms of the noble families in Yorenth's castle town. If they'd had more time, Kyr would've loved to break open a few and see what sorts of things the highborn thought were important enough to stash down there.

She'd certainly never had anything so precious in her life.

One chest in particular, a small yet elaborate reliquary, caught her eye. The thing was covered in enough jewels to feed her for life.

Beyond the shelves, a stuffy, torch-lit room opened up before them. The bronze holding vault containing the coin to cover withdrawals for the week lay at the far end of the room behind two locked doors.

Another bit of luck for them.

There was a whole underground labyrinth of family vaults down here as well, but the masters of the Guild of Bankers foolishly built the substantially more valuable mark, the holding vault, right near the staircase for no other reason than to shorten their walk to retrieve patrons' coin.

As Sylas had explained it, the first two doors would be simple cylinder locks, but he'd been unable to give her much information about the vault lock itself other than it was likely spelled.

Magic was highly controlled in the queendom and spelled locks were a rare thing, but *of course*, Kyr thought, *the queen and her council can make an exception to their rules when it comes to protecting the nobles' valuables.*

Kyr knew she would have only a few precious minutes to examine the lock and crack it before the first guard rotation, when it would be quickly discovered that no work was being done and that their packs of bricklayers' tools were, in fact, empty.

She looked back at Grym.

'Superstitious nonsense,' he always said whenever he saw her and Vasha the night before a job doing their rituals for good luck—lighting candles for the Spirits, tucking a harpy feather in the left boot. He didn't believe in luck or rituals, only skill and practice.

Kyr started working on the first door, applying just the right amount of tension with her tools and listening as the pins aligned with the shear line. It opened easily for her, and Fenrow stayed back to keep watch as she deftly unlocked the second door.

Kyr had been called cocky before by new recruits to the guild and had replied that she had every right to be. She imagined the four of them returning to the guild with their packs overflowing and smiled to herself.

Now they stood before the vault itself, the door nearly twice her height, and she was not a small woman.

They'd arrived without much difficulty at all, and Kyr cursed herself for thinking how well it was going.

A big head brings bad luck.

Adorning the door, covered with years of verdigris and engraved with whorls of odd symbols, was an ornate, equally tarnished lock. The first thing she noticed were more strange symbols, just like those on the door, covering the face of it.

Perhaps this is all part of the spell?

'Careful touching those sigils,' said Fenrow. 'Who knows what magic the Soloriens or their lackeys are capable of.'

Kyr studied it for a moment longer, but she didn't think she'd ever seen anything like it. She played with the ring on her thumb and breathed deep, focusing herself. Her fingertips felt like they were buzzing. She was going to have to be exceedingly careful not to provoke any of that unpredictable diviner's magic.

She knelt down and began.

Instantly, a sense of familiarity came over her, her fingers moving by memory.

Click, CLICK—

One pin down. A self-assured smile played at her lips.

It was only a matter of moments before the next pin clicked into place.

Too easy, she thought.

A minute passed as she worked at the third pin.

'Come on, Kyr...' Fenrow called in a low voice.

'Shh!' she hissed. *Spirits damn it.*

She gritted her teeth, feeling for the third pin to slide into place as she eased her tool along the keyway.

She let out a string of unintelligible mutterings, then huffed under her breath. 'Worse than serrated pins...'

Then she felt it. That sharper sound, a confirmation. Only two more to go by her estimation.

Fenrow poked his head around the door, every line of his

face deeply etched with frustration. Vasha shrugged at him. Kyr felt her face growing hot the longer she worked at the damned thing. It took her another minute, but she heard the final pin click into place and triumphantly stood to pull open the door.

Kyr swore under her breath.

There, on the handle, was a matching, inverted symbol, something she'd seen an illustration of in a book Sylas had given her ages ago. She remembered what kind of rare lock it was just a moment too late.

A whistling lock.

A shrill whine burst forth, sending them reeling as they covered their ears.

'Fen, shut it up!' Grym snarled.

Fenrow pushed Kyr aside and pried the faceplate off with the point of his dagger. Studying the revealed mechanism, he grunted in frustration before smashing his dagger into it.

The whistling stopped.

'Interesting method,' said Vasha, a smirk on his face.

'Shitkickers, all of you!' Fenrow snarled at them before storming out of the chamber.

Vasha sighed, raising his brows. 'He's in a bit of a mood, isn't he?'

A moment later, Fenrow returned. 'It's fine,' he said, smoothing his thin, blond hair back. 'No one heard. We're lucky those oafs upstairs are even stupider than you lot.'

They heaved open the door and rushed inside the vault, where Kyr and Vasha began stuffing their packs with gold sunmarks and silver moonmarks.

'Hope this gold is what Sylas is expecting,' Vasha said. 'Don't get me wrong, it's a lot of gold, but . . .' He shrugged.

'It better be what he's expecting,' Fenrow shot back, handing a pack to Grym.

Footfalls of a guard's sabatons sounded on the staircase

above the first landing.

'Shit,' Grym muttered, spinning around to glare at Fenrow. 'I thought you said we were good, Fen!'

Fenrow scowled. 'We *were* good, Grym.'

'Shouldn't you be itching for a fight, dear Grym?' Vasha leaned against the vault door, looking disinterested as usual and wholly unconcerned about the approaching guard.

'Only dead strongarms have ever itched for a fight,' Grym growled back at him.

Kyr didn't let herself think about how messy their escape was about to be. Botching a job because of a lock with some stupid magecraft on it? She'd never hear the end of it.

Kyr, Vasha, and Fenrow slung their packs over their shoulders.

'Hey!' a voice shouted from the outer chamber, before the guard's footsteps hurried back up the stairs, no doubt to alert the others.

Grym took off after the guard, catching up with them on the first landing by the sound of it. Kyr heard him roar with frustration, the guard cry out, and a crash of armor against stone.

'Shit,' Kyr whispered. One minute earlier while she'd still been messing about with the lock and Vasha would've likely been able to play it off somehow, one minute later and they'd have been gone. *Of course the guards come at the worst fucking time.*

'You get the guard?' Fenrow asked as Grym returned, his large form shadowing the doorway.

'Yeah, she's not getting back up,' Grym answered. 'Braids.' He shook his head. 'Too easy to grab. Got to keep it short like Kyr's.'

Kyr grimaced, brushing her dishwater blond hair out of her eyes and readjusting her heavy pack.

'Always going straight to violence,' Vasha said. He grabbed his pack and they made for the door.

'Got a better idea, Vasha?' said Grym.

'I'll get the last pack,' Fenrow said, before disappearing into the vault.

It was only mere moments before another set of boots sounded on the stairs. Kyr could only guess that guard had been one of a pair, and now her partner was wondering why she hadn't returned.

'Pack it up!' Grym whispered harshly, grinding his jaw. 'If I have to fight, you better take the lot.'

'Fuck's sake,' said Kyr, stumbling out of the vault and looking frantically around the room. 'We really are in a Spirits-damned stone tomb down here.'

Seconds later the outermost door slammed open, nearly off its hinges judging by the sound of squealing metal. A faint yell. More footsteps.

There was no way out but through the guards. The glow of torch fire traveled along the hall toward them, casting long shadows on the wall.

'You have no way out, thieves!' a guard yelled.

Grym stood in the doorway, the blade he held at his side coruscant in the approaching light.

'Shit, we're done for.' Fenrow fingered one of the daggers at his belt.

'No, no,' whispered Kyr, her eyes flicking around the room as she placed a hand on the rough limestone wall of the chamber and mentally readied herself for a fight. She tried to steady her breathing, but it was coming in rapid swells, her eyes wide.

Grym darted from the room with a growl as swords clashed, the sound of clanging metal ringing out through the stone chamber.

Guards burst past him, shouting for the thieves to drop their weapons, halberds pointed and swords raised. Vasha dropped his dagger and held up his hands, ready to negotiate.

Fenrow did too, but more guards followed, ready to attack.

Though Fenrow tried to sidestep an oncoming swing from a guard, the sword still grazed his arm, causing him to wince as blood leaked through the rip in his tunic.

Grym returned then, pulling an unseen guard off Kyr who had closed in while she'd been distracted by the fray. He bashed the guard's head against the wall, then turned to cross blades with another.

Kyr froze, watching the melee. They weren't stopping. *Why weren't they stopping?*

These guards, it appeared, were not here to take prisoners. The panicked feeling clawing up her throat disappeared, her desperation turning to quiet resolve.

'No,' she repeated under her breath, her eyes wildly scanning the chamber walls. 'Not like this.'

She closed her eyes. *Not like this.*

At first, there was only a faint rumbling. Then the walls began to shudder violently, and the ceiling suddenly cracked open. Rubble crumbled down upon them, releasing a cloud of dust that cast the chamber in a disorienting haze.

Grym let out another grunt, twisting as he tried to avoid falling rock, but he was too slow. A mass of stone collided with his head, and he crumpled to the ground, his head snapping to his shoulder with a sickening crack, spraying the floor with a mixture of blood, brain, and bone.

The air quickly became choking with the tang of spilled blood, and Kyr fought down the acrid taste of bile in her throat. She'd always hated the smell.

'What's happening?' a guard yelled, barely audible over the sound of the chaos.

The rumbling grew louder, and the stone floor began falling beneath their feet. Kyr's ears rung. The growing rent in the earth swallowed Grym's body up, along with several of the guards, their guttural cries rising from the darkness like cliffwraiths in bards' tales of the Outlands.

'Climb!' Kyr screamed, as the floor began to collapse beneath their feet.

Using the vault door as leverage, the three of them quickly hoisted themselves up through the sundered ceiling, feet kicking at whatever purchase they could find on the rough wall, before the floor could completely give out beneath them. Two guards clambered after them, one grabbing on to Fenrow's foot before he kicked the poor fucker off.

The wall buckled and collapsed, dooming the guards below. Heaving themselves over the lip of the broken floor, they scrambled to their feet and took off running down the same empty hallway they'd come in by, toward a seldom used door for couriers that Sylas had made sure they knew about in case they needed another way out.

They passed the archway where Vasha had flirted with that guard. The hall was empty, the man likely somewhere below.

'Such a shame,' Kyr heard Vasha lament under his breath.

Stumbling out of the counting house, the trio was momentarily stunned by bright sunlight, distant shouting, and the cries of gulls carried on the sea's salty breeze.

All around them, a vast sheet of fine grit from the ruined tower clouded their vision. It took a moment for them to orient themselves, coughing amidst the spreading haze, before Kyr spotted wooden scaffolding across the alley, climbing a manor house like ivy. Screams began echoing from the courtyard behind them.

Her heart kicking in her chest, the three of them hastily scaled it, and took off across red-tiled rooftops, looking over their shoulders the whole way back to the Sledge. Their escape was a blur of heat rippling on the horizon and ever-distant yelling from the direction of the commerce district. Her thoughts came in flashes, of falling rock and Grym's crimson blood.

She couldn't make sense of what was happening to them.

Only when they crossed under the clematis-covered gates of the Keep's courtyard did they slow, all pausing in a dazed shock for a long moment.

Fenrow turned to Kyr. 'We should be . . . dead! What in the Spirits Six did you do back there?'

'What do you mean what did *I* do? It was some kind of . . . I don't know, earthquake,' she breathed, all of them gulping down air after their mad escape, '. . . landslide, or . . . something.' She doubled over and dropped her pack from her aching shoulders.

Fenrow watched her resentfully, his brows pinched. 'Kyr, *you* did that. The wall cracked where you touched it. Your hand, it—it had this weird shimmer to it.'

'I didn't *do* anything!' she shot back. She'd fucked up with a lock *one* time and he was turning on her? 'Grym is fucking dead, Fenrow. And you're blaming it on me?'

'I know what I saw. They'll be coming for us soon thanks to you,' he spat. 'The Sun's Own can't ignore something like this.'

'You're panicking. It was just shitty timing. Right, Vasha?'

Vasha hesitated, looking between the pair. 'Lady Kyr,' he began, 'I don't know what that was, but as you can see, the rest of the city appears . . . quite undisturbed.'

His ridiculous nickname for her usually made her laugh, but now it only made her feel hollow, further removed from them somehow.

Wanting to look anywhere but at the two of them, she glanced around, finally taking in the ordinary surroundings of the Sledge—the wrens chirping, miners walking past the Keep's entrance, heading home from a day's work. Her heart ached.

Vasha blamed her too?

Before she could reply, Sylas came storming out of the guild manor, the wooden door slamming behind him.

'What the fuck! Runners tell me half of the commerce district is in ruins!' He stopped short, his formidable gaze flickering between the three of them. 'Where's Grym?'

The silence that extended between them suddenly had a weight to it. The ache in her chest turned to a sharp panic as she thought of Grym, somewhere under all that rubble. There would be no retrieving his body, no telling him she was sorry she'd failed him. He was simply gone.

Fenrow's pale skin flushed with red hot anger. 'He's dead thanks to *her*.'

'Fenrow . . .' Vasha warned, his guttural Saerian accent thick with emotion.

'What?' Sylas demanded. His eyes bore into her, and she hated herself for it, but she cowered.

'Fenrow, come on,' Kyr said gingerly, anxious to make him understand. If she could just explain—

She reached out to put a hand on his shoulder but he backed away from her, his hand flying to the hilt of his dagger. Kyr blinked, looking to him, then to Sylas.

Where once they had regarded her as one of their own, now Fenrow's and Sylas's eyes were cold and unfriendly, their mouths curled in unfamiliar sneers. Vasha avoided her gaze entirely.

She tried to tell herself it would be alright. She would explain the whole thing to Sylas, then go to her quarters, clean the blood and dust from herself, mourn Grym . . .

She reached for her pack, but this time Fenrow drew his dagger on her. She felt the muscles of her face involuntarily twisting with a mixture of hurt and anger. Though the dagger remained in his hand, she felt just the same as though he'd carved out her heart.

'I didn't kill him,' she said quietly.

'Alright, one of you tell me what the *fuck* happened back there!' Sylas yelled.

'Kyr picked a spelled lock that alerted the guards to us, and then she brought the fucking building down on top of us! Grym didn't make it out. That's what happened. I'm telling you, she has magic,' said Fenrow.

'*Magic*?' Her voice rose in disbelief. 'No one has magic that can do *that*, Fenrow.'

'I know what I saw.' He stared her down, dagger still at the ready. He wasn't going to be convinced. 'She's a danger to the guild. They'll come for us. Probably already are.'

Sylas's eyes roamed over her with a calculating expression. It was an expression she'd seen many times before when watching him weigh risks and assess threats. Only this time, she was the threat.

She knew Sylas would go to any length to prevent unwanted attention on the guild. She had seen him kill without remorse, do whatever he pleased without a second thought. And she did not think their history would spare her.

Kyr staggered back and fled into the teeming city streets, as swift as the late summer breeze rolling in off the Wravellian Sea.

'Kyr, wait!' Vasha called after her, but she just kept running.

2

KYR

KYR HAD BEEN HIDING out ever since, trying to lay low and keep out of sight. But there was only so much moldy, worm-eaten bread one could tolerate. She just needed enough coin to fill a pack with some food—*real* food—some soft Telhavi cheese, a stuffed flatbread or two, maybe a few slices of candied orange, and some of those clams she liked. Oh, and maybe a little of that nut brittle that Reza sold down by the docks.

Nothing too extravagant.

She had simply gone to the morning market in Yorenth's dye district to case a few stalls. And maybe it *was* getting a little boring spending all her time alone, with no one to talk to.

Coin and food. Once she had a little, she could catch the next corsair's vessel out of the city and put all of this behind her.

She passed a man in rags, whose hollow eyes seemed to have forgotten even himself, scavenging amongst discarded off-cuts between the dyehouses. It had rained the night before, unusual for that time of year, and all of his meager belongings were waterlogged and damaged. Kyr looked at the ring on her thumb and took it off, handing it to him.

'This should fetch you a new cloak or, at least some good ale,' she said warmly, pressing it into his hand. He didn't look at her, his eyes still unseeing, but the man closed his fingers around it nonetheless.

The steps in front of her were lined with offering bowls for the Spirits, but she couldn't remember the last time anyone had left anything. It'd only get stolen these days, anyway.

As she made her way deeper into the city from the dock district, wending through Yorenth's serpentine, hilly streets, she felt a presence at her back. She stopped and peered down the adjacent alley.

Tucked in an alcove off of the street was a statue, and she wondered if those were the eyes she had felt on her back. She still disliked something about the Solorien statues scattered about the city, erected for the deified members of the royal family and their virtuous displays of magic.

Like most in the Sledge, Kyr was still waiting to see any of that magic do any good for them, if it even existed at all. Maybe she was just jaded after all the time spent memorizing the statues' inscriptions as a child, just to get a piece of stale bread from the Solarum's keepers.

She knew the statue's inscription without looking:

So Solq blessed Farnah Solorien, for such a servant was she to her people, that she made Light from Darkness, Seeing from Unseeing, and brought forth Vision from Air to guide them through the Dreaming.

Kyr turned away from Farnah's stony visage and tossed a cursory glance over her shoulder—but found only an ordinary bustling street, with vendors hawking their wares and city dwellers hurrying on their way. The smell of spiced tea and the mudflats at low tide rose with the sun-warmed air, already stifling at this early hour in a city so far south. Overhead, a woman strung washing on a line as a group of Sun's Own made their way to the Solarum for their morning rites.

In the distance, Kyr could already hear shouts from the marketplace. She much preferred the glowmoth-lit night market, heady with cool sea breezes and the thick, acrid scent of glass fires, but her now-former guildmates frequented it too, and she couldn't risk being seen by anyone who might report on her whereabouts to Sylas. With any luck, they would all think she was somewhere far beyond the city walls by now.

Kyr continued down a narrow alleyway, one of a few lesser-known shortcuts, sticking to the shade as much as possible to hide from the strong sun that already beamed overhead. As she passed by quiet shopfronts, beneath dyed sailcloth draped across the alley in a feeble attempt to keep the streets cool, that unshakeable, wary sense came over her again.

She hoped she was imagining the quiet that fell over the place, making her feel suddenly like prey. It was a sense she had grown accustomed to as a child in the Sledge, an instinct that told her it was time to leave and do it quickly. Whether it'd been another, bigger urchin trying to swipe what little she did have, or other more unsavory characters lurking around the docks after the day's work was done, Kyr learned early on to listen to her gut. Still, she loathed the feeling, and part of her wanted to search the alley and kick in the teeth of whomever she would find.

Instead, she slowed her breathing and made herself focus, playing with the ring on her finger. *Can't draw attention right now.*

Kyr turned around and, as she did, caught the edge of a black cloak whirling behind a recess in the alley as someone ducked behind it.

She swallowed hard. *Spirits damn it.*

Kyr knew those long black cloaks, as all brigands did. Knew they'd probably be coming for her eventually.

Thought I had more time.

Sylas had often called on the Rooks—cowled, masked, and

clad all in black—to get rid of wayward thieves or political opponents who wanted to crack down on the guild's dealings. Just as she thought, she'd become a liability to the guild, with Sylas clearly wasting no time hunting her.

Well, Kyr ap Sand wasn't going to go down without a good and bloody fight.

Her need to be vigilant made it easier to ignore the pang in her gut that Sylas, who she'd spent nearly her entire life with and thought of as something like a father, could so easily discard her. Sure, he'd been cruel over the years—you don't become the leader of one of the most notorious shadow market guilds on the continent without cruelty—but he'd also been indisputably kind, teaching her all sorts of things beyond thieving and lockpicking. He'd given her everything.

Kyr clenched her jaw and waited, then, remembering the draughts Rooks often drank to improve their hearing, slipped off her boots, walking on silent feet to the tavern one door down.

The raucous chatter and laughter within the dimly lit, smoke-filled establishment felt so at odds with the fear blooming in her chest, and the gnawing urge to flee that rose up within her. A man stood in the corner was handing out pamphlets and yelling loudly, going on and on about the Spirits and their imminent return to the world that they had long ago forsaken.

'My fellow Sentinels! Yorens! We stand upon a precipice! The Mad Queen may have abandoned us, left us to toil in our mines and forges, to fight in her wars, but Solq has not abandoned us! The Spirits *have not* abandoned us!'

With spittle flying, eyes filled with fervor, and hair unkempt, many of the tavern's patrons dismissed the man's words, but he was undeterred.

'Careful, old man,' chided a patron. 'You'll be locked up

for words like that. Or worse.' He turned to the man beside him. 'Thinks Solq's going to come down, and what? Imagine!'

The graying fanatic turned to him. 'Let them show their cruelty! You'd show respect to a monarch who feasts while you starve, and yet, where is this respect for our land, our home, and those who shepherded it?'

The patron frowned and, seeming to have no good answer, waved a hand, dismissing him.

Kyr turned away and watched as, moments later, the shadowy, cloaked figure from her periphery began searching the alley.

If she weren't so preoccupied with life and death at that moment, she might've found it amusing that he was unaware she was now watching his slow, measured steps as he surveyed the shadows. He angled his body toward the alley across the way and pulled a small vial from his cloak. The sheen of a blade caught the light as he applied the contents to it, providing all the confirmation she needed.

Kyr was being hunted.

She'd heard of the effects of pawn's malady, chosen poison of the Rooks. As a paralytic it was quick, but it killed slowly—perfect for lengthy interrogations, the promise of an antidote drawing a confession from most. She strained to see more of him but could make out nothing else distinct through the clouded windowpanes.

'Five starmarks for an ale,' the barkeep, a squat man with liver spots on his face and wisps of gray hair, said to her.

'No, thank you,' Kyr said offhand, still watching out the window.

'An' it's ten for the chair,' he growled.

She sighed and stood, a scowl darkening her face, and began pushing her way through the packed room to the back door, heading out into the crowded streets again.

Knowing he was lurking a street over made her consider her next movements carefully. The market was just ahead, with jaunty music and the shouts of auctioneers and bidders already reaching her ears. The best chance of losing the Rook would be to disappear into the throng.

Kyr wove through the market square and peeked her head around the corner of the alley, but there was no sign of the Rook. She made her way by a fabric stall, in one swift movement dropping her old shabby cloak to the ground and pulling a couple yards of lupine-dyed wool with her while the stall-keeper's back was turned. She fashioned the wool into a new cloak with her old brooch, a stolen treasure that she'd managed to keep hidden from Sylas, and continued shouldering her way through oblivious marketgoers.

A performer of lesser magics danced about in front of her, releasing a flutter of luminescent butterflies into the air, much to a group of children's delight. The strange multi-colored things danced around before vanishing into air. The performer had probably been purchased from her parents as a child by the queen, as most children discovered to have any diviner's abilities were, her power used and siphoned away until all that remained was reduced to party tricks and fool's work. Or so the rumors went. And she'd probably been told it was an honor to do so, too.

Was that to be Kyr's fate now, too?

No sooner had the thought occurred to her than she was shaking her head, huffing a low, skeptical laugh.

No, Fenrow's full of shit.

Kyr reached the other end of the square and still didn't see the Rook anywhere. A man with a wooden crate strapped to his chest selling dates passed by, and she eyed them hungrily. In her periphery she saw no black cloaks, felt no eyes on her.

Sighing with relief, she pulled the wool over her in a makeshift hood and turned a blind corner, where she bumped straight into a man's hard chest.

'Oh!' she yelped.

A low, sonorous voice. 'Looking for me?'

Shit. Sylas had clearly paid more for one of the better assassins. She knew in that moment she'd been an idiot to underestimate this one. Her heartbeat thumped in her ears as she realized she had no weapon but the throwing knife in her boots, which were currently tucked behind some crates back by the tavern. *Shit. Shit. Shit.*

'I thought so,' he said with a cruel smirk.

She seized his arms as he lunged for her, but she was weak from hunger, and a sharp point at her flank sliced through tunic and skin.

'Don't struggle,' he muttered.

Trying to get some leverage to break free of his grasp, and with his dagger still pointed at her ribs, the man's eyes suddenly disconnected from hers and took on a faraway look, the jaundiced whites of them growing wide with shock.

He dropped the blade, and Kyr shoved him to the ground, wasting no time scrambling across loamy earth to grab the weapon. This time as she reached for the large, wing-shaped pommel of his dagger, she saw it.

The shimmer Fenrow had mentioned, faintly rippling the air around her hands.

The Rook began clawing at his throat, a wild expression on his features as his eyes went from rage-filled to panic-stricken. His nostrils flared and his lips began taking on a strange blue tinge. He collapsed then, his long dark hair spilling over the cobbles. She waited for the assassin to cough or sputter, to get back up and grab her and finish what he'd started, but his chest never drew breath again.

Gasps echoed through nearby onlookers, and she could hear feet scuffing on stone as others tried to get away. From her.

'Murderer!' a beggarman shouted at her.

'What did you do to 'im?' yelled a woman in a yellow head-scarf, looking down on the square from the window of an attic room. Kyr put pressure on the wound at her side, trying to hide her face from their stares and the body at her feet.

'Fuck, fuck, fuck,' she cursed under her breath.

She quickly turned and pulled the makeshift cloak tightly around her, looking for the nearest escape route. She hadn't meant to do anything but defend herself, but she'd learned twice over that no one cared what she'd *meant* to do.

Again, Kyr ran. Her scrambled thoughts tried to make sense of what had happened, and again no other explanation came. No explanation other than magic. She ran all the way back to the docks, to the loose sewer grate behind a derelict boathouse she'd scouted out as a hiding place if she ever really needed one.

Kyr never thought of herself as someone who'd run from anything. Now she didn't know what she was.

Need to stay hidden for a while, she thought to herself as she settled into the filthy, mildewed alcove that was to be her home until she could discreetly find passage out of Yorenth.

She'd expected the paralytic to take hold of her before she even reached the docks, but strangely, she felt more tired than anything else.

Behind a grate to her left, a rat bolted by in the darkness, and Kyr's stomach growled. She thought of her seven-year-old self, and the promise she'd made to that girl. With a sigh, she wiped the Rook's dagger on her sleeve, watching the shadows.

Desperate times.

3

ATLAN

THE RECLUSIVE PRINCE drummed his beringed fingers on the desk where he sat, hunched over another old text Saartho had selected for him. This volume discussed ancient designs for some kind of machinery activated with magic, when the Spirits worked with the artisans of Yorenth to build all kinds of fantastical inventions. Yorenth's royal library still had a small selection of texts from the time the Spirits walked the land, many describing strange mechanical innovations lost to time. Now he sat in this stuffy attic room of the palace most days, poring over them because of magic he never asked for.

'*Fucking* magic,' he huffed under his breath, shaking his head. When his magic had first appeared one sweltering morning in his ninth summer, he'd thought it a blessing from the Spirits themselves.

Everything his mother always told him, about how they were descendants of Solq himself, how everything they did was in service to a grand ideal of humanity that would herald their return, seemed true in that moment. His mother had looked upon him so fondly that day, she'd almost seemed proud. Now he knew better. She wasn't proud of him, she had just found a new weapon to wield.

At least his magic protected him from her somewhat, and the older he got, the less she seemed to notice him at all. Now in his twenty-ninth summer, he still couldn't believe he was the one stuck in one of the royal library's secluded studies, and his brother, Vyktas, was the one down in the field practicing maneuvers with the guard every day.

I'm no scholar. He sighed and shut the tome in front of him, pushing it aside.

His mind was wanting to wander anyway, so he let it take him back to memories of the field, and then to his first ever battle— the Battle of Kingdom's Fall, as it would come to be known.

When he was sixteen, he found out he was being sent to the war camps with several of the foremost knights of the Sun's Own to aid in the fight against the Eradomin, a hostile people to the north who had, for unknown reasons, waged war with the woodland clans and fiefdoms, throwing the region into chaos. His mother had her eyes on expanding the Realm of the Sentinel then, and he was to aid her to that end.

He'd camped and fought alongside men and women that he looked up to as being made in the image of the Spirits. He'd dreamed of glory.

How easily deceived I'd been.

Part of him felt disgusted with himself for what he'd believed back then. What he'd done. Another part of him still didn't care about anything but fighting.

Those thoughts carried him further, to the raucous dueling pits of the Sledge. Throwing a couple starmarks to the smudger while he wrapped his other hand with his teeth, he would pass the deafening crowds screaming for the prince. They knew he would deliver a bloody show.

It was then that Atlan's focus narrowed to a tightening deep between his hips, and he felt his erection pressing against his trousers.

Shit.

If he was to get anything else done, he needed to release this damn tension. He loosened the strings at his waist and settled into the chair, freeing his cock and gripping it tightly at its base. He began moving his hand, up and down, quickening his pace as he reveled in the feeling before a fight. The ritual of removing the poultice from his last fight's injuries, so full of adrenaline he couldn't even feel the pain anymore. Then the fight itself, a frenzy of keeping his guard up until he could find an opening on his opponent.

Atlan grunted on an exhale as darker thoughts came to him. The many shades of blood, its scarlets, maroons, and burgundies. He could still hear some of the screams he had silenced over the years, like an echo from a far-distant time, and he understood the fear he instilled on the battlefield.

Fuck, that got him close.

Like some kind of carrion insect, in his right mind, in the light of day, he would crawl back beneath the refuse, these thoughts disgusting him as he knew they should, but in the dark, alone—

He leaned back in his chair, almost about to finish, when a door slammed down the hall. He stilled and listened for a moment for the footfalls of a guard, or worse, Saartho, but instead heard another distinctive, horrifying sound. One he'd committed to memory years ago. The deadly soft steps of his mother's slippered feet scuffing the stone on their way to his chamber.

'Fucking shit,' he muttered, anger and embarrassment flooding him in an instant as he stuffed his painfully hard cock back into his pants and flipped open the tome in front of him to some arbitrary page.

It was only mere moments before his mother strode into the

room in a ripple of pale golden silks, not even bothering to knock or announce herself. He scowled at her.

'A sour look already?' she said dryly. 'What have I done this time?'

'A little respect for my privacy would be nice,' he muttered, instantly hating how childish he felt.

She crossed the small space to him and bent down so they were eye to eye. With a delicate touch, she brushed a lock of his hair, black just like hers, away from his face. Try as he might not to, he still flinched.

'My son,' she said, her eyes roaming over his face. 'No one would've said so much as a prayer for you if I'd decided to leave you shackled to a tree up in the mountains as soon you showed a glimmer of magic. They fear you, but I saw your potential for greatness. We both know how that turned out. You are here by my grace alone. How easily you forget that.' She sighed and rose to standing, smoothing out her dress. 'Do not tell me I cannot go where I please in my own palace ever again.'

He was frozen by her words, aware of an anger and bitterness within him but unable to reach his emotions. He hated her all the more knowing she was the only one who had that effect on him.

His mother deftly ignored his empty gaze, as she always did, walking past where he was seated to perch on a divan in front of a pair of bookcases. Dust swam in the buttery evening light streaming in through the narrow windows at her back, igniting the edges of her unbound hair in golden fire.

'We have more important matters at hand than your endless capacity to sulk. I debated whether to even tell you, but, well, Taryq thought it best.'

'How kind of him,' Atlan grumbled.

She narrowed her eyes. 'After all, it does, I suppose, concern you.'

Atlan rested his chin on the palm of his hand. 'Are you going to tell me or not?'

His mother smiled, but the expression didn't quite reach her eyes. 'A report came in from the outpost on the road to Bellgard.'

Atlan straightened. 'Bellgard? We just defended our trade route with them from a mountain ogre attack.'

'Indeed. Apparently, several Sun's Own and the contingent of the Noblegard you fought with were all found dead. Though not from an ogre attack. Their corpses were ... on fire. As you well know, if it had been ogres, we would have found nothing but bones.'

'*What*?' he blurted, his brows furrowing.

'Still are on fire, actually. The crowners can't get anywhere near them. They're all still lying on the road.' She paused, picking at one of her long nails. Atlan thought they looked like talons. 'I need you to go and see the bodies, tell me if it's mage-fire like the council suspects. Rain, pails of water sent with caravans from the city, nothing has been able to put out the flames.'

'You think there's a rogue mage? Another Singer?' His thoughts felt suddenly scrambled, a thousand questions coming to him. He rose and paced to the other end of the room. 'Were there reports from the survivors? Maybe it's another blight.'

She folded her hands. 'There were no survivors.'

Atlan stopped his pacing and turned suddenly to face her. 'How long have you known about this?'

Her eyes flicked up and her lips pursed as she considered the question. 'Since Minodas?'

'Since *Minodas*?' he scoffed. 'Men I've fought with, men I swore I would protect, have *died* and you didn't think to tell me immediately? A fire threatens the main road out of the city and you think it can wait *three days*?'

Vyktas, who followed their mother everywhere like a dog,

surely knew of the report too, and apparently hadn't thought to tell him either. He remembered playing in these very rooms with Vyktas as a boy. How great the rift between them had grown.

Did Wren know? He clenched his jaw.

His mother drew a line in the dust on the end table next to where she sat, then rubbed her finger on a cushion with a look of faint disgust. 'It took a day for the messenger, of course, but beyond that I wasn't sure whether to tell you because I knew you would react exactly as you are.' She frowned at him. 'And don't be ridiculous, there are no other Singers.'

'You know that's not true.'

She bristled at his words but ignored them. 'Besides, the dead were a few new recruits, and the rest Bellgardians.' She said this with a wave of her hand that made his blood boil. 'We have an agreement with Vizier Rumail, yes, but there was simply nothing we could've done. He doesn't need to know about our difficulties with the blights. When you go to Bellgard, you won't tell him, either.'

Atlan knew a threat from his mother when he heard one.

'I deserved to know as soon as we got word of it,' he said, his voice so thick with venom he could almost feel it coating his tongue.

'We? If you bothered to come to council meetings, maybe you would have known sooner. But you're too busy fighting or fucking, apparently, so I'm telling you now. Satisfied?'

'I am not—'

'Please. Wren tells me about your little trips to those disgusting brothels by the mines. You can't seriously think you're being discreet, can you?'

He exhaled sharply and ignored the comment. 'So you do want me there after all, then?'

His mother smirked. 'Well, I would think that any noble that wants to be considered for the Sun's Own, let alone

Captain of the Guard, would be there no matter what anyone else thought.'

He hated it when she did this, when she played like her word on things wasn't final. Like he could've shown up when her mood was against him.

The smile he returned was tight-lipped. 'You're right, Your Radiance.' He practically choked on her royal title. 'I should've been there.'

Before she could reply, more footsteps sounded in the hall. Hurried, this time. The frantic shuffling grew closer and closer until an out-of-breath guard appeared in the doorway.

'Your Radiance,' said the man, an older man named Erwat, who, Atlan knew, had been part of the Sun's Own for the better part of his life. Normally stoic, he'd never seen a guard with his experience look so flustered, especially not in front of the queen. 'Your Radiance,' he began again, still catching his breath. 'There's been an attack on the counting house!'

She stood immediately. '*When*?'

'Just over an hour ago, I'm told. Prince Vyktas has gathered the advisors in the throne room. They need their queen.'

Her silks brushed against Atlan as she passed him to follow the guard. When she got to the hall, she stopped suddenly and turned. 'If you're finished being sullen, you're going to make us late.'

Any retort he might've had for her had died in his throat with the news, so he simply followed her and Erwat out the door and down the tower steps.

He knew better than to ask questions about her sudden change of heart in wanting him to be present at official meetings. Though his mind was reeling, he understood well enough—she could never say it, but his mother was asking for his help the only way she knew how, by demanding it, and that could only mean one thing. Something very bad had happened.

'The counting house is in *ruins*, Your Radiance! Eighteen guards and nobles dead! The Guild of Bankers is demanding someone answer for it, and I need to give them something,' pleaded Sol Rywin, a man with graying black hair, and his mother's advisor to the Guild of Bankers. 'Even if it was an act of the Spirits, like the strange weather and the fires, they want someone to blame. I can only put them off for so long.'

They were seated in the council room, located off of the grander throne room but still spacious and lit by hundreds of knight's votives. The limestone chamber was open on all sides with the Yoren Mountains to the north, the sea to the west, mudflats to the south, and sandbanks to the east. An elaborate mosaic of the sun over mountains covered the ceiling and floor.

Through stained glass doors behind them, Atlan could see knights kneeling at a distance in the hall. Just another one of the ways his mother made herself feel superior. She'd decreed soon after her reign began that Sun's Own present in the palace were to kneel in silent reflection outside the main chamber of the castle whenever she held important meetings and events. At least had the sense to relieve some of them of the nonsensical duty so they could aid those in the commerce district, apparently still caring enough to project a glimmer of a beneficent image to their people.

Atlan returned his gaze to the desperate advisor and wondered what his mother would say.

He knew she couldn't say who was behind the suspected attack on the Guild of Bankers, because she didn't, nor could she say the Sun's Own were taking action, because they weren't. They were well and truly unprepared.

Another contingent of the guard was preoccupied with strange blights south of the city walls for weeks now. Villagers were reporting fog that never dissipated, rivers that had stopped flowing, and other bewildering accounts. He wouldn't have believed it either if he and his men hadn't seen it for themselves. Ogre and wyvern attacks were also increasing, threatening valuable trade routes into the city.

It was as if the wild creatures of the realm knew something they didn't.

Atlan stood against the wall beside his mother's seat counting down the minutes until he could practice with Sun's Visage, his family's famed glass blade, in the yard. He preferred to be anywhere but at court and council meetings, but Captain of the Guard was a title to be proud of, and something he could actually see himself doing each day without wanting to off himself.

That is, if his mother would ever officially bestow upon him the title she so enjoyed withholding. At this point, after his exploits in the field, the Sun's Own already looked to him with reverence—he was Captain of the Guard in all but name.

'I can assure you, Sol Rywin, we will have answers for you soon. We are doing everything we can. I have spared no relief. Many of my personal guard are down there now searching.' She folded her hands primly in front of her. 'We must first mourn the dead and begin repairs. Most importantly, we must have patience when dealing in matters of the Spirits, for we do not understand their reasons.'

Sol Rywin looked displeased with this vague nonanswer but nodded and took his seat. Everyone in the room knew this had nothing to do with the Spirits, but his mother still had a contingent of powerful nobles and soldiers loyal to her, and with her penchant for throwing anyone who disagreed in the dungeons, no one dared cross her.

Yet, anyway. Atlan had his suspicions that her advisors were talking behind her back instead.

Atlan heard his mother on late nights as he was returning from the Sledge, pacing her bedchamber, muttering to herself.

'What are They trying to tell me?' he would hear her plead, as she frantically ordered her court diviners to pull more cards or recheck the die they had cast.

Her long black hair which she normally kept neatly tied back and hidden from view, as was the fashion in Yorenth, now fell down her back in wild tumbles. Her eyes had taken on an equally feral look since she had begun staying up until all hours of the night, trying to understand why all of this was happening.

His grandmother's rule, and great-grandfather's before that, had been times of peace and prosperity. But now, at a time when they were already unpopular due to their wealth, all of this turmoil was doing them no favors.

'This is not the only evidence of further activity,' she began solemnly. 'There has also been an attack on the Western Road. I suspect it is another blight. Atlan will lead a party of Sun's Own to scout the region and quell any magical agitation there.'

Atlan's head snapped to where she sat before he managed to suppress his reaction.

'With all due respect, Queen Attiqah,' said Sol Errol, another council member, 'you say that we do not have to worry about other mages, that the Realm has a handle on those with magical abilities, that your son is a sign magic is returning to the Solorien line.' He paused. 'And the Solorien line *only*.'

'And yet the 'magic' causing these blights must be coming from somewhere. Are you not concerned there is more to this than this—this chaos? What about the rumors of mages in the Free North? Should we not be considering all possibilities?'

The queen narrowed her eyes. It was subtle, but Atlan was attuned to her shifting moods. 'I understand your concerns, Sol Errol, but as you and I both know, we maintain detailed records of anyone known to possess but a drop of magic, and our knowledge extends beyond even our citizenry. I can assure you, whether this was an accident or a new manifestation of the blights, it would require more magic than any mortal could catalyze.'

A lie. Though she would never admit that to anyone, not even herself. He knew she was afraid of what he could do. He'd wondered if there could be others like him when he was younger, but even Saartho had his doubts.

'We would've seen evidence of power like that by now,' he'd said.

As for what happened in the commerce district, Atlan thought it was probably just a natural event. Something having to do with the bedrock or the groundwater. Pure, normal, nonmagical misfortune.

The queen continued. 'The Spirits have always been active in our world. We may not always feel it, but their presence is always there. It is much more likely that this is their work, that the blights are a form of divine communication we must seek to understand, than a mage outside the Solorien line with that kind of power.'

Sol Errol's chair scraped along the floor as he stood with a start. 'So the Followers of Their Return are correct, then? Is that it? That is tantamount to heresy!'

The queen's eyes grew furious. 'Of course not!' she bellowed.

The room fell silent.

'You dare speak to me of heresy?' Her voice turned mocking. 'Those charlatans want the common people to believe that the Spirits would return simply to 'save them' from their poor, unfortunate lives in this safe and virtuous city. One that they forget affords them many freedoms other places in our world would not. That is not the purpose of the Spirits. They are not here for petty matters of mankind, but for guiding action far beyond our understanding. To believe otherwise, *that* is heresy.' She looked at each of her council members, but none returned her cold gaze.

Sol Errol took a deep breath and flattened his hands on the table. 'Is it not another sign of unrest that the common people believe that to be so?'

'Sol Errol!' Vyktas snapped. Atlan rolled his eyes.

The advisor raised his hands. 'I merely ask the questions that are on the minds of many in this room. They just won't admit it.'

'Vyktas, take your seat,' Queen Attiqah said, holding up a hand to her son. 'If any of you have any concerns about order in my queendom, you will bring your concerns to me. Sol Errol, I will excuse your outburst this time because you have brought valuable information to me about a lack of trust amongst my advisors and council members, but if you speak out of custom again there will be consequences.'

She continued. 'Yes, the blights are alarming. Yes, we do not know exactly what is causing them. The Followers of Their Return are a small sect of radical zealots that I could crush at any moment if I wished to, but it's really the last of my concerns.' She extended her hand in a nonchalant expression. 'The Sun's Own works diligently to find anyone with magic. There is no one, in any of the lands—not Sentinel lands, nor Northern lands—with the gift of magic from the Spirits, except for my son.' Her eyes locked on Sol Errol. 'Above all, you would do well to remember that you only know what I deem necessary for you to know. There is often more to these matters that your betters have already considered.'

'Now,' she breathed, turning her attention back to the room. 'I must speak with my sons for a moment. Leave us.'

More stalling, then.

Atlan watched them all file out of the room, all except for Sol Taryq, who clearly thought he had a blanket invitation to be wherever the queen was, and was apparently right about it, too.

With the advisors gathered in another room, the court

gossiping would begin. At least with the catastrophic damage to the commerce district and Sol Errol's objections, Atlan and his *eccentricity*, as they called it, would probably not be the subject of rumors this week.

Now would come the moment that his mother dangled the captaincy in front of him yet again so that he would do her bidding and travel to the outpost. He told himself he would not be so easily manipulated anymore, but his resolve tended to slip through his hands like so many grains of sand the moment he was face to face with his mother.

The queen stood and began walking to one of several large archways at the back of the room that opened to a balcony high over the city. In the distance, a vermilion sunset melted into the horizon, the Yoren Mountains like jagged teeth in a bloodred mouth. His mother watched the setting sun nervously like a bad omen.

'This couldn't have happened at a worse time,' she said, removing her crown and scratching at her head in what was, for her, a remarkably human gesture. 'First those Followers of Their Return start prophesying in the streets, putting lofty ideas in the common folks' heads, and, apparently, my advisors' heads too. Then the attacks outside of the city, and now Yorenth itself is in danger.'

Vyktas put a comforting hand on her shoulder, and she reached up to put her hand over his, giving him a brief smile.

Atlan strolled out onto the balcony, and a great shadow passed overhead. The air swelled, a sudden whooshing followed by preternatural silence.

Wingbeats.

His mother's phoenix, Tanwen, landed gracefully on the stone balustrade and fussed over her grip on it. In her talons she held a small scroll.

'What's this?' their mother said, not bothering to hide the annoyance in her voice like she did with her courtiers. She snatched the scroll from the creature's grasp and tore open the seal.

Atlan had always had a bleeding heart for Tanwen. As an adolescent he would sneak into her chambers to feed her mint he'd stolen from the palace kitchens. She had a certain look in those yellow marbled eyes of hers that captivated him, and even now he ground his jaw at the sight of the fetters and harness his mother kept on her. One day he'd see the inquisitive, sensitive creature freed.

'What does it say?' Vyktas said, ever the impatient child, peering over their mother's shoulder. Atlan leaned against the balustrade, ruffling Tanwen's feathers with one hand, waiting for whatever horseshit was likely coming their way now in the form of this note.

'Just a response from Wren. I already sent her a message to go to the counting house. She's getting me a list of names, those who could be involved.' She read more of the note and scoffed. 'She's not found anyone who could be of use yet. This list is all just Sun's Own, noble families, and laborers.'

'Well, there's no one to find. Is there?' Vyktas asked cautiously. 'It was the Spirits.'

'Darling, don't be so foolish. It's unbecoming. I've instructed Wren to look for anyone with lesser magics—it should be easy enough to find someone to give them. There was a bricklayer with a tattoo . . .' She looked over the note. 'That's unusual. Perhaps she had a record. We need to check with the jailer. That could work.'

'But won't that undermine what you just said about the Spirits?'

Atlan huffed a laugh and Vyktas shot him a look, his lip curling up angrily.

'Must I explain everything to you,' muttered their mother. 'It doesn't matter what the true cause was. People always want someone to blame. What I say to my advisors is one thing, what

I say to the people is another. My advisors know this.' She gave her younger son a pointed look. 'I would've hoped by now that you would understand this.'

Atlan turned toward Tanwen, who cocked her head and let out a soft chirrup. He laughed and brushed the feathers at the crown of her head back.

'Atlan,' his mother said, handing him the note. 'This takes precedence over the blights. I name you Captain of the Guard —use our resources, meet with Wren as soon as she returns, and find me someone responsible.'

Atlan blinked, looking down at the note, then up at his mother.

'Congrats, brother.' Vyktas smirked, clapping a hand on his shoulder as he walked back to the vestibule leading to the throne room. Atlan ignored him. His brother always did lose interest quickly when there was no longer anything to gain from the conversation.

'You mean this?' he said, looking at his mother and trying not to appear too eager. Usually, some ceremony came with being chosen for such an honorable position, but he didn't care that his mother would never honor him in that way if it meant he would walk out of today's council meeting Captain of the Guard after all.

She glared back, assessing. 'Don't make me regret it.'

4

THE LOST ONE

'STARLINGS . . . yellow castle . . . mirror in the fortress . . . flight.'

Pale, thin fingers traced depressions in the stone. Had they done that? The etchings felt worn and soft against their fingertips. Old, now. Older than the years themselves. They tried to remember, but it was getting harder and harder.

Sister. Yes, they had one. Last time he was here he had told them that. Then he had left them again, but not before drawing the interlopers to them.

'Listen, starlings.' Their trilling let the Lost One know when the interlopers were near. The swirling, murky night grew deep, cocooning all.

'Starlings . . . yellow castle . . . mirror in the fortress . . . flight.'

5

ATLAN

'WHAT BRINGS a prince to these humble quarters so late at night?' Wren half-smiled, her eyes tracking Atlan across the empty palace kitchens.

The low-ceilinged space glowed with candlelight against the darkness that threatened to consume the edges of the room. Outside, the night was moonless and opaque, making the lonely corner of the palace feel far away from the rest of the world somehow. Like a room in someone's dream.

'I'm fucking hungry, that's what.'

He knew she was really asking why he never ate with his family at court, but he was in no mood to get into family history. Especially not with someone he didn't know if he could trust. He sat down next to his mother's spymaster at a long table, some dates and a half-eaten flatbread in front of her. He hoped she couldn't smell the wine on his breath.

It seemed he was always encountering her like this. In the daylight, in official council meetings, she was nowhere to be seen. What's more, Wren was relatively new to court. She'd been a recruit to the city guard that had proved herself particularly apt at gathering information, and his mother had a discerning eye for anything and anyone that could benefit her. Atlan thought his mother should be more interested in *how* exactly Wren was coming up with this information, but she always was short-sighted. Greedy.

Wren rolled her eyes, tucking a short dark brown curl back from her face. She watched him eye the various courses from that night's meal, then pile some quail and lentils onto his plate. 'Eating like that before a fight's going to slow you down.'

He didn't answer her.

'Aren't you going to ask me how I know you're going to the Sledge?'

'Let's see, because you know everything? Probably were looking through my keyhole this afternoon.' He reached over and grabbed a handful of dates from her plate.

Wren snorted and shook her head. 'So is tonight a celebration, or your first night on duty, Captain?'

'A little bit of both, I suppose.' He picked up a carafe of wine and drained it to the dregs.

Wren raised her eyebrows. 'That kind of night?'

'That kind of night.'

He knew he was being obtuse, but better he come off as an arsehole than drunkenly give her information to go and report back to some clandestine ally of hers. Or worse, his mother.

'Shouldn't you be happy?'

He turned to her. 'What, don't I look happy?'

Wren returned a leveling gaze that he could hardly stand to look at.

When he turned back to his meal and didn't say anything further, she continued. 'I used all my contacts to try to find someone with lesser magics near the counting house, you know, someone who might've really had something to do with it—'

Atlan frowned. 'No one had anything to do with it, Wren.'

She shrugged, arching her eyebrows playfully. 'Anyway, all

the names I got were either nobles or laborers at the counting house. Maybe it really was just an act of the Spirits.' She took a bite of a date. 'You'll just have to find someone to satisfy Attiqah —but it shouldn't be too hard, plenty of unsavory characters down at the docks. You know, someone who deserves it.'

Someone who deserves it.

He hadn't wanted to think about what he was really doing, but Wren's words forced him to. By bringing someone to his mother for this, he knew he would be sentencing them to die.

Wren seemed to sense his darkening mood. 'Finally going to get that fancy white cape?' she joked.

Atlan let out a half-chuckle. 'I doubt it. Anyway, all I care about is that I have her blessing to act, I don't need all the fanfare.' He paused his feasting for a moment, pulling a piece of parchment, her message, from his pocket and tossing it onto the table. 'Who are these bricklayers you mentioned? Crowner's records at the chancery indicate the body of only one bricklayer was found.'

Wren knit her brows. 'Hm?' She finished chewing. 'Well, they're still looking through the rubble. There was a fissure in the earth, several feet deep. They might find more bodies.'

He nodded. 'Maybe, though they've found many already. Humor me. What did your people say they looked like?'

'Well, a few witnesses noticed two of them in particular. A man and a woman, both with blond hair, which is probably why they stood out. The woman, she was with the three men who everyone described as ordinary laborers, but she had a tattoo on her hand,' Wren indicated to her own hand, 'and only Birds have tattoos. You'd be surprised at how many people in the Sledge are involved in that kind of thing.'

Atlan nodded, scrawling something on the parchment and tucking it back into his pocket. He piled more food onto his plate.

'So,' she drawled. 'I'm looking at Yorenth's new protector, then, is that it?'

He rolled his eyes and studied her for a moment in the dimness. Her lips were glossy from the sugared dates. It made him think about how they might taste.

He knew what she wanted, and if it would stop her prying, maybe he would give it to her.

Atlan turned to face her fully, locks of his hair falling around his face, shielding everything from view but her. Her wide, bright brown eyes. Full lips. 'You always ask this many questions?'

'I could ask less of them,' she said, shrugging, and he watched as her own gaze traveled down his face and stopped at his mouth. He reached for her.

Their kiss was a fiery, quicksilver thing at first. She grabbed his shirt, pulled him toward her. In that moment, he thought he might be able to do this. Clumsily, they rose from the table, his calloused hand gripping her throat as he backed her into an alcove. A copper pan clattered off the cupboard to their right, but he didn't care about being heard. His hands were at her hips then, lifting her onto the windowsill with ease.

He had her mostly naked when the damned thoughts began their assault. The ones he tried to banish day in and day out, and most of the time, succeeded. The ones he kept locked away until he could resist them no longer.

Memories of gore, the same screams he'd been hearing in his head for years, nights he tried so hard to forget. He felt them there, menacing the outer bounds of his mind.

Wren reached for the ties on his trousers, but he stopped her and shoved her back, shame flooding him. He wasn't going to be able.

She looked up at him, confused. 'What's wrong?'

'Nothing.' It came out angrier than he meant it to. He

opened his mouth to try and explain himself when the clock in the Solarum tolled midnight. 'Spirits damn it, I'm already late.'

'You're leaving?'

He didn't even look at her as he grabbed his cloak and headed for the door.

She called after him, 'Atlan, what the fuck!'

Sols Tyran and Wrasar were waiting for him at the stables, and he was glad to have their company.

With his men, he was someone admired, not someone to be feared, studied and prodded, nor cast aside. Emotions he couldn't identify swelled in his chest as he mounted the horse and took off at a gallop, but he swallowed them and readied himself for the evening they had planned.

There would be time to feel everything when he was breaking some glassworker's nose.

6

ATLAN

A<small>TLAN</small> <small>TIED</small> his brown gelding to a post outside the
weatherworn limestone building that housed the dueling pits.
A chill traveled on the night air, unusual for Yorenth, though
not uncommon in the endless desert to the east.

He, Tyran, and Wrasar pushed past a group of teenage boys
crowding the entrance to the staircase that led deeper into the
building.

'Y'know they used to duel with *magic* here!'

'Yeah, right, Celan,' one of his companions said, nudging
the boy in the side. 'You still believe in tall tales?'

Atlan smiled to himself. He knew he'd probably had a
similar conversation with one of his friends when he was a
child, and then his magic had come in and he'd wondered
whether the old stories were indeed true. All anyone had to go
on were recorded oral histories and a few tomes that were
spared from the firestorms that destroyed the Library of Yoren a
century ago.

On the small landing halfway down, he looked up at the
stars through an open hole in the roof, tiles shattered on the
dirt floor below.

It was then that the pungent, tangy smell of sweat and blood hit him. The thick walls of the expansive cellar reverberated with the sound of crowds screaming over the fight currently underway. Most pit fighters were commonfolk who found that if they had a knack for violence, they could make a lot more coin than they would toiling away in the forge, or in the city's open markets.

Atlan was usually the only noble, and a prince at that. His fights were some of the most popular in the Sledge, and his family turning a blind eye to him most of the time meant he could get away with such behavior.

'The Prince is here!' whispered someone standing off to his right.

The whispering only grew as he prowled across the room to the far end of the pit, where he took off his armor and undershirt and began wrapping his hands for the first round.

Fighting for sport in Yorenth was as old as time, and highly ritualized. One had to be trained both in unarmed and armed combat, for if no one went down in the first round, a second round was fought with wooden weapons. From there, steel. A death match, depending on the skill and determination of the contenders. Atlan could recall many grievous injuries to noble sons who were too proud to yield.

'You ready?'

Atlan relaxed at the sound of Tyran's voice. His oldest friend. He was the only one who didn't go easy on him out of fear during training as new recruits. They'd been friends ever since. Tyran had snuck food to him in the dungeons, they'd seen front lines together, gone drinking underage at Knight's Rest—

'Always.' Atlan looked around at the refuse scattered about him. 'Well, except—have you seen my sheep grease?'

Tyran turned from where he had piled up all his armor. 'Have you checked your arsehole?'

Atlan offered a sardonic chuckle in response. 'Clever, Tyr.'

'It's right here,' he said, a sideways grin on his face, handing it to him.

From the haze, a mix of amberleaf smoke and chalk dust, emerged a stocky, balding man with a long, ruddy beard knotted with various charms and beads. The crowd swelled and silenced as he raised his hand.

'And now, good people,' he rasped, 'without too much delay, the fight you've been waiting for!'

'Up you go, prince,' Tyran gestured toward the ring, slapping Atlan on the backside as he passed.

Roars and screams filled his ears, but he could make out no faces in the darkness that surrounded the brazier-lit ring. He squared his shoulders and rolled his head, his neck cracking loudly, skin prickling with the rush of being back in the pit. His world shrank to the inexorable now.

'The Lion of Yorenth fights Fierabras the Feared!'

More cheers suffocated the air in the room, but he could barely hear them. His opponent entered the ring too, a wiry but muscular man with a long beard and hair trimmed close to his scalp. He gave Atlan a feral smile, showing off several missing teeth.

Atlan's thoughts began moving in flashes. Heat rolled off the fires roaring away in the braziers. Every muscle in his body coiled like a spring, the relentless knot in his core replaced with a warm tension. He felt the involuntary curl of his lip.

They lunged for each other.

Without even thinking, Atlan could sense the openings he might take. His fist connected with his opponent's jaw first, knocking him back several steps, but Fierabras was undeterred and launched forward again with brutal, heart-stopping speed. It was like he'd hardly even felt the blow. If Atlan had had a moment to think, he might've recalled the black amaranth addicts that lingered around the old cistern entrance in the Sledge.

But he had little time to think as he barely dodged his opponent's attack, retreating to the side of the ring.

He felt a swelling in his chest. *Fucking Six.*

He had to be careful in fights not to let his emotions get the better of him, spiraling in an unwitting display of magic.

He dodged another attack, then countered with a hard swing to the man's right flank. Again Fierabras staggered back, but he still didn't look the slightest bit pained or tired. Finally, an opponent that got his blood rushing. A wicked smile crossed his face. He always liked to spend this round tiring his opponent out, frustrating them before they picked up their swords. They traded blows for another minute, much to the rowdy onlookers' delight.

Atlan was preparing to draw him in with a feint when a bell echoed through the amphitheater, and the announcer spoke again. 'Fighters, draw your weapons!'

Had the round gone that fast?

He raised his wooden waster to his opponent in a salute, softly kissing the hilt, and slashing down to the side. When the bell sounded again, he set his feet and assumed farmer-threshes-wheat, a stance with his blade held low and behind, leaving his dominant side exposed. This form was defensive, an open invitation to attack.

Fierabras charged at him with a ferocity that Atlan deftly parried. Fierabras quickly reassessed, moving into viper-strikes-field mouse, blade held high and at the shoulder, with the point extended and aimed at Atlan's face. He advanced, slowly cycling his stance from the right to the left, then left to right, the ironwood blade making tight, gentle arcs.

Atlan noticed his opponent's furrowed brow, tight jaw, and practiced footwork demonstrating a soldier's strict adherence to the forms. He smiled to himself. This opponent was full of surprises.

Fierabras's cross-cutting was intended to make Atlan guess where the first strike would come from.

Too tight, he thought. *Let's loosen him up.*

The world around him shrunk further, and there was blessed silence in Atlan's mind. Just he and his opponent, and the promise of violence.

As his opponent made another cross-cut, Atlan advanced. Fast. Fierabras remained outside of striking distance, but he wasn't the target. Atlan hewed a powerful middle cut at the other blade's tip as it passed by, and with a crack, added to its momentum.

His opponent stumbled, the first bit of shock registering on his face since he'd entered the ring as his own motion was used against him, his body and blade pitching in the direction of Atlan's swing. He was left suddenly exposed.

Time slowed. By now, the crowd was but a distant buzz. The flames illuminated a myopic world. Instead of attacking, Atlan himself retreated into viper-strikes-field mouse. He stood still as a statue, waiting for him. Fierabras gave an almost imperceptible nod, acknowledging the reprieve. He recovered, holding his blade out defensively in thorn-of-the-rose. There was fear there now.

We can't end it that quickly. Atlan smiled. The fighting lust was upon him.

Atlan felt himself become a blur of motion, feinting from one opening to another, allowing his opponent just enough time to parry before cutting at another opening. His opponent's eyes grew wide as he struggled to keep up with Atlan's onslaught.

He cut away, retreating just outside of measure, again adopting farmer-threshes-wheat.

'Again!' Atlan yelled, brows furrowing in a fearsome expression.

Fierabras inched forward, blade quivering slightly as fatigue began to set in.

Atlan would end it now, the climax having been built. He waited for his opponent to enter the proper distance and then—

He was suddenly jarred back into the world by an uncanny feeling, the hair standing up on the back of his neck. His gut twisted back into that sickening knot with a surge of reality. His awareness flickered to the crowd.

Thinking instead of moving, he tried to recover, hitting his opponent again hard in the flank. Fierabras doubled over and grunted, a mingling of pain and frustration, then retaliated with another uncontrolled attack. It was just what Atlan needed. He sidestepped and prepared for the opening his stumble would create, angling to knock Fierabras out with one blow to the skull.

The braziers at the ring's edge were burning lower, and there in the sea of faces, he was suddenly drawn to one face in particular. More like, some short blond hair being brushed out of someone's face by a hand. A hand with a Knave's tattoo.

Could it be?

That distraction was all his opponent needed. Fierabras struck, and his sword cracked against Atlan's forearm with a sickening snap. Atlan suddenly staggered backward, then stumbled to the ground, blinded by pain.

He was seeing in flashes again, but it was nothing like the adrenaline of fighting. He stared at his arm, something clearly broken, feeling as if he'd just been struck by lightning. Tyran rushed toward him, while Wrasar was engulfed in chaos after an onlooker threw a punch at Fierabras.

My sword arm? He blinked.

The announcer yelled something, but he couldn't hear it.

Half the crowd seemed to ebb away from the ring all at once like a sea-tide, as the other half joined the burgeoning brawl.

Tyran said something he couldn't hear over the shouts from the crowd, and as he hauled him to his feet Atlan was still searching the crowd for that woman with the tattoo.

'I saw her!' he yelled, breathless. 'She survived!'

Could she really be here? The woman with the tattooed hand?

Tyran looked around. 'Who?'

'Take this!' he grunted, frantically pulling the note from among their things and shoving it against Tyran's chest. 'Find her! Go!'

He grunted, shoving Tyran off. The movement sent another blinding flash of pain through him. He'd barely gotten the words out as a wave nausea rose in his gut.

Mercifully, Tyran left him to go pursue the woman, who had now disappeared into the surging mass. Atlan muscled through the crowds and staggered up the steps of the dueling pits, a cold sweat breaking out on his neck, his vision tunneling.

Fuck.

He needed to see Sika, get this set, get something for the pain. As he broke out into the cool night air, he sighed in exhausted resignation. With no way to get back on his horse, he began the long, agonizing walk to the palace on foot.

7

KYR

IT WASN'T the first time Kyr had awoken to the cold bite of a dagger at her throat, but it was one of the more inconvenient times in recent memory. She'd found herself in her fair share of predicaments by this point in her life, though she had to admit, the current one still wasn't as frustrating as that time in Quormanth when she'd been caught with the duchess and was forced to flee a frenzy of outraged, halberd-wielding guards out a third-story window.

And just when things were getting interesting, too.

The duchess's skin had been so soft, and her hair smelled of the night-blooming roses that part of the river valley was famous for. Sylas never let her forget how badly she'd fucked that one up.

'Hello, boys,' she said, giving the armored men kneeling over her a lazy grin and rubbing the sleep from her face with the back of one hand. 'Can I help you?'

She would've preferred to have been lying in a soft feather-erbed in an inn somewhere, a beautiful woman asleep next to her and the marks she'd stolen hidden safely away before the Sun's Own caught up with her. But as her bleary eyes took in her surroundings—the slimy stone ceiling of a sewer tunnel above the men's heads—she was rudely reminded that that wasn't her life anymore.

Her gaze traveled downward, studying the weapons they had on them, their armor—the livery of the Sun's Own, but not as clean as most of the guard kept their regalia. And they had their visors down so she couldn't see their faces.

Cowards.

The men didn't speak, merely hauled her up before Kyr could even react, one of them reaching for something at his belt.

They didn't seem likely to tell her, but in her gut she knew this was about the market. *It has to be.*

She quickly tried to use her magic—maybe this time she'd drown the bastards in a flood of wastewater from these filthy tunnels—but they immediately clasped a set of manacles with a strange iridescent tint around her wrists. That serene feeling of resolve that swelled in her chest and traveled along her very bones right before she'd summoned her magic in the past sputtered out completely, leaving a strange emptiness she'd never felt before.

'Don't try anything,' grunted one of the men. 'Those manacles are forged from bismuth alloy. You'll not be transmuting anything with those on.'

Transmuting? She couldn't help the puzzled expression that came over her face. *Is that what happened to the Rook?*

'She's a sand rat,' muttered the other guard. 'Probably doesn't even know what any of that means.'

Kyr kissed her teeth. *Sand rat!*

The men hauled her up and began attempting to force her down the darkened corridor. Kyr responded by hauling her manacled hands skyward and bashing one of the men over the head. He stumbled, and as the other guard spun around, she headbutted him. Kyr reached for the Rook's dagger still stashed in her waistband, but the other guard was already up and on her again, shoving her into the slimy wall so hard she felt the impact rattle her teeth.

He gripped her chin. 'I don't care who you are. Do that again and you'll find yourself at the bottom of the canal.'

She fought back the urge to spit in his face. The other guard was on his feet now, trying to stop the bleeding from his nose, and they grabbed her again, taking special care to bruise her arms.

She gritted her teeth. 'Gentle-knights, I really don't know what this could be about. I was just minding my own business down here in these *lovely* sewers,' she said as they half-dragged her along toward the daylight streaming through the grate that led out to the docks.

They pointedly ignored her.

'Ah, strong, silent types then?' she continued, glancing between them and rolling her eyes, a small, amused smile at her lips. 'Alright.'

She thought back to that day in the market. She was sure she'd covered her tracks after the incident, what with how many times she'd made sure no one was following her, but apparently not well enough. Had she been recognized somewhere?

So many mistakes lately. Now she could only hope they wouldn't cost her too dearly.

'Kyr's like a cat,' Vasha always said. 'Nine lives and all that.' By her estimation, she'd probably used about four of them by now, so she knew she would find a way out of this.

Her mind began racing. To the Sun's Own, the Rooks were just other criminals. Surely, the Crown and its underlings had better things to spend their time on. As far as they were concerned, Kyr had been cleaning up the city for them. They'd probably make her rot in a cell for a while and then let her go quietly.

She took a deep breath, reassuring herself, but a pit had begun to form in her stomach. *They couldn't know about the counting house, could they?*

As they emerged into bright sunlight, she realized how covered in grime she was. And she still didn't have her Spirits-damned boots. They traveled down winding back alleys and along the city's fetid canal until Yorenth's castle town came into view above them. She'd never seen this district in the daytime, only at night as she furtively traveled its shadows doing Sylas's bidding.

She felt the stares of well-dressed nobles she passed like a brand, instead focusing on the hymns echoing from the Solarum. *Pretty bits of music.* She'd have liked to learn an instrument in another life. There she went again, thinking about other lives. *Definitely getting too old for this.*

They began heading deeper into the upper district, and in the daylight the flourishing excess of the nobles of Yorenth was startlingly apparent. All of the homes and monuments were limned with mosaics or gold, gardens were plentiful with trees so heavy with fruit that much of it fell and was left to rot on the ground, and as the sun climbed overhead, many leisurely retreated to private baths or shaded verandas to escape the heat.

Kyr watched blackbirds scatter from the eaves of a nearby roof and thought of the sorry Rook. *Serves him and Sylas right.*

She sighed, wondering what he was doing at that very moment. Would he hear about this? Would he still look for her? The answers filled her with a confusing mixture of hope and worry. Perhaps anyone else would deem it insanity, but Kyr thought maybe she could still reason with him. She knew, deep in that rotted heart of his, he cared for her.

The turn to the guardhouse was just ahead. She'd been there once before, as a kid, to break out a fellow Knave. It had been laughably easy, too. Worrick was the man's name. He'd probably been about her age now, and he'd been caught when the first mate of a crew had gone back aboard their ship to retrieve their captain's forgotten pipe. He found Worrick with some false ship records, a forged letter from the port master, and a bottle of imported whiskey at his lips. Worrick was none too pleased about being rescued by a child, but he came along.

When the men pulling her along didn't take the turn to the guardhouse, Kyr's stomach dropped. The palace came into view, looming over them, for all its gilded edges like a dark cloud. Then, to her horror, the guards shoved her through a set of gates like a mass of golden tridents and up the colossal set of steps leading to the palace.

'Hey, I didn't do anything wrong!' she yelled, thrashing as she frantically tried to break their grip on her.

'Yeah, they always say that,' sighed one of the guards as they forced her along with them, faces completely indifferent, revealing nothing.

There were only a few reasons commoners were ever brought to the royal palace, and none of them good. Kyr tripped on the limestone steps, as if her feet had a mind of their own to carry her far away from there.

They shoved her past ascending columns carved with all sorts of symbols—blazing stars, elaborately dressed men and women with wings, serpents with three heads—before shuffling through an impressive alabaster archway at the top of the stairs and into the cavernous palace.

Tapestries of armored warriors killing ogres and wyverns with swords engulfed in burning light lined the walls, telling tales of the royal family's supposed ancestry. Soloriens commanding armies, even a massive work of embroidery depicting the queen as a flaming phoenix with knights bowing to her.

Everything in Yorenth was named for the Solorien family, for the supposed magic they had once wielded, the gift Solq—

the Spirit of dawn, fire, and luminescence—had once given them. The power of their line had apparently all but dried up these days, and no one had seen the royal family perform magic in at least a century.

Kyr sneered up at her surroundings. *What a load of crap.*

They came to a set of grand doors made of colored glass, and Kyr knew it had to be the throne room that lay behind them. Something was very, *very* wrong.

She knew well she had done something she shouldn't have —by all accounts she'd done a lot of that over the years—but what business was it of the queen's?

'Listen, whatever you think I did—' she started, but the guard to her right jabbed his fist into her gut, causing a nauseating ache deep in her stomach that made her retch. That put a swift end to any further pleading from her.

The doors heaved open, and there at the end of a long, richly colored rug woven with strands of golden thread, with knights and advisors surrounding her, sat the queen on her glass throne. The throne room was open to the outside, but without much of a breeze it did little to quell the oncoming mid-day heat.

Queen Attiqah Solorien of Yorenth, rumored to be mad— and carrying on a bold love affair out in the open with her former captain of the Sun's Own, a handsome warrior named Taryq—ruled the Realm of the Sentinel with a gilded fist. King Osimar Solorien could generally be seen sitting a noticeable distance off to the queen's side somewhere, apparently content to be draped in silks and jewels and to feast on spiced meats and cheeses.

The queen was perched on her throne like a bird, her long neck, black hair and near black, lightless eyes reminding Kyr of the Rook once more. Subtle wrinkles lined her eyes and bracketed her mouth, and she wore kohl and red ochre on her face, as was common among the highborn. She was dressed in an elaborate black gown that drowned her small figure, a golden lace collar framing her visage. In one hand she held a scepter, in the other, a black lace fan which she was vigorously waving.

'Your Radiance,' said one of the guards as they approached. 'This is the fugitive.'

The fugitive?

'Ah,' said the queen in a low, husky voice that surprised Kyr. 'Yes, let me have a look at her.'

Though she'd grown up in the slums all her life, Kyr never felt more like a pauper as she was shoved, covered in grime, bare-footed, and weak from days of scrounging for food wherever she could find it, toward the regal woman. Still, she met the queen's scrutinizing gaze.

'What is your name?' Queen Attiqah asked, an unnervingly soft and kind smile on her face.

At first Kyr didn't want to answer, but then she thought of the guards and their fists so close at her side, and she did not think she would be the first commoner to be beaten for amusement by this lot. 'Kyr ap Sand.'

'Ap Sand?' the queen said, her eyes showing the slightest hint of surprise. 'No family at all?'

Kyr shook her head. Unless you counted all the other lost children of caravanners who shared the name, some of whom ended up in the Knaves' Keep.

'You will address Her Radiance properly,' snapped one of her knights, a man with tanned skin and long blond hair the color of straw.

The queen held up her hand. 'It's fine, she knows not the ways of court.' She hummed to herself, then leaned toward one of her advisors. Kyr could just barely make out the end of what she said as she began pulling away. '. . . but I don't see it, do you?'

The man looked Kyr over in a way she didn't like, then turned back to the queen.

'If she does have the gift, it's worth an inquiry. It won't matter either way to the guild.'

Whatever *gift* they were talking about, Kyr knew she certainly didn't have it. If they were talking about the strange happenings that had turned her life upside down, then she'd hardly call that a gift.

It was then that Kyr noticed a man about her age, maybe a little younger, standing off to the right, behind all the others. His brown skin and long black hair were so like that of the queen's.

Holy shit. She tried to stifle a laugh, but it bubbled up anyway.

The entire room went silent as everyone turned to look at her. She straightened, looking down at the floor, and they turned away again.

That really was Prince Atlan in the Sledge, not just some gimmick to sell more tickets to the pits. She'd never been able to get a good enough spot to see the royal family on festival and feast days, nor had the time to see 'the Prince's' matches before. She thought it all theater, that there was probably just some man from a middling family who looked enough like the Prince.

The only other things she knew about him she'd heard from bards and criers. There was plenty of talk in the taverns about how the older prince was rarely seen at royal events and estranged from the rest of the family. He was out of favor with the queen, and it was said she preferred her younger son, Vyktas, a child of her dalliance with Sol Taryq.

The queen and her men continued talking in hushed voices about Kyr while she stood there at their mercy. In the distance, through open arches before an enormous stone balcony, Kyr watched the hazy sun as it began its descent behind the mountains. From there, you could see all of Yorenth. The lower city, like the base of a spire that held up the castle town and palace at its point, was surrounded by barren lands that stretched out all around for miles. If these sanctimonious lunatics didn't kill her, she was getting out of this place for good.

'Vyktas,' murmured the queen, motioning the blond-haired knight who had reprimanded Kyr over to her. *So, the rumors are true, then.*

The older prince, Atlan, stood still as stone. His black linen shirt and leather trousers, though well-tailored, were so noticeably different from his brother's gold-trimmed armor and long saffron-dyed cape emblazoned with an embroidered sun. His right arm was in a reed splint from the nasty blow he took at the fight. The way the older prince's eyes watched his mother and brother betrayed his interest in their conversation, but his face remained emotionless, and he never spoke.

The queen continued a hushed conversation with Vyktas for a few more moments, laughing several times with her son and periodically glancing over at Kyr.

With nothing else to do, she studied the Solorien throne more closely. It was made of thousands of pieces of colorful glass so that when light reflected off of it, it cast iridescent light across the vast room. *Lovely, certainly,* but Kyr couldn't help but look at it and wonder how many workers in the Sledge contracted grey lung all for a pretty chair for her to sit on.

With a raspy clearing of her throat, the queen turned back to everyone present. 'Yes,' she said, and began nodding absent-mindedly. 'Guards, take Kyr ap Sand to the palace dungeons, and'—her piercing eyes traveled down to Kyr's wrists—'who has the key for those?'

The guard to Kyr's right stepped forward.

'Atlan,' the queen said, gesturing for him to retrieve the key without looking at him.

The guard approached the prince casually, dropping it into

his gloved palm. Kyr wondered whether that was out of some unspoken disrespect or, rather, because they were close friends.

Before she could think much more of it, Queen Attiqah turned and spoke to a woman Kyr had not noticed before, and this time Kyr overheard.

'We'll soon see if she is who he thinks she is.'

Kyr's eyes frantically looked around as several knights began closing in.

'Wait!' she yelled, but the queen's offended face flicking over to her was enough to make her swallow her words. There was something quietly threatening in everything she did, and Kyr knew she was well beyond fighting back now. Her chance of escape was back in the sewers, not here.

She readied herself to be taken away.

I know when I'm outnumbered.

The guards dragged her away again, out the way they came and then down, down, down. All the way to the royal dungeons, usually reserved for traitors, prisoners of war, and the like.

And now, Kyr too.

8

KYR

'YOU'VE REALLY GONE and done it now, Kyr,' she muttered to herself. She held her manacled hands up to the darkness and, in a moment of frustration, roared and slammed them against the wall. Wearing these damned things was pure torture. She had a corrosive itch deep in her chest that had proven impossible to soothe.

Is this magic? Is this what it's supposed to feel like?

She wondered if she was stuck like this, cursed to feel this way forever. Even more vexing—had that feeling always been there, deep within her, and she'd just never noticed it? She sighed, pushing her racing thoughts away.

Kyr settled into the corner, still aching from the guard's gut punch. She'd already searched the cell from top to bottom, scouring it for anything she could use to pick the lock on the manacles, but found nothing. Not even a twig in the dirty, sodden hay that covered the floor.

How had they even learned she had magic in the first place? She assumed they had somehow connected her to the guild's job at the counting house, and certainly they'd be able to get a clear description of her from any number of people at the

66

Tyrdas market, but no one in the lower city believed in magic. Not magic like that, magic that could kill.

What did they know that she didn't?

She leaned her head back against the cold stone and tried to ignore the hunger and the ache in her cheek that was sure to bruise. She had almost nodded off when she heard voices and footsteps nearing her cell.

Someone in armor visiting at this time of night? *Not good.*

Kyr startled awake, sitting up just in time to hear the padlock on her cell door clatter to the ground. Two Sun's Own entered.

'Ap Sand,' a familiar voice called. It was one of the same men from earlier, the one who had shoved her up against the wall in the sewers.

'Come to get a little more of your anger out?' she replied.

He exhaled, not quite a sigh. 'I'm sorry about that. We weren't sure who we were dealing with.' The man removed his helmet, revealing a shaved head and thick black beard. 'Call me Wrasar.'

'And who did you think you were dealing with, Wrasar?'

The man shrugged. 'You tell me.'

Kyr crossed her arms and leaned the against the cell wall. 'You want my life story, or just the fun bits, highborn?'

He smiled, but it was a humorless expression that made her feel more threatened than anything else. 'We've heard some rumors. How about starting with those? And I'm no highborn, I was born in the Sledge.'

Kyr chuckled. 'Ah, I see.' *Bootlicker.* She looked him over. 'Not an ap Sand though, I take it. Your parents must be proud.'

'Ragpickers. They are.'

Kyr nodded. 'Then you know I can't have heard much of anything useful to nobles, let alone royalty.' He opened his mouth to protest but she kept going. 'Rumors do fly in the Sledge, but I hardly expect you want to know about mine contract feuds and who's skimming off the top of which gold piles.'

'Oh, that's where you're wrong,' Wrasar said, scratching his beard. 'I'm very interested in hearing anything a Knave has to tell me.'

'That so? And if I told you I'd heard the Sun's Own gather together and perform dark rites beneath the palace?'

Wrasar's smile was so faint, she could really only see it in his eyes. He cocked his head. 'Very funny.'

Kyr smirked. 'Listen, I'm always happy to oblige, but I don't have any idea what you boys are talking about. You're going to have to be a little more specific.'

Wrasar leaned in and she looked away from the scrutiny in his gaze. 'I think you do. I think you know a thing or two about what happened at the counting house, and I think you know a thing or two about magic.' Her head snapped back to him. Wrasar raised his brows in a smug expression.

Shit. She expected this to be about the Rook, and now she'd given herself away.

'Kyr, right?' She said nothing. 'Kyr, your friends in the Sledge ratted you out. You're already facing execution for the counting house, but telling us about your magic, it might help you. Save you, even. The queen has a keen interest in the magical.'

Kyr felt a cold sweat break out on her neck and sat up. She swallowed hard. 'I wasn't even at the counting house. I'm only a sand rat, remember? I'm not even allowed in that part of the city.'

Wrasar regarded her coolly. 'You seem to be having problems with your memory, Kyr. You fit the description of someone seen at the counting house when it collapsed. Yet you're here, alive. How?'

'I'm alive *because* I wasn't anywhere near it. You've got the wrong person.' She thought about telling them the truth—it seemed she was pretty much fucked either way, but as panic rose within her, her Knavish sensibilities took over. Sylas's voice in her head.

If you're ever caught, deny everything. Then she thought about the words he always said next. *I will come for you.* Each time she thought of him, her heart broke all over again.

'Allow me to jog your memory a little further, then,' said Wrasar. 'Anyone who was there would have to know something. The counting house isn't just collapsed,' he said, giving her a pointed look, 'it doesn't exist anymore. There's a rift in the earth so deep we haven't reached the bottom. The crowners likely won't recover all of the bodies. The west tower is gone. Diviners were sent to the area, but their magic . . . it doesn't *work* there.'

Kyr whistled low. 'That sounds pretty bad. Seems like you're looking for someone who knows a lot about magic.' She shrugged. 'And I know nothing.'

'We thought you might say that. Listen to me. If you don't want to talk to us, that's fine.' Wrasar's body visibly loosened, but Kyr didn't feel any less tension. 'But someone else might come in here next, and they might be nicer than me, but they might not be. They might be much worse. I suggest you tell us what we want to know, and that way we can all be done with this.'

She looked from him to the silent guard behind him and grinned. 'On to threats already? Not how I'd handle it, but I'm sure you know what you're doing. Send your friend in, I sure as shit have nothing to say to you.' Kyr stretched out her legs and placed her hands behind her head, then closed her eyes.

Wrasar rolled his shoulders, an annoyed expression on his face, and he crossed the room to stand over her. 'We know it was you at the counting house. We know you displayed magic, Kyr. You did it out in the open, for Spirits' sake. You were *hiding* in a *sewer*.'

She couldn't tell if that second comment was in reference to the counting house, the Rook, or both. If they knew about both, her situation was far more grave than she had realized. She thought of the people in the commerce district and the market and wondered which of them had informed on her.

'Oh, did I forget to tell you? I became an acolyte of Solq last week and gave up all my worldly possessions.'

Wrasar's shoulders sank slightly and a different kind of tiredness tugged at the corners of his mouth and eyes. 'I tried to reason with you, Kyr. If you won't talk to me, then I have nothing to relay to the Captain of the Guard and the Queen. There's nothing I can do for you.'

She raised her chin. 'I don't need you to do anything for me.'

Wrasar shook his head and motioned for the other guard to follow him. The door slammed shut, and then she was alone again.

———

That night Kyr dreamed of the Keep. It was an ordinary day there. She woke up early because Erich, the scoundrel, had a woman in his room. After a hasty bath, she woke Vasha and they went downstairs to eat breakfast—oranges and coffee, like always.

In her dream she could even smell the chocolate, acidic smell from their cups and feel the latent heat that the sunbaked air of Yorenth never seemed to lose, even at night.

'Sylas is looking for you,' said a shorter, broad-shouldered woman with long black hair, one of the new recruits, though Kyr didn't know her name. It was one of those oddities of dreams where she was sure she knew the person, but upon waking realized she was never real, only an amalgam of the memories of different people.

'Wonder what he wants with you at this Spiritsforsaken

hour,' Vasha grumbled. He would've slept until midafternoon if he'd had any say in the matter.

'Let me guess . . . probably wants me to break into something. Ooh, or sneak in somewhere!'

Vasha's lip curled up around the edge of his mug. 'How original.'

She chuckled and tried to steal orange slices from his plate. Vasha swatted her hand, and while he was distracted, she stole the whole unpeeled orange out of his other hand. He scowled beneath his unruly mop of peppery curls.

'I'll see you later?'

'Fine.' He waved her away.

She passed through the courtyard archway into the shadows of the den of the Knaves' Keep. It was rumored the Keep had once been a shrine to a fire mage of Solq, and you could still see it in the crumbling frescos, the old ceremonial braziers lining the halls.

She entered the third room down the hall on the left, and found Sylas hunched over a series of letters from runners, thieves, and nobles alike. Hundreds of clothbound books lined the wall at his back, mostly ledgers and stolen records. She'd looked through a few of them before on rare occasions when Sylas left her alone in the guild's archives, but they were mostly filled with boring, coded messages about business dealings in Yorenth.

'You sent for me?'

Sylas looked up at her, with his usual mild annoyance at first and then, beneath that, a sly twinkle in his eyes that betrayed his love of her. 'Ah, there's the pup.'

'What do you need me to do?' she said as she fell into a chair in the corner of the room and began peeling the orange she'd stolen from Vasha.

'There's no job,' he said, straightening some papers against the desk. 'I wanted to see you. To see how you're doing.'

Kyr tilted her head. He never talked like that. 'I'm fine,' she answered, sounding more standoffish than she meant to.

'Of course you are.' He sat, the wooden chair creaking as he reclined in it. Even from here, she could smell the tobacco, soap, and wine on him, like always. 'My Kyr. You're always fine, aren't you?'

Kyr stopped peeling the orange and studied him. He stared back in that steady, unflinching way of his, as though he already knew what you were thinking and was just waiting for you to say it.

By the window, a kestrel rattled in its cage. Sylas kept several birds, something which had always unnerved Kyr. She thought they should be free, flying high above the city.

In an instant, Kyr was transported, imagining what the city would look like from above. If you were to enter Yorenth through its gates, it felt dizzyingly claustrophobic, like an anthill. But from above, one could see how expansive it really was. A few struggling farms out in the marshes surrounded the lower city gates, that by now had mostly turned from crops to grazing animals in ever-dwindling flocks.

She flew out over the Sledge, a kaleidoscope of straw- and tile-roofed buildings which abutted the narrow dock district and the Wravellian Sea. From this vantage, she thought she might be able to see all the way to Saeria. Yorenth's castle town coiled above the lower city like a watchful serpent, and its eyes were the palace itself.

Suddenly, a tearing sensation gripped her chest, and Kyr wanted to cry, to scream. She saw flashes of wilderness, rain on darkened windowpanes, before returning to the Keep. Sylas was still looking at her. She tried to speak, but found she had no voice.

Kyr woke up cold and alone.

9

ATLAN

ATLAN OPENED his eyes to the sight of his mother sitting at the foot of his bed, looking more than a little displeased. His father, oddly, was there too, sitting in the armchair in the corner and staring idly out the window. A rare appearance without a goblet or a falcon in his hands.

'How are you feeling, son?' His father had a cautious look.

'Fine,' Atlan answered, a bit bewildered. His eyes narrowed as he watched his father look to his mother, as if for a signal of what to say.

'The dueling pits again?' Osimar asked. 'Now, you know that's no place for a prince.'

'A prince?' he said, looking between them. 'A prince has duties, responsibilities. A prince trains with the blade and takes lessons with all of the royal tutors. Last I checked, I stopped all of that when I was, what, seventeen? I haven't been a prince in over a decade.'

Osimar's eyes brightened, offended. 'Your mother is queen, and I am king. You will always be a prince, Atlan.'

Atlan raised his brows in a challenge to that.

His father sighed and produced a small vial from his

pocket. 'I'm told your arm set nicely. Sika wanted me to give you this.'

Ah, he thought. *So that's one reason for this charming visit.* Sika hadn't been in the infirmary when they'd set his arm, much to his disappointment. They still didn't want him seeing her, despite it being years since the last time he'd touched a sedative.

'As you know, alchemy's never a perfect science. There will be some unpleasant side effects,' he said awkwardly, 'but it should heal the bone quickly enough for you to resume your duties.'

Atlan eyed the vial hesitantly but took it. 'What's this about? I know the two of you didn't come here simply to give me a potion Sika could've had delivered.'

His mother straightened like a snake seeing its opportunity to strike. 'You are responsible for plenty, or are you forgetting your duties already? Osimar gently placed his hand on her arm, but Attiqah withdrew from his touch. 'What information do you have for me from that beggarwoman?'

And the true reason reveals itself.

The woman Tyran and Wrasar captured after his disastrous fight was a Knave—a thief—not a beggarwoman, not that any of that mattered to his mother. They were one and the same, lower than low. He'd been so in shock at seeing her, how she fit the description Wren had given him exactly, that he hadn't thought about what he was really doing.

Condemning her to death.

'Well?' his mother prodded. 'I made the long walk all the way here, I expect you have something to tell me?'

A dry laugh escaped him. 'And I suppose the infirmary was too far a walk?'

Her face hardened. 'Again with this? I already told you, the queen must be seen as a patron of the arts. The portraitist was already waiting. I can't shirk my duties just because you let some cretin off the streets break your arm in what, may I remind you, is conduct very unbecoming of a Captain of the Guard.'

His father blithely nodded along.

'Mm,' Atlan grunted, a sarcastic non-answer.

He fought off any reaction to the memory of his disastrous bout and the long night in the infirmary that followed and took a deep breath. 'I had some of my men to speak to Kyr ap Sand last night. She claims not to know anything about the attack on the counting house, nor her magical abilities from those rumors in the Sledge.' He shrugged, wincing at the pain that shot through his shoulder and arm. 'I'm continuing to search—'

The queen's glare seemed to sharpen somehow, making her look more like a force of nature than human. 'You *sent* your *men?*' she asked harshly. 'This is important for our family's future, Atlan! For the future of my rule!'

There it is. What really matters.

She exhaled sharply. 'I suppose I have to do everything for this family.' Atlan looked at his father, but he was looking intently at a gold-thread rosette on his mantle. 'It doesn't matter who this woman is. This is about our family's legacy, which I am trying to protect!'

'Oh, yes, legacy,' said Atlan mockingly. 'Always looking forward to what you can gain, to how you'll be remembered. Commissioning portraits and statues of yourself for people who aren't even *born yet* to gawk at a hundred years from now, when none of this will matter!'

His mother bored into him with her eyes. 'The people who are yet to be born determine our immortality. I thought I raised you to understand this, to be like our great ancestors, but it would seem that somewhere along the way, my firstborn son became a lazy, unambitious lout.'

'Are you going to chime in, Father?' Atlan scoffed.

'Listen to your mother,' was all he said.

Atlan shook his head. They could call it 'unambitious,' if they wanted, but he refused to see it that way. In his eyes, he simply didn't do what they wanted him to do, and that infuriated them. *Who decided their way of doing things is the only way?*

He tried to explain himself. 'I thought that—'

'Enough,' his mother snapped. 'I don't care what you thought. Anyone who even *might* have magic is a threat to the Crown until they are under our boot. Come, we are going down there.'

'What, now?' he protested.

'Yes,' she answered sternly. 'And you will come with me to learn how you should have handled the situation. If she's the thorn in my side that's been causing all of this, I will find out.'

———

Atlan hated the claustrophobic dungeons even more now than he had when he was a boy. They frightened him then, but as he grew older the place took on the same melancholy, suffocating temper of all the terrible memories he had acquired within their buried walls.

As he passed under the limestone archway at the bottom of the narrow staircase that pitched down into the earth, he wondered if his mother ever thought of those times she sent him here as punishment. If she did, she never spoke of it.

The sight of the oubliettes still made him forget himself and go someplace else in his mind. A wretched moaning drifted up out of one of them and Atlan tightened his good hand into a fist until he thought his fingernails digging into his palm might break the skin.

'Your Radiance,' muttered a Sun's Own just ahead, straightening from his position leaning against the doorway at the entrance to the cells, clearly surprised to see them both there at all, but more than that, to see them together.

'Martiq,' she ordered. 'Where is my new prisoner? Take us to her.'

'Kyr?'

The queen pursed her lips, an expression Atlan had seen many times before. He knew from experience she was irritated that the guard had referred to the prisoner by name, as if it undermined her somehow.

'Yes,' she said curtly.

Martiq nodded hastily and they followed him down the corridor, past cells occupied by creatures that used to be men, their eyes empty and skeletal backs hunched over. Most of them were political prisoners of some sort, people who had done everything from hiding lesser magics from the Crown, to preaching something she disliked about the Spirits, to those that had murdered guards, even set fire to the Solarum.

Martiq's bulky armor and flowing cape made his movements clumsy in such a narrow space, and his mother's skirts dragged along the walls on either side. The dungeon was built like a maze, confusing to navigate if one did not already know their way, and with it being underground, the only light came from torches lining the walls, making it all the more oppressive.

Atlan flicked the key to the magic-deadening manacles still around Kyr's wrists between his thumb and forefinger. He knew magic. It loved passion, craved rage with nowhere to go. If Kyr truly did have some kind of power, they were playing a dangerous game keeping her locked up.

They walked for what felt to Atlan like hours down never-ending, labyrinthian halls, before coming to a stop in front of one of many indistinguishable cell doors. Martiq, whose face was damp with sweat, either because of nervousness or the stifling air down there, pulled a large, hammered iron ring dripping with keys from his belt. He unlocked the door.

'Your Radiance,' Martiq said with a bow of his head, but the queen stopped him with a raised hand as he turned to go.

'Wait. I suspect I'll be needing you a moment longer.'

Martiq shifted nervously on his feet but followed them into the dank cell.

Kyr sat in the far corner, opposite a bucket reeking of shit, studying the manacles at her wrists. In the light from the torch outside, Atlan could see the sheen of sweat lining her brow. 'Another visit? To what do I owe this pleasure?' she said without looking up.

This wasn't an act. There was not a hint of fear in her voice. If he hadn't already known, Atlan would've guessed she was an ap Sand right then. To him, Kyr seemed as fearless as they come.

'I understand you must be angry,' the queen began.

'Angry?' Kyr huffed a laugh. 'You think this is my first time being thrown in a locked room by someone who thinks I'm nothing but a . . . what was the phrase your men used? Sand rat? I might've been angry a long time ago. To be honest, I don't give anger much thought anymore.'

'I understand,' the queen said, nodding. Kyr finally looked at her. 'You're rebelling against this world. It's been unfair to you, as it is to many.'

'Oh, save it,' Kyr challenged. 'Whatever lines you've rehearsed, they aren't going to work.' She blew out a breath through her nose. 'You nobles are insufferable. I don't know what ideas you've gotten into your heads about who I am, but I can assure you, I'm nothing. Just a thief, who killed a murderer. Do with me what you will, but please, don't make me listen to this drivel.'

Killed a murderer?

His mother clasped her hands together. 'Look at that, we're already getting somewhere. Who did you kill, Kyr ap Sand?'

For the first time, Kyr's expression faltered. She'd just

admitted to something, and it was clear they knew astonishingly little about it.

'What? Isn't that what I'm here for? The Rook?'

'There were no Rooks at the counting house,' said Atlan.

His mother cut him a furious glare for interrupting.

'It seems there's some confusion,' his mother continued. 'What there *is* little confusion about, however, is your use of magic at the counting house. You're going to tell us about how you detonated it, and then you're going to demonstrate your magical abilities to us. We can discuss the rest of your life of crime after that.'

'Whoa,' said Kyr, putting her hands up. 'I did not *blow up* the counting house. And I already told the others. If I knew how to summon these abilities you and everyone else seem to think I have, I would. But I don't. Not to mention these,' she said, lifting up her shackled hands, 'kind of makes it difficult.'

'I see you do not want to cooperate with our inquiry,' said his mother, frowning.

Kyr gave her an incredulous look.

Queen Attiqah raised her chin, a faraway look falling over her eyes, as though she were seeing something at a distance. 'You are being charged with hiding your magic from the Crown. This is a serious offense.' The queen's eyes snapped back to Kyr. 'However, if you were willing to demonstrate your abilities for us and explain how you discovered them and how long you've known about them, we could discuss a potential pardon and a place among the court's diviners.'

'So, this is what happens to the court diviners,' Kyr remarked. 'Service or death.'

His mother smirked. 'Something like that.'

Kyr turned away from them. 'I told you, I don't know anything about the counting house. The Rook fell dead at my feet. Others on the street, they said I killed him. I hardly touched him.'

'Martiq,' the queen huffed, gesturing to where Kyr sat. The conversation, Atlan knew, was over. Her patience at an end. It was in that moment he wished, like he had so many times before, that he wasn't so attuned to his mother's moods, knowing exactly what she was about to do before she did it. He would trade his titles, his riches, his men all, not to know.

Martiq hesitated only a moment before charging across the room as though he was already trying to get what he was about to do over with. He reached down, grabbing Kyr by her shirt, and hit her hard across the jaw.

Kyr's lip split open instantly, blood speckling the wall behind her and draining bright ruby down her chin.

'There's the tyrant,' Atlan heard her mutter.

He was staring at the floor, but for some reason, he couldn't turn his back on her. He heard the next blow. And the next. And another after that.

Atlan didn't want to watch a moment longer. He began backing toward the door, but his mother grabbed him and shoved him forward, gesturing to the key in his hands with raging, animalistic eyes.

Memories echoed in his head. *Do as I say. Do as I say.*

'Again,' she said, looking on solemnly. Atlan slowly stepped toward the manacled and beaten thief, who was now curled over against the wall like a wounded animal just trying to survive the onslaught.

He grabbed her by the wrists and unlocked her manacles.

'Again, Martiq,' the queen ordered when the guard hesitated.

With her hands free, Kyr stood and tried to ready herself to block the hit this time, but having to squint through the blood that poured down her face slowed her down. Atlan knew what that was like. Head wounds bled a lot.

The guard hit her harder this time, and Kyr spit out a piece of a tooth onto the stone before slumping backward against the wall. Atlan could only stand there, his head turned away.

Just as the queen was about to order another blow, the cell lit up like a brazier had been set alight. Martiq yelped and staggered back, and Atlan's eyes flashed to the source of the glow.

The Knave was on fire.

There, engulfed in flames in the corner of the cell, her clothes did not burn, her hair framing her battered face was not singed, and as she sank to her knees, she did not cry out. She did not make a sound.

He realized what was happening. She wasn't *on* fire, the air around her was combusting as she protected herself in a cloak of flame. Small flames burst from the ether, licking at nothing. Burning out and then reigniting, over and over.

She's changing the composition of the air around her?

Sweat beaded on Atlan's face, but he barely noticed, so in awe was he of such a unique display of raw magical power.

The queen's brows were pinched together, her bewilderment and irritation plain, but Atlan thought he saw something else beyond the flames dancing within those black eyes of hers. Something he'd never seen before.

'Now, was that so hard?' said Attiqah.

Just as quickly as the flames had come, they winked out and Kyr lay exhausted in the dirt and straw scattering the floor. She wiped the blood from her face on her arm and grunted.

It was then that she first glanced at him, and he saw the wild tenacity in her eyes. The kind of grit that only comes from having to figure everything out on your own.

A fellow fighter.

In a rage, his mother spoke. 'It seems we have a confession on multiple accounts—'

'Your Radiance,' Atlan said quickly, leashing the excitement in his voice. It was risky enough interrupting his mother when she was like this, but something in him made him press further. 'Might I confer with you for a moment?'

His mother glared at him before relenting and nodding, leading him away toward the cell door.

Atlan leaned into his mother's ear as they turned away from Kyr. 'I believe her. I don't think she has any idea about how to use her magic unless she's forced to. She's the most powerful mage we've come across yet. Let Saartho and I train her. I can keep a close eye on her and report to you about her progress. She may prove useful in helping us control the blights. And I know you've had your eye on expanding the Realm. With training, she could be a powerful weapon.'

'Control them? What if she's the cause of them?' his mother whispered harshly. 'Especially if she doesn't know what she's doing. That makes her a danger to us!' The queen's voice was low but frenzied. Still, Atlan could see she had begun thinking. 'She could be a powerful asset to our army in the future, true, but I have you. Another mage outside the family? It's too great a risk.'

'She's not just a mage, and you know it. Only a Singer can do something like that.' His mother's caliginous eyes flicked to Kyr. 'Please. I can control her with the manacles if need be. She's too great an advantage to execute for nothing.' He hoped he was convincing, because in truth he hadn't any plan to use those horrid things. His mother clasped those manacles around his own wrists when he didn't obey her. The way your magic guttered out as soon as they were placed on you, it was like an itch you could never scratch. Even though the way he spoke sickened him, he knew it was a language his mother would understand.

The queen studied him intensely for a moment before nodding once. 'Fine. You have my permission. But I expect you to be at council meetings every Tyrdas. I want to know everything you learn about her, and if she makes any move against us, I'll have Tanwen picking at her intestines before the day is out.'

Images of his mother on the battlefield with Tanwen flashed through his mind, and he sighed, nodding solemnly. Perhaps tonight would not end in more suffering.

The queen strode over to Kyr and looked down at her, arms folded. 'Kyr ap Sand, I have a proposal for you.'

'I can't wait,' Kyr said, somehow managing an almost smug expression despite her bloodied, harrowing appearance. She was rolling something between her thumb and forefinger, and Atlan realized with no small amount of horror that it was the piece of her own chipped tooth.

'Because you have already faced enough punishment today, I'll not acknowledge your disrespect. But make that mistake again and it will be your last. My son, Prince Atlan, has graciously offered to train you in the way of your magic so that you may better serve the Crown. You will reside in the servant's quarters and have daily training sessions with the prince and the royal historian and master diviner, Saartho Ulam. They will report to me on your progress. If you do anything to harm the Crown, attempt to escape, or otherwise sow mistrust, the punishment will be death, which you've only just so narrowly avoided, so I suggest you do as you're told.'

Kyr nodded primly, opening a blood-red mouth. 'It would be an honor, Your Radiance.'

Atlan lowered his head—otherwise, he didn't think he could hide his smile at the fawning Knave.

Was he truly meeting someone else who could do the same frightening things he could?

He almost chuckled as he thought about how angry Vyktas would be at the thought of another Singer, and a Knave at that, in the royal house. And for Atlan to get to spend time with someone who might understand him, someone outside of his miserable family?

He didn't care if she hated him and his family just as much as he did. As he left the cell, his smile grew.

10

MOTHRIL

THE TORTURER DID NOT FEEL the rope burning his palms as he tied off the rowboat at the hidden entrance to the citadel tunnels. Scars had covered his hands since his adolescence, the nerve endings there all but destroyed. He looked down at the wooden belly of the boat and noticed a dagger lying there, a personal effect of the man he'd just thrown overboard. He picked it up, eyeing the initials, *S.o.E.* engraved just above the crossguard, then tossed it into the basin. He never bothered to learn their names anymore. It was easier, not knowing what the initials stood for. Instead, he often found himself remembering their eyes. The emotion they held when they were so full of hope, the way the pupils dilated with fear. And then, something beyond all of that, as he brought their bodies into the light, humble in their regard of the sky.

The morning fog created an opaque screen on either end of the tunnel he'd docked at, and he relished the feeling of knowing he was unseen. It was almost as if he didn't exist, which was exactly how he preferred it. That, and it shielded him from the harsh light he so rarely saw these days.

His cloak whispered against the cold stone at his feet, as he ascended the familiar steps from the towpath into the tunnels and stooped under the doorway into darkness black as night. He hardly even felt the churning of his stomach anymore as he made his way into one of the lower chambers, a feeling that used to sicken him on the way to his day's work.

The bloodied figure tied to the rack off to his right was dimly lit by the glow of ancient Eradomin blood magic along the walls, and he moaned in fear as the torturer's shadowy form entered. The rust-colored, faintly glowing markings made most Wiccars too fearful to even enter the tunnels, which meant most days he was alone from sun-up until dusk.

He could hear the man trying to shift away from him as much as his wrecked body would allow, but still he ignored him as he heaved his tools onto the table, unfolding the leather case and running his hands over the metal implements inside. As he selected a thumbscrew and a small blade, the man screamed a strangled cry through his undoubtedly sore throat. Still, Mothril didn't turn. It was as if he hadn't even heard him at all.

He spent several long moments sharpening the knife, focusing on the *snick* of the stone honing the metal's edge rather than the muffled cries of his victim. He hardly acknowledged those who came to his chamber now. For one, there were too many of them to even recall, but he learned long ago that it was the only way he would be able to do this work.

Just flesh and bone.

Finally, the torturer turned to face the man, who had soiled himself already. That was expected. What was not expected was the presence of the Prime's foremost Elder, Melsze, and a young woman.

Melsze beheld him with a look of pure disgust, while the girl's eyes were wide and filled with fear. He was used to that look from Melsze's previous visits down here. As for the girl, he'd never seen her before.

'Oh. I am not used to an audience,' Mothril said, his face flat and voice soft.

'We aren't here to *watch*, you deviant,' Melsze scoffed. Mothril remained expressionless, saying nothing. Melsze sighed. 'You're being relieved of your duties here.'

Relieved? Mothril's post hadn't changed in years. Neither had his father's. It wasn't supposed to change.

He felt an expectation of confusion or anger, but the feeling itself never came. Still, Melsze's declaration startled him. He had *become* his work. He'd had to.

'Wh—What do you mean?'

'I know you'll miss your vile little freak's den,' Melsze sighed. 'But the Prime has decreed that you are to guard Whispess Oria's room. Starting right now. If I could answer your questions, well, I still wouldn't. But I can't, so that makes asking them doubly useless.'

The Whispess? Mothril furrowed his brow. Why would the Prime want someone like him near her, of all people?

'There must be a mistake. You're sure of this?'

'Regrettably,' Melsze said flatly. 'Lyra will show you the way to her quarters.' The girl stepped forward, and Mothril's eyes darted to her shaking hands. She quickly placed them behind her back when she noticed him staring, but then his eyes went to her torso rising with rapid breaths.

He was so used to looking for signs of discomfort in others. *She's nervous.*

'Can I bring my things?' he asked after a moment.

'Can you *bring your things?* You mean your creepy little torture tools? You'll not be bringing anything of the sort near the Whispess!' Melsze said, aghast.

Mothril nodded. 'I'll just—'

'Your *belongings* will be brought to your new quarters. The Whispess has recently had an . . . episode, so you must go immediately. Her maiden will explain once you've arrived.'

With that, Mothril left his chamber behind without so much as a look over his shoulder. He lumbered along behind the girl in silence, after she'd hopelessly tried to make painful conversation with him for the first minute or so. Turns out he and a girl no older than her twenty-first winter had absolutely nothing in common.

They reached the surface and crossed a short bridge over a glass-like pond, rippling with drops of rain between the lily-pads. Rivers ran like creases in a palm through the entire citadel, which occupied one level in its entirety, from the water-falls that sat stoically at its back to the lake and forest's edge to the south. The entire place had been in disrepair for decades, and the clans lacked both the knowledge and the tools to do much to save the intricate stonework. Instead, they lived at once like kings and paupers, in their crumbling fortress in the woods.

The pair approached the Prime's quarters, empty now except for the Prime, the warlord Edril Sil, and his daughter, Whispess Oria, since he, in opposition to the usual custom, refused to take another wife after Lady Felith died. Mothril had briefly served as a hired swordsman in Lady Felith's service, but he had never met the Prime except in passing.

Edril Sil had come to prominence decades ago from murky origins, seemingly rising from the Northern mists themselves to lead the Wiccars in battle. He had been instrumental in turning the tide against the Eradomin, and tales were still told of his ascendant charisma in battle, his very presence seeming to elicit great valor in men.

His marriage into an illustrious Wiccar family shortly after-ward legitimized him among the clans. Mothril's father met with Edril Sil when they first arrived at the citadel, striking some kind of deal that was still a mystery to him. When his father, torturer and executioner before him, had needed an apprentice, Mothril's fate was sealed. He'd been in the tunnels ever since.

What reason had the Prime for changing things now in his thirty-eighth winter? He was too set in his ways to learn the habits of a new post.

Mothril's mind raced as they hurried along in the intensifying rain. Watchful pines as tall as hill giants towered impassively over them, deepening the lightlessness cast by an already clouded sky over the central bridges of the drowned courtyard. It was then that the girl made another attempt at conversation.

'The Whispess has been having nightmares,' she started awkwardly.

'Dreamsight? Bad omens, you mean?' Mothril asked. Everyone here knew the strange seer's work the Cailir family was capable of. It was why they were in power. In ancestral times, legend said, they frightened the other clans so much that all of them deferred to the Cailirs, or the Callers as they were sometimes known, on everything. Most of the clans still believed they called down visions from the Fäendhmar, the worldbeings.

Of course, there were also the obvious advantages of having powerful seers like them lead the Wiccars. They were, after all, the only ones who could see ahead, foreseeing battle outcomes and other eventualities important to the clans' new and fragile alliance, and their independence from the southern Realm of the Sentinel.

The girl shook her head. 'Not exactly. Warriors have been . . . attacking her as she sleeps. They travel with the visions but are separate from them somehow. Like they're drawn to her dreams. And when she wakes, the injuries they inflict are still there.'

'What?' Mothril felt . . . genuine shock for the first time in many years. He'd never heard of such a thing.

'Yes,' she whispered. 'That's why the Elders want you watching the Whispess—'

'How am I supposed to guard against phantoms?' he muttered.

'No,' she said quietly. 'Not to protect her. To prevent her from leaving. Whispess Oria has made several escape attempts. The Elders have grown concerned.'

Mothril watched the girl's expression, but her face betrayed nothing about how she felt about any of this. *Quick study.*

'What does the Prime make of this?'

She shook her head, freeing several loose strands of hair about her face. 'I wish I knew. The Prime is more likely to tell you than I, or even the Whispess. Her visions must remain pure. All I've been told is that the Prime and the Elders seem to think something terrible lies ahead for us, and that it has something to do with that relic the Elders are enamored with.'

Mothril had heard of this relic—a mirrored, dimensional surface said to contain secrets of great power locked in memories of its beholders throughout history. Each piece of the mirror was said to be, essentially, a small, shattered piece of crystallized memory.

Countless rulers sought it out as a way to immortalize their greatest strengths, from alchemy and divination to martial prowess, hoping to retrieve it again in the afterlife, which they believed to take place on another plane of existence, where the worldbeings dwelled.

'They seem certain that the Whispess's visions are the key to understanding all of it. So, he insists that she have them, no matter the great personal cost to her,' Lyra added.

Strange. Mothril knew Prime Edril Sil to be a shrewd and cunning man, but he had always loved Felith and their daughter. *He must be truly worried about something.*

The Wiccars had defeated the Eradomin years earlier, banishing them from this plane of existence entirely, so Mothril wondered why he still insisted on defending the relic so desperately. There were many questions he wanted to ask, but instead he simply nodded once and continued up the short flight of curved steps to the Whispess's room.

Eventually, as the stairs wove into the structure, they came to a small inner landing, with a low table and high-backed wooden chair in front of a faded stained-glass window. The colors it threw across the floor were faded and melancholy somehow. As if the light itself were lonely.

'Whispess?' said Lyra as she gently opened the door. Mothril loomed behind her in the doorway. Not knowing what to do, he ran his scarred hand along the doorframe, looking anywhere but at the wan figure in the four-poster bed.

The room was cluttered with furnishings—preserved butterflies in glass, maps and tapestries, a harp, ink bottles, beautifully-bound books, a gallery of her life.

'Lyra,' called a soft voice.

'Yes, it's me, my lady,' the girl answered, rushing over to her side.

Mothril stayed back, looking around the shadowed room. Large cathedral windows lined the length of the wall opposite them, letting in dull, pearly light that cast the room all in gray. Outside, rain now fell in sheets.

Lyra glanced back at him, looking unsure. 'Your . . . new guard is here too.'

'Oh!' said the Whispess, jolting up from the bed with a start.

'Not so fast, Oria,' Lyra cautioned, laughing a bit, as she reached her arms out to support her rise from the bed.

Two things occurred to him then. The Whispess and Lyra had forgone titles, so they must be closer than they were letting on. There was also a cane propped against the bedside table. He cocked his head. *Hers?*

He'd seen glimpses of the Whispess when she was younger —around her twentieth winter, maybe—whenever it was he was last summoned to the castle for an execution or to report on some bit of knowledge he'd pried from someone. Back then, she had seemed so spirited and full of life.

That had been long ago now, though—he hadn't been inside the upper citadel since the Prime began sending Melsze to him. Melsze told him it was because he made the Elders and guests of the clan uncomfortable.

And this is who's been escaping? Not likely without the help of her maiden here.

Now, he understood that his presence here was a hostile one. He supposed that things had not really changed as much as he'd thought. It seemed he was still there to frighten. To intimidate.

A gentle voice drew him from his thoughts. 'Welcome,' said the Whispess.

She appeared from behind the sheer curtains hanging on all sides of the bed, and Mothril was shocked by how much she had changed from that memory of her. She had a swollen lip, a bruised cheek, and stitches running from her temple to her nose on the other side of her face, along with several other, older scars. Wisps of red hair, and some curious blond strands at the crown of her head, had come loose from her braid. She looked like Death Herself.

He realized he was staring. 'Right. I'll, er, be just outside.' He'd already spoken more words that day than he had in the previous six months.

'Wait!' she called after him. She laughed slightly—a curious, musical sound. 'Won't you tell me your name? If I'm to be guarded night and day I at least want to know who my captor is.'

'Mothril of-Arcandras, Whispess,' he answered, with a hasty bow of his head. He knew his voice sounded flat and forced. It was often how his words came out when he didn't know how he was feeling. He paused for a moment, and again words came out of him without thinking. 'And I'm not your captor.'

'Aren't you?' When he didn't respond, she said, 'Please do call me Oria.'

He tried the name out in his mouth. It didn't feel right, but he didn't know what else to say, so he simply nodded, and went to go stand at her door.

11

KYR

KYR WAS PISSING with the door open when the chambermaid came in. 'Spirits Six!' she yelped, reaching to slam the door shut. 'Don't you knock?'

'Terribly sorry,' said the woman through the door. 'But, well, the prince is waiting outside. He was going to come in himself, but I told him I didn't think that would be a good idea.'

'You're Spiritsdamned right. Would another hour of sleep kill these people?' she muttered, pulling on her leather trousers and washing her hands in the small basin provided to her.

She had to admit, at least the servant's quarters were quite the step up from an underground prison cell or the sewers. The place even had a wooden tub. If only she could get some water for it. At least they'd brought her enough yesterday to scrub most of the grime of the past week off her and given her some clean, well-made clothes.

Kyr could practically feel the chambermaid's apprehension through the door. 'I'll tell him you're ready, then?'

'Yeah, sure, if you can't just make him go away.' She heard the woman hurry out the door, and Kyr scowled at her reflection in the tarnished piece of metal hung on the wall. The muscle in her arms had already begun to atrophy with the weeks of little food.

Last night at the servant's dinner, even with a bruised face, chipped canine, and split lip, she'd practically eaten an entire roast. They'd all stared at her with faces ranging from bewilderment to disgust. She wasn't winning hearts here, but she didn't care.

She already had friends. *All gone again.* Why bother making more?

Kyr had just finished lacing up her trousers and begun wrapping her breasts in a loose cloth, her shirt lying on the floor at her feet, when the prince barged in.

'Shit, sorry!' He quickly turned away, fumbling for the door. 'Iba said you were ready.'

Kyr chuckled. 'Relax, little king. I'm not shy, and you're not exactly my cup of tea anyway.'

'What? Th-that's not what I meant.' He scowled, his face reddening ever so slightly. 'And don't call me that.'

'No?' Kyr teased. 'Oh, shit, that's your brother, isn't it?'

He stared at her, mystified. Kyr would've enjoyed goading him further, but by the look on his face and that broken wrist, the little king was having a difficult enough time of it as it was. He waited for her to finish slipping her shirt over her head before awkwardly shoving several books he'd been carrying under one arm into hers.

'What's all this?' she complained.

'You do know how to read, right?' Atlan said. Kyr looked up, ready with a retort, when she saw the sarcastic expression on his handsome face.

They watched each other for a long moment, then slowly began to grin and then, inexplicably, to laugh.

'Yes, I know how to read,' Kyr replied, a smile still on her lips. She held the books out before her and read the spines. *A History of Magic, The Transmuter's Atlas, The Fall of the Spirits, v. 1.*

Transmuter. There was that word those guards had used again.

'Well, then that's today's work,' said Prince Atlan, smirking.

'Fuck me, I didn't realize the queen's little deal meant I'd have to spend all day reading. Might've reconsidered . . .'

'Believe me, I didn't want to read them either. But it's either that or listen to Saartho go on and on for hours. Trust me, this is better.'

She nodded, studying him. 'Ah, Saartho, that's my other new shadow, isn't it?'

'Don't worry, he's a mostly interesting, mostly friendly, and very well-studied shadow.' He winked at her.

She brushed her hand over the cover of *A History of Magic.* 'When do I get to meet him?'

Atlan didn't answer, but she could feel the prince's eyes on her. Kyr looked up. 'What?'

'It's nothing,' he said, shaking his head.

She couldn't help but laugh. 'No, tell me.'

He looked at her a moment longer, as if debating whether to say what was really on his mind. 'I don't quite know what to make of you. To be honest, I'm surprised you're even willing to speak to me. When I walked in that door I was prepared for you to—'

'Take a crack at you?' Kyr grinned.

'Well, yes. Aren't you . . . angry?'

'What? About taking a beating?' Kyr chewed her still swollen lip and gave a small shrug. 'You highborn aren't my first, and you certainly won't be my last. Besides, that guard, Martiq? He punches like he's afraid to get hit. Wasn't so bad.' She bared her teeth. 'Will need to do something about this, though.'

'I can take you to the royal infirmary this afternoon. For what it's worth, I'm sorry. I don't . . .' He paused a moment, before walking over to the door and closing it. 'Agree with the queen's methods.'

'Why don't you say something about it then?' Kyr asked plainly. 'I mean, you're the prince.'

Atlan nodded. 'If only it were that simple. When I was younger, I certainly tried but, spend enough nights in the palace dungeons and you eventually stop trying. That's kind of what they're made for, crushing the spirit and all that.'

She'd do that to her own son? Kyr whistled. 'Your mother sounds like a real piece of work.'

The prince looked dumbfounded, as if he hadn't been expecting her to say that. Kyr worried for a moment she'd said the wrong thing, but as quickly as the expression appeared it was gone. 'You have no idea.'

He paused for a moment as they stood there, quietly assessing one another, then continued. 'So, listen, I brought these up here figuring you'd want to be alone, rather than with a bunch of stuffy nobles, but you're welcome to come down to the library whenever you'd like. That's where I'll be all day. There are even more books there. You're going to *love* it.'

Kyr rolled her eyes but couldn't stifle her laugh. So far, she despised the Solorien court, just like she'd expected, but she could find a way to get along with anyone with a good sense of humor. 'I was confined to the Sledge cistern, then thrown in a cell for days on end, and then stuck in this room for another very long night. You think I want to be alone after all that?'

'Er, right...' he said awkwardly.

While Kyr didn't think she'd ever grow fond of being around royals, there was an unpretentiousness about Atlan that made him tolerable, and she sensed a darkness, a sadness about him like a shadow around the edges of his eyes.

After so many years in the Sledge and watching people from the shadows, she'd developed a pretty good read on people, but that didn't mean she wasn't still going to be cautious. Still, he seemed to possess no malice and it appeared he had about as much disdain for authority as she did, judging by the tense relationship he seemed to have with everyone else in the palace, save some of the guards.

The sly smile returned. 'You're not getting rid of me that easily, little king.'

Atlan looked relieved. 'Maybe Saartho can speak at our last rites after we die of boredom. Follow me.'

Kyr slipped on her new boots, the most comfortable pair she'd ever had, and started after the prince out the door. 'You know those two guards that brought me in?'

'Yes,' the prince said warily. 'I'm sorry about that.'

'Now, those two, I'd really like to take a crack at.'

He looked at her sideways. 'Can't blame you. If I were you, I would too. As for those manacles, I'm sorry about that too. I know the feeling. Like you'd rather claw off your own skin than tolerate them another moment.'

'That's exactly it! What're those damned things made of?'

'Bismuth alloy.' She looked at him, recognizing the words the guards had said to her. 'Don't know exactly how it works. They're from the First Age, but they do something to the ability to communicate magically with your surroundings. It's like they . . . *absorb* it.'

She frowned. 'They made me itchy.'

They broke into laughter again.

As Kyr followed him down the narrow hall to a spiral staircase, she memorized her surroundings. While having her every move watched by the prince was apparently going to be less unpleasant than she'd expected, that didn't mean she wasn't going to be prepared to leave at a moment's notice if things went south. She might've also been making note of all the valuables worth stealing in the place. Old habits.

'So, you practice magic or just read about it?'

'Only a few times, mostly out in the desert. If I were to practice it, *truly* practice it, I'd need a place the size of this palace I could level if something went wrong.'

'You've done that too?' Kyr said, before remembering how vehemently she'd been denying any involvement in what happened at the counting house.

He looked at Kyr double. 'Fucking Six, it was you, wasn't it?'

'I—'

Atlan's mouth quirked up, a strange expression that made him look at once both amused and sad. 'I lost some great men and women that day.'

Kyr eyed him warily. 'Shit. I'm sorry.'

'I don't blame you, Kyr. I know firsthand how hard it is to control. In fact, it's pretty damn impressive for your first time.' They began walking again. 'I only vanished some fruit off a tree.'

'Where did the fruit go, I wonder?' Kyr asked as they approached a set of large brass doors. She paused, thinking back to the doors of the counting house holding vault. The last time she'd been with her guild family. The last time Grym had been alive.

She pushed those thoughts away, glancing at the prince. 'I'm sorry about your arm, by the way. That looked like a painful blow.'

'Not my proudest moment,' he sighed. 'What were you doing there anyway? You must've known the Sun's Own would be looking for you.'

'I was *so* bored,' Kyr said, half-laughing, half-whining.

'You're joking,' the prince said, a riotous laugh escaping him.

'I wish I was. I'd given the Sun's Own the slip so many times in my life, I guess I got a little cocky.' Kyr shook her head. 'Which has been happening a lot lately.'

'You and me both,' Atlan said, gesturing to his arm.

'How did they even find me? Your men, I mean.'

'Got informants in the Sledge,' he said, smirking.

'Bastards,' Kyr muttered.

The royal library was massive, one of the few rooms in the upper palace that wasn't open to the elements. Brass shelves filled with thick, deckled-edged tomes lined the walls, going all the way up to the domed ceiling. There was an oculus at its apex, meant to be the sun in the mosaic surrounding it. It cast a lonely beam of light onto a matching mosaic of Yorenth on the floor.

'Ah, there they are!' cried a man with broad, wizened face. His eyes were kind and bright, and his cropped black hair was heavily streaked with gray. 'My magicians!'

'Erm . . .' Kyr gave Atlan a sideways glance.

'Kyr ap Sand, this is Saartho Ulam, royal librarian and historian,' he said with a sigh. Kyr liked that the prince introduced her by her full name. Most people shied away from the ap Sand surname because they felt bad. She liked that he treated her like every other person.

'I already know all about you,' he said, smiling kindly. 'We've another Singer in our midst!'

'Singer?' Kyr said, looking from him to Atlan.

'Mages, diviners? You're like them, only more powerful. Able to call on the Spirits. Atlan,' Saartho said, scoffing, 'have you told her nothing?'

Atlan held up both hands. 'I had to get her out of the dungeons first.'

Before she or Saartho could reply, a voice came drawling from behind them. 'The dungeons that you got her *in* to?' Kyr turned, and saw Atlan's brother, Vyktas, entering the library.

His flaxen hair, olive skin, and golden livery made it seem as if the sun itself were in their midst.

'Do you have something you'd like to say, little brother?' Atlan said, still with his back to Vyktas.

'Just that it's quite . . . funny, really, that you're acting like it wasn't you who gave the orders to bring her in.'

'Aw, looking out for me?' Kyr mocked.

'I'm speaking to my brother, sand rat,' Vyktas shot back.

Kyr rolled her eyes. *Always with the rats. Can't they think of anything more creative?*

'No,' Atlan said. 'Let's hear what she has to say. What do you think, Kyr? Speak freely.'

'I think there's a chance I can trust a man who knows what it's like to wear manacles. I can't say the same for you,' she said, looking at Vyktas.

Vyktas clicked his tongue. 'How positively tragic.' He smiled at his brother. 'You two deserve each other.'

Atlan was moving in an instant, slamming his brother into one of the towering bookcases with his good arm. Kyr appreciated that about the older prince, too—his ability to push through the pain he was assuredly in.

'Not in the library, please, boys,' Saartho cried, clearly more worried about the books than anything else.

Kyr leaned toward him, muttering, 'Are they always like this?'

'Afraid so,' Saartho said, before going to straighten some of the books they'd jostled.

Atlan stared into his brother's eyes for a moment before letting him go. 'Of course I brought her in. I had to. Kyr needs training. Now, if you'll excuse us, we are discussing said magical training. Something you wouldn't understand.' He stepped away. 'Best run along.'

Vyktas smirked. 'I simply came to see how things were going. It's bad enough you convinced mother to let some thief off the streets into our home, but if she were to hear what fast friends you two are becoming . . .'

'Out!' Atlan boomed, pointing to the door. 'Now!'

Vyktas whistled softly and backed toward the door. 'Easy,

brother. I didn't mean anything by it. It just seems strange that you'd enjoy the company of a mass murderer, seeing as you mucked up becoming one yourself so spectacularly. Didn't think you had it in you, really.'

'What?' Kyr said, looking from Vyktas to Atlan.

Vyktas glanced at her sardonically, before disappearing back out into the darkened hall.

'I'm sorry about that,' Atlan said. 'My brother thinks because he bests men in the palace yard that that means he's someone important.' He rolled his eyes. 'He's never even been outside of Yorenth.'

'Now then,' Saartho said, clearing his throat in annoyance. 'Let's refrain from any further scuffles, shall we?'

'Sorry, Saartho,' Atlan replied.

Kyr looked at him blankly. 'Why did he call me a mass murderer?' She blinked. 'How many people . . . ?'

The look Atlan gave her was more sympathetic than she was comfortable with. 'Kyr, he doesn't understand magic.'

Saartho watched the exchange with interest but said nothing.

'Okay,' she said, still waiting for him to answer.

'Eighteen people, Kyr.' Visibly cringing, he added, 'So far.'

Saartho raised his brows, seeming to understand then.

Kyr's face flushed, felt hot. 'What?'

'I'm sorry. I know you didn't mean to.'

Kyr looked away quickly to hide the burning hot tears that began to fall down her cheek and wiped them away with the back of her hand. 'Shit.' She knew it had been bad, but . . . *shit*.

'Do you two need a moment?' Saartho asked.

Kyr turned back to them then, her eyes welling with tears. She wiped at them again. 'No, it's fine. Please, continue.' There would be time to break down later, to do something—anything —about the damage she had done, but right now she knew she needed to understand what was happening to her if she was going to prevent her magic from ever getting out of control again.

Saartho was eyeing the tomes in Kyr's arms. Hesitantly, he spoke. 'I see you've already picked out quite the selection for her, Atlan. Very good. But first, you must have many questions.' Another tear fell down her cheek and Saartho took the tomes from her, placing them on a nearby desk. 'Well, I suppose I can start with telling you what you are.'

'What . . . I am?' Kyr echoed.

'A Spiritsinger! Or Singer for short. It's most curious, indeed. You see, in our current age, we believed the gift of greater magics to be one granted solely to the Solorien family and its heirs. But you've come along and quite upended that! Most curious . . .'

Ah, so that's why Vyktas and the queen hate me so much. That and my being born in the wrong part of the city.

'Have you shown any magical abilities before all of this?'

'No, never. The guildmates and I, most folks in the Sledge, really, didn't even think magic existed beyond the tricks those performers at the markets do. And rumors about the queen.'

'I'd love to hear those,' Atlan murmured.

Kyr sighed. 'I'll tell you later, preferably over the strong drink I'm going to need after all this.'

'Oh, magic does indeed exist!' Saartho exclaimed. 'We no longer have the formal records of it, but before the Oracle of Yoren, my teacher, died—this was years and years ago, mind you—she was able to preserve many of the oral histories of the magic wielders of antiquity. In fact, it used to be almost commonplace. We have a book on this somewhere I can give you . . .' He began eyeing the shelves nearby.

'Saartho,' Atlan prompted.

'Right, yes. You see, we don't really understand why magic seemed to die out in the formerly magical houses. But early in the Second Age, it did. It's been nearly a century since anyone showed more than a drop of magic. Then Atlan came along, and then, well, you.'

'You're saying that—are you sure?'

'Atlan told me of your time in the queen's dungeons,' said Saartho, his distaste of Queen Attiqah plain in the curl of his lip, 'and the crowners gave me their report on that dastardly Rook. Quite sure.'

'What did the report say?'

'Asphyxiation,' Saartho replied. 'A lack of air. Yet you never laid a hand on him.'

Kyr couldn't hide the pain from her face at what she'd done to these people. Even though it had all been done in self-preservation, she'd still killed so many.

She let a certain numbness take over, just until she could get through this conversation. 'Spiritsinger . . . why Singer?'

'Well, this is an educated guess more than anything, really, but I can assure you, I am well-studied. The Histories, some of which mention lost ancient texts, refer to the magic wielders of the First Age as Spiritsingers. For reasons unknown, these Spiritsingers were granted magic by the Six Spirits—Solq, Tellurn, Riparus, Crescian, Aerith, and the Lost One, who may or may not be a Spirit of Northern mythology named Calligone.' He cleared his throat. 'Magic that allowed them to manipulate each of their essences which, really, amounts to all matter in the world. They were able to concentrate these essences, sometimes having an affinity, a gift from one Spirit in particular. We believe the powers work almost like a kind of vibration, hence the name 'Singers.''

He continued, waving his hands at a vision only he could see. 'The Spiritsingers of the First Age could raise mountains, level cities, feed the hungry, divert rivers, all sorts of things. It was said to be a remarkably prosperous and harmonious time in our history. I suspect you and Atlan are heralding the return of them.'

'My theory? The Spiritsingers were magically-imbued guardians, who walked the land ensuring the Spirits' creations were safe in times of peril. Scholars believe there was a time of great scientific and mechanical advancement long ago, and that much of this was lost when the Spiritsingers disappeared. Likely, they were related. Atlan can tell you about the book he's currently reading, there was once a kingdom far to the south that utilized magical machinery for all manner of tasks. If it weren't too dangerous to travel there, you wouldn't find me here, but on an expedition to see the ruins! I've selected a few more texts . . .' Saartho reached up and plucked another book off a shelf, 'that may help us better understand and find the answer to all of these questions.'

Guardians. Kyr chafed at the word. *I'm nothing like them.*

Saartho set the book on top of her ever-growing stack. 'You like to read, I hope?'

She heard Atlan's low laugh behind her.

Kyr sniffled. 'Love it.'

Saartho said something to Atlan then, but Kyr couldn't focus on their voices anymore. Eighteen *people. And the Rook makes nineteen.* It was almost too much to bear.

Atlan placed a hand on her shoulder. 'How about that drink?'

12

ORIA

ORIA STEADIED HERSELF, gripping her cane tightly in one hand. Her pain was always at its worst in the morning. Despite it, she feared feeling better, when color and life would return to her skin, feared when her bones did not ache, because she knew her father would call for her. She knew she would give up some of her essence, again and again, to give her father her vision.

Bracing her other arm on the bedside table, she made sure her feet were steady under her and then slowly rose from the bed.

Lyra had helped her fasten her long hair in braids, but then, like every day before the new moon, left Oria and took her siblings to pray at the Circle of the Elders. Oria had wondered what the prayer rites were like since she was a little girl, not that she'd ever thought much of the Fäendhmar beyond wondering at their existence, but as the Whispess she was not allowed to go—her visions were reserved only for occasions deemed necessary by her father.

I wonder if he is still angry with me.

She reached for her cane, passing by her father's old swords hanging on the wall. She always avoided looking at them, fearing to catch her ruined reflection in the gleaming metal. This time, she looked. She didn't know why. It was worse than she'd expected, not because of her injuries, but because of the loss of something in her own eyes. An unrecognizable mask peered back at her.

Her and Lyra's last escape attempt had gone about as poorly as it could have, and she wasn't sure she'd get another opportunity. She wasn't sure she wanted one, deserved one.

She turned and took a deep breath, steeling herself for who she knew she would see on the other side of her door, and emerged from her chambers.

He was like a statue, a gargoyle in the dreary morning light of a Northern winter, drawing all light to him, like a lone warrior in a field of snow.

Mothril didn't speak, only raised an eyebrow as if to say, 'What do you think you're doing?'

'I'd like to go to the greenhouse,' she said summarily.

He studied her for a moment and then said, rather matter-of-factly, 'Alright.'

'Alright?' *Well, that was easier than expected.* 'I thought you'd put up more of a fight.'

She couldn't figure out what to make of him since they'd met. He said little and showed even less emotion, only slight displeasure creasing the lines of his face, and he was so soft-spoken.

She'd gone to say goodnight to him the night before, and he'd looked at her in such a strange, intense way. Yet his face remained unreadable, and she wondered if it was from years of practice. Years of gruesome work. She wondered what it felt like to do such things, what must be in one's heart to cause pain, to loop the rope around another's neck and snuff out their life.

His voice drew her back to the moment. 'Why would I want to fight with you, Whispess?'

Not knowing what to say, she laughed awkwardly. Most of her past guards were like a puzzle, figuring out what they liked and making them trust her was a way of ensuring her safety. She worried Mothril's enigmatic disposition would prove a maddening challenge.

He rose from his chair, blocking all light from the window at his back. 'I meant it when I said I'm not your captor. Melsze said I'm to guard you, beyond that he wasn't exactly forthright with your father and the Elders' wishes, nor their reasoning.' Then quieter, he added, 'And I haven't answered to anyone in a long time.'

'What of your loyalty?' Oria asked, surprised.

'Loyalty,' he mused, stepping closer to her and straightening his cloak. In the narrow landing above the staircase, he felt much closer, swallowing everything up in his looming presence. 'Loyalty is a two-sided coin, Whispess. Something the clan leaders and monarchs the world over seem to have forgotten.'

It was dizzying, the questions that came to her then. She thought of asking him what kept him here. She wanted to know his history with her father. She wondered what a torturer knew of loyalty, what he knew of the world, but instead all she said was, 'Do you dislike my father and the Elders?'

'I'm not sure 'dislike' is the word,' he said pointedly. She waited for him to elaborate, but all he said was, 'Come. I'll follow you.'

Oria studied him, then raised her brows. 'Shouldn't you be escorting me?'

His eyes shifted about the room. 'I—don't know where the greenhouse is.'

'How long have you been one of my father's men?'

His usually mercurial gaze was unflinching. 'Twelve years. And the ten before that as a mercenary.'

Twelve years, and he's never seen the grounds?

'I see.' She couldn't help her curiosity about his life. Many hours alone in her chambers had left her desperate for any conversation. 'And before that?'

He took the leather strap of one of his gauntlets between his teeth and tightened it, muffling his words. 'No need to exhume the past.'

She flushed slightly, feeling as though she'd gone too far with her prying—tempering her curiosity had been a problem since childhood.

Oria made her way to the top of the staircase. 'Could you ...' she trailed off, unsteadily lowering herself down a step with her cane while trying to move her dress, which trailed along the floor, out of the way.

The light from the candelabra beside the stone banister cast his imposing shadow on the wall opposite her. Then, startlingly, cold chainmail brushed against her linen sleeve as Mothril's armored hand reached under hers. He began walking slowly beside her down the steps.

She wondered what this gentleness would transform into if Mothril had to do his duty and prevent her escape. After the last time, her father had told her it was the most shameful thing she could do to her people at a time like this. The ultimate abandonment.

'I don't understand why the Prime thinks you need a guard,' Mothril said suddenly.

The statement surprised her. 'Well, during the day, when I'm in my right mind, it isn't a problem. It's the nights that are difficult.' She sighed. 'Being a seer has proved ... difficult lately. I don't know how much you were told—'

Mothril nodded, but his face took on a pensive look. 'Lyra mentioned something about your injuries,' he said.

She nodded. 'I don't like talking about it.'

'My apologies, Whispess.'

She smiled, but it was strained. 'You can call me Oria, you know.'

'I meant no offense, Oria of-Cailir.' The cold morning wind bit as they entered out into the gray North.

'So formal.' Oria smiled then looked away, watching leaves float swiftly on the river that traced from the courtyard out into the basin. 'It's alright. You have nothing to apologize for.' She paused. 'It's my own feelings I'm thinking about. I sometimes think that all people ever see when they look at me is weakness.'

He was looking ahead, out at the water. 'Many will see weakness and fail to notice its constant companion. The fighting strength to keep going.'

Again he surprised her, and she felt laid bare by his words. He hadn't denied her feelings or tried to diminish them. He simply put the truth plainly.

It took the better part of an hour to cross the drowned courtyard and pass under the fortifications leading to the lowland clearing where her people grew the few hardy plants that survived out here. It seemed such an unnecessary struggle to her, to try to put down roots in a place like this. Perhaps they were safer against attack, but she had the sense something had been lost, too.

She led Mothril to the small garden bordering the first reaches of the great Northern forest, where a solitary greenhouse stood beyond virid hedges and an old, moss-covered stone wall. Like the rest of the old Eradomin castle and many of the houses in the surrounding village, the greenhouse was overgrown and crumbling.

Oria always had to be careful when she visited, for broken glass and thick roots covered the old stones at her feet. It was as if the forest was trying to eat this place alive, to return the clans to their wild-dwelling ways.

'I love it here,' Oria said, turning to face him.

He nodded, looking up at the glass ceiling high above. 'Peaceful.'

She hummed in agreement. 'I used to come here often when I was younger, when I had free rein of the citadel.' She turned to look through a broken pane into the woods beyond. It was a gray day, clouds hanging low in the sky over the drooping pines and rocky ground. Thin, spindly thickets, weak from the lack of light, swayed in the wind at the forest's edge to the south.

She crossed the greenhouse to the apple tree growing against the far end, its branches breaking glass and poking in through the spaces left behind. A summer-ripening variety, there were still one or two that hadn't fallen to the ground and begun to rot. She plucked one, and bit into its sour flesh.

She turned to find Mothril running a hand over a cast iron disc in the center of the room. 'I wondered about that when I first saw it,' she said. 'Melsze once told me it's a sundial. I don't know why they'd need one here, though.' She gestured to the dreary weather outside.

'They say the nights have grown longer and longer in the North,' he replied impassively. 'I remember the difference from my childhood just a couple decades ago. It seems the weather was once more hospitable too.'

'Yes,' she agreed. 'Melsze says the same, and that there never used to be such frequent storms. I've often wondered if we've angered the Fäendhmar somehow with our quarreling with the other Northerners. All this warring and in the end, it only hurt everyone.'

He grunted in response, and she turned back to the window and the unbroken world beyond.

It's going to rain soon, Oria thought. Her mother always used to say she had a good sense of the weather's temperament. She took another bite, staring out at the vast wilderness.

A creature darted from the undergrowth, vulpine, it seemed

at first, but lacking the characteristic orange fur. Instead, it was made of twigs and leaves, with juniper berries for eyes, as if the forest had come alive. Oria's brow furrowed. It sniffed the air, then moved in a strange, shimmering, rhythmic fashion toward a burrow at the base of a tree, where it disappeared into the leaves, as if it had never been there at all.

Oria opened her mouth to say something, but nothing came out. She shook her head. *I must not be getting enough sleep.*

She leaned forward, studying the area more closely, but saw nothing beyond an ordinary hedge.

'Whispess?' Mothril asked. She stared for a moment longer, and when she turned to him, he was watching her intently with those fathomless eyes of his.

'I—'

His own gaze moved to the forest's edge. 'What is it?'

She shook her head, unsure of what to say. 'I thought I saw some kind of animal, a fox, maybe, but it was just wind through the brush. I must be more tired than I realized.' She felt Mothril's eyes boring into her with a torturer's vigilance.

'I doubt it was a fox. There are hardly any of them left in the woods up here.'

'You're right, it must've been something else. Or maybe nothing at all.' She gave him a small, unconvincing smile. 'I think I'd like to return to my chambers now.'

'Of course,' he said, and bowed his head, then led her back toward the moss-covered citadel in the distance.

13

ORIA

EVER SINCE SHE WAS A CHILD, Oria never missed a chance to attend her father's meetings with the Elders. These meetings, which were once held in their clan's sacred dell under the stars, now took place in the citadel temple, grand and airy like the Sentinel cathedrals she'd heard stories of. As Whispess, her presence was important, but she wasn't sure she'd ever feel worthy.

What had she done but stay in her bedroom, dreamwalking each night, providing vague details of visions that only served to strike fear into the hearts of her people? She was weak otherwise, her body broken, her thoughts and memories clouded by the restless sleep of nightmares.

Oria listened as the Elders said their prayers to the Fäendhmar, thick smoke of incense filling the room as they knelt and touched their palms to the stone. Intended to connect the devotee to the worldbeings through physical touch, she didn't think it seemed to have the same effect inside this lonely dwelling, away from the mountains they called home.

She wasn't to participate in these prayers, but still sat at the head of the Elders, as if she were someone of consequence. It was the Elders who were mighty warriors, skilled trackers, and brilliant tacticians, with her father the greatest among them. Whatever fears their people had, he had a way of reassuring, even inspiring, them. When they were lost, he guided them. Whatever their needs, he succored them. She wondered if she would ever be able to do the same. The one gift he had not been given was their family's ancestral one. He could not see ahead.

'We have had our share of misfortune, none can doubt that,' said her father, his voice gentle and soothing as ever.

He sat in the crumbling cathedra at the head of the derelict stone chamber, broken columns on either side of the dais, a waterfall rushing behind the window at his back, and looked out at the Elders, now seated on low chairs. Many wore their day-cloaks which covered their faces. The stale white light shining in dulled his red hair, like hers, and light gray, almost pearlescent skin. Medallions carved with ancient symbols on the obverse, an eye on the reverse, were braided into his hair.

'And yet, Whispess Oria's dreams have been more peaceful as of late, and though the Far Clans have not returned our summons, I see no reason to concern ourselves yet. If the Eradomin had returned, she would have seen it. She has had visions of them, yes,' he conceded, 'but in them they are still specters.'

'Whispess, is this true?' asked Elder Sybil of-Swythe, one of the few whose faces she could see through her own veil. She shifted uneasily, her silvery armor creaking. Her face was creased by her well-lived years, with deep furrows around her brow from a warrior's concentration. Elder Sybil led the Order of the Bear, one of their most skilled orders of knights.

'Yes,' she said. She opened her mouth to qualify her answer, but when she saw her father watching her, she decided against it. It *was* mostly true, she supposed. They had indeed only appeared as specters, but something haunted her about one of the Eradomin she kept seeing. She didn't know what it was, but he was different somehow. Touched by reality.

He had begun affecting her waking life, in a way none of the others did. One recurring dream was particularly difficult for her to relive, but she knew if she wanted to be of use to her people, she had to.

She woke each time in a field, somewhere the silty, grassy knolls gave way to a patchwork of pines and granite outcroppings mantled in thick, sooty mists. Her father had always said her mother had possessed great magic, often casting a protective shroud over Wiccar warriors in battle. Perhaps this was meant to symbolize her power? But then whose eyes was she seeing through?

She was a warrior, she thought, maybe even a prince. She knew she wasn't herself. Laying on the ground, she would hear a soft thumping, as if the heart of the earth beat in her ear. The rhythmic sound grew louder, closer, and there were voices. Voices on the wind, and then—

The specters closed in, drifting slowly from the mist. Spectral cavalry, like manifestations of the wind clad in armor, they watched her from the edge of the trees. At first, she'd tried to flee, but she never seemed to be able to put any distance between them. They chased her through the misty wood, and each time, as a tower came into view above the rise of a hillock, they caught her. Always, the same one caught her.

She didn't care to think in any depth about what followed, how he marred her flesh and drank blood from her in some kind of sickening ritual. Then she was slung across his horse's withers, her cheek against the thick, black coat of its shoulders. She knew not where they meant to take her. Somewhere surrounded by vast, unbroken desert. One thing she knew for certain was that she had to get to that tower.

She never did.

Her father's commanding voice broke her reverie. 'Melsze,

send a party of knights and trackers to the Far Clans. We will meet with them on the road and put Elder Sybil's mind at ease.'

'Thank you, Prime,' Elder Sybil responded, bowing and returning to her seat.

'Thank you for your council, Elder.' Edril Sil nodded conciliatorily. 'You're right. It has been too long without hearing from them. Still, it's likely they've already left on this year's pilgrimage, and we will find that all is well.'

Sybil started forward. 'It just seems strange that they didn't send someone ahead. My warrior-sisters and I—'

'Perhaps they did,' her father cut in. 'The roads are more dangerous to travel now than in years past.'

'This is true,' Melsze added. Sybil narrowed her eyes at him, a subtle yet rare show of emotion for the stoic knight.

She wasn't even sure if her father or Melsze had caught the small change in her expression, but it stirred something in Oria. 'There has been one strange thing about my dreams.'

The room filled immediately with the sound of creaking and groaning wood as the Elders shifted in their seats to look at her.

'You should've said so, my dear.' Though her father spoke with a term of affection, his face was drawn and voice curt. 'Go on, tell the Elders. What is it?'

'I saw the same man again, and—'

He stood. 'Who?'

'I-I don't know. He's never given me his name,' she said, flustered. 'He—'

'He is still walking with the wind? Like you said?'

'Yes, but—'

'That is good at least. And the Erángal?' Irritation flared in her at her father's constant interrupting, but she only shook her head. That, at least, seemed a relief to everyone in the room. 'Then we will need to attempt another rite soon.' Her father's gaze was apologetic and yet, she knew there would be no arguing with him. Times were too dire to relent. 'Rest Oria, prepare yourself. You need to be able to study this man when you see him again.'

She nodded. She had seen the Erángal once before when she was in her tenth winter. It had been a frigid night, her father telling her stories of the worldbeings.

'Little Fäen, come here,' he said. *He sat in front of the fire on a low stool, furs beneath his feet in what would later become her father's war tent.*

Oria had had another nightmare and awoke looking for her mother.

'Your mother's gone scouting again.'

'Why?'

'Because there are people who want to hurt us, but worry not, she will find them. We will do everything we can to protect you.'

She curled into his lap, looking at the cover of the book he was holding. 'What are you reading, father?'

'It's a book of poetry. Would you like to hear some?'

She nodded.

He told her of how the worldbeings gave to her ancestor, a Cailir, a relic for safekeeping. 'She threw down her crown, her sceptre all, for the lure of Calligone's e'er lasting eye, beheld the door to worlds, did I, innumerable, one thousand sides . . .'

'Beautiful,' she breathed. He smiled down at her. 'The 'everlasting eye,' what does that mean?'

'It's a reference to a very ancient artifact. It belongs to our people. They'd see that taken from us too.'

'Does it really have a thousand sides?'

He smirked. 'Would you like to see?' Her eyes grew wide, and he ruffled her hair, much shorter then. 'Come.'

She followed him to a trunk, fitted with several locks, at the far corner of the tent. The ensorcelled locks required not only keys, but the touch of a talented magician who could quell the magic they would release upon opening.

Her father did so—Oria barely sensing the fleeting magic like a hint of fear at the edge of her psyche, and then the lid swung open. Her father grinned as he reached in, removing the cloth to reveal a peculiar, transparent object. It looked almost like nothing as he held it, but every so often you could see the edges did not quite match their surroundings.

'It is only a small piece of what it used to be,' he said. His voice sounded full of regret.

She shifted in her chair, the beads of the veil she wore to hide her injuries rattling with the movement. She'd started wearing it when the dreams got worse—the last thing she wanted was for the Elders to lose confidence in her, or to see how unwell she really was. It was similar to the day-cloaks they wore, though more elaborate, so no one questioned when she suddenly traded in her flowing dresses for the cloak and headdress.

'Return to your chambers. Your new guard will escort you, yes?' her father asked and turned to look about the room. 'Where is he?'

Mothril stepped forward from the far wall and bowed his head. 'Prime.'

'Ah, Mothril of-Arcandras, is it?' said Edril Sil, giving him a tight-lipped smile.

'Yes—'

'Your father was a great man. It's a shame what happened. From the Far Clans, was he not? You and he were part of that free order that became Felith's service?'

Some said the Far Clans bred with giants. Looking at Mothril now, she wondered if that was indeed true.

'Yes, it was an honor to serve Lady Felith.'

'An honor,' Edril Sil repeated, raising his brows, an almost mocking smile forming on his lips. 'What manners! I wouldn't have expected that from someone who has spent their life in the tunnels, prying secrets from those who would be our enemies. Putting them to *death!*' She noticed the gleeful grin on her father's face and wondered if he was taunting Mothril somehow. 'Quite the life you've lived, Mothril of-Arcandras.'

'I go where I'm needed,' Mothril replied stoically, revealing nothing further about the strange interaction.

'Well, it's good to finally put a face to the name. It looks like you're settling into this new role well.' Her father leaned in toward him and lowered his voice, but she could still hear every word. 'As I hope Melsze has already told you, my daughter can be quite confused after she's had one of her dreams. She needs someone with a firm hand.'

Oria watched Mothril's blank expression carefully, but he showed no sign of how he felt about what her father said to him.

He turned his attention back to Oria. 'Go, rest. I'll try to see you before the rite if I can.' He parted her veil and gave her a kiss on the cheek.

Oria steadied herself with her cane, then followed Mothril out of the room.

14

ATLAN

ATLAN WENT to Kyr's room to find it empty. Panic rose within his chest for a moment, until he saw a note sitting on the bed.

Beat you to the library, little king! I'm going to be the smartest thieving rodent in all the land!

Beneath it was a crude stick figure drawing. One with long, dark hair and a tiny head—himself, he assumed—and another with short hair, a giant head, and whiskers, surrounded by books. Atlan chuckled and shook his head.

He'd taken her to the infirmary after their meeting with Saartho, and promised to bring her the bottle of wyvern whiskey he'd hidden in the palace kitchens so they could have that drink—

'It's made with *wyvern piss*?!' Kyr said, incredulous.

'Only the very best,' Atlan had replied, as seriously as he could muster. But when he returned with it, she was nowhere to be found.

Crossing the courtyard later that afternoon, he saw her feet dangling over the ledge of the palace cupola, beneath the green-tiled dome of the servant's quarters, and figured she needed to be alone.

Perhaps she didn't trust him with the truth of her feelings, and she had every right not to. At least it seemed she was in better spirits now.

He found her in the library, though she wasn't poring over a book. She was bent down in front of the polished brass face of a doorknob.

'What are you doing?' he asked.

'Oh,' she said, laughing as she turned to look at him. 'I was trying to see my new tooth. How's it look?' She grinned, showing off the new gold tooth she'd earned courtesy of Martiq.

'Dazzling.'

'You flatter me.' She sighed and returned to the table where a book lie open, its pages covered in maps. 'It'll take some getting used to knowing I've got enough gold to rent a room at Knight's Rest in my mouth.'

'You go to Knight's Rest often?' Atlan asked. 'I used to go there a lot in my youth, back when I thought I'd be some hero.'

'Oh, come on, that attitude'll get you nowhere. You can still be some big hero.'

He laughed softly. 'Right. What are you reading?' he asked, nodding to the book. He sat at the table.

'The Fall of the Spirits,' she replied, scrunching her nose. 'Nasty business, the end of the First Age.'

Atlan smiled. 'Mm. Have you read the part about the firestorms yet? Saartho thinks those were a similar kind of blight to the ones we've seen now, only—'

'I've heard talk of those,' Kyr interrupted. 'In the guild they think it's all being caused by the queen's diviners, you know, to sow discord.'

'I wish my mother were that sophisticated in her thinking,' Atlan mused. 'Alas, we truly don't know what is causing the blights. My mother would tell you we've angered the Spirits, but like some scholars of the First Age, others believe they are caused by rogue mages. With all the rumors about the North, who can say? Though, you mentioned rumors about the queen before...'

'You want to hear them?' she said, leaning in conspiratorially. 'Is it true she buys children with small magics?'

He leaned forward too, an amused smile playing at his lips. 'Yes and no, I suppose. The court diviners are made up of those in Yorenth with small magics, however they're usually more than willing to leave their lives behind for the prospect of a life in the palace. No coin required.'

'What do they think of you, I wonder? I mean, what you can do?'

'I don't know. They've always been sequestered in a separate wing of the palace. I've had little interaction with them. To many, though, my abilities are just another rumor. Of course, they're more likely to believe it than those without magic, but whether they have time to even consider it is another thing altogether. My mother's kept them quite busy as of late.'

'I see.' Kyr fingered the pages of the book idly. 'It's the same in the Sledge. Half the people believe in the magic of the Solorien line, the other half think it's a bunch of nonsense.'

'It's definitely not nonsense,' he murmured.

'When's the last time you used magic?'

He eyed her, wondering how much to say about his magic. After all, except for lessons with Saartho, he so rarely got to the opportunity to talk to anyone about it at all. 'Years ago, now. Not since my days as a soldier.'

'Aren't you curious if anything's changed?' she asked.

'Sometimes,' was all he could think to say.

'I still think we should be practicing magic, instead of just reading about it. We need to be prepared. Atlan, I . . .'—her voice grew quiet—'I don't want to hurt anyone again.'

'Practicing it doesn't mean you won't hurt anyone,' he answered solemnly. Kyr looked at him, eyes full of questions, but she didn't press further.

He would've told her if she'd asked. He would've told her about the last time he'd gone out into the desert with a contingent of the Sun's Own. He'd been so full of rage that day after a fight with his brother that he'd immolated the straw dummies they'd set up out there for him to practice on. Almost in unison, the men closest to them began shrieking in pain as their armor heated to the point of glowing. Confused and in a panic, they ripped off vambraces and greaves, but not before they were left with horrendous burns.

Atlan still couldn't eat roast pig, for the smell reminded him of that day. It was one thing to hear about what magic could do, and another to witness it.

'Well, I guess this is the next best use of our time, then,' she said.

'I know you're curious about it,' he said. 'I promise you, it's better to learn about it this way than by making a mistake firsthand. You're about to get to the best part, the theories about where Spiritsingers went and all of the First Age relics they wielded to help channel their powers.'

Kyr raised her brows. 'I think I need something like that.' She looked down at the page. 'Why don't you stay here, hm? In case I have any questions?'

He smiled and pulled out an ornate green ledger, a translation he'd been working on with Saartho for the library. 'Alright. I would be surprised if you didn't have questions. I'm sure this must all be a lot to take in.'

'It is, but it's also a relief, in a strange way.' Atlan nodded, understanding the feeling. 'It makes me feel like at least there was a reason for all that's happened. Maybe now I can offer something to the world, instead of just taking from it.'

'Well, I know you likely don't have too high an opinion of

the Sun's Own, but there's always a place for you among its ranks, if you're interested. I like you, Kyr, and not just because we've been thrust together like this. I think you'd make a great warrior.'

Kyr laughed softly. 'Thanks for the offer, but I'm afraid my next steps are still a long way off. All of a sudden, I feel like there is so much I don't understand about the world.'

Atlan smiled. 'I understand.'

'You talk of me not trusting you, but what makes you so quick to trust me?' she asked, looking at him inquisitively.

'I don't know, it's just a sense. If I had to guess, I'd say it comes from my soldiering days. Fight in battles long enough and you get a sense of who you'd like at your side.'

Kyr nodded. 'Well, I appreciate that. I may not have stumbled upon a particularly honorable profession, but I like to think I've lived by somewhat of a code. There are others, in the guild, you know, who have no code. They'll do anything. Those ones always scared me.'

'Mm, I know the type.' He wondered if she could tell he was talking about himself.

He looked down, thumbing the edge of a page. *Not like that anymore.*

'Anyway, enough talk. I can't say I'd fit in with the city guard, but I wouldn't mind a few sword lessons, if you'll have me. I've practiced with shortswords and daggers most of my life, but I've never really had to use them.'

'That'll take little convincing from me. We can train after we're done in the library most days, if you'd like.'

Kyr smiled. 'Deal.'

15

ATLAN

ATLAN AWOKE LATE the following morning. The sun had already risen almost to its apex in the sky, throwing sunbeams swimming with dust across his bedchamber. He propped himself up in bed and rubbed the sleep from his eyes, the silken sheets falling from his bare chest. Outside, he could hear the shouts of guards practicing in the training yard. Their morning drills were long over by this point in the day—by now they would be sparring.

He never regretted his choices at the Battle of Kingdom's Fall, but he did regret the loss of his life as a warrior. He could've lived forever as a lowly, nonmagical foot soldier. There was safety in the routine of it, in a skill that he could hone to perfection. Having complete control over himself.

His eyes traveled to the small vial his father gave him on the table beside his bed. He flexed his fingers, breathing in the pain one last time, then sighed, uncorked it, and downed the sour-tasting solution.

Atlan got dressed and prepared himself for another long day in the library, even though he would probably get little done besides laughing with the Knave. Soon, at least, he would no longer have to deal with the pain in his wrist. He would've let it go on longer the way he liked to, but this reminder of his most recent failure in the dueling pits nagged at him.

The hall was eerily empty of staff, which usually meant Taryq or his mother was about. Like a predator prowling through a forest empty of birdsong. As he came around the corner of the staircase, he heard the faint harsh sounds of a hushed argument.

'You will do as I say!'

His mother. The sound of something shattering.

'I'm sorry!'

Vyktas. And it sounded like he was crying.

On silent feet, he made his way to the door and looked through the crack in it. 'Oh!' said his mother, throwing up her hands. 'I gave you and your brother everything, and this is what I get.'

Vyktas turned away and began shaking, trying to hold back his tears.

'For the love of Solq. What is happening to this family?' She turned to face him again. 'Here I thought I was raising two strong sons who would carry on our legacy. Sons that history would remember as warriors, as victors! Instead, I get one son who failed at the critical moment in battle, dooming our endeavors in the North, and now sulks around my castle, angry at *me*, for his own shortcomings.'

Atlan's jaw ticked.

'And here's my do-over, throwing a tantrum like some ill-tempered child.' She crossed the room and grabbed ahold of his chin. Vyktas shut his reddened eyes tight, preparing to be struck. Her voice was cold and empty of emotion. 'I've changed my mind. You're not ready.'

She released Vyktas, and he cowered among the columns in front of the bookshelves that lined the walls of his mother's study. 'Go back to your boyish brawls and your nobles' daughters. Your father will handle it.'

Not Osimar, Atlan knew, but Taryq, despite his mother's insistence that everyone go along with her delusion that Atlan and Vyktas were born of the same father. Only in private did she acknowledge the truth.

Atlan had never seen his brother leave a room so quickly. He stepped back from the door and tried to pretend he hadn't been eavesdropping, but Vyktas nearly ran right into him just outside.

He was looking at the floor, his body wound tight. 'What are you doing here?' he sneered.

'Are you okay? I heard—'

'I don't know what you think you heard, but it's nothing,' Vyktas hissed through gritted teeth.

'Vyktas—'

He pushed past Atlan.

'Hey!' Atlan called after him, following him up the stairs and grabbing ahold of him by his cape. 'What the fuck happened in there?'

'If you were listening, then why are you asking? You heard, I'm not ready for real battle.' Though he hid it well, there was such deep pain in his brother's voice.

'Real battle? What *battle*? What is Mother planning?'

'Spirits, she really has shut you out.' He sneered, clearly gloating, but Atlan didn't take the bait. 'She's fucking paranoid again, Atlan. She's back to her designs on Bellgard. Says they're looking into the blights more and more, and since Vizier Rumail knows about *you* and what you can do, he's going to blame us. She wants to make the first move.'

'That's absurd! Bellgard is our ally.'

'Oh, I've tried telling her.' Vyktas had a crazed, tired look in his eye Atlan had never seen before, except in the mirror. It caused a pang of some unknown emotion somewhere in his chest.

She was destroying him too.

'Did she . . . ?' The weight of the question settled over them. They never talked about what their mother did.

His brother exchanged one knowing, heartbreaking glance with him. 'No more than the usual. A slap here, a paperweight thrown at my head there,' Vyktas said with a wave of his hand, 'you know how it is, I'm sure.'

When he saw Atlan's livid expression, he rolled his eyes and added, 'She missed.'

He and his brother had never quite gotten along, resentment clouding whatever friendship might've formed between them, but still, something in his brother's eyes made him fucking furious.

A singsong voice interrupted his thoughts. 'Little king! I'm going to know more than you if you don't get your ass down to the library! Pentaculum this, and Pentaculum that!'

Vyktas gave him a look as if to say, 'What is wrong with her?'

Atlan grinned. 'Over here, Knave!'

'Ooh, a game of hide and seek?' she called back. The sound of her footsteps began traveling toward them, and then she came bounding up the steps.

'Oh,' she said, stopping short when she saw Vyktas. 'Both little kings.'

'Saartho's got you reading about the Pentaculum, huh?'

'Yeah, it's actually pretty interesting.'

'Pentacu-what?' said Vyktas, raising his eyebrows and glancing between the two of them.

'Oh, it's some ancient artifact the old historian's got a thing about. Created by the Spirits during the First Age and all that.' Kyr sighed, leaning against the wall. 'He claims it's going to save us all from the blights and whatever else is coming down the pike.'

'Well, where is it?' Vyktas joked.

'Ah, that's the funny bit,' Kyr replied.

'It's disappeared,' Atlan cut in. 'Probably just the stuff of myths.' He wondered what Kyr and Saartho talked about. Obscure historical artifacts didn't have much bearing on a modern Spiritsinger's understanding of her magic.

Kyr shrugged, then looked at Vyktas again. 'You okay?'

'Why do you care?'

'I guess I don't, particularly. But I know what someone looks like when they need a G.F.D., hm?'

'A G.F.D.?' Vyktas mocked.

'A good fucking drink.' She winked. 'What do you say?'

Vyktas looked at Kyr like she'd grown three heads.

'Oh, come on. You're not really going to tell me you're too good for a drink with me with tearstains on your cheek. I know a place down by the docks with ale that'll knock however it is you're feeling right out your ass! Bet I can drink you under the table, too.' She turned to Atlan. 'And you still owe me one.'

Vyktas looked at Atlan, and Atlan couldn't help but laugh. He gave a feeble shrug. He couldn't remember a time when anyone had talked to his brother that way. Atlan was sure Vyktas was going to tell them to fuck off, but to his surprise, he said, 'Can't believe I'm agreeing to this. Let's go.'

The queen was nowhere to be seen as the trio made their way to the gatehouse. With a nod from him, any patrolling Sun's Own took no notice of them as they made their way down the steps at one of the palace's side entrances and out into the lively streets.

For Atlan, it was a trip he was used to making. His brother was less sure of the idea. He and Kyr couldn't contain their laughter as Vyktas clutched the hood of his cloak tightly around his face.

'You'll be fine,' Atlan teased.

'Are you joking? Half of Yorenth is fighting over scraps, I can't imagine we're popular right now.'

'True,' Kyr cut in. 'But they blame each other for that. You little kings are something to aspire to.' Her lips twisted into a wry grin. 'And besides, I didn't know what you two even looked like before I got dragged into the palace. No one'll notice.'

'Is that true?' Vyktas's mouth fell open. 'You didn't know?'

'Yeah,' Kyr scoffed. 'People, at least in the Sledge, have other shit to worry about. You know, food and fresh water, a roof over your head, that sort of thing.'

Vyktas scowled at her and turned to Atlan. 'You put up with this kind of talk from her?'

Atlan shrugged. 'I prefer when people tell me the truth.'

They arrived at a squat building sat right on the sea, with a rotting veranda jutting out from the back of it. Lazy waves lapped at the stone barricade it sat upon, and rather than a door, they passed through two strips of linen hanging in the entranceway.

It was dim inside, lit only by a hearth in the back corner and the soft rays of late afternoon. The bar was on the left side of the room, with a small kitchen against the window-lined wall behind it. A kettle steamed away, and seated at small tables tucked into alcoves near the fire were dockworkers chatting and laughing. The sight was ... peaceful.

The chatter stopped. The barkeep turned around.

'Well, if it isn't Lady *fucking* Kyr!' yelled the barkeep, a tall, broad man with a rosy complexion and full beard.

Atlan nudged her. '*Lady* Kyr?'

'Oh, yes,' she said, grinning. Beside her, Vyktas looked surprised not to be the one getting recognized.

The man barreled around the bar and pulled Kyr into his arms. 'We thought you were dead!'

There were eyes on them now, and even though he could tell Kyr was uncomfortable she played it off. 'Nearly, but not quite, Haskil.'

'You're the talk of the whole Sledge! Word is you got hauled off to the palace and—' He stopped abruptly when he saw the two faces beside her. 'Spirits Six, it's—'

Kyr hushed him. 'These fine gentlemen and I would like a drink. Pyromancer's, if you've got it.'

Haskil blew out a breath. 'It's on the house so long as you'll tell me the whole story later.'

'Deal,' she replied with a wink. She leaned in close to him. 'Oh, and uh, you'll tip me off if you see any runners?'

Haskil's face wrinkled in confusion, but he nodded. 'Sure, Kyr.'

They settled in the far corner under the stairs, away from the rest of the patrons, their table filled with a pitcher and mugs and a book Kyr had purloined from the library and hidden under her cloak.

'Alright, Vyktas,' Kyr smirked. Vyktas eyed her as he poured their drinks. 'I'll hold your hair back when you puke.'

Vyktas looked at Kyr over his mug, narrowed his eyes, then downed it in one go. He made a pinched face and coughed. 'Ugh, you drink this vinegar?'

'Happily,' she replied, a lazy smile crossing her lips. She turned to Atlan. 'You want some?'

He held up a hand. 'No thanks.'

She got him some water instead, and he took it gratefully. He would've liked to join Kyr and his brother, but whatever Sika had given his father was starting to work, and he was beginning to think he would be sick enough from that alone.

He'd been fed plenty of alchemical experiments during his time as a soldier, some worse than others, but he still wasn't used to the feeling. Each time was a new experience, and now a strange, tingling sensation was overtaking his arm. Bone reknitting.

Better be working, he thought. The waves of nausea deep in his gut appeared to be the unpleasant side effect his father had mentioned.

'What's the book?' Vyktas asked, as Kyr pulled out a leather-bound volume and placed it on the table with a thump.

'Oh, well after I finished reading about the basic history of Spiritsingers, Saartho's had me studying theories about magic's disappearance based off of some ancient notes by an Oracle.'

'An Oracle?' he asked, taking another swig and openly cringing at the taste.

'You're moving fast. I'm helping him translate sections of her notes written in Borean Poet right now.' Atlan leaned in, taking small sips of water, desperately needing the distraction of the conversation.

Kyr nodded, gulping down ale. 'Mm, the Oracle of Yorenth.'

'Ah,' said Vyktas, 'I vaguely remember learning some of that language in my lessons. I don't know how you do it all day, brother.'

'I manage,' he said, a bit more bitterly than he would've liked, partly out of bitterness and partly because of the sickness in his gut worsening by the minute.

Atlan watched the two of them get increasingly drunk, with Vyktas making the occasional barbs at Kyr that she brushed off. Nothing seemed to bother her, and Atlan wondered how she managed it. He knew she had anger in her—he'd seen it—but she never let it get to the core of her, a quality Atlan both envied and admired.

'Now, now, before you and Vyktas get too drunk, indulge my curiosity, Kyr, ' he began. 'Why does Saartho have you looking into the Pentaculum? He hasn't mentioned that thing to me in ages.'

Kyr's mug was halfway to her mouth—she frowned and lowered it to the table. 'Oh, he had some moment of brilliance the other day. Said he thinks it might be related to our magic somehow. I asked him to explain it, but he just wandered off, talking to himself.'

'Six,' Vyktas said, slurring the word slightly. 'You're so *serious* all the time, brother. Can't leave the magician talk alone for a day, eh?'

Atlan glanced pointedly at Vyktas, then looked back at Kyr. 'What did he say? He's never really mentioned it much to me, beyond lecturing me about the Histories. Not in regards to my magic, anyway.'

'Apparently not,' Vyktas said to himself, eyeing his mug and draining it. He groaned softly, then slumped against the wall and closed his eyes.

Haskil appeared then, and placed a small bowl on their table in front of Kyr with a smirk.

Kyr looked at it, then looked gratefully up at the barkeep. 'Thank *fuck*! Little k—I mean,' she cleared her throat, looking awkwardly between Atlan and Vyktas. 'Listen, you have to try this.'

'What is it?' Atlan asked. As he leaned forward, the room spun.

'It's Reza's nut brittle,' Kyr said, smiling. 'Thanks Haskil, you're the best!' He clapped Kyr on the back then disappeared back into the kitchen.

Atlan smiled back, but something was off. He looked down at his mug of water, furrowing his brows. He gave it a sniff. *Definitely water.* He took another sip to be sure, but as he looked up, again the dizziness. The grain of the wooden walls shifted and swirled with each movement. He felt . . . *drunk.*

Hastily, he tossed a few pieces of the nut brittle into his mouth, hoping it might sober him up.

'Calling it quits so soon, Vyktas?' Kyr drawled.

Vyktas lurched upright, slowly opening his eyes. 'You . . . wish. Another round!'

Haskil peeked out at Kyr, who subtly shook her head. Vyktas slumped back over.

'He's got no business challenging anyone to drinking contests.' Kyr said through a mouthful of nut brittle. 'Anyhow, Saartho thinks the Pentaculum has something to do with the balance of magic in the world. That it's either protecting it, and failing, or fiddling with it somehow, causing, uh, anomalies.'

Atlan blinked, trying desperately to pay attention. 'Like the blights?'

Kyr nodded. 'And, well, me.'

Vyktas opened one eye at that. 'That ex—plains it.'

'Something you'd like to say?' Kyr returned a mocking smile.

'I *knew* you ssstole our family's gift. There's simply no way—'

'Careful,' Kyr tutted. 'Or I'll singe that pretty blond hair with some of your family's gift.' She reached out and grabbed a strand of Vyktas's long hair. He slapped her hand away and Kyr let out a satisfied laugh.

'Written accounts of the First Age tell us what each Spiritsinger could do was not the same, they each, er, *we* each have our own unique relationship to magic, but it's all—it's all connected. A common thread . . . runs through it,' Atlan said, hoping he was making sense.

'So, what *can* you do?' Vyktas asked Kyr, laying his head on the table.

'Wouldn't you like to know?'

Vyktas smiled and closed his eyes. 'You're funny, Knave. Funny . . . criminal . . . person.' Rapidly descending into a stupor, he began snoring softly.

Kyr smirked. 'Looks like I win.'

Atlan couldn't help but laugh. 'Yeah,' he slurred slightly, 'looks like it.' She slammed her mug down triumphantly. Vyktas, still softly snoring, hardly reacted.

'Kyr.' Atlan's head was swimming.

Kyr carried on. 'Anyway, Saartho wanted to talk to you about it too. Next time you're in the library.'

'Kyrrr,' Atlan repeated.

'Hm?' she asked, looking more than a little bit out of it herself.

'Taste this.'

She looked at him like he was a madman but took his mug of water and drank it. 'What are you playing at? It's water. Trying to sober me up already?'

He blinked at her. 'It's water, right?'

A short bark of laughter escaped her. 'Yes, it—' She leaned toward him. 'Are you mad? Wait. Are you drunk? Your eyes are all . . . glazed over.'

'I-I might I think be.'

Kyr's mouth dropped open. 'Off of water? Is this what you're using your magic for?' Laughter overtook her. 'World's *worst* Spiritsinger.'

Her laughter made him laugh, too. 'Kyr,' he tried, 'I'm serious. My father gave me something to mend my broken arm, and I think I'm having some weird reaction to it.'

Or maybe this was Sika's idea of a joke.

'Well, is it working?' she said, lifting his arm.

'Spirits, Kyr!' he shouted, but his arm no longer hurt. He looked at it. 'Huh.'

She slid the water back toward him. 'So, your arm is better, and you've found a loophole for the world's cheapest drinks for a night. I fail to see the problem.'

Atlan shook his head, laughing. Vyktas, still in a stupor, shifted in his seat. He glanced at him. 'Kyr, about what Vyktas said—'

Kyr waved her hand, but her face took on a fragile quality. She swallowed. 'Oh, don't worry about me.'

'Kyr, the counting house—I mean, you didn't know a thing about magic—'

'I know,' she said, nodding too quickly. 'Look, we better get him back to the palace, hm? You two'll be fine, but Her Radiance could have me hung by dawn if she so desired.'

Atlan wouldn't be put off that easily, but they did need to be getting back. The last thing they wanted was Wren, Taryq, or their mother noticing their absence, and the last thing he wanted was to be known as the prince who vomited in front of an entire tavern full of subjects. Kyr chatted with Haskil while Atlan dragged his semiconscious brother out the door.

The sun was setting over the sea, and Atlan watched it, his brother's head on his shoulder, and felt a kind of feeling he'd never experienced before in his life. Alchemical mishaps aside, it was something akin to what he imagined contentment was like. Nothing but shining sun and cloudless skies on the horizon.

Kyr stumbled out into the street and the two of them carried Vyktas along home with them. In the dark, with the hoods of their cloaks pulled over their heads, they were like any drunken friends shambling home after a night out.

The cool air of the palace was a balm. Atlan took in a deep breath and wondered how long this drunkenness would last as they hurried up the stairs unseen and settled Vyktas in his bed. Atlan pulled his boots off and considered trying to get Kyr to open up once more.

He looked over his shoulder from where he knelt. 'I know you don't want to talk about it, Kyr, but when you do, I'll be here.'

She nodded almost imperceptibly as she toyed around with some trinkets on Vyktas's desk and leafed through some of his books. She opened a drawer and looked in, then shut it.

Words seemed to pour out of her unwittingly. 'I'm a villain to some, Atlan. I have to accept that. It's different from when I was a Knave. That was a world where everyone was always trying to get one over on the person next to them. It hardly mattered whether someone went without marks or jewels. In fact, if they left them lying about, who's to say they didn't deserve it? Lives are a different currency entirely. That much I know.'

Atlan didn't know what to say. He had learned the hard way what it was to trade in lives. Without another thought, he stood and started toward her.

'What are you doing, you drunken bastard?'

Atlan pulled her into an embrace. Kyr's arms extended in shock at first, but then he felt them slowly close around him.

'Have you ever killed anyone before?' he asked, voice quiet.

She exhaled, her body loosening. Her voice was just as soft in his ear. 'No. I'd come close a few times, but I never . . .'

'It's sickening, I know. Like a hard pit that sits,' he reached between them, placed his hand against her sternum, 'right under here. And it eats away at you.'

'Yes,' she whispered.

'I know,' he said softly.

Her voice, which had been tight and strained now unspooled in ragged breaths. 'I didn't mean to. I didn't want to.'

'I know.'

They stood like that, both needing the comfort of a kind touch, for a long while. Her tears bloomed on his shirt, and Atlan felt the effects of the potion begin to slip away. Kyr broke away first, wiping her cheek. He took a deep breath.

'I tried to drink it away, the other day, and again today. Usually that works. But I can't stop seeing their faces. Those guards. We were robbing the place blind. The guild's had its eye on it since I was just a kid. The Sun's Own caught us, which was my fault, I guess, and . . . and that's when I brought the whole place down. My friend *died*, Atlan. I don't even know why it happened. But one of my guildmates said he saw something strange about me, a shimmer, like, around my hands.'

'The aura,' Atlan murmured.

'Aura? Yeah, something like that. Anyway, the guild kicked me out, and I guess I deserved it. Had it been anyone else, I would've wanted them out too. Too much attention, too much potential for disaster. But then Sylas . . . he sent a *Rook* after me, the fucking bastard. After everything I've done for him!'

More tears welled in her eyes and she looked away. 'Shit, sorry . . .'

'Spiritsinging is tied with emotion, Kyr. Something which humans are notably terrible at controlling, even in the best of circumstances.' They both laughed softly at that. 'It's why everyone's so afraid of magic, of the blights. It was an accident. Not like what I did, which Vyktas so kindly pointed out, though I've had my fair share of magical mishaps too.' He glanced at his brother's sleeping form. 'I went into battle knowing the harm I could cause, and I caused a lot of it before I, as he put it, 'mucked up.''

He could tell they both had more questions, but there would be more time for that later between studying and training. 'Come on, dangerous magicians liable to bring down the city need to sleep, too.' He gestured toward the door. 'Hm?'

Kyr blew out a laugh and nodded, and they walked out of the room, arms around each other's shoulders.

Sometimes he worried his fast friendship with Kyr was nothing more than an illusion—a shaky, feeble thing built on a cheap agreement with his mother. Did they truly understand each other as outcasts, as fighters?

At moments like this he needed little reassurance. Already Kyr treated him like more of a friend than most. She didn't care about titles or what he could do for her. She had her own life— if the palace ceased to exist, her world would keep turning. He had a feeling Kyr's world would find a way to keep turning even if the Spirits themselves stopped weaving the world's harmonies tomorrow. What the two of them had was purer than any mere alliance or shared affliction.

They simply liked each other, against all odds.

16

ORIA

A FIRE DANCED AWAY in the hearth before Oria's bed, casting flickering shadows about the room. Outside, one of the Northern Lands' near-nightly thunderstorms wrought havoc on the land.

With Lyra's help, Oria changed into a long robe and melted into the soft down mattress and straw-filled cushions of her bed.

It always took her a while to calm her body after sundown —her thoughts consumed with what she had seen the night before, or else anticipating what awaited her. It brought her some measure of relief knowing that what she saw did not always come to pass. The smallest of changes made in response to her visions could, after all, sometimes head them off altogether. She thought again of the fox and, though it seemed to have nothing to do with Eradomin warriors, wondered if it was some kind of sign her dreams were creeping more and more into her waking life.

'I have a surprise for you,' Lyra said, a mischievous glint in her eye.

'What?' Oria asked, her expression growing curious as she noticed Lyra was holding her hands behind her back.

Lyra produced a small book, handing it to her, then leaned in close and whispered, 'I stole it from the scribes.'

'Lyra!' Oria gasped. 'You didn't.'

The leatherbound cover was weathered, the paper yellow, but she could make out the faded title well enough. *Poems of the Eradomin, vol. III.*

'I didn't realize the scribes had preserved any of the old Eradomin volumes, let alone that they'd leave one lying about.'

'Well, you're supposed to have a writ of tomes, but after meeting with your father, the scribes are always so busy. They never notice me,' she said, a proud smile still gracing her lips.

Oria returned the expression, but despite herself couldn't ignore the anxiety in her chest that her friend had taken such a risk for her. 'Lyra, we could get in real trouble for this!'

'Don't worry so much,' she said, laughing. 'No one saw me.'

Lyra knew she was curious about Eradomin poetry, particularly that which was still written in the original Borean Poet language.

'To understand a people, you must understand their legends,' her mother had once said.

She did want to understand the Eradomin, but more than that, she wanted to understand the catalyst that had called these scattered peoples to war, not merely the tempered reasons her father gave her. The skirmishes were terrible. She'd witnessed their aftermath firsthand as a child. Beyond that, the bone-deep worry in her father's face conveyed further concerns he had not divulged.

'I can't thank you enough for all you do for me,' Oria said, 'but I can't have you risking yourself for me like this, even if you want to.'

Lyra squeezed Oria's hand. 'Nonsense. Goodnight, my lady.'

Oria smiled and resolved to bring it up with her again

another time. 'Goodnight, Lyra.' She settled into the mass of pillows at her back.

Lyra made for the door, but it swung open on its own, a large figure shadowing the threshold. Mothril bumped against the doorframe, one hand awkwardly on a longsword at his belt, seeming unsure of himself. The simple tunic and cloak he'd been wearing before had been replaced with a guard's regalia—pauldrons, chainmail that fell to his hips, wool trousers, and massive steel-toed boots.

Oria stared at the sword now sheathed at his side, no doubt given to him by Melsze or another of the Elders. To use against her, she realized.

Both Oria and Lyra looked at him expectantly. 'I'm to make sure you stay awake,' he said abruptly. 'For the rite tomorrow.'

Oria winced. She hadn't wanted to tell Lyra until the last moment.

'Another rite? Already?' Lyra said, aghast. She crossed her arms, looking between Oria and Mothril. 'But it's only been a fortnight since the last time. You're not ready!'

'Lyra,' Oria said soothingly. 'It's alright. I'll just rest longer afterward. He said he'd give me more time in between after this.'

Lyra pursed her lips.

Each time Oria was summoned by her father, Lyra became more upset than she did. Growing up in this wrecked castle, far from the mountain peaks and starlit skies she knew in her youth, Lyra had been her only friend, the only witness to the whole of her life. Just as she was to Lyra's, whose duties prevented a real life of her own, too.

Oria gestured for Mothril to sit in a chair by the fireplace. 'Please.'

'Thank you, Whispess.'

Lyra looked at Oria with widened eyes, and Oria nodded almost imperceptibly, letting her know she'd be alright. The two of them shared a subtle, unspoken language, made up of glances and gestures, that they often used to check on one another.

Still, Lyra lingered by the door for a moment before whisking through and shutting it with a soft *click*. Oria knew Lyra was mistrustful of her new guard simply because of the position he'd been made to fill, but strangely, she couldn't quite arrive at that same thinking herself. As much pain as her circumstances brought her, she had her duty, and he had his.

Mothril sat in the corner, his face half-lit by the glow of the fire. Occasionally, lightning would strike somewhere outside, and his full face would be illuminated. He had bluntly cut white hair that fell around his face and shoulders, hooded eyes, and a broad nose. His skin was a shade of pale gray like most Northerners, but that hair, it was a rare trait among her people. Their hair didn't change as they aged like the few Saerians she'd met, so white hair meant white hair at birth.

After a few awkward silent moments passed, Oria forced herself to say something. 'Well, I think I'll read then.' She opened the book of poems in her lap. 'Would you like something to read?'

'I'm not much of a reader.'

'Oh,' Oria said somewhat sheepishly. Except for their walk to the greenhouse the other day, getting Mothril to speak had been like getting blood from a stone.

He looked at her and, shifting uncomfortably, added, 'Haven't really had the time.'

'No, of course.' Feeling silly, she quickly began reading.

Soon, the only sounds were the storm raging outside, pages turning, the crackling of the fireplace, and Mothril occasionally shifting in his chair. It was a more comfortable silence than she'd expected. In her book, she studied a fragment of a poem that was once set to music.

En-wasted, once-remembered lands
lay gilt footsteps aye false shadows,
a-fraught with beasts, silver sword-winged foes,
rulers of none aye a fatalistic deceiver
no soon to gain the favor of crows.

The Lost One, herald lay the wellspring that flows,
across a ship'less sea lay a thousand years,
aye none to remember,
sept the watchers on Sarthura's Rim
the truth-seeker, the Queen, shall return.

We watchers know the wanton'ness o-lost mages
We watchers seen it burn
en-take within its hungry soul,
the lifeblood lay a god.

The World-Swallower aye its many faces
mirror-song to what it cannot possess
A leviathan's promise
Born a-white crow, we watchers, we watchers know

Her eyes glanced along Mothril's form in the corner, his wide shoulders, the corded muscle of his forearms where he had rolled back the sleeves of his tunic, his long legs. He had taken his gloves off, and she noticed the shine of scarred skin in the firelight.

If he was used to living with scars, maybe he wouldn't think her face was ruined the way everyone else did.

She tried to read again but found her attention back on him. 'You were my father's torturer before this?' Of course, they both knew she knew the answer to that, and she couldn't think what had made her blurt out such an absurd question.

He seemed startled by her brusqueness, his eyes flicking

over to her while the rest of his body went rigid. 'I—I can wait outside, if you'd prefer.'

'No, I didn't mean it like that,' Oria said quickly, reassuring him. 'You don't make me uncomfortable, Mothril,' she added.

'I understand,' he muttered, before stopping, halfway risen from the chair. He looked at her with an intense, appraising gaze. 'I don't?'

'No.' She met his eyes, thinking about why that was. She supposed she had spent her life around dangerous folk—the Prime, knights-errant, warriors. She'd always had a gentle nature in the face of such bloodthirst, and it seemed nothing could destroy that within her.

Mothril turned woodenly back toward the fire.

'Did you always expect to be . . . in that line of work?' As soon as she said it, a wave of embarrassment coursed through her. *Oria, shut up, shut up!*

'No,' he said sharply. She waited for him to say more, but he didn't.

'No, I suppose not,' she said quickly, trying to recover any common ground. 'But . . . you are doing a—a necessary service for the protection of the clans.' She could feel her entire face flushing.

'No,' Mothril said again, only more bitterly this time.

'No?'

He was looking away from her, into the glowing coals. He shook his head. 'It's not necessary, and I'm not protecting anyone. What I do, it shouldn't exist, but we've decided that it needs to.'

'Well,' she started, playing at the hem of her chemise, 'then why do you do it?'

'I tell myself, so no one else has to. But the truth is, sometimes, when I'm tying a real bastard to the rack while the flames heat the poker, I'm enjoying myself.' She broke his gaze, embarrassed. He smirked and turned back to the fire.

Several silent moments passed before she tried again, if not to settle her curiosity than to at least make the mood in the room less discomfiting. 'So, what did you want to be? When you were younger.'

He looked thoughtful for a moment, and then his scowl returned. 'I don't know, I think when I was a boy I wanted to be an artisan or something like that.' He huffed a laugh.

'I don't think it's silly. I love art, especially music.' She turned and looked toward the corner of the room where a harp stood. 'I could play you something, if you'd like?'

Mothril said nothing, still gazing into the fire, but as Oria crossed the room and sat at the harp, she could feel his eyes on her.

'I'll play you one of my favorites.'

She began plucking a melancholy tune, one of the Eradomin songs she'd memorized when she was allowed to study with the scribes. Her father had put an end to that several years ago. He felt having access to the books was inviting Eradomin influence into their lives, and more importantly, her dreams, but Oria always found their songs and writings beautiful and felt drawn to them somehow.

Growing up, she always hoped that one day there would be peace amongst the Northerners and she could study the books openly, but that day never came.

The harp's notes floated on the air between them and, as he listened intently, she felt closer to Mothril than she ever had speaking to him. She looked at him a few times as she played, his eyes flashing to hers and away again, and thought he looked more at ease, too. The angle of his shoulders eased and something softened around his eyes.

As the song ended, Mothril sat up. 'You're going to make me fall asleep if you keep playing like that. Was that your plan?'

Oria smirked. 'Was that a joke from my stoic guard?'

There, on his lips, was the faintest ghost of a smile.

She stood to make her way back to her bed—she could walk short distances without her cane most days. Anything longer than that, though, and her back and legs would ache for days.

When Oria was first injured, she'd been assured that the damage to her body would heal in a day or two. After all, dreams weren't reality. It was all merely a reaction to her visions, an unusual effect of the strange seer's magic she was capable of. But when they lingered, even festered, the healers became frightened and confused. Her father sat her down—asked her if she was willing to continue the rites.

'Of course,' she'd said. She wanted to be Prime one day. She had to show strength.

She would never tell anyone that in the deepest hours of the night she wondered if it was all worth it. It was during one such night she had first tried to escape.

Passing the fireplace, her foot caught on a crooked stack of books piled near the foot of her bed. Her stomach dropped and she braced herself for the fall.

'Whispess!' Mothril sprung from his chair.

'I'm alright,' she called out as her hands and knees connected with the floor, but he was at her side instantly, his arms bracing her. She readied herself for the uncaring pain of a guard's touch, a man's touch, but he was surprisingly gentle.

'I can call for Lyra,' he said, slowly helping her to standing and guiding her back to the bed.

She clenched her teeth against biting pain. 'No, really, I'm alright. It's not an infrequent occurrence these days, I'm afraid. Since my injury.'

He sat down with her, looking her over. 'I see,' he said, before realizing he was sat on the edge of her bed. He quickly stood and stepped away.

Oria rubbed her knee. 'Sometimes I think I don't need my cane.' She smiled weakly. 'I suppose you might not have heard, spending all that time down in the tunnels. These rites, like the one tomorrow, and my dreamwalking, they cause me a great deal of pain. After so many, I became permanently injured. The healers think it's my spine. Of course, now my legs have become affected, and my'—she winced, feeling her body lock up around the pain—'my neck, my hands.'

He gazed once more into the fire, burning low and illuminating the edges of the room in spasming orange light. 'Surely the Prime wouldn't continue to allow something that would maim his only child?'

She cast her eyes downward. 'If he cares, it's outweighed by my ability to tell him where the remaining Eradomin are.' She didn't realize the bitterness in her words until she'd said them, and when she looked up, he was looking at her strangely. 'It's why I tried to . . .' Oria's voice died away. 'But I know he needs me. The clans need me. Escape seems a good idea some nights, but when morning comes I feel terribly guilty.'

Mothril returned to the chair by those ruby embers. 'I know the feeling. Of obligation to your clan, I mean.'

Oria looked up at him, surprised by his sudden interest in conversation, but also pleased that they had found something it seemed they could relate to each other about.

This time, after a moment, it was he who spoke. 'You really see them? When you're dreamwalking?'

She nodded. 'Yes. I'm a different person each time, though I know not who. I see through their eyes. The Eradomin, they only ever appear as these spectral figures, like I could put my hand through them if I got close. But when they touch me, it's real enough.'

Mothril said nothing, but the knuckles of his hand gripping the arm of the chair went bone white.

'I find myself wondering about who these people are that they're after. The dreams are so vivid, my days and nights bleed together. It's hard to distinguish between them and reality sometimes. I wish I knew what it all meant, if only so I could stop thinking about it constantly.'

'What do you think it means?' he asked.

She worried her lip. No one had ever asked her that before. 'Sometimes I think maybe I'm seeing something from another time, another world, even. Other times I'm sure I must be in the North. Father and the Elders tell me my visions are so important because if the Eradomin were to appear in my dreams as flesh and bone, like us, they believe it would mean they have returned to this plane, no longer in hiding.'

'Is that why you're reading their words?'

'Yes,' she said with a bit of a laugh. 'Looking for answers, I suppose.' She sighed and set the book down beside her.

'Well, I wouldn't worry. Everyone knows the stories,' he said, letting out a breath. 'They're out there still, in the woods, in hiding, retreated into their own dream worlds, but,' he reached over and poked at the logs with the fire poker as he shook his head, 'no, I don't think so. They've all gone to ground.'

'Why do you think that?'

'You spend a lot of time wandering when in a free order. They're not out there.'

A free order. That was the polite term for it. Most thought of them as traitors, people who had left their clan—one of the Far Clans, usually—to go out on their own. They became wanderers or mercenaries at best, thieves and murderers at worst, to be able to live that kind of life in so harsh a place as the North. Oria wondered what Mothril's father had done to be accepted back in, let alone be given any kind of position having to do with the Prime, even an undesirable one.

'Did you like being a knight-errant?'

'In a way. It was a hard life, but we were free, that was for sure.'

She thought about saying they were free here, too. Then she

remembered she couldn't make it out of the citadel if she wanted to. She didn't know if the shame of her and Lyra being returned to her chambers by knights with swords drawn would ever fade.

Still, she had it better than most in this rugged part of the world. So, though she was bound by duty, she'd settle for its constraints on her freedom if it meant being needed by her people.

'Do you remember when we still lived in the hills?' she asked suddenly. 'I was only a child, and the visions tend to cloud my mind. I have so few memories, except for the last few chaotic years, yet I miss it.'

'Yes,' Mothril said, fixing his eyes on her. 'I remember it often.'

'The bonfires at Golh were always—'

'Like the old ways again.'

She smiled. 'You know of the old ways? It seems you're more of a student of the shared Northern Histories than I am.'

He laughed, low and rumbling, but said nothing further on it. 'What are these rites like?' he asked instead, glancing over at her curiously.

Oria again found herself surprised by how his time underground affected his knowledge of how Wiccar ways of life had changed, especially since the Fall.

'They're quite elaborate,' she said, the small smile on her face falling. 'They're held in the old clearing, the one for prayer. The Elder-knights will be there, my father and his council. I practice a kind of total sensory loss, so that I can focus only on the vision I receive. Sometimes I sleep, sometimes it's more like a trance. You will see things . . . happen to me.' He looked at her with such intensity then that she urged, 'But you must not react.'

'What kind of things?'

She crossed her arms, pulling herself into them. 'I'd rather not talk about it. You'll see soon enough, anyway.'

When she saw him bristle at this, she said, 'You would not be the first guard unfamiliar with the rite to try to intervene. Promise me you'll stay with Lyra.'

He shifted in his chair, wood groaning, to look squarely at her. 'I make no promises, Whispess.'

'Why not?' Oria questioned, affronted.

'Because I won't break one.'

She frowned, wondering what exactly he meant by that, but he had turned away again, becoming transfixed by the lightning outside.

Oria turned back to her book, reading several chapters as the night grew around them. They talked on and off throughout the night about various subjects, with Mothril carefully dodging questions about his past, until the sun broke over the horizon.

Oria watched the light of dawn creep over the room until it reached the door, then slid to the edge of the bed. Breathing deep and with the help of her cane, she rose, bone-weary, to face the day. Mothril had nodded off at some point in his chair, and her cane hitting the stone woke him with a start.

'Shit,' he muttered, squinting in the white light of the brightened room. She stifled a laugh and, to her shock, he smiled. 'Do me a favor, Whispess? Don't mention that I fell asleep.'

Her lips curled into an amused smile. 'Don't worry, my ever-watchful guard, your secret is safe with me.'

17

THE LOST ONE

NO STARLINGS TODAY. Darkness ebbed from them—no one would be coming, at least not in this corporeal realm, where they slept away the hours, seldom waking to look out over unchanging grounds, the horizon always the same. Each day they prayed to see something new, something that would mean they weren't forgotten. The dreams changed all that. They used to have dreams often, as all mortals did. They must've.

Where will we go this time? There was a time they thought the glimpses of another world were all a past life. They had been someone once, someone with a family, born into darkness.

Yes, they remembered.

Riding into battle through a field of burning asphodels, under the cover of an unnatural night. The Seven Years' Night. One for each sibling, the last one for them. They were the youngest rider their mother's army had ever seen.

Kharupan would be their sanctuary. They would be safe.

Never before had they seen their mother afraid. Not when she emerged from her slumber clutching them to her breast, not in the face of a most ambitious mage, and never on the battlefield, except that day. It was, after all, the first time their world had been visited by other celestials. It was the first time they had ever been threatened, and their mother was not accustomed to it.

'If I do not return, be good. Watch over your kin, and most importantly, watch over your father. I worry for his sanity if this day does not go our way. He will never ask for your opinion, but you need to guide his hand as I have done. Be wise about it. Most of all, be good.'

They thought about it. Were those the last words their mother had ever spoken?

No. Wherever she was taken, she was kept alive. There was another of their blood, too. When the dreams came, they could feel the other of them, out there in all the world's ophidian tendrils.

18

ORIA

M OST WOULDN'T KNOW IT, because Oria was the only one sat up in this room all day, but if someone stood outside her door just right, you could hear every word they said. She heard Lyra and Mothril come up the stairs, then pause outside her doorway.

'Does the Whispess usually take her meals in her chambers?' Mothril asked, followed by clattering sounds of someone handling a tray.

'Yes, nowadays,' came another, softer voice.

Not Lyra, then.

'W-when Lady Felith was alive the Whispess and her maiden ate in the dining hall with her and the other Elders. I-I suppose such frequent trips across the grounds would be a lot for her to manage at present.'

'I see,' came his reply. Then the door opened, and Oria watched with no small amount of amusement as Mothril brought her meal to her.

'I very much like having a guard as attentive as you,' Oria said, greeting him 'Was that Lunafrey?'

Mothril scowled slightly. 'Mm. Said she made your favorite.'

Oria grinned, reaching straight for the pastry. 'She's so good

to me, especially when each meal feels like it might be my last.'
Oria sighed. 'I love redcap pie . . .'

'Redcaps?' said Mothril. 'Aren't those poisonous?'

'Not the mushrooms,' she said, laughing. 'You've never tried
a redcap? The berry?'

'Can't say that I have.'

'Oh, well, you have to! Come here.' She speared a bite with
her fork and held it out to him.

Mothril grimaced, raising a hand in protest and backing
toward the door. 'Really, Whispess, I can't—'

'You'll like it!'

He looked downright pained. 'I can't taste your meal.'

Oria smirked. 'Think of yourself as my cupbearer. Besides,
it's my dessert, and I'm ordering you to.'

He sighed, then leaned in and tasted it. After a few
moments, he looked at her askance. 'It is good,' he said,
nodding.

Smirk turned to satisfied smile. 'Told you.'

'Right.' He cleared his throat and made for the door.

'Won't you stay?' she asked, before he could rush out like he
tended to do.

'Haven't you learned by now that I'm not much good for
conversation?'

'Nonsense. I like talking to you.' She turned her attention
back to her meal. 'I can't believe you've never had a redcap
before. Not even living in the wilds?'

He sat reluctantly in his usual spot by the hearth. 'No, but
we were well aware of redcap mushrooms.'

'Mm.' She nodded, swallowing a mouthful of pie. 'Though
they're not the most poisonous you'll find in these forests.
Bleeding violets, now those could probably kill a man your size
with just a stem.'

He looked at her dubiously. 'Know a lot about poisons, do
you?'

She smiled and gave a slight shrug. 'I've read quite a few books on toxic plants and mushrooms. I used to make tinctures and poultices for the knights, too. I believed one day I'd become an Elder-knight myself, known across the North for her deadly poisons.'

'What interested you in them?'

'I don't know,' she said, picking at her food. 'I guess I'm glad I learned about them, it's probably the only way I'd have of defending myself now if the Eradomin were to return.'

'Not necessarily,' said Mothril. 'Have you ever used one of these?' he asked, producing a narrow dagger from his gambeson. It was unlike any she'd seen before. The metal had a dark gray tint to it, and the hilt was engraved with some kind of inscription.

'No,' she said, a bit nervously. 'Is it a throwing knife?'

'It is. Dagger, throwing knife, you can use it in a few different ways. Do you want me to show you?'

She nodded, so he rose and came to kneel beside her bed. Even kneeling, his eyes were level with hers. He held the knife between them.

'There are a few ways you can grip the handle. Here.' He took her hand in his. 'You can either grip it like this,' he said, placing his hand over hers and extending her pointer finger along the spine of the knife, 'or like this,' he said, showing her another grip with two fingers and the palm of the hand. 'Firm, but relaxed.' He rubbed his thumb across the joint of her first finger, softening her grip.

Holding it the way he showed her, she felt no ache, and there was no locking up of her fingers. Oria stared at her hand in amazement.

'Come,' he said, gesturing for her to stand. He helped her from the bed and they went to the far wall of her small room.

'Try throwing it at the side of the bookcase.' When she

looked at him out of her periphery, he added, 'Don't worry, you won't damage the books, and no one will notice.'

She looked intensely at the grain of the wood, trying not to think about how close he was, and how he smelled of rivermint and pipeweed.

'You want to be about this distance for the best possible chance to hit, say . . . eight feet. When you throw it, you're going to think of it in terms of rotations of the knife. Using this first position,' he said, adjusting her grip again, 'you can throw it without the knife rotating, and you won't have to worry too much.'

His hand ghosted across her hip. 'This leg forward. Now, when you throw it, stay relaxed. Think about putting your momentum behind that finger.'

She took a deep breath and threw the knife. It let out a satisfying *thump* as it connected with the wood and was left sticking out of the bookcase. She gasped softly.

'Good.' Mothril, always so stoic, had a small, satisfied smile on his face. 'A little poison on this knife, and you're a force to be reckoned with, Oria of-Cailir.'

She pulled the knife from the wood, then sat back down beside the wooden tray. Mothril drifted over to her. She turned the knife over in her hand, admiring it, then handed it back to him.

'Keep it.'

Her eyes met his. 'Are you sure?'

He nodded. 'I never want you to feel like you're defenseless.'

Oria looked down at it again. It felt like power in her hands. 'Thank you.' She ran a finger along its edge. 'I suppose this wouldn't be much help at close range, though.'

'You'd be surprised.' He eyed her, considering his words. 'It's not about strength at that point, but the swiftness and accuracy of your strike. May I?'

She nodded, and he moved the tray from the bed, then sat beside her. 'Lie back.'

She did so, relaxing into the soft pillows behind her despite the nervous fluttering in her chest. Then, achingly slowly, Mothril moved closer until he was nearly on top of her, his body heavy over hers. He reached down and tightened her fist around the knife with his own hand.

He began speaking softly. 'Even pinned like this, you still have openings. Here,' he said, moving her hand into position so the knife pointed toward his ribs at his left side. 'I can do nothing to block this if I want to maintain my hold on you.'

His face was so close.

'You may think I have the power in this situation, but once quick stab here, between these ribs, or here,' he said, moving her hand to a spot at the base of the neck, 'and you'll mostly have to worry about rolling my corpse off of you.'

He let go of her hand, and she realized she was breathing hard. She removed the knife from his neck.

He huffed a laugh. 'That's enough lessons for now, I think.' For a fraction of a second, he hesitated, then lifted himself off of her. 'Come, I'm sure they're expecting us.'

19

ATLAN

'COME ON THEN, LITTLE KING.'

He couldn't help but smirk as Kyr comically danced about a couple feet away, waggling her longsword out in fool's guard as if it were a cock.

Atlan waited until it seemed like she was distracted by her own antics to attack. He feinted high, and Kyr registered a look of surprise, but her feet were ready, so she met him in a bind. Atlan sidestepped, striking at her neck. Kyr whirled away from the blade and inside, blocking his arm and kneeing him in the gut.

He stumbled backward with a hearty 'Oof,' landing in the dirt, clutching his stomach. 'They teach you to fight dirty in the Sledge,' he bit out.

She closed the gap between them and pressed her thumb between his thumb and forefinger. Instantly, the pain lessened.

'It's a pressure point,' she explained. 'And they don't *teach* you anything in the Sledge. You learn from doing. On instinct.' She laughed. 'And you learn the most from the times your instincts are dead wrong.'

'Right, I almost forgot for two seconds that you're such a lionheart.' He brushed the dust off his linen trousers.

Kyr snorted. 'And I didn't realize that royals had such an appetite for dust. Thank you for the reminder.'

'Anytime.' Atlan couldn't remember the last time he had enjoyed himself this much, even with Tyran and the rest of the Sun's Own he'd grown close to over the years.

'You headed to that council meeting now?'

'Unfortunately, it was part of my deal for keeping *you* alive,' Atlan said, poking Kyr in the chest.

Kyr looked at him with theatrical adoration. 'See, I told you you could still be some big hero.'

Atlan smiled, his cheeks aching. 'Listen,' he said. By the way Kyr raised her brows and leaned in, he knew she had picked up on the playful curve of his lips, the rebellious look in his eye. 'You should come. I know a place where you won't be seen.'

'Little king,' she *tsk*ed. 'Are you sure this is information you want to be giving to a Knave?'

'If the Knave happens to be a friend.' He winked, and she smiled wide. 'Come on, come with me to the council meeting. We can laugh while my mother's advisors make a show of wringing their hands over the fate of citizens they don't even give a fuck about.'

Kyr planted her practice sword in the loamy earth, then followed Atlan to the council chamber.

It was another grand, high-ceilinged room in the palace, with airy archways, half-melted votives, and gold-threaded tapestries, which, Kyr remarked, all looked the same to her.

Atlan showed her to an alcove off the chamber's mezzanine where she could listen and not be seen, then took his place with the courtiers below.

'The Wiccars?' came the queen's low drawl. 'We will never have anything to do with the 'Free North.'' The last two words sounded like an insult when she said them.

The Free North was an endless plague on his mother's legacy, with the Wiccars being the only people to withstand the might of the Yoren army. The added fact that they were disorganized, roaming fighters, who often attacked in smaller groups and still won, only deepened his mother's humiliation and dissatisfaction.

'I understand your position, of course, and I share it,' said Sol Eyria, 'but they are said to have magic—'

'We've been over this,' Queen Attiqah snapped. 'Superstition, all.'

The room fell silent as the councilors looked anywhere but at their queen. Sol Eyria alone pushed further. 'You must be able to understand that your council is concerned when another mage of small magics was uncovered in our very city during this inquiry.'

Queen Attiqah scowled, seemingly annoyed at even having to entertain these questions. 'Inconvenient timing to be sure, but the important thing is, she was found and has agreed to become a court diviner.'

Atlan looked up at Kyr's hiding place, and saw her brows furrow at the lies his mother so confidently and comfortably told.

'And Sol Taryq? What does he think?'

'He thinks what I tell him to think. If you're asking whether he has found anything of note regarding the blights to the west, more pressing matters have delayed his trip to Bellgard. In his stead, Prince Atlan will travel there later in the week.'

He made eye contact with Kyr then, looking just as confused as she was at this sudden change of plans. The thought of leaving Kyr behind in Yorenth caused a pang of emotion in his chest. He worried for her safety if he was not here.

'What could possibly be more pressing?' Sol Eyria urged.

'I am speaking,' Queen Attiqah barked. 'Sol Taryq has

found the traitor responsible for the attack on the counting house. The true traitor to the realm, not that lowborn who was simply hiding her magics from the Crown.'

Sol Rywin cut in, barely able to contain himself. 'You mean this?'

'You will have good news to deliver to your guild today, Sol Rywin.' The room filled with murmurs. 'Bring him out!'

Atlan saw Kyr rush toward the balustrade overlooking the room then, remembering she was supposed to be hidden, crouch back down.

Two Sun's Own dragged a disheveled man into the room as the advisors and nobles present gawked. Unkempt dark brown curls framed his brows, and his cheeks were pockmarked with scars. He couldn't be older than his twenty-second summer.

'Roqlar Elaurien, a glassworks apprentice and former royal diviner, was seen in the vicinity of the counting house the day of the attack, and had on his person glowmoth silk dust, an illegal alchemical substance known for enhancing the abilities of those with small magics. We believe that, while his skill is nothing out of the ordinary, structural issues with the counting house—it was undergoing renovation after all—are mainly to blame for the scale of the destruction. Furthermore, he failed to report for duty as a court diviner the day of the attack.'

'Please,' Roqlar sobbed. 'I didn't—'

'You will be silent!' the queen shouted, her face contorting.

Atlan could only look at Kyr. The expression she wore was both sorrowful and determined. She met his eyes and shook her head.

'I extend my heartfelt gratitude to the Sun's Own and Sol Taryq,' the queen continued, turning proudly to where Taryq stood by her side, 'for their efforts in apprehending this dangerous criminal.'

The advisors whispered amongst themselves and nodded along, satisfied. Atlan saw the sickened expression on Kyr's face and immediately felt a sense of guilt. They were going to execute an innocent man for something she did. Nothing more than an accident.

He thought about what he would do if Kyr weren't there. He might not even be at the council meeting at all. He'd hear from some crier about this man's execution, and that would be that. But Kyr had opened his eyes.

How had he lived like that?

'Roqlar Elaurien has been found guilty by Sol Taryq's review. His execution is set for tomorrow afternoon.'

Quickly, Kyr rose to a crouch and dashed behind the mezzanine's benches, out into the second-floor hall.

Atlan turned to look at Taryq for further explanation, but he only wore a slight smile on his face, pleased with himself. For years Atlan had felt he was competing with Taryq for his mother's attention, and he couldn't deny he'd grown to hate him for it. At first, he'd been something like a father, or at least a friend, to him, until he fell out of favor with his mother. He then fell out of favor with Taryq too, ever the ambitious noble.

Amongst the chaos of the unexpected news, his mother consumed with the council's questions, Atlan quietly left the chamber to find Kyr.

When he reached the second floor, he found her just down the hall from the mezzanine's entrance, vomiting into a planter. She looked up at him, glassy-eyed.

'How easily I've let myself be taken in. If I'd thought about it for more than a fucking minute, of course something like this was going to happen. Of course the queen needs an explanation. A scapegoat for what I've done.' She wiped her mouth on the sleeve of her linen shirt, then sank down to the floor. 'Come on, Kyr,' he heard her whisper. 'You're fucking losing it.'

She looked like a caged animal. Like she would gnaw her own arm off if it meant getting out of the palace faster.

'What was I thinking, hanging around with Spiritsdamned

royals who would use me and anyone from the Sledge as it suited them?' She buried her face in her hands. 'Spirit's sake, Grym would be so disappointed in me. This is no place for a thief, for a—a kid from the docks. Weighing lives like that . . . I'm just a nameless daughter of caravanners, Atlan. I'm not supposed to be here.'

She staggered to her feet, looking like she wanted to flee.

Atlan stepped toward her, his eyes softening. 'Kyr . . .'

She ignored him.

'Kyr, listen to me—'

Kyr turned on her heel and advanced a step, an unreadable expression on her face. 'What is it, little king? Come to tell me how this can all be explained away? You lot seem to have a rationale for everything. What? Let me guess, I should stay because I've got magic that can be used for the greater good, or some such bullshit?'

'What?' Atlan's eyes were unwavering. 'No.' He could hear yelling coming from the council chamber, and cocked his head toward the sound. 'Kyr, I came to tell you 'fuck these bastards.' I've been told all my life that I have a duty. That I have power that can be used for 'the greater good.' No one ever defines what that is, by the way. In my experience it usually amounts to whatever the person saying it has decided is valuable. Worth maintaining.'

She watched him with wary eyes.

'This is what they do. My mother. Taryq. He'd sacrifice anyone to improve his position.' Atlan scoffed. 'They tell me I will be someone remembered by history. A victor. What they really mean is that I should shove any feeling of distress, any dissonance down, and maintain our family's consolidation of wealth, our power, at all costs. Maintain, maintain, maintain. What good is 'duty' when the whole thing it's in service of is a broken, churning behemoth that eats people alive, like that fellow in there, just to keep itself going?'

Kyr's shoulders fell as she calmed, and she smiled weakly. 'I knew your anger in the dueling pit had to come from somewhere, I just didn't know you were such a renegade.'

'I've felt this way my whole life, witnessing my mother do as she pleases, *destroy* as she pleases, with no one to stand up to her. I-I wish I were stronger, it's who I want to be, but . . .'

'But the whole thing's like some great machine, like you said. We're but small screws in it, Atlan.'

'Screws can come loose.'

Kyr looked at him, eyes red-rimmed, and raised an eyebrow. 'What did you have in mind?'

20

MOTHRIL

A TEMPEST THREATENED the simmering skies above the clearing.
In front of Mothril, the Whispess watched the great oaks
swaying in a frenzy overhead, closed her eyes, and breathed the
petrichor of the ancient ritual grounds in deep.

He thought of all they had talked about the past several
nights and wondered if he'd said too much to the Prime's
daughter.

Surprising even himself, he found he enjoyed her company.
The more he learned about her life, the more he admired her
for all she had dealt with in her young life. And then there was
that song on the harp—she'd played it beautifully.

From their conversations, he'd learned Oria had barely
broken free of the yoke of childhood when the Battle of Kingdom's Fall happened, when Edril Sil usurped the ancestral
home of the Eradomin, ending the Wiccars' nomadic ways. She
had believed what they all had.

Eradicating their enemy would provide them protection,
seclusion, and a homecoming. Edril Sil's vision for their people
was like a faith then, a fervor. Only recently had that faith
begun to wane. Like him, she didn't agree that warring had

brought them much of anything. Her reasons were different than his, but that they agreed at all was surprising. He didn't know what to make of her, the ruler's daughter willing to sacrifice herself, and all the while concealing something of an apostate's spirit.

'It's time, Whispess,' said a guard to her left. Mothril stood beside him at her back.

'Here,' he said, handing Mothril a strip of white fabric. 'It goes around her eyes.'

'Are you alright, Whispess?' he asked, voice low. She shied from the sound of his voice so sudden by her ear, but nodded.

Mothril hesitated a moment, then gently lowered it over her eyes and tied it, careful not to touch her.

'She needs to be led down,' said the guard.

He let out a grunt of acknowledgement. Next to her, Lyra whispered, 'I'm here.' Oria gave her hand a squeeze in answer.

Lyra walked ahead of them toward the lower circle, and they began their slow descent to the shaded clearing, past ghostlike troops of Elder-knights in gleaming argent livery, woolen day-cloaks, and veils, who stood watching from the surrounding cliffs.

Sweet smoke clouded the air as they passed braziers lit with incense, and the knights began chanting a low, wordless hymn.

They passed by rows and rows of knights, unseeing statues, as they descended farther, when Oria finally left his side to walk out to the clearing's center and kneel at a stone altar there.

Mothril watched as she attuned herself to the soft earth, pressing her palms into the grass.

The dark clouds above gathered quickly then, and the heavens cleaved opened, pouring rain down upon the sacred wood, pattering off armor and stone, nearly drowning out all sound. Oria sat back on her heels, her body slackening.

Mothril noticed that most around him had their eyes closed or heads down, but he couldn't take his eyes off the Whispess.

She slumped to the ground, lying on her back, her dress and cloak nearly soaked through. He tried to study her expression, to understand an inkling of how she was feeling, but couldn't make out the details of her face through the downpour.

As he lifted his hand to shield his eyes and get a closer look, a scream shattered the air. If the sound hadn't come from her direction, he'd have thought it came from some kind of wraith.

He started forward, but Lyra grabbed his arm. 'Do you want the Prime to have you swinging from a tree in the Cloakwood?' she snapped. Her words didn't register. 'A guard that steps out of line is as good as dead.'

Mothril looked back toward the ritual circle to see red blood bloom on Oria's cheek from an illusory slash. She sobbed, dragging herself along the ground, as if trying to back away from something.

He cocked his head, remembering one of his father's teachings. 'A weapon is not only a tool, but a responsibility. We must cut away our ties to our past, and never commit ourselves to one eventuality over another.' He felt a sudden tightening in his chest as he thought of this, and his bloody past. *Another tie to cut away.*

'Eildroth!' she screamed. Gasps sounded from above at the terror in her voice.

Mothril knew that name.

'It can't be,' he whispered. Every draft rustling the leaves overhead, each gust of storm-tossed air, captured his focus.

Oria's body was dragged, pulled by nothing but air, as if someone had her by the hair. Suddenly her body jolted, and her arm twisted sharply. He knew instantly that her shoulder was dislocated. The blood on her cheek was gone then, as if lapped up, and another slash formed on her chin. Her other cheek.

He took another step, unconsciously finding his sword, but not to cut away any threads.

'What are you *doing*?' Lyra whispered, reaching for him again.

He pulled his arm from her grip, his face a mask of grim determination. 'They don't know what might come through.'

Mothril entered the clearing.

21

KYR

THEY'D PUT some distance between themselves and the palace, not just because Atlan was rightfully paranoid about someone overhearing what they were about to discuss, but also because they could never quite breathe easily within its imperious walls. When Kyr mentioned this to Atlan, he replied that the palace had a way of doing that.

She and Atlan sat now amongst the sun-bleached ruins of an old beacon at the southernmost tip of the docks. It was late in the evening by then, and the heavens were torn asunder by the glow of an infernal sunset.

'How did you find this place?' Atlan asked, after they'd climbed the old, rotting stairs to the tower's roof. It felt almost as if they were outside the city, the way the shoreline connecting this place to the rest of Yorenth's shipping district had almost completely eroded. The only way to reach it now was a small footpath through dense scrub brush along a steep hillside.

Kyr sat on the edge, and Atlan stood behind her. 'I've been coming here for as long as I can remember, even before I was a

Knave. It's always been my spot.' She squinted as she looked out at the dark waves.

Atlan said nothing, a comfortable silence extending between them. Kyr looked back at him, noting the way his face looked unrestrained, and yet sadder somehow.

'When I needed to get away, when I needed a night without waking to someone trying something, I'd come here. If all the food I could eat grew on trees out here, I would probably never leave.'

Atlan smiled, joining her at the tower's edge. 'Thank you for showing it to me.' Kyr turned back to the sea, an odd feeling coming over her. It felt strange to be showing the prince a piece of his own dominion, and yet he'd thanked her as if it was hers.

'So, how exactly does one start a conversation about what the queen would deem a hostile act?' she asked.

'A hostile act in the face of insanity is something entirely different to the sane. We begin by discussing the next steps.'

Her voice grew bitter. 'I won't let Elaurien die.'

'I know,' he said, nodding, 'which is why when we leave on that inquiry into the blights, we're taking him with us.'

'We?' Two thoughts occurred to her then. She hadn't expected the prince to be such a willing accomplice, but also, she wondered how much of a wanted woman this was going to make her. Would she ever be able to return to Yorenth?

'Yes,' he said, matter-of-factly. 'We're going to Bellgard, to the translators at the Archives there. They're likely our last hope of finding out what the Oracle's notes mean, and they have a more complete record of oral histories than the royal library here does. We should speak with Saartho. I'm sure he will have guidance for us.'

Kyr picked up a pebble and tossed it into the sea below. 'First, you'll need to speak with your mother.' It came out more as a regretful statement than a question.

He nodded. 'I know. It's best if I let her think this visit to the outpost on the Western Road is routine. Before she realizes we're gone, and Elaurien with us, we'll be halfway to Bellgard and out of her reach.'

'How do you think she's going to react?' Kyr asked, biting her lip.

Atlan looked off into the distance. 'With how unpredictable she is these days, I can't say for sure. She'll have Taryq and my brother to steady her. As for whatever comes next, we'll save that discussion for after our visit to the Archives. We don't know what we're going to find, after all.'

Kyr nodded. 'You'll be able to get to Elaurien?'

He turned back to her. 'I can get us as far as the cell door . . .' His dark brown eyes connected with hers.

'Oh, no,' said Kyr, putting her hands up. 'I'm already in trouble!'

'Trust me, I wouldn't involve you if I didn't have to. I can get most keys to the palace dungeons, but not this one. We're going to need a guard's signet ring, and your talented fingers.'

Kyr burst out laughing.

Atlan cracked a smile. 'What?'

Kyr shook her head. 'Nothing.'

He shrugged. 'I'll have horses ready at the stables too.'

Kyr sighed. 'It's as good a plan as any, and it is nice working with a prince.' Her expression saddened slightly, and Atlan caught the shift.

'Are you alright?' he prodded.

'I'm fine.' She gave him a reassuring smile. 'I was just thinking about how this is going to change things.'

'It will,' Atlan agreed, face growing serious. 'But you've made me realize it's about time I did something with all this knowledge and power, rather than just squandering my days. Saartho has been telling me I've seemed restless for some time, too.'

'Ah, you're always so hard on yourself. You weren't squandering them. You have to think of it as preparation. Every moment has prepared you for what comes next.'

'Very profound. Maybe in another life you wrote Solorien verse in the Book of Dreaming.'

Kyr snorted. 'Doubtful.'

With a sigh, Atlan placed his hands on his knees and stood. 'Alright. I should go speak with Her Radiance then. We'll need to be ready to go tomorrow.'

'You're sure about this, Atlan?'

He fixed her with a steady gaze. 'I am.'

Kyr's face turned solemn, her voice steady. 'Alright, go. I'll meet you at the library like usual?'

'See you then, Knave.'

She gave him a playful nudge and looked out at the sea once more, hearing his footsteps recede. She knew she should be getting back to the palace as well, but she'd missed this place. She'd memorized the line of the waves along the rock-face, knew all the contours of it. She'd seen how the sea fennel spread along its crevices over the years, the crooked pine beside the path growing farther and farther over the cliff's edge. She'd spent many nights comforted by the solitude of this place, the worries of the city a world away.

A scraping noise sounded below. Someone was coming up the stairs.

'I thought I told you to run along back to the palace, little king,' Kyr said, laughing, as she looked over her shoulder.

A figure appeared out of the deepening night. It was not Atlan.

It was Sylas.

22

ORIA

THE SOUND of horses circling faded away to pattering sheets of rain, and a voice shouting out into the storm. She felt as if she were between worlds, the vision she'd seen fresh in her mind and yet, there was the feeling that something had not yet dawned on her. She had been torn from her vision, and awareness of the present was still far off.

'Seize him!'

Her father's voice.

Then, much closer, a hoarse but gentle voice. 'Or— Whispess?'

She writhed at the person's touch, reaching for them as she rolled over on the sodden ground, and nearly screamed.

'Stay still,' came the voice again, steadier this time. It had the serious tone of someone working at something. 'I need to put your shoulder back in the joint.'

Her tear-stung eyes opened, focused at last, to the scene before her. It was not the man called Eildroth speaking to her. Mothril's looming figure knelt over her, rain sluicing down his face and armor, his pale hair sticking to his skin.

In her periphery, she could see Elder-knights rushing down

the steep path to the clearing. She tried to remember what happened, but exhaustion descended on her like a heavy fog. Instead, much as it pained her, she focused on maintaining the sharpest moments of her vision for her father's questioning later.

The warriors on the wind had appeared again, this time across large swaths of barren land. But it wasn't her they were searching for. They passed her by, charging toward a kingdom made of gleaming yellow sand, far in the distance.

She blinked and found herself in a room—airy, something comforting about it—in a tower high above snow-capped peaks. Thin lancet windows filled with bright sunlight. One of the warriors entered, and for the first time, he spoke directly to her.

He'd given her his name. Asked her if she wanted a drink of water. Said she must've come a long way.

Then, suddenly, she was returned to the forest clearing she often found herself in. He did not seem to recognize her. The ritual that she so feared began. Incense. Daggers. His body over hers, tasting her wounds.

'Forgive me,' Mothril said, and before she had time to process his words an unearthly pain swallowed her whole, followed by swift relief. She was distantly aware of a horrible sound she made, and yet she barely registered it.

'Mothril,' she gasped, eyes wide but unseeing in the shock of it all. The rain slowed as she looked at him. His face was expressionless, but his pale grey eyes were piercing.

Again, she found herself wondering what the emotion was behind them. It comforted her, somehow, the familiarity of studying him.

The rain slowed. Footsteps spattered across the wet ground towards her, and then Mothril was pulled sharply backward. Someone else grabbed under her arms and she was thrust painfully to her feet.

'She's injured!' Oria heard him yell.

She turned to see him being held by three knights, a blade to his neck.

'You dare interrupt a sacred clan rite?' boomed her father's voice. 'I'd heard rumors about you, Mothril of-Arcandras, I was warned that you were growing restless!'

Oria looked between them, shouting, 'Father, please! He only wanted to help!'

'Help?' her father asked venomously. 'My daughter, you've always had such a soft heart. Do you know who this man is, really?'

She looked at Mothril. 'Yes, I kn—'

'No, I don't think you do.' Edril Sil's voice was calm, but there was an undercurrent of warning to it. 'Maybe you know that he and his father were part of a free order. But did you know that they were the only survivors of the Ronin clan?'

Several gasps sounded from the Elders gathered around them. What happened to the Ronin was a pervading mystery amongst the Wiccars.

Edril Sil nodded slowly. 'He and his father claimed they were set upon by bandits, but no trace of anyone else nearby was found. We searched for days. I tend to believe what everyone else does, that they callously murdered their clan Elders.' Edril Sil turned as he said this, glancing at the onlookers higher up on the cliffs, before turning back to her. 'Did you know that? Perhaps he's told you he was forced to torture as apprentice to his father, but . . . no, it's who he is.' He spat the words.

'He and his father tried to make it in a free order because killing is what they do. Rathwil came crawling back to us, of course, with his boy in tow.' He sneered at Mothril. 'The Northern wilds are unforgiving.'

Oria looked at Mothril, whose gaze had never broken from her.

'I agreed to let them in only by the grace of your mother. She was tricked, blinded by how they had protected her once, but I knew it for the gambit it was. The only suitable place for them was down in the tunnels, which is where I would've thrown them if it weren't for Felith's pleading. So, we came to a compromise.'

Edril Sil approached Mothril, who was still only looking at her. 'And do you know what else?' her father continued, his voice imbuing the clearing with a sense of unease. 'The Ronin had many children. All were found dead. One of the Elders, their daughter was about your age at the time. When my knights found her, she had no eyes. Only pits of dried flesh remained.'

For the first time, Mothril's brow crumpled, and Oria saw what looked like guilt in his eyes before he closed them. Oria backed away.

Edril Sil continued. 'You may be wondering why I let such a man get so close to you, my beloved daughter. It was so long ago now, and I thought knowing how much he and his father were indebted to our clan meant he would take his new, improved post as a gesture of good faith and behave accordingly. That, and it's never a bad thing to keep a closer eye on those you don't trust. I was wrong about one of those things, but right about the other, it would seem.'

'Father, please,' Oria began, attempting to smooth things over, to return everything to the way it was. 'Can't you see that this was similarly a gesture of good faith on his part? He has never seen one of our rites before. He knows not the ways of—'

Her father scoffed. 'You're just like your mother. No, I cannot allow it, I will not—'

'Listen to me!' Oria pleaded.

'You will be silent! Perhaps this insolence on your part is his influence as well.' Her father looked at Mothril as he said his next words. 'Melsze will be so disappointed to hear you did not turn out as he'd hoped.' He sighed. 'I can see now that it was a mistake to let this beast near one so impressionable as my daughter.'

Oria felt her face grow hot.

'I know who Eildroth is,' Mothril said suddenly.

Oria's eyes flicked to him, widening.

Her father cocked his head and then, to Oria's surprise, chuckled. 'Oh, this is interesting. Please, beast, enlighten us all as to why *you* know an Eradomin name.'

Mothril's eyes darted from him to Oria and back. 'Only if I am able to continue as part of this clan and as guard to the Whispess. She is right, I-I have never seen one of these rites before. I was concerned for her safety and acted, that is all.'

'That is all?' Edril Sil mocked, raising his brows. 'You think your meddling doesn't affect all of us? My scribes have studied Oria's dreams. Her visions come in narrow windows, often following new moons. Who knows when we will next be able to glean critical knowledge from them?'

Edril Sil's face darkened, and he pitched his voice lower. 'I should kill you where you stand.'

Oria was stunned. Her father had learned more of her visions and hadn't told her about it?

Mothril, undeterred, challenged him. 'If the name dies with me, you will never get the answers you seek.'

Her father's lip twitched. 'Alright, Mothril of-Arcandras. I assent to your proposal. Let's see what you have to say for yourself.'

Oria sighed with relief.

Her father waved his hand. 'Guards.'

Immediately, Elder Efja pulled a cloth across his mouth, gagging him.

Mothril bucked, his massive form sending her and another knight to the ground. He whirled around, but a third knight already had the point of his blade at his throat.

Oria thought she saw his eyes dart toward his sword in the grass, assessing the distance. His jaw ticked, and he straightened, allowing the guards to restrain him.

'You said you'd let him go! Please, there's no need for this!'

Edril Sil didn't look at her. 'I said nothing of the sort. I need to find out why he's been withholding this from us. Sybil, escort the Whispess back to her chambers, and see to it that the healers attend her.'

'This isn't fair!' Oria cried out, mustering as defiant a voice as she could.

'I really think it's more than fair,' her father said, giving her a gentle pat on the cheek as he passed by. 'I will come see you later, I want to hear all about what you saw.'

With that, Oria was led out of the clearing by Sybil, as Mothril followed, surrounded and bound.

23

KYR

'COME NO CLOSER,' Kyr said, moving to her feet in an instant.

He was really here. Sylas, in the flesh. He wore the same old brown cloak she always liked searching the pockets of as a child. Mostly, she found spare coins or keys, toothpicks or a prayer book, but another time she found a marble that changed color when it rained, and another, a set of brass knuckles.

'Kyr—' he crooned.

'How did you find me? Were you following me?'

He looked like shit. His normally bright eyes were dull and sunken, like he hadn't slept in days. She noticed a ring he always wore—a fat ruby surrounded by carved obsidian—was missing from his left hand.

'Would you believe me if I told you I went on a walk, innocently, and saw you from the docks? I always look at this tower when I pass by. It reminds me of you.'

'Atlan?' Kyr called out, ignoring him.

'Atlan? How familiar.' He looked down the path below them. 'Mm, I saw him. He didn't see me, though. I have so many questions about your association with the prince, but that's not what I want to talk about right now.'

'I don't have anything to say to you.'

'Kyr, I'm not here to hurt you,' he said, and she almost wanted to believe the familiarity of that warm, gruff voice.

'Maybe I'd believe you if you hadn't of sent that Rook,' she shot back.

'Can't you understand the position I was in? He wasn't supposed to hurt you, he was supposed to bring you back to me.' He took a step closer, shaking his hair from his face, revealing that thick, pink scar along his forehead.

'Most people don't send assassins for that. Was the poisoned blade part of your plan, too?'

'Poison?' Sylas wheezed. 'I'd hardly call a draught of dreamless sleep *poison*. Besides, I'm not most people.'

He grinned, and she saw the gold tooth at the back of his mouth. Now she had one to match.

'You always were a slippery one. I had to send the very best. But I heard he was no match for you.' His grin turned surprisingly fond, like he always looked in her best memories of him.

Her killing the Rook must've made him proud. He'd always said he never thought she had it in her to kill.

'I don't care why you sent him after me. He attacked me. I had to defend myself, I—'

'You don't have to justify it to me,' he said, holding up his hands.

'I'm not trying to justify it!' She felt tears welling up again. '*You* let me go that day. I know you, Sylas. I saw the way you looked at me. I thought after all these years I'd spent at your side, you knew me better than to think I'd be any kind of trouble for the guild. I thought you could at least do me the courtesy of letting me go in peace, but instead a Rook corners me in the market, and now I can't ever get back who I was before that day!'

'You think I was looking at you that day with malice?'

'What else?'

He looked at her appraisingly, opening his mouth and then closing it again. 'Kyr, I couldn't let you go because, you see, that wasn't the end of our story. You may think you saw cruelty in my assessment, but it was only shrewdness. Someone with magic, despite the attention your little mishap could've brought, is still someone useful to me. More than that, I care for you, Kyr, as if you were my own.'

'Oh, don't,' she said, looking away.

'Vasha misses you too. You know, he didn't leave his room for four days after you left. I think he's still angry with Fen and I.'

Spirits, I miss him, she thought.

The sun had sunk below the horizon now, and the shadows grew a deeper blue. Dusk was more appropriate for Sylas, anyway. He looked out of place in the light.

'I'm not coming back to the guild, Sylas. I don't care if you try to kill me a hundred more times.'

'Kyr,' he said, his expression both humorous and frustrated. 'I don't want that. What will it take for you to believe me?'

'Nothing. It's too late.'

'Then will you at least allow me to explain my reasoning a little further?'

She eyed him, anger still tensing the muscles of her face, but she said nothing. It was as much of a concession as she would give him, if only to satisfy her curiosity.

'You've always had a good eye. I'm sure you noticed the many lockboxes and reliquaries and such on your way to the vault.' She didn't answer, and Sylas sighed. 'There is a lot more kept in the counting house vaults than marks.'

'What are you saying?'

'I'm saying I miscalculated. There was . . . something I thought was kept in the holding vault. My information is rarely incorrect. In this case, it was. It's been happening more and more as of late.'

Kyr felt her heartbeat quicken, like her heart itself knew Sylas never revealed information without expecting to be owed for it. 'We got everything that was down there. We did what you wanted.'

He paused, raising a brow. 'You think I needed more gold? Kyr,' he tutted, 'you're smarter than that.'

A moment stretched out between them. 'Well, it's all buried in rubble now, so I don't know what you want me to do about it.'

He looked at the ground. 'Yes, that was unfortunate. I'm sure you must feel quite guilty over Grym's death.'

'It was an accident,' she nearly growled.

'Oh, a terrible one,' he said innocently. 'No, there's no changing what's already happened. We can only move forward.'

'*We?* So sure of yourself . . .'

'I see it's rubbed off on you,' he shot back.

Just then, the breeze off the sea picked up, blowing their hair about and sending seed pods flying off the cliffs into the water.

He smiled, and it was neither kind nor unkind. 'The gold was lovely, I've no complaints about your work other than the . . . obvious mishap, but, as I've said, it wasn't what I was expecting.'

'Out with it,' Kyr spat.

Sylas gave a subtle shrug. 'Alright. Kyr, you ever wonder about our guild's complete dominance over the Realm? I mean, we've got the best of the best. We never fail at our job. Until the last one, that is.'

'You trained us well.'

'Mm. I *chose* well.'

'What's that supposed to mean?'

Sylas looked down at his feet. It was an unusual sight for the guild leader who always stood proud. 'There was a relic that

I thought would be hidden in the vault. After all, outside of Bellgard the Soloriens possess the largest collection of texts on First Age artifacts, and they're the ones with the might to bring them home. I was sure they had it.'

'What's the relic?'

He squinted up at her. 'It's called the Pentaculum.' Kyr stilled, trying not to show interest. 'The descriptions of its physical appearance are varying, but it's said to contain magically ciphered memories of the First Age. That of kings, Kyr, warriors, the Artificers.'

Kyr crossed her arms. 'The Arisen Rexus and all that? Many-eyed beasts turning everything to ash, you really believe that? The Artificers are a bedtime story, Sylas.'

He shrugged. 'To some, maybe. To others, there are truths hidden within these stories. I believe these many-eyed beasts are an allusion to a powerful artifact. One mirrored relic, perhaps.'

Kyr considered this. 'What did you plan to do with this Pentaculum, once you got ahold of it?'

'Well, there are so many possibilities, aren't there?' he answered slyly.

She raised a brow. 'If you think I'm going to get information on this for you from Atlan, you're wrong.'

'I thought you might say that. I've always appreciated how headstrong you are. But it's not just me interested in its whereabouts, I should think you and the prince would like to find it, too.'

'And why is that?' she asked defiantly.

'Kyr, I don't just go about plucking random orphans off the street,' he said, looking at her from under his brow. 'When I found you that day by the forge, I felt something. An upheaval, of sorts. I have something of an *attachment* to the Spirits. Well, one in particular, I should say.'

Sylas turned away from her, facing the city docks. 'Before

you laugh it off, think about what I'm saying. Think about why we've always done so well together. Think about how when we enter a room, all the pieces fall into place. No . . . *chaos* to be found. Or perhaps a better way of putting it is, chaos collared.'

'Are you telling me I've always had magic?'

'In a manner of speaking.'

'And . . . you do too?'

'Not like you.' He smiled wryly. 'Each of us contains within us the ability to tap into our world's natural magical field with devotion and study, but a rare few have always had access to otherwise latent domains of the Spirits. Many years ago a much, much younger thief devoted himself to Crescian, you know. And not always just to get ahead.' He folded his hands behind his back. 'Mm, twenty-three years have taught me much.'

'But I'm rambling. You are one of those I speak of, Kyr. A direct conduit. For everything you see around us. All of it, sifted through Crescian's influence. Your intentions, your emotions, that matters too. After the counting house, it all made sense, what I felt about you all these years, why when I put you on jobs all the events turned in our favor. Like lock and key, so to speak.'

Kyr could only stare at him blankly. He'd never spoken so openly with her before, and he'd never sounded so Spirits-damned cabbage-brained. 'Sylas—'

He turned to face her, and there was a helpless look in his eyes that startled her. 'Let me finish. I am risking much by telling you this. Crescian is lost to me. Everything I've built is at risk, but much, much more importantly, she is at risk. I need her, and so do you, if you wish to continue using your newfound magic. The Pentaculum may well be the only remaining source of answers regarding the Spirits and the magic of our world.'

Kyr scoffed. 'Sylas, you sound mad!'

'And isn't that how you felt when you collapsed those walls?' Kyr fell silent, and a knowing smile formed on Sylas's lips.

'There is a whole *world* of magic, Kyr. And only those of us who can see it can protect it. Now, all I can do is suggest you heed my words tonight. I'm sure our Lady of Chance will guide us back together when the time is right. It's good to see you well.' Sylas nodded, then turned and disappeared back down the steps from which he came.

For the first time in her life, Kyr was speechless.

24

ORIA

THE STARS in the cloud-scattered sky almost looked like the gossamer canopy of her bed. She reached for blankets beneath her palms, but her hands came up clutching dried leaves and earth.

'No,' she whispered. She blinked, looking around, and came to realize where she was. A cold sweat broke out on her forehead, her neck.

In the distance, she could see the lurid orange of a fire against the dark night. She was lying on some kind of animal skin with a makeshift shelter made of tree limbs and brush off to her right. The dwelling looked so much like the ones she had grown up in that she stared at it, lost in remembering, until the sound of a snapping twig broke the spell.

She saw only shadows.

'She's awake!' called a woman's voice.

Oria sat up, trying to get her bearings. Moving her hand blindly in the darkness, she felt the handle of a knife. Mothril's knife. She held it clandestinely at her side.

'She is not running?' asked a deeper, male voice.

'No,' replied the woman. 'Perhaps she has not fully attuned herself to this form.'

'A Daughter of the Veil? Unlikely.'

She saw the shadowy figures drawing closer, but against the firelit woods she could make out nothing to indicate who they were. The man advanced on her suddenly, and she swiped at him with the knife, but it didn't connect with flesh. Instead, a jagged tear formed in the night, pouring thick columns of quicksilver starlight. It was as if she had slashed the very fabric of her vision itself.

'Is that—? No, it can't be!' the man's voice roared.

The light began to gather in bright pools on the ground at her feet, illuminating the forest. Oria lurched away from it, shutting her eyes against the harsh glow.

When she opened them again, she was huddled against the headboard of her bed in the citadel. She blinked, still breathing hard.

What kind of knife had Mothril given her?

Oria looked down to find it still dripping starlight, sparkling droplets beading on its edge before fading away, the light diffusing to darkness.

25

ATLAN

SAARTHO'S small quarters off the library were surprisingly sparse—a small cot in the corner surrounded by books and a desk covered in parchment beside a large stained-glass lantern were the only furnishings of note. He stood by the desk now in a long sleeping gown, studying the two of them.

Kyr had come running to Atlan, banging on his door in the middle of the night. He didn't know how she got past the guards at the entrance to the royal family's quarters. If he'd doubted his boisterous friend was a Knave before, he didn't now.

She'd told him of her encounter with Sylas, how he knew about—and appeared to be actively searching for—the Pentaculum.

They'd gone immediately to see Saartho.

'A messenger of Crescian?' Saartho asked, repeating Atlan's question. 'I've never heard of such a thing. That doesn't mean he isn't telling the truth. It's a curious thought.'

Saartho yawned, rubbing the sleep from his face. 'As for why a powerful black market guild leader is looking for the Pentaculum? I imagine it's the same reason any authority would be happy to be in possession of such an object. Power. Imagine the knowledge it contains in the hands of one who wants to dominate,' he said, glancing at Atlan, 'or in the hands of the apathetic ruler, who cares little of their own destruction. But, in the hands of those who would honor its knowledge, it holds the promise of great progress. Not just for Yorenth, but for the world.'

'That's exactly what I'm saying!' Kyr exclaimed. 'If there's a relic out there that could tell us about the First Age Spiritsingers, its safekeeping should be our priority.'

Saartho furrowed his brow, musing. 'I haven't come across any texts referring to the Pentaculum as some sort of arcane codex. But . . . it does remind me of another curiosity from our time at war in the North. I remember reading the testimony of a captured alchemist—the woman was quite mad from her experimentation with psychoactive tree sap . . .' He shook his head. 'Anyway, did I mention that this alchemist was in personal service to the Prime? Fascinating man, although I never met him personally. Very dedicated to the sciences.'

'Saartho,' Atlan prompted.

'Oh, yes, right.' Saartho scratched his head. 'The alchemist was largely incoherent, but kept going on and on about a mirror with strange properties. She said it would look within her and, in turn, produce living reflections. That it could see through 'false veils,' whatever that means.'

'Wait,' said Kyr. 'Sylas said something about a mirror.'

Both Atlan and Saartho looked at her then. In the shadows of the historian's darkened room, their meeting suddenly took on a clandestine air.

Atlan nodded. 'Saartho, Kyr and I are leaving. Something is shifting, I can feel it. Cunning-folk grow restless. Clearly, the North seeks answers as well. We certainly don't want the likes of Sylas or my mother finding this relic. When she gets word of it, she'll demand it, and I'll have to deny her. When that happens, this could all collapse.' Atlan paused. 'And to tell you the truth, Saartho, I won't mourn it. Maybe it would be best if we didn't put out the fire and simply started again from the ashes.'

'My boy,' said the wizened historian, 'two idealists can't put an end to a crown heavy with the weight of a thousand years of tradition. I know you resent how you've been treated, and you have every right to feel that way, but—'

'But what if we could?' Kyr interrupted. 'Burn it all down, I mean.' Atlan looked at her, uncomfortable in his agreement with Saartho's gaze fixed on him. 'Sometimes all it takes is for someone to light the first torch.' She shrugged. 'The Sledge has been ready tinder for a while now.'

Saartho turned to Kyr, horrified. 'There hasn't been a rebellion in Yorenth in hundreds of years!'

'Then maybe it's time,' Kyr shot back.

Atlan cut in then. 'Saartho, wouldn't it be nice to conduct research that would benefit people, without the constant meddling of the Crown? To be able to study these things openly? You could be in correspondence with the archivists in Bellgard, travel instead of being isolated, stuck here at the whims of a petulant tyrant!'

Saartho frowned, turning to him. 'If you leave, if you undermine her like this by freeing a convicted treasonist and seeking a powerful relic behind her back, there's no telling how she might react. You will be putting the entire region at risk!'

'She would not do something so rash,' said Atlan. 'She is barely maintaining her authority with the council.'

Saartho nodded. 'Well, the library will always be safe with its wards, but Kyr,' he said, furrowing his brow, 'surely you can imagine how this will affect the Sledge. If Attiqah is going to take out her rage at being thwarted on anyone, it will be them.'

Kyr crossed her arms, looking away. 'Then she risks upsetting Councilman Thay.'

'All of this over one prisoner's fate? Are things so bad?' Saartho asked, looking between them. 'You will be king one day and then—'

'Vyktas will be king one day,' Atlan corrected. 'Besides, I hardly want to be a prince. Everyone knows it. I understand the privileges my position in life affords me, and duty I can handle, but not when it's in service of *this*.'

Saartho raised a brow. 'Atlan, is this because of . . . ?'

'Kingdom's Fall?' Atlan asked dryly. He exhaled sharply through his nose. 'No. Maybe that's where I first gave it all more than a passing thought, but this has been a long time coming, long before then.'

'Now Atlan, you know I would never doubt what you can do, but are you sure you're ready? You're a man of high learning, yes, but are you ready in here?' he asked, taking a step forward and tapping Atlan's chest. 'I know I don't need to tell you this, but what you and Kyr can do, it cannot be controlled. The structure here, your routine, it keeps not only you, but all of us, safe.'

His thoughts blackened at the mention of his 'safety,' and the unwelcome images that word conjured in his mind. The vastness of the desert. Blood speckling the sand. Sightless eyes. Atlan leaned against the wall, focusing on the pattern of the lamplight. 'The way I see it, nowhere is completely safe, and we need this relic.'

Saartho's erratic gesticulating drew his attention. 'I implore you to think about this! Have you considered what you will do once you find the Pentaculum?'

'We will return to Yorenth as soon as we can. What else?' Atlan said. 'We need to study its potential, and we'll want your guidance.'

'Do you really think she will just let you return with it, no questions asked?' Saartho questioned, his face wrinkled in disbelief.

'If she will see reason. She *must* see reason. If not . . .'

'If not?' Saartho prodded.

'We will go to Bellgard. Perhaps to the mages in the North.'

'And do what? The two most powerful mages this Age has ever seen cannot hide themselves away in the corners of the world!'

Atlan scoffed. 'So then I'm to obey? Just do what I'm told? Let others starve and die, in service of my family? A leader should never have their subjects do what they would not. That's the first thing I was taught. How things have decayed . . .'

'What about your new position as Captain of the Guard? What about the Sun's Own?'

'I love my sisters and brothers in arms,' Atlan began, 'but it's not enough of a reason to stay and support what my mother plans, the path she has *clearly* chosen.'

He pressed his hands together. 'I've two letters for Tanwen. One to my mother, telling her I left early to look into the blights on the road. That will buy us some time. The second for Tyran, telling him the truth. I believe he will understand and act in my stead to protect the Sun's Own from any retaliation, any of my mother's scheming.'

Atlan put a hand on Saartho's shoulder. 'You know I've wanted to leave for a long time. Well, the opportunity has presented itself.'

'Atlan,' said Saartho, placing his hand over top of Atlan's. 'I'm not saying you would not have your supporters in this. In truth, there is little left I can teach you. We both have known this for some time. I've seen you growing restless. If you want to go, I cannot and will not stop you. But at least let me give you something. When are you going?'

'Elaurien's being murdered tomorrow afternoon,' said Kyr.

'Regrettable,' Saartho muttered.

He made his way slowly across the small space, to the shelf above his desk. 'I knew this day would come. I just didn't think it would come so soon.' He shook his head. 'I always find we have so little time.'

From behind another book, he produced a large, leather traveler's journal, its pages waxed to protect it against the elements.

Atlan watched him, recognizing the ledger. 'I'm sorry I won't be able to help you finish the translation.'

He smiled at him. 'That was only to test your knowledge, Atlan. This is my personal copy, and the only translated copy of the Oracle's personal notes that exists.'

Atlan could do nothing to hide his surprise, nor his excitement.

'It pains me to let this go from the safety of this place, but this was meant to be a guide, not to collect dust. The Oracle of Yoren did much research on magic in our world. Almost all of our understanding comes from her. She knew much more than you two or I ever will.'

Saartho paused, letting his hand fall across the faded cover and smiling faintly. 'If you're to become rogue mages, this will teach you what I cannot.' He opened it to the first page. 'Now, rumored by some to be a kind of idol-like object, the Oracle believed the Pentaculum could harness free magic in this world. It may be the key to solving the blights, to helping the both of you be able to use your magic in the way past Spirit-itsingers did. Less chaotically. Other sources don't describe it at all, other than to say you will know it when you lay your eyes upon it. One Saerian account says it is the wind itself, and if you travel to the Edge of the Seas, it will whisper its secrets to you.' Saartho smirked at that.

He opened the book to a marked page and showed them the symbol. It looked like an eye. 'She identified a single symbol, a description, mentioned over and over again in texts and stories, not only from Yorenth and other Sentinel city-states, but from Saeria, and Old Era. I suspect this is some kind of sigil marking places of mystical significance.'

'Why didn't you tell me this sooner?' asked Atlan.

'Things have shifted significantly since Kyr made her abilities known. Besides, there was always little we could do to look into it from here, and I dare not risk the queen finding out. But Atlan, Kyr, you two hold the key to why magic has returned. That much has always been clear to me. You two hold the key to controlling it, perhaps harnessing it. Sylas's revelation only reinforces that. If you find the Pentaculum, you will have the greatest chance of anyone to uncover the secrets of the First Age.'

'So, does this translation mention anything about where to find the most important relic of our Age?' Kyr asked, wasting no time.

'Indeed,' Saartho mused. 'For the curious mind.'

'What's that supposed to mean?'

Atlan braced himself for what he knew Saartho would say next.

'A riddle. It is our most promising and only description of the relic's last known location.'

In answer, a loud squeak sounded from the corner of the room.

Atlan and Saartho turned to see the Knave flopped across the historian's bed, her face buried in the crook of her elbow. 'I fucking *hate* riddles.'

26

MOTHRIL

DARKNESS GREETED Mothril's aching eyes as a familiar friend. He was back where he belonged, and in another sense, altogether different from the man who had occupied his time with instruments of pain.

His brief time above ground could never have undone the years he spent here, how his eyes instantly adjusted to the lack of light, the cool, moist air that clung to him like a film. And yet, there was an undeniable tether now, somewhere deep inside of him, to the world which he could not sever.

Despite their agreement, he did not anticipate seeing the sun again. He breathed deep, trying to empty his mind, but thoughts of the tether, of her, continued to assail him.

'He's awake.'

'Melsze?' Mothril mumbled. He tried to turn toward the voice and realized he was restrained. Then he remembered how he'd gotten here, slowly, like grains of sand falling into formations in his mind. His face felt swollen. He figured he had a black eye.

Melsze came into view then and pointed to something Mothril couldn't see. 'Which dosage?' came another voice.

'Is the Whispess alright?' Mothril asked.

Melsze clicked his tongue as he studied his face. 'Don't tell me you've begun to care for her.'

'Just tell me,' Mothril grunted back.

Melsze looked at him disparagingly. 'She's fine. Regardless, that's not what we're here to discuss, is it? Much as I hate being back down here with you, you know things I intend to reveal. Things that would be useful to the Prime. You understand that I can't let you go until I know more.'

Mothril's skull pounded, his eyes able to open only slightly. He focused on the crosses and whorls of blood dried on the walls. 'I understand.'

He nodded again to his mysterious assistant, who handed him a small vial. 'Do you know what this is?' Melsze asked.

Mothril eyed the sickly green liquid with black seed pods floating inside. 'Since when have the clans been able to get Saerian lotus leaf?'

'The Prime has traveled extensively,' Melsze replied, almost off-handedly. 'It seems you have, too. You've piqued my curiosity once again, but we'll get to that later. Surely, you know of its magical properties, then? Saerian lotus leaf is a truth serum, it rewards honesty by being expelled quickly through the urine. Exhibit dishonesty, however, and it will turn to a thick black sludge in your belly, burn its way through your veins. Normally, it won't kill you, but someone of your stature ... well, we had to give you a larger dose.'

He grabbed a fistful of Mothril's hair and wrenched his head back, forcing the bitter liquid down his throat. Mothril choked and sputtered at its acrid taste as it burned its way down his esophagus.

'I promise you, I get no pleasure out of this, unlike you.' He paused, rubbing the stubble growing on his chin. 'Let's start with an easy one, shall we? Who is Eildroth?'

Mothril breathed in deep. He could do this. He was no

stranger to pain. 'The Prime isn't reading up on all those books he's hoarded if he doesn't know the answer to that.'

'The answer only, please.'

'A famed Eradomin warrior.'

'*Famed*? My.' Melsze smirked. 'How do you know that?'

'I read about it in one of those books.'

'The scribes have been letting you in? I'll have to talk to them about that.' He knelt down. 'Those books are written in a very old dialect of Borean Poet,' Melsze said accusatorily.

He nodded. 'They are. I learned it in the free order.' His stomach began to burn. 'We came across some old men, Sentinel exiles. One was a scholar of languages.'

'I don't believe you,' Melsze said, staring him down.

'Isn't that the point of the lotus leaf? You don't have to.'

'How's your stomach feeling?'

Mothril grimaced and looked away, his eyes meeting the old wooden table that still had some of his tools on it. He looked at the thumbscrew. When had he last used that? *The shepherd who'd been withholding her yield from the clan? The man who'd abducted an Elder's daughter?*

Melsze stood. 'Did you really think blathering on about something you read in a book would be enough to satisfy the Prime? To restore your position?' He shook his head. 'You know something, and I intend to find out what it is.' Mothril took a deep breath. A small, awkward laugh escaped him. 'Is something funny?'

'No.' He was thinking about all the time he'd spent in Melsze's position. He was thinking about how he'd earned this, and he would not shy away from the pain.

'You might find the pain of lying funny now, but you won't in a moment, I assure you.'

Mothril shifted in the chair, focusing on the pain spreading out from his core along his veins. It was a burning that came in waves, like nausea. It almost felt good for a moment before growing to a sickening, all-consuming fire that he thought might tear him apart. Then, like a fever, it broke, and he was able to take a breath.

'So, you know Borean Poet, and you *read* about an Eradomin warrior, who Oria just so happened to see in her first rite since you've been her guard. Just a coincidence?'

'Yes, but I've heard stories as well.' Mothril inhaled sharply through his nose. Cold sweat had already begun forming on his brow.

It felt like his organs were corroding. *Maybe they are.*

He had little experience with alchemy in his own torturous ministrations.

Oria might hate him for what he was about to do, but he had weighed the options in his mind. It would spare both of them the most pain, and it might be the only way to gain favor with the Prime. Perhaps it was selfishly more helpful to him in the immediate moment, but now that he knew what Oria was, he would see her free of this place. That, and he'd admitted something to himself during that rite, when he saw her being dragged along the ground, broken and fighting against specters.

He cared for her more than he wanted to admit.

'While Oria slept, I went into her room,' Mothril spat out as bile burned his throat. 'She has books, ones I take it she's not supposed to have.'

Melsze made a mollified sound. 'I see.'

'There's . . .' he nearly stopped himself. 'A book of Eradomin poetry. It mentions him. Not by name, but the description is enough to recognize him from stories.'

'What stories?'

Mothril struggled to control his breathing. 'In the . . . free order.'

'The free order, yes, tell me about that.'

'When our clan was attacked, my father and I had nowhere else to go. We joined some men who were itching to leave the

Far Clans when they passed through our camp on their pilgrimage.'

What dosage had they given him? He was dying now, he knew it—at any moment, the accursed potion flowing through him was going to burn clear through to the skin revealing his lies.

'What were their names?'

'Mora, Sorril, and Wyroth.'

'Of?'

'Mora and Sorril of-Iais, and Wyroth of-Bane.' That little bit of truth was a balm, it felt so good just to have the acid in his veins cease its burning, if only for a moment.

'You give up their names so easily when you know we will question them. Why?'

'Because all of them are dead.'

Melsze snorted humorlessly. 'Dead men don't answer questions, do they?'

He watched Mothril closely the same way Mothril had watched countless others in this room, looking for signs of distress and lies—heavy breathing, sweating, the way they curled into the chair, into themselves, and then finally fell open like a broken doll when they couldn't take the pain any longer.

He worked to control all of those things in himself now and wondered how much Melsze could see. The pain had continued building on itself and was so intense he felt he was choking on his own swallowed scream.

'How did they die?'

'Mora,' he breathed, 'fell into an icy river. Sorril and Wyroth were killed.' Another deep inhale. 'By bandits.' Everything in his body sang for him to speak more truth.

'That must've been difficult. Losing more of your kin to bandits.'

'It was.'

'And what a strange feeling, to find yourself the survivor again.'

'It was.'

Melsze leaned in, looking at his pupils, Mothril knew. *Melsze knows more about pain than he lets on.* 'Eildroth ... why do you think he is significant?'

'He leads a sect of the Eradomin. It's ... it's in the books. If the Whispess is seeing him, then it's important. He may be trying to commune with her somehow. Or to stop her, to distract her from seeing something else. I don't know.'

'You don't know?' Melsze asked, dubious eyes flickering to the assistant who still stood behind him.

'I told you I knew who he was. I've told you. Everything I've learned about the Eradomin are from her books.' He reeled as the fire rose within him and washed over him. Still, he continued with his lies. 'She ... she has not left her chambers since I've been her guard. I've done as the Prime has asked.'

'Why did you interrupt the rite?'

'She was in pain.' *Truth*, his body whispered. *Keep telling the truth.*

Melsze circled him. 'There are ways to see if the toxin is working, you know. Your veins will run black—so strong is the effect that it can be observed simply by looking at the skin.'

He drew his finger along Mothril's forearm and ripped open his sleeve. Mothril looked down, knowing his lies were about to be revealed, no matter his efforts.

'Hm,' said Melsze. His arm looked ... *normal.* His skin was the pale gray it always was.

Mothril strained against the pain, closing his eyes. 'The Eradomin ... are ... gone.'

'What makes you say that?'

'I saw the last of them die.'

Melsze grinned. 'Now we're getting somewhere. When?'

When Mothril hesitated too long, Melsze ripped his sleeve

farther, searching for evidence of his lies. 'They were killed by the Far Clans.' His strained words came between gasps of breath. 'Ronin . . . we weren't attacked by bandits. It was Eradomin cavalry. They . . . we fought them off. My father and I . . . hid. That's how we survived.'

Melsze's face was impassive. 'Interesting. Why not tell the Prime upon your acceptance into our clan? Did you not think he would want to know about a clash between his people and the Eradomin?'

He could tell Melsze didn't believe him, but it didn't matter. He had to give him something. 'I don't know. It was my father who met with the Prime upon our arrival. Perhaps they did discuss it, and *you're* not privy to all the information the Prime has.'

Melsze didn't like that. He grabbed Mothril's jaw and jerked his face toward his. 'You're sweating. Burning up? Perhaps you half-giant Ronin have some strange immunity to this toxin and that's why it's not showing on your skin.' He let go.

'I expect the others on the road said something too.'

'Not one mentioned Eradomin cavalry. However, they did mention two outlanders, faces they didn't know, who claimed they were from the Ronin clan. The last survivors of a bandit attack.'

'Well, we didn't think it wise to cause panic along the entire road, but I should think someone saw something. The signs of the Eradomin were all over our camp. We figured there had been an inquiry afterward.' He stared back at Melsze. 'It was common knowledge then that there were still Eradomin scouts scattered across the wilds. In all the chaos of our arrival, we didn't think to mention a few dead ones.'

'What signs?'

'The brush was flattened all the way to the river crossing, then no sign of them.'

'At the time you believed there were still scouts out there, but now you say these were the last of them. How do you know?'

'There hasn't been an attack since.'

Melsze nodded. 'I will relay this information to the Prime. Once your face has healed a bit, so as not to upset the Whispess, and *if* the Prime accepts your answers, you will be returned to duty. But don't think this is the last discussion we will have about this. Despite the evidence you're telling the truth, the Prime doesn't trust you, so neither do I.'

Mothril only nodded. He just wanted him gone so he could collapse.

Melsze turned to his mysterious assistant, who had stayed silent and out of sight the entire time. 'You're not to tend to his injuries unless he starts bleeding profusely. Nothing to eat or drink until tomorrow.'

Melsze turned back to him. 'Despite what you say, the Whispess seems to have taken a liking to you. You may think that a good thing. Actually, it is the most dangerous thing she could do and, ironically, at this present moment it is the only thing keeping you here.'

Melsze turned his back, and Mothril felt the dried blood on his lips crack as they curled in the faintest smirk.

Melsze left, shutting the door behind him. Mothril exhaled, shifting away from whoever stood behind him and letting himself relax, if only slightly. He let out a breath and looked down to see the veins in his forearm running black.

27

KYR

MIDNIGHT'S STARS twinkled overhead like mischievous jester's eyes watching the Knave and the Prince, who hurried from alcove to archway, shadow to shadow, on their way to the Tower of Yorenth.

'Told myself I was done with heists,' Kyr grumbled.

'It's not a heist,' Atlan replied. 'We're merely . . . paying someone a visit.'

'Am I going to have to pick a lock?'

'Maybe.'

'Then it's a heist.'

'We're not *stealing* anything.'

Kyr rolled her eyes. 'Only a person!'

'*Freeing* a person, Kyr. It's not the same. Now, *shh*,' he said, making a hushing motion with his hand. 'There will be guards up here. Just let me talk to them.'

'Don't *shh* me,' Kyr retorted. Atlan returned an eye roll.

A pair of Sun's Own guarded the outer staircase that led to the upper floors of the tower. 'Prince,' the man said with a deferent nod.

'Ah, Sol Errik, Sol Peria,' Atlan replied, a careless ease to his

204

voice. Kyr thought he looked stiff in his matching livery. 'Here to see the prisoner in the tower cell. I've got a signed letter from Her Radiance.'

She stifled no small amount of surprise that Atlan had managed to lie well enough to get such a letter. In another life, he would've made quite the Bird. Atlan glanced at her out of the corner of his eye. He handed the sealed letter to the guards and nudged her as if to say, *Yes, I did come prepared, actually. Thank you.*

'Sol Taryq didn't tell us anyone would be coming,' said Sol Peria. Atlan seemed to tense at the mention of his name. The guard eyed the two of them, lingering on Kyr far too long for her liking. 'And who's she?'

'This is Kyr ap Sand. She's under my watch.'

Sol Peria gave her a quizzical look. 'She joining the guard or what?'

'No,' said Atlan, his voice growing stern, 'and frankly, this is none of your business. Now, are we through?'

'Yes,' said Sol Errik glaring at Sol Peria and quickly stepping aside. 'Please.'

'Thank you,' Atlan said, plucking the fake letter from Sol Peria's hands as they crossed the threshold.

'Wait,' said Sol Peria. 'Isn't she the woman who Martiq took to the dungeons last week?'

'Sol Peria—' Atlan began, his voice tense.

'The very same,' said Kyr. 'Pleasure.' She extended her hand.

Sol Peria's face twisted in bewilderment. 'I'm not shaking the hand of a Knave. Atlan, what's the meaning of this? We free ruffians now?'

'Peria,' Atlan warned.

Kyr shrugged. 'Your loss.'

Peria cocked an eyebrow, incredulity plain on her face. '*My loss?*'

'Could've told the little ones someday that you shook hands with the infamous Kyr ap Sand. Ah, well.'

Peria's brows wrinkled in confusion. Sol Errik chuckled and extended his hand.

Perfect.

Atlan stepped on Kyr's foot. 'We'll be on our way then.'

Kyr made a brittle smile back at him.

They entered out onto the stairs, dizzying with no railing, passing torch after torch hung on the wall as they climbed the tower.

'That was a little much, wasn't it?' Atlan asked her once they reached the tower's zenith.

'What? I got the ring,' she said, holding Sol Errik's signet ring up to him.

Atlan barked a laugh, shaking his head. 'And here I was going to try and press clay into the mechanism.'

'I told you, you're working with a professional.' She grinned. 'Besides, have you not thought about it?'

'Thought about what?'

'Well, I guess you're already a prince, so maybe it hasn't occurred to you. But if we leave Yorenth,' she began talking low, 'if we really do this, we're going to be written about in the Histories. Do you realize that?' Kyr waved her hands. 'The Prince who stole away with a Knave!'

'Oh, please. How many times do I have to tell you? I am only still here because my mother fears it would be a bridge too far to disappear me herself. Now she doesn't have to. Truly, I don't know why I didn't think of leaving sooner. I'm sure she's already got plenty of excuses to give the council as to why I'm gone.'

They rounded the corner to the door leading into the upper chambers, and Kyr paused. 'Are you going to miss it?'

'What? Being prince?'

'No, I know you won't miss that,' she laughed. 'Are you going to miss the Sun's Own? Being Captain?'

'Will you miss being a Knave?'

Kyr looked down at her feet. 'Some things about it, maybe, but on the whole?' She shook her head. 'Nah . . . if you'd asked me a couple weeks ago, the answer might've been different.'

'I think we've both outgrown our lives here, Kyr.'

'Where does one go up from princedom?'

'That's the thing, I don't want to go up. I don't belong there.'

Kyr threw an arm around him. 'Come on, then. Get down here in the dirt with the rest of us, eh?'

Atlan chuckled, pulling her in toward him.

They passed several more patrolling guards—a few eyed them with curiosity but, it seemed, as a rule, no one questioned the prince.

Finally, they rounded the corner of a lonely, moonlit hall, at the end of which lay Roqlar Elaurien's cell door.

Atlan approached first, studying the lock on the door. 'Looks like it's your time to shine, Knave.'

Kyr groaned. 'Really don't see why you couldn't get the key for this, little king.'

'Mother keeps the key to this door on a string around her neck. This one, and the royal vaults. Only a good picklock with a stolen signet ring is opening this.'

Kyr inspected the lock quickly for any pesky engraving. Nothing. *Guess they don't expect anyone to make it this far with a lockpick.*

Atlan held the signet ring in place on the indentation in the lock while Kyr worked.

This time, it went how she'd expected it to go back at the counting house.

The door swung open to slats of moonlight falling across a sleeping figure. With no time to waste, Atlan trudged in ahead of her, knelt down, and shook him awake.

The man—rather, a boy, really—woke with a start, and Atlan clasped a hand over his mouth. '*Shh*, or they'll hear you. We're getting you out of here.'

Roqlar made a muffled sound of confusion through Atlan's hand.

'The less you know the better.' He cocked his head to Kyr, who stood behind him, and gave a wry smile. 'She wants you out, and I do what she says.'

In the deep blue beyond the tower, the Solarum tolled a very late hour.

'But you're the, the, Prince Atlan, and . . .' Roqlar breathed through Atlan's parted fingers, looking between them. Atlan stepped back, slowly.

His eyes reeled with questions, but Kyr could see he thought better of it. 'Six, I-I don't have much of a choice in trusting you, do I?'

'I assume you have some way to get the three of us down from here and through the gates in one piece?' Kyr asked, much to Elaurien's visible alarm.

Atlan nodded. 'I do.'

'Can I ask what it is?'

'I'm going to scatter us,' he answered simply.

They were on the first landing of the outer staircase when Atlan clamped a hand over Kyr's bordering-on-hysterical laughter. 'And you call yourself a thief. So damned loud.'

Kyr continued snickering. 'I'm sorry—it's just—Spirits, the guild would fucking love this. I mean, you're going to make us *fucking* invisible! Do you know how valuable something like that is?' She bit her lip to stop from laughing again. 'If I knew how to do that, it would be everyone else's problem. Six, I would be insufferable.'

'Alright, it's going to feel a little . . . funny.' He turned to Roqlar. 'But I'm going to ask you to trust me again. Take my hand.' Roqlar did so. 'Whatever you do, don't panic, and don't let go.'

He turned to Kyr. 'Now, if Kyr will just behave normally until we're past Sols Peria and Errik, this should be a breeze.'

Kyr gave him a mock salute.

Atlan took a deep breath. 'Here we go.'

Roqlar vanished on the wind like grains of sand off the peak of a dune. Kyr's eyes widened, but Atlan thrust her forward and down the tower steps. The idle conversation between Peria and Errik drifted up toward them.

'I hope it won't be like that tomorrow, I think I sweat all the way through my gambeson,' Errik said.

'Where's your posting tomorrow?'

'Tower again,' he sighed.

Kyr came down the steps first. She cleared her throat, realizing she didn't know what to tell them. Fortunately, Atlan pushed past her. 'We're done here.'

'How was Elaurien?' Sol Errik asked.

'He's dying tomorrow. How do you think?' Atlan replied dryly.

'Right. It's too bad, isn't it? He seems a nice fellow.'

Atlan gave a flat smile. 'Mm. Well, goodnight.'

Errik and Peria nodded. Kyr winked at them as she passed by.

When they rounded the corner to the lower stairwell, Atlan took her hand too. 'Ready?'

'Nope!' she said with a shit-eating grin.

Kyr couldn't make sense of what happened next. She felt as though she were everywhere at once, experiencing all things—part of the sky, and yet, part of the ground that had been beneath her feet. She felt a wholeness, and yet split into a million different pieces, like light reflected off the faces of a many-sided diamond.

They made no sound. Wherever they were, whatever space

they occupied, they were beyond that. She sensed them passing through space, moving along the course of a track. Somehow, she knew Atlan's hand was in hers, but she couldn't feel its form. There had been no sound, nothing to indicate what had happened to them. They were everywhere, and simply gone.

She saw through fractured vision. Moonlight, limestone, firelight. Insects chittering in the night air. Nothing felt real, nothing was definite, and then she blinked and, like it had never been, she was back in herself, in the world as it should be.

They were on the street outside the tower, in the shadow of it.

Kyr burst into laughter again. 'Atlan, what the fucking Six was that?' Roqlar gave a small smile, like he wasn't allowing himself to feel too optimistic yet.

'Amazing, isn't it? I'll tell you how I learned about it when we're on the road. Now let's go.'

They clung to the shadows, shielding the world from view with hooded cloaks as they made their way through an unlocked wicket in the city wall.

She could see the stables now. Atlan mentioned he knew the stablemaster in his youth, knew he'd be in a drunken stupor by this point in the night.

All was quiet as they snuck into the stalls, securing saddle-bags Atlan had stashed there to three horses. A gentle wind whistled through the open doors, carrying on it the sound of crickets and the grasses swaying. Roqlar mounted the first horse, his face seemingly permanently stuck in a state of amazement.

Then Kyr noticed the rustling grasses grew louder, but the wind did not. The grass was being crunched underfoot.

'Someone's coming,' Kyr whispered.

Atlan stood still as a statue, listening. The footsteps stopped outside the entryway.

'Solq's Light, I'm done for,' Roqlar's hollow voice whispered.

Slowly, Atlan crept toward the sound. He leaned with his back against the wall and pulled his longsword from his belt, preparing to surprise the person. A shadowed figure came into view. Atlan whirled around, and smashed the person into the wall, putting the blade to their neck.

They let out a high-pitched yelp.

Kyr was stunned. She and Atlan spoke in unison. '*Vyktas*?'

'Brother, please lower the sword from my neck.' Atlan did, and Vyktas brushed himself off. 'Thank you.'

'The other prince,' Roqlar whispered, his mouth hanging open. He leaned down to Kyr and said nervously, 'Why is the other prince here?'

'Great question,' Kyr replied.

'Were you following us?' Atlan asked, and Kyr could hear the barely contained fury in his voice.

Vyktas seemed to be weighing his answer. 'Yes, but—'

'What do you want? If you tell mother about this—'

'No, no! That's what I was going to say, if you'll let me finish. I'm not here to cause trouble! I-I want to go with you. Take me with you, wherever you're going.'

Atlan studied his brother's face in the dim. 'You can't be serious.'

'Deadly, I'm afraid.'

Atlan's jaw ticked. 'No. This is already going to piss her off, I can't have her sending the Sun's Own after us because you're gone too.'

'You really think she's going to let you go? She may despise you, but you're her most valuable asset. You're going to have all the might of the Realm after you whether you take me or not.'

'It's guaranteed if I take you.'

Roqlar ground his jaw. 'I hate to impose on my heroes, but I would really, *really* like to get out of here.'

'If you don't let me come with you, I'm going to follow you. And I've never left Yorenth. I might die in the desert, or—or be set upon by highwaymen! Then she really will blame you. She'll kill you.'

'I'd like to see her try.'

'She'll get manacles on you somehow. Besides, I already left a note saying I was going with you.'

Kyr saw Atlan studying his brother. He seemed truly torn. 'Oh, let him come Atlan. The more the merrier.'

Atlan sighed, looking between Kyr and his brother. 'Fine. We don't have time for this. But no whining, you do as I say, and I'm going to need a full explanation once we're on the road.'

Kyr patted Atlan on the back. 'I'll ride with you.'

The four of them arrived at the old crossroads under a bright crescent moon. To Kyr, the night felt sacred, like the beginning of something. Atlan and Kyr came to a stop, and Roqlar rode up beside them.

Atlan turned to him and nodded once. 'This is where we leave you. Good luck.'

Roqlar stared at them for a moment, sawing the reins. 'I don't know what possessed you, I don't know if you were Spirit-sent, but thank you. I-I won't forget this. Wherever I go, people will know Prince Atlan Solorien as kind and righteous.'

Behind him, Vyktas looked off into the twinkling night. Then Roqlar nudged his horse forward and took off at a gallop eastward. To where, they knew not.

No one had seen them. No one knew a thing. The Princes of Yoren had slipped through the hands of the Realm, and the only other Spiritsinger and most wanted man in Yorenth with them.

As Kyr watched Roqlar disappear into the night, she thought she could almost feel the screws of the monarchy's gluttonous machine loosening.

28

ORIA

IT HAD BEEN several days since the rite, and Oria had been awake only twice. Once to eat and have her wounds healed, and once because of that bizarre dream. Her father still hadn't come to ask her about her vision.

What could possibly be more important? she wondered.

This morning, the bright dawn streaming through the panes pulled her from her dreamless sleep, and she opened her eyes to see the table beside her bed empty. She sat up, a bit too fast for her joints, which protested the movement with popping and creaking. She looked around hazily for a moment, then froze. Her shelves were empty. And there, by the cold fireplace, sat her guard.

Mothril had been returned to her.

Upon noticing she'd awoken, he quickly rose to standing. Before he could protest, she threw the covers off, pushing herself to her feet and rushing over to him.

She reached her hand up to the faded injuries on his face, but thought better of it, and only made it halfway. 'Are you alright?'

'I'm fine, Whispess.' Still, she looked him over. He had an old bruise on his cheek, and she could tell there had been swelling around his eye, too, that had since gone down.

'Who did this to you?'

'Mostly Efja,' he said, grinning faintly. 'She's a good fighter.'

She nodded, still looking over his face with wide eyes. Her voice came out as a barely audible whisper. 'You're okay.'

Then, as if a spell had been broken, she cleared her throat and stepped away from him, returning to her bed.

More questions swirled in her head. She wanted to ask him about his past, about Eildroth, about the dagger. Instead, she found her eyes lingering on the shelves at his back.

'Where are my books?'

'Your father's men took them.'

His simple, easy answer shocked her. 'What do you mean? When?'

'Yesterday.'

'Why? How could they possibly—Mothril, you told them?'

His face was answer enough. 'I am sorry, Whispess. I had to.'

'You had to take away my only source of enjoyment?' Her voice was shaking. She'd given everything, *everything*. Couldn't she keep just one thing for herself?

She looked at the empty shelves now, the dust that was already beginning to line the empty spaces. *An apt metaphor for my life*, she thought. 'How could you?'

Despite everything she knew about his life before, she'd thought his intentions with his treatment of her were, if not pure, at the very least without spite. Now, with all her father had told her about him, she didn't know what to think. Perhaps she didn't know who he was at all.

He opened his mouth to speak, then closed it again.

'Why did you tell them you knew anything at all? Why didn't you just say nothing? Why couldn't you stay with Lyra?'

'And watch you be hurt? I've done that enough in my life.'

His vehemence silenced her.

Mothril stood, opening his mouth to offer further explanation. Instead, he closed it again and turned his back to her. 'There is more danger present than you know, Whispess.'

Oria knit her brows. 'What's that supposed to mean? You're talking about my clan, my family. I've lived with these people all my life.'

Mothril sighed, giving her a frustrated look. 'That's not what I meant, but you can't deny that these rituals—'

'I love my people. I've given everything I have to them,' she argued weakly. 'They would never hurt—'

Mothril turned around. 'Look at yourself!' She was stunned to hear him yell. His chest was rising and falling rapidly. 'It's happening slowly, right now. You just can't tell because they take from you little by little, fragments at a time. It shouldn't be like this, Oria. You should be out there, the wind in your hair, laughing—'

'Oh, don't tell me you've suddenly grown a heart.'

As soon as she said it, she was consumed by regret.

Mothril's face, which had been swept up in emotion just moments before, fell calm and flat, but his eyes—the way one peers through a mask—looked to her like those of a wounded animal. He returned to the chair, not looking at her. 'I didn't do what your father says I did.'

'Why should I believe you? Why should I believe anything you say? Since you've been here, you've barely spoken, and *everyone* knows what goes on down there in the tunnels—you said it yourself, you've *enjoyed* it!'

'There is a lot you don't know about me, Whispess.'

'Then *tell* me!'

He looked frozen.

'Tell me, Mothril,' she urged him.

He stood abruptly and walked to the door, unlatching it before pausing like a phantom on the threshold.

'Forgive me,' he said, his voice almost a whisper, and shut the door behind him.

———

After that disastrous rite, there was a constant anxiety to the air. A droning in the distance. Everything felt ephemeral. The storms grew in intensity. Oria was grateful for her guard's frustrating silence over the days that followed, because it meant they could ignore all they'd said or left unspoken, ignore all that had happened since the rite. Mothril tried to speak of it only once, on their walk which had become part of their daily routine by then if it wasn't raining, which it often was.

'Oria, I only told them about the books to protect you.' They were in the greenhouse again, and Mothril was studying the sundial, as he always did. He drew a finger across its face.

'I fail to see how I'm any better protected than I was before.' She plucked a rosehip gone to rot from a bush and let it fall to the ground. Mothril didn't argue with her. Apart from that, they spoke only when they needed to. Several times Oria stood just inside her closed door, thinking about how sorry she was for what she had said.

After leaving the gardens that clouded day, they passed by the entrance to her father's halls—a great, stone room with simple columns and a mezzanine overlooking the Elders' meeting table.

'Oria?' her father called. 'Is that you?'

'Yes,' she replied, nearing the door and peering in at him through the narrow opening.

Without looking up, he waved to her. 'Come here, please.'

Once she had a hand on the door, Mothril pulled his arm

away, following behind her at a distance. Her father leaned against the table, bracing himself above a map of the continent south of the old Eradomin wall. He spoke in a low voice to a veiled Elder at his side. 'Thank you for bringing this to me. Go, I will meet you and Sybil at the gates later.'

His hair was tied back at his nape, and he wore cloth instead of his usual scale armor, his robes billowing around him, falling the long way to the floor at his feet, next to which a juvenile river wyvern was sleeping. Studying the wyverns that inhabited the Northern peaks had been an interest of her father's for as long as she could remember.

'Is everything alright?' Oria asked.

'Hm? Oh, yes,' he said. 'A messenger has reached the Far Clans and it seems all is well. Nothing to concern yourself with.' He rolled up the map. 'My daughter,' he said, giving her one of his genuine, warm smiles. 'Come closer, let me have a look at you.'

She approached him gingerly, and he reached out and tugged her closer, raising a hand up to her cheek.

'This is healing nicely,' he said. An observation, but with some distant air of satisfaction. He was referring to the cut on her face from the rite.

She nodded.

'I'm sorry, my dear. You know it pains me to see you like this.'

Another nod.

'Just say the word, and we won't do it anymore.' This wasn't the first time he'd made her that offer. He often gave her the chance to refuse her visions, to take a draught of dreamless sleep and forget it all each night.

He asked, because he knew she'd refuse. He knew his daughter was loyal to a fault. She didn't want to see more war, more displacement, more starvation. Once she'd nearly taken him up on it, and then that very night she dreamt of an ambush at the citadel. She told the Elders, and knights were able to intercept the attack.

'I'm alright, Father. Really.' Behind her, Mothril shifted on his feet, making the floorboards creak.

'Good, good.' His eyes flicked to Mothril. 'It's good that your guard is here as well. He may be useful. I want to know more about the vision, about Eildroth.'

Oria nodded. 'It started the same way as always. I'm in the wilderness, searching for something. I hear them in the distance, the howls of their beasts, the horses. They were looking for something too, but I never found out what. Eildroth came to me, in a tower room. He told me his name. Before I could ask anything further, I was transported elsewhere. To one of the rituals.'

Mothril stilled.

'What did the tower look like?'

'It was an ordinary room. But there were mountains surrounding it. They had snow on them.'

'And one of them spoke to you, this is new?'

'Yes.'

'But nothing else has changed?'

She nodded, and he looked at her expectantly, waiting for her to offer more detail.

'He told me his name, and then he told me that he has been looking for me. He called me Daughter of the Veil.'

She felt Mothril's eyes on her. Her father's eyes widened slightly, yet his face wrinkled in confusion. 'He did? I will have the scribes look into this. Mothril, what do you make of this?'

'The Veil is said to be ruled by Calligone. In one of the myths, Eildroth looks for the Fäendhmar to repay some kind of debt. I know little else.' *Had he been reading her books?* She thought of how little he slept. *Is that what he told them?*

Edril Sil made a sound of gruff acknowledgement and looked at Oria. 'Was there more?'

'No, the vision was . . . interrupted,' she said, looking over her shoulder awkwardly.

'I see.' When the Prime looked at Mothril, he did not hide the displeasure on his face. 'Perhaps he would be more useful as a scribe.' He turned back to her. 'Oria, we must discuss those books in your room.'

'Father, it merely gives me something to do. I promise I wasn't trying to do anything wrong.'

'I know, my kin. I also know someone must have brought them to you, because I know you're not sneaking into the scribe's halls.' Oria began to protest, but he stopped her. 'And you don't need to tell me who it is. That doesn't matter now. But it simply is too dangerous for this knowledge to be elsewhere, where it could fall into the hands of someone less well-intentioned than yourself.' He looked pointedly at Mothril. 'And my intention is not to chastise you, but we have long known that having outside information taints your visions. Perhaps this is why you have been seeing the Eradomin so often.'

'You're right, I'm sorry,' Oria admitted.

He nodded. 'Then you can understand, my little Fäen, why I can't allow you to roam the castle freely like this anymore.'

At first, Oria thought she'd misheard him. 'What?'

'These walks to the gardens and the meeting hall, they aren't good for you. There is purity in isolation for seers like you. Besides, I see how difficult it is for you, getting around with that thing,' he said, flicking his eyes to her cane. She looked down at it. 'From now on, you're to stay in your chambers unless you're washing up, or I summon you. Does this not sound reasonable?'

'Father, no, I—'

'I'm so proud that you always put our people before your own comfort.' Why did he always look so sympathetic, so understanding, when he did these things to her? As if he didn't have a choice.

'Please, father—'

'Whispess, you're looking paler as we speak. Mothril, escort Oria back to her chambers, please. She needs rest. And she is not to roam the citadel grounds anymore, is that understood?'

Mothril glanced at Edril Sil. He seemed to hesitate, then grabbed Oria by her arm. His strength startled her at first, but his grip was deceivingly tender.

'Please, father,' she tried again. Her father wasn't even looking at her. She had never felt so exhausted, so defeated and small, in all her life as Mothril pulled her away and out of the room.

She heard the door shut behind her.

'Whispess,' Mothril said. She looked up at him, into the shelter of his frozen river eyes. Mothril's hand let go of her arm, then traveled down, softly, slowly, to brush against her hand. The barest touch. 'This need only be temporary. Just say the word.'

It was as if the comforting touch of his hand loosed something within her.

'What are you saying?'

His gaze flickered to the door. 'I'm saying I'm your guard, Oria. In the truest sense of the word. A protector, not your captor. I want you to remember how you feel right now. Not out of anger, or petty revenge, but as a source of power. Something you keep in here,' he said, that same touch fluttering along her collarbone for the briefest of moments. Her eyes glanced with her inhale to where his hand had been. 'Just for yourself. A reminder of sorts.'

He watched her with an intensity that mesmerized her, and Oria noticed his eyes darken preternaturally. 'Mothril?'

'They think they can keep you prisoner, but you're more powerful than any of them know. I have no qualms about burning this entire fucking place to the ground. You need only say the word.'

Oria regarded him in stunned silence, feeling both strangely comforted and afraid. Not quite of Mothril, but of the uncommon power she felt radiating off of him.

Who are you, Mothril of-Arcandras?

29

MOTHRIL

MOTHRIL MOVED EASILY, comfortably through the dead of night. He looked into Oria's room, her flank rising and falling with the soft breaths of someone sleeping deeply. By that time, even the calls of the frogs in the courtyard were silent, everything blanketed in that insular darkness of a midnight in the Northern woods.

He lingered for a moment, watching her, how her posture held none of that pained rigidity it did in the daylight. She looked so serene, like one should when they were sleeping, and he wondered how long it would be until a nightmare came, snatching away even that respite from her.

It must be exhausting, he thought. He'd sometimes deprived prisoners in the tunnels of sleep—it was one of the few things that made grown men sob and beg. *Why was that?* he wondered absently.

Slowly, he shut the door and made his way quietly down the stairs, entering out into the courtyard. The cool humidity before a thunderstorm was thick in the air as he headed toward the guard's chambers. He kept to Night's perfect embrace, sure that if another guard spotted him they'd eagerly report his abandoning his post to Melsze. After seeing him put many of their friends to death over the years, they despised him.

He'd been washing up earlier that morning when he noticed a window on the third landing of the watchtower, which could be opened outward onto a small parapet above the citadel gates. He watched the window now as he approached the tower like a shadow. The posting at the gates was least favored among the guards. Long hours awake, with the likelihood of anyone daring to approach a Wiccar stronghold being less than nothing, made for an incredibly boring watch.

The guard's chambers were empty now just like the rest of the citadel, the men posted at the gates the only souls still awake. It was quite the feat getting his large form through the window without his armor scraping on its stone edges, but he managed it, and soon he was sitting high above the lonely fire occupied by the four guards below.

'Hey, Balodan,' one of them called out. Something about the man, with thinning hair and glossy scarred skin across his lips, was familiar. He didn't know his name, but he was a guard the others seemed to dislike almost as much as they disliked him. 'Heard you were with Sybil last night.'

Leaning against some crates stacked against the wall, a tall, burly man with cropped black hair looked up from where he was sharpening his blade and snickered.

'Well?' the man continued. 'How was she?'

'Drim, shut the fuck up,' he replied without looking at him.

Mothril pulled a pouch of amberleaf from his belt, packed it into his pipe, and lit it from the torch hanging on the wall just inside the window. He inhaled, lay his head back against the wall, and looked out at the penumbral forest surrounding the citadel. The tension of the day traveled out into the ether with the smoke, and for some reason, he thought of the last night he'd spent as a knight-errant in a free order.

It had been a night something like this, only he'd been

down there with the other men, around a fire just like theirs. They'd been hiding out in some ruins after robbing a Saerian caravan, eating their stores and drinking their fill of looted wine.

Sorril's mood was dark. His brother had died the month before at the river crossing, and in truth, the rest of them— Sorril, Wyroth, Rathwil, and Mothril—had barely survived the winter themselves. In some places, the snow had been waist-deep, and winterfowl and hare were scarce. One night they'd dug into the heavy snow for shelter, and Mothril was sure he'd lose his toes come first light. The memory made him shudder even now and look to the fire below, suddenly envying its warmth.

He drew on his pipe again, closing his eyes, when he thought he heard his own name. Or maybe they were just talking about the moonmoths out at this time of night.

He looked over the edge. '. . . the big lumbering oaf,' said the man called Drim.

Mothril smirked. *Definitely him.*

'The Prime ought to have him put down, s'what he should do. Should've seen how many guards it took to get him back underground. Melsze had me give him lotus leaf. I didn't even want to do it. I thought the fucker was goin' to bite me!'

So, this was Melsze's assistant?

'I mean, what's he *thinking* lettin' someone like that near the Whispess?' Drim puffed out his chest. 'Now, me, I'd make sure the Whispess was *well* taken care of.'

'Even with that ruined face?' another man asked.

'You can always snuff out the torch,' he replied, laughing.

Mothril exhaled and looked more intently at the men, the smoke curling away into the darkness. If any of the guards bothered to look up, they would surely see the red-hot bowl of his pipe, his glittering eyes in the darkness, watching them, but they didn't.

Men are always so unaware of danger.

The fourth man spoke. 'I heard the Whispess almost escaped last time. Nearly made it into the forest with her maiden. I'll bet having a professional murderer for a guard quashes any further hopes of that.' He laughed as he said the last bit. Mothril felt his lips curl into a smile, and not a friendly one. He leaned in, eyeing them closely.

'I still don't think he should be let loose around the citadel like he is,' said Drim, shaking his head. 'I heard he killed his whole family out in one of the Far Clans, an' his father only got him the post here 'cause he needed to find a way to sate his bloodlust.'

One of the other men laughed and shook his head. Their conversation moved on to idle chatter, and Mothril finished smoking what amberleaf he had left. It must've been nearly four o'clock in the morning by then, the citadel empty and quiet.

He reached into the pouch he kept his amberleaf in and pulled out a rusted charm, engraved with his initials, *M.o.A.* It had been a knight's keepsake his father had given him, and for years he'd wondered why he kept the sentimental thing. Perhaps he was waiting for the perfect moment to disencumber himself of it. He held it by the chain over the fire below, then slowly let it slip from his fingers.

By the time the guards' voices rang out below, questioning what had just fallen right beside their fire, Mothril was already across the courtyard.

30

ATLAN

THE WESTERN ROAD snaked along ahead of them for miles. Beside the prince, Kyr squinted, looking out at the vast reaches of arid land and the endless sea, rippling in the heat waves on the horizon. After riding through the night, they stopped in some sparse shade to water their horses.

'Do you think she's already sent someone after us?' Vyktas asked nervously.

'I'd be surprised if not,' Atlan sighed.

The pair had talked on and off since they'd been clear of the dunes that led out into the Barrens. At first, Atlan had been concerned with Vyktas's reasons for following them, but as the night narrowed to the trio and the road, they fell into comfortable conversation. He'd misunderstood his brother, he realized. Vyktas wasn't there to spy or ruin his plans, he wanted adventure. Maybe he'd had a little too much fun drinking with him and Kyr the other day.

The wind danced over the empty terrain, whipping through their cloaks. Kyr turned. 'Well, we can't stop here long. We can probably be seen all the way from the mudflats in this spot.'

Atlan made a sound of acknowledgement, pushing the

226

thoughts of bounty hunters from his mind. 'Agreed. We head on to the outpost, then?'

Kyr nodded before retrieving an apple from one of the saddlebags. 'Then onward to Bellgard.' She retreated to the shade of the lone tree nearby as Atlan pulled a waterskin from his bag.

Vyktas watched her go, then turned to his brother. 'What's in Bellgard?' Then, more quietly, he added, 'Why did you want to leave?'

Atlan studied him. 'For one, Mother's gone too far—' He took a swig of water.

'Mother's always gone too far,' Vyktas interrupted. 'Something's different now.' He looked over his shoulder at Kyr. 'Is it her? What do you two even talk about?' Vyktas's eyes widened. 'Are you two *in love*?'

Atlan choked. 'Six, no! We're friends, that's all. Maybe it's the Spiritsinging, but we just understand each other.'

Vyktas's eyes dimmed, his easy smile faltering. 'Oh. I see. Well, good thing we won't have to smooth over any secret trysts between the future king and a Knave.' He brushed some dirt off his cloak.

Atlan chuckled. 'Clever.'

'What? What did I say?' Vyktas said distractedly, focused on a small stain he'd found.

'Now that we're away from Yorenth, surely we can be honest with one another? You know Mother never planned for me to become king. It was always going to be you, Vyktas.'

Vyktas dropped his cloak, the stain forgotten, and looked at him, incredulous. '*Me*? I know Mother says things like that to get a rise out of you, but you're the eldest! The Sun's Own, the council, everyone expects you to be king.' His face grew serious, and he lowered his voice. 'One of the reasons I wanted to come with you is to talk. Even the council is starting to think she's not fit to rule. I suspect they plot against her as we speak.'

'Who?' Atlan pressed.

'I don't know for certain,' said Vyktas, 'but I have my suspicions. I've seen things, brother. I'm not a child anymore, I observe more than people think.'

Atlan blew out a breath. 'All the more reason for me to have left. Now that we have some room to breathe, we can speak freely.'

'Does that mean you'll tell me what's finally pushed you over the edge?'

Atlan regarded him with a flat expression. 'When our family plays our games, we play them with other people's lives. I don't want to ask anyone else to die for the good of the Realm.'

'Well, I don't either—'

'Maybe not,' Atlan cut in. 'But do you turn the other way when we go to war, when people are executed, when we send Sun's Own to their deaths?' Vyktas began to protest, but Atlan cut him off. 'You do, and so do I. We believed there was a reason for it, and that was enough to satisfy us. But you know, deep down you know. The rest of your nights, when you're trying to sleep, you'll know you've infringed on something precious. Maybe violence is inextricable from a world where others have what others do not, but there has to be something I can do. There has to be something else besides this.'

Atlan searched the horizon. 'I have to face what I've done, and I can't do that under the thumb of our family. That's what's changed. It's what I admire about Kyr, she doesn't shy away from things.' As he said this, he gestured toward the Knave who was balanced precariously over the watering hole's edge, using the placid surface as a mirror and vigorously picking at her teeth with the tip of a dagger. One by one, apple seeds rippled her reflection.

'Did she . . . eat the core?' Vyktas said under his breath.

Atlan cleared his throat.

He continued, slowly turning away from Kyr. 'With two

powerful mages out of her reach, Mother will need to be careful. She will need to listen, and that's if I even go back.'

Vyktas was aghast. 'You're not going back?'

Atlan shrugged. 'I'm not king, and I've no desire to be the spare, blindly following orders.' He patted his gelding. 'Yorenth's people will always mean something to me, but I can't countenance my role in our family any longer.'

'So *Lady* Kyr's turned you against us, then? Is that it?'

Atlan huffed a laugh. A memory came to him. He was fifteen, and he'd caught Vyktas praying to the Spirits for magic like his brother had, kneeling between the stone benches in the Solarum. Vyktas hadn't seen him, but it brought Atlan no small measure of joy knowing his brother wanted something of his so badly. Now, he realized his brother wanted to understand him.

'I'm not against you, Vyktas.'

'You're not? You were going to leave without a word.'

'Vyktas—' he started, but Kyr approached them. He wasn't sure what he was going to say anyway.

She ambled over, balancing the dagger on its tip before flipping it once and putting it back in its sheath. She tousled Vyktas's hair. 'Hate to interrupt, but we'd better keep moving. I've traveled this road before once—there's a spot farther west we can make camp. It's near the Outlands but, well, you two are good with a sword, right?'

'Aren't we staying at the outpost?'

'The outpost's deserted and half-burned, Vyktas,' Atlan replied. 'But this place sounds good enough.'

'We can't camp this close to the Outlands! There are ogres, and wyverns, and who knows what else!'

Kyr's eyes flicked to his belt. 'Better keep that dagger close then.' She patted his cheek. 'Aim for the eyes.' She grinned, and Atlan couldn't help but laugh. She seemed so undaunted by everything, and he hoped maybe some of it would rub off on him.

They rode on, the sun sinking lower and lower as Yorenth grew small in the distance behind them. They'd seen no one all day—the roads were even less traveled than they had been a month or so ago when Atlan had ridden out with a detachment of Sun's Own and Noblegard.

When everything was different. He was going through the motions of being a soldier, but even then, as he and his men traveled farther from Yorenth, the fresh air became intoxicating. His thoughts cleared, and it felt like he could get a breath in for the first time in months. The same sensation enveloped him now, even as he left his home with nothing but what they needed for the journey to Bellgard.

Nameless in the desert, he felt more himself than he ever had in a city of his mother's sycophants.

Night fell, and they led the horses to a forested part of the Outlands' foothills. There were no villages in the desolate lands between Yorenth and Bellgard, and few ventured beyond city walls these days. This dense outcropping of trees was the only sheltered spot along the road for a long way in both directions, and had there been more travelers, Atlan might've expected to cross paths with them here. They settled into a quiet glade that was just inside the forest's bounds, but felt altogether separate from the road they had just been traveling.

While Kyr got a fire going, Atlan and Vyktas followed an old path that came to a short ledge overlooking the valley, and in the darkness he could see fires burning. The strange, rhythmic flickering of magefire was unmistakable. These fires were the same ones his mother had mentioned to him, the ones that had been burning for weeks now.

'Is that magic?' Vyktas asked. 'It looks unnatural . . .'

Atlan nodded. 'It is. How it came to be, that's the burning question. So to speak.'

'Let's go down there—' Atlan put a hand out to stop him.

'No. You may think you're eager to see magic up close, but trust me, you're not. It's incredibly volatile.'

'I don't need you to watch over me,' Vyktas snapped. 'I'm perfectly capable of handling myself.' Vyktas started down the ledge, and Atlan pulled him backward by the collar.

'You're the one who wanted to come with us, so you answer to me. I'll not be responsible for your death!'

Vyktas shrugged him off. 'You need to have control of everything, don't you? Fine, I'm going to bed.' He headed back toward camp. Atlan followed him, but by the time he reached camp Vyktas was already in his tent. Kyr sat alone by the fire holding a dried fish skewer.

'He was in a bit of a mood,' she said, raising her brows. 'What did you do?'

'He's always in a mood. I swear, one moment I think we might finally be able to understand each other, and the next he's back to his arrogant, childish self.'

'Can you blame him?'

Atlan's lip curled and he scoffed. 'What's that supposed to mean?'

'Nothing, really. He clearly looks up to you. I think he wants to impress you.'

'Vyktas doesn't care about impressing me.'

Kyr shook her head, her mouth full of fish. 'Mm,' she swallowed, 'I don't know, seemed pretty upset about whatever you just said to him.'

'Give it another day or two sleeping on the ground and he'll wish he'd never come in the first place.'

Atlan sat down next to her, reaching for a piece of fish, causing Kyr to swat his hand away. He laughed and laid his head on her shoulder, looking up at the stars.

'It's strange. Earlier today he was asking all these questions, too. I think he's jealous of you.'

'A prince, jealous of me? You two really ought to learn to appreciate your lot in life more,' she quipped.

'I won't argue with that,' Atlan conceded. 'There's just so much he doesn't know. There are things he thinks he understands, but he wasn't there.'

'Like what things?'

'Well, the Battle of Kingdom's Fall, for one. He was just a kid then, but he's heard all the stories, so he thinks that makes him a soldier. He wanted to go down there and see the fires, Kyr. I mean, he has no *idea* how dangerous magic can be.'

'He mentioned that before, in the royal library.' She turned her head slightly, looking down at him.

'I suppose you want to know about it,' Atlan sighed.

'Only if you want to talk about it.'

'I don't particularly, but . . .' Atlan looked over at Vyktas's tent. 'Maybe it would be good to,' he murmured, mostly to himself. Kyr handed him another piece of fish, prompting him. 'Since the day my magic came in, my mother considered me her secret weapon. When the clans began fighting with the old rule in the North, the Eradomin people, my mother saw an opening.'

'Of course,' Kyr muttered, and Atlan laughed softly.

'Exactly. So, we joined with the Wiccar clans, hoping to overthrow the Eradomin with them and, when the clans were at their weakest, subjugate them, too. Their old citadel is this place called Castle Forlorn—not the name they gave it, obviously, but it's the name that stuck with Sentinel commoners due to its near-mythic reputation.'

Atlan shifted against her. 'Anyway, I was sent to the front. I thought I was there as a soldier, to prove my might in combat and make a name for myself as a warrior. Of course, my mother had another idea, one she didn't deign to make me aware of. I wasn't there to practice my swordsmanship or protect my brothers and sisters, I was there to use my magic. To destroy, utterly.'

'Shit . . .' Kyr threw the skewer into the fire.

'She had acquired this strange new herb, from Old Era. It amplifies magical power, grows like a weed there, I heard, on some sacred ley line. She ordered her men to use it on me. They held me down, forced me to inhale its smoke.' Atlan's face took on a faraway look. 'They didn't have to hold me for long, though. I liked it. I'd never felt anything like that before. A part of me I hadn't known existed wanted more. I felt like I could bend mountains to my will. Maybe I could have. She'd already had me in shackles for days, and at that time I had much less training, and well . . .'

He felt Kyr tense against him. 'You erupted.'

'Something like that,' he said, with a resigned expression. He nestled closer to Kyr. 'It's hard to describe. My body became like a wellspring of magical energy, only amplified. Or at least that's what I heard. My body was gone in that moment. We never found my armor, my sword. My will was a pyre, the Northerners fodder for it. I ignited their very blood, boiling it beneath their skin. Their bones were nothing but gray ash. In that moment, I saw myself on countless battlefields, the North ablaze. It was then that horror creeped in at the edges of my consciousness. That's when I saw Solq. He took me in his embrace and bore me far away from the battle. Time was as nothing under his wing, radiant in the skies far above the field.'

He looked up at Kyr. 'He spoke to me, you know. Not aloud, it was more like, I suddenly knew deep within me that this wasn't the right path. Solq only advocates for lighting the darkness. I realized then that I was in a clearing, somewhere in the forests surrounding the citadel. Behind me was a line of charred foliage. When I arrived back at the barracks, without clothes, covered in dirt and ash . . . I never beheld such fear and bewilderment.' Atlan's face twitched. He turned away, sitting up and drawing his knees in. 'Taryq whisked me home immediately. My mother questioned me for days but, ultimately, she viewed it all as her greatest failure. Here she had the most powerful tool in the known world, a son with magic to rival the Spirits, and he wouldn't do as she said. I kept thinking about Solq. I didn't want to sow any more destruction. Rumors of what I had done spread and, well, I was mostly left alone after that.'

Kyr reached out and held his hand. They sat there as the fire dwindled, saying nothing. It was more comforting to him than any words she could've said.

31

ORIA

Thunderous hoofbeats.

'No,' Oria breathed.

She was surrounded by darkness, like her own unknowing reflected back at her, but it wasn't a nighttime kind of darkness, rather specks of black that moved as one swirling behemoth, absorbing all sound. The drumming of galloping steeds vanished as quick as the sound had reached her, and for a few horrifying moments all was silent.

She felt different this time. Her hands, somewhere in all that darkness, felt softer, like a fine dagger rather than a calloused, blunt instrument.

'You cannot hide from us, Shadowed One!' The coarse, deep voice rang out from below.

As she stepped forward, the air cleared, and Oria realized she was in a high tower like the kind from stories she'd heard of the Southern Realm, surrounded on all sides by wild lands. Surrounded on all sides by Eradomin. The one in front who had called up to her took off his helmet.

Eildroth.

He was tall and broad, with pale gray skin like hers, only

now she could see he had scaley black markings on one side of his face, almost like scabs spreading from his beard to his brow. Stoneflesh. A disease common to the Eradomin people that the Wiccars had a natural immunity to. His hair was thick, some of it braided, and tied back beneath a furred hat. All of this was dulled by his translucent appearance—still a specter, thank the Fäendhmar.

'You are routed, there is no escape!' he yelled again. A legion of ghostly figures, more than she had ever seen before in her dreamwalking, encircled the tower. Suddenly she felt an urge to speak but, not knowing who she was, couldn't find the words. She reached for Mothril's knife but it wasn't there. She had left it on her nightstand.

Before she could react further, she startled awake. Somewhere, she knew, so did another.

She heard the rushing waterfalls outside in the distance, saw fireflies blinking on the other side of the glass. She was awake and back in her chambers. Oria sighed and reached for a tincture on the table by her bed, promptly knocking it over. The sound of shattering glass broke the thick silence.

'Shit,' Oria cursed, then scolded herself for speaking that way.

The door immediately swung open.

'Whispess?'

What is he doing awake at this hour? she thought. *Doesn't he ever sleep?*

'I'm fine, Mothril.'

He didn't move. 'I heard a noise.'

'Yes, I was going to take some sleeping draught. I had another dream,' she explained, 'but I knocked over the bottle, and . . .' Oria trailed off.

Without a word, he crossed the small space and knelt by her bed, collecting the pieces of broken glass.

'You don't need to do that,' she said sheepishly.

'It's fine.'

She sat up, a bit too fast, and bit her lip against the twinge in her spine. 'Be careful. How can you even see the glass?'

'I've been awake for a while. My eyes are already adjusted.'

'Mothril,' she began hesitantly. She heard the pieces of glass tinkling, though he didn't answer her. 'Mothril,' she said again. 'I-I'm sorry. For what I said to you. Before.'

He looked at her, and though it was dark, she saw a curious expression flash across his face before he regained his usual composure. 'You have nothing to apologize for, Whispess.'

'Of course I do. You were only trying to help, and I treated you horribly. I wasn't in my right mind. I've not been myself, and I—'

He placed the broken pieces on the table, then leaned down farther, nearly bowing his head to the stone. Was he *sniffing* the ground?

'What tincture is this?' he asked.

Puzzled, she answered, 'It's for my nerves. So I can sleep again after having one of my visions.'

He made an appraising grunt and then asked, 'Was it a bad one?'

'Mothril, I'm trying to say that I'm grateful for you. For your friendship. You're more than a friend to me. I-I mean, you've been an exemplary guard to me, which is what I meant by more than a friend.' She continued to stammer, her face growing hot.

He shifted, letting in a slant of light from the doorway, allowing Oria to make out the plane of his cheekbone, the outline of his nose, his mouth. 'I'm honored.' He chuckled softly, his lip quirked up almost into a playful smirk. 'So, was it a bad one?'

She was grateful for the change in subject, even if she didn't like dwelling on her dreams. 'It wasn't so bad. I mean, not in comparison to the other visions I've had. I wasn't hurt.'

He nodded. 'But my father won't be happy. There were more

Eradomin than I'd ever seen before. Wind-walking, but still
…'

'Interesting.'

She hugged her knees into herself. Why did he insist on
being so obtuse? Lyra had always told her she was easy to talk
to, so why didn't Mothril feel the same way?

'I've been meaning to ask you, that knife you gave me, I had
the strangest dream about it.'

His black eyes watched her in the dark. 'What do you
mean?'

She leaned over and pulled it from a drawer beside her bed.
Turning it over in her hand, it looked so ordinary. 'Where did
you get this?'

'My father,' he answered plainly.

'In my dreams, it protected me.' She looked up again. 'From
the Eradomin.'

He took a step forward. 'It did?'

'Mm, it—it was like it tore the sky open,' she said, throwing
her hands up.

He went frighteningly still. 'In your dreams?'

Now he was making her nervous. 'Yes.'

'Did anyone see you?'

She shrank into the pillows, feeling like she'd done something wrong. 'I-I don't know, it was a dream! I heard the voices
of a man and a woman, but I couldn't see them. You sound as
paranoid as my father.'

She heard him exhale. 'I'm sorry, I—' He stepped forward
and lowered himself again by her bed, his back to the table. He
looked up and behind, so she could see the right half of his
face. 'Do you trust me?'

She thought about his question. What her father revealed
about him *had* frightened her, and yet, Mothril was here, mere
inches away, alone with her in her empty chambers. And she
wasn't afraid of him. She was familiar with the sense one gets

when another person is dangerous, like a crackling in the air, but she'd never sensed it from him. All she felt when she focused her weaker, waking seership on him was a heavy burden of mourning, and a deep longing.

'I don't know what to think.'

He paused for a moment, watching her. 'I make you nervous.' His head tilted, like an animal's. His voice faltered. 'You're afraid.'

'No, I'm not.'

'Your hands are shaking, your pupils are pinpoints, and I can see your heart beating in your chest.'

'You *cannot*,' she snapped. 'It's black as a moonless night in here.'

'Tell me. Are you afraid of me, or are you afraid of what you saw in your dream?'

How did he do that? Always getting straight to the heart of matters, like he could read her mind. With him, there was no pretense.

She paused, considering his question. Perhaps her words said in anger had done more damage than she'd realized.

Oh, don't tell me you've suddenly grown a heart.

Shame flooded her. He did make her nervous, but not for the reason Mothril expected, and she wasn't about to admit the truth, even to herself. 'It's not that I'm afraid of you, Mothril.' She paused. 'I just don't know what to think. About any of it. My visions, the clan's future, *my* future. I feel so kept in the dark. Right now, though, I don't want to fall asleep again.'

'They won't come here.'

'How could you possibly know that?'

He took a deep breath. 'Trust me.'

Crossing her arms, she said, 'Mothril, I don't understand. How do you know that? Did you figure something out? From one of my books?'

'Those aren't the questions you should be asking. The question you should be asking is why you feel compelled to continue doing something that is so clearly destroying you.'

'It's my duty. An *honor*,' she offered, but even she could tell there was no heart behind her words.

He stood, retreating to the doorway. 'What you are able to do is something that rulers the world over would hunt to the edge of the world to possess. The Prime knows this. But you're not a possession. You should be cared for, protected, treated with the utmost respect. Not shamed for your sacrifice, suffering and hidden away from the world.'

For once, she didn't have a retort for him. His words caused a deep pain behind her collarbones, and she wondered if this is what the poets and scribes meant when they spoke of heartache.

He put a hand on the doorframe and glanced over his shoulder. 'Sleep, Oria. I'm right here. No one is going to enter this room on my watch.'

32

KYR

SNAPPING twigs and crunching leaves woke Kyr just before dawn. Next to her, Atlan slept, one arm slung behind his head and the other across his chest. She leaned over him and poked her head out of their tent. Fog blanketed the forest, and for a moment Kyr feared one of the blights had reached them— she'd heard word in the castle of mist that befell entire towns and would not burn off—but she could see the rising sun through the trees.

She heard rustling to her left and turned to see Vyktas's tousled blond head poking out from his tent.

'Vyktas!' she whispered, and he turned to her, rubbing the sleep from his eyes. 'I heard a noise. Was it you?'

'I heard it too,' he whispered back. 'It wasn't me. It came from that direction,' he said, pointing ahead of them. 'Why don't you go look?'

'Me? You go!' she snapped.

'You're the hardened criminal!'

She narrowed her eyes and emerged from the tent in only her undershorts and a cloth binding her chest. 'Fine.' In her right hand she adjusted her grip on the ornate dagger Atlan had given her from the royal armory.

She heard the rustling again off to her right, and slowly rounded in that direction, circling whatever the source of the sound was. Kyr paused, scanning the mist-obscured wood as she stepped on silent feet, tensing against the chill morning air. *Nothing.*

The feeling of her warm bedroll still clinging to her, she was ready to dismiss the sound as an animal, but out of the corner of her eye, she saw movement. As soon as she turned, there was a blur of movement, and something swung down, pinning her to a tree.

A woman in an orange robe, loose on top with tighter bindings around her legs, dropped to the ground, holding a sword-point to Kyr's neck. She had gold beads in her black, braided hair, and a calm, knowing look in her eyes. As if this were normal for her.

'Who are you?' Her voice was soft but sure.

'Who's asking?' Kyr replied.

'You can call me Two-Trees. I want to know what you're doing in our nullah.'

'Two-Trees,' Kyr said on an exhale. 'As lovely as it is to meet someone as charming as yourself this way'—she glanced down at the gleaming metal under her chin—'I think you may want to lower that thing.' Kyr's voice quieted to a whisper. 'There's a very angry, very violent prince behind you.' She pointed over her shoulder.

Two-Trees turned her head to find that Atlan was at her back, his sword arm outstretched. What happened next was almost too fast for Kyr to comprehend.

Atlan backed away suddenly, his eyes growing wide, his gaze drawn upward.

'Atlan, what are you—'

Behind her, the tree began to uproot itself, as though it had a mind of its own. Wood creaked and groaned, and with a *whoosh* of leaves, Kyr felt herself being lifted, ensnared in the tree's branches.

'Kyr, don't—' Atlan's words were cut off by another limb lowering to snatch him up too.

'What the fuck kind of trees are these?' Kyr shouted.

'I suggest you stop squirming,' said Two-Trees, 'or its hold on you will only get tighter.'

'Well, then tell it to stop!' Kyr yelled back.

'It will, once I know who you are and what you want. The nullah feels my suspicion, my fear and trepidation.'

'*What the Six?*'

All three of them turned toward Vyktas's voice.

'Who is he?' Two-Trees asked, whipping around to face him. The bark dug deeper into Kyr's skin.

'Who are *you*? Atlan, Kyr, why are you up in a tree?' said Vyktas, squinting up at them, half-startled, half-bemused.

Atlan called down, 'Please, Two-Trees, is it? We mean no harm. Let's just talk.'

Kyr glanced over at him and could see his boots and trousers completely wrapped in ever-expanding tendrils of new growth.

Two-Trees assessed them. 'First, you'll tell me what a mage is doing here.'

'*A* mage?' said Vyktas, appalled on their behalf. 'This is the Prince of Yorenth! He's the most powerful mage in the realm!'

Kyr would've tried to signal him to *shut up*, but her hands were bound.

'Is that so? It seems your prince was not even able to call the forest. Besides, I wasn't talking about him.' She paused. 'Though now the strong smell makes sense,' she added, under her breath. 'I was talking about her.'

'How did you know we were mages? Wait, the *smell*?' called

Kyr, still trying not to look down at how far off the ground she was.

'You reek of magic. Mages always smell *terrible,* like a wet dog.'

Kyr scoffed. 'I do not! Now him, maybe, but I'll have you know I bathe *regularly!*'

Atlan's laugh seemed to break the tension somewhat. Two-Trees studied them.

He called down to the mysterious woman. 'We did not mean to intrude—we are only travelers, on our way to Bellgard. Do you know it?'

Slowly, Kyr felt the tree release its grip, creaking and swaying as she felt her feet touch the ground.

'We do not venture near there, though I have heard of such a place. The people there practice the Misguided Way, stealing from what is plentiful to make useless objects and ugly struc-tures. But you, you *can* commune with the Spirits, although weakly. Interesting . . .'

Behind her, Atlan was lowered to the ground too.

'Yes, the Misguided Way,' Atlan agreed, brushing off his shirt. He hadn't even had time to button it. 'Tell me more. Who are you? Are you out here with others?'

'Of course. All of us who follow Their Return live here.'

'Spirits, you're Followers of Their Return?' said Kyr. Two-Trees turned to her, nodding. 'You believe the cities should be destroyed, rulers deposed, that sort of thing?'

'We don't believe in destruction, only creation. Destruction has its part in it, but it is nothing like what you speak of. It is not for us to tell those of the Misguided Way that they are wrong. They will learn that one day, when they can no longer escape their endless cycle of destruction. We keep to ourselves, and whoever would join us, may.' She looked Kyr up and down. 'How do you know of us? I have not seen you before.'

'There's a band of you lot in Yorenth. They're a real thorn in the queen's side.'

Atlan nodded. 'She and her advisors have been increasingly worried about them of late. She thinks those ideas of yours are going to lead to rebellion.'

Two-Trees shook her head. 'I do not know these people. We would never go to Yorenth. They are pretenders.'

Kyr shrugged. 'It's always interesting what travels in from the road.'

'How did you learn to do that—before?' asked Atlan, changing the subject.

'Notice my fresh scent, it is not like what *you* can do, if that's what you're asking. To those of us who have lived out here our entire lives, it is how we commune with the Spirits and the world we share with them. We do not issue each other commands. We sense, and they respond. Of my sisters, I have a natural inclination toward it. It is why I scout.'

'Your sisters? And where are they?' Kyr questioned.

A smile crept across Two-Trees's face. 'They're here right now.'

Kyr, Atlan, and Vyktas each looked around as several women emerged from behind trees and brush in all directions.

As they moved closer, Kyr took them in. A woman with long, deep brown hair and a profile that whispered of ancient statues. Another with sun-lightened curls who smiled warmly at her, though Kyr noticed the knife gripped in her hand, painted with bloodred symbols. In her periphery, she noticed yet another woman with inkwells for eyes and black hair to her waist. Kyr lingered on the curve of her waist, the defined muscle of her legs.

I never want to leave this place, she thought.

'Witches . . .' Vyktas breathed, and Kyr had to stop herself from laughing.

'Witches are a myth, Vyktas.' Glancing at Two-Trees, she

added, 'And on that note, most think the Followers of Their Return are a cult.'

'*Kyr*,' Vyktas whispered harshly.

'They can believe what they like.' Two-Trees shrugged. 'But if you're here to scout this nullah on behalf of your queen, I have to let you know, your people will die out here. Not only because it is a place sacred to us, but because the land will not let you.'

'We're not here on behalf of anyone,' said Atlan. 'We are headed to Bellgard to speak with the archivists there. We only thought this a safe place to camp.'

'Do they know about what you can do?' she asked.

Atlan tilted his head, his brows furrowing. 'A curious question.'

'It is not every day a stranger comes to our nullah, let alone three mages.'

Vyktas stepped forward, a tight-lipped smile on his face. 'Oh, I'm not a mage, so if you're planning to further imprison them in thorns, I assure you, you can spare me.'

Two-Trees smiled. 'This is your brother?' she said, turning to Atlan. 'He is funny.'

'How'd you know?' he asked.

'You have the same smile.'

Atlan looked at his brother, who rolled his eyes at him.

Two-Trees continued. 'I ask of their knowledge only because people who are aware of the destructiveness of mages tend to be less welcoming, particularly in cities.'

'We intend no destruction, in your nullah or in Bellgard,' said Atlan. 'We might have more in common than you think. We too seek balance, through a better understanding of what we can do.'

Kyr recalled what she knew about the Followers of Their Return, at least in Yorenth. They often spoke of life in the First Age, when people lived in small communities in connection with the land around them. Spiritsingers were nomadic then, agrarian sages who roamed the land dispensing wisdom to their communities and maintaining equilibrium in nature.

If they could demonstrate this to Two-Trees, perhaps they could put her at ease. 'We want to see what they have at the Archives about Spiritsingers,' she said.

'Spiritsingers?' The way Two-Trees was watching her now betrayed her interest, just as Kyr hoped. 'What do you know of them?'

Kyr leaned toward Atlan. 'Show her.'

'*What?*' he whispered back.

'Trust me.'

Atlan eyed her warily, then sighed, resigned to the Knave's plan.

The air began to shimmer around him, iridescent crystals of light reflecting and consuming him, and then he was gone. Scattered.

Kyr found it endlessly fascinating, watching magic, seeing Atlan's skill before her very eyes, especially now, after knowing what the sensation was like firsthand.

'Atlan!' Vykas yelled, looking around for him.

Somewhere, a gasp sounded from the underbrush. Kyr turned, realizing they were being watched by even more people than they could see.

Two-Trees's face was filled with wonder. 'You were not lying. You are more than just powerful mages. Matter . . . it listens to you.'

In an instant, Atlan was back at their side.

'Brother, what *was* that?'

'Scattering, I've always called it. I stumbled across a description a while back on how to do it, how to hide particles of yourself amongst others in the surrounding environment. It was written on an old piece of parchment folded within the pages of a book on sea wyvern migration. When I told

Saartho, he snatched it away, 'for study and preservation,' he said.'

Vyktas stared at him, like he was seeing his brother in a completely new way.

'You are—' Two-Trees began.

'Spiritsingers,' Atlan finished.

What Kyr said next, she knew, was a gamble, but one she hoped might yield information from a mage whose magical knowledge might be less fractured, isolated as they were here.

'We have the notes of the last Oracle of Yoren, and we need all the help we can get making use of them to the fullest. That's why we need to see the archivists.'

Two-Trees's eyes widened. 'My foremothers knew of her. You carry them?'

Kyr nudged Atlan, who nodded and produced a small book from his cloak. Two-Trees took it eagerly from him, flipping through its pages. Part of Kyr wondered if it was a good idea to be showing such a thing to a stranger, but Two-Trees had made it more than clear they needed to respect her and her sisters' wishes if they hoped to leave this forest alive.

'Where did you get this?' she asked.

'My teacher, Saartho Ulam,' Atlan said. 'He tells me Bellgard has a large collection of oral histories dictated by the Oracle. We're hoping they might be able to fill in any gaps in our understanding of these notes.'

Two-Trees nodded, still looking through the pages. 'If you are going to Bellgard, you should know the road ahead is dangerous, more so even than last week. A clutch of wyverns has made their nest on the cliffs.'

'Wyverns?' said Vyktas, looking like he'd faint.

She nodded. 'I can escort you, under one condition.'

'Lady,' said Kyr, 'I am at your command.'

Two-Trees snorted. 'I have my own reasons for wanting to know more about your Spiritsinging, but I cannot travel to these Archives. You will tell me of the knowledge you acquire from this place, and I will make sure the three of you get there and back unharmed.'

Kyr looked at Atlan, who was studying Two-Trees.

Vyktas, who had ventured closer, spoke then. 'I know she *did* just recently attack you with the might of the entire forest, but it might be nice to have another person on the road. Safety in numbers and all.'

Kyr was still looking at Atlan. She broke out in a grin. 'The more the merrier?'

Atlan scowled at her familiar words. 'Oh, fine.' He sighed. 'Alright. We accept.'

Two-Trees said goodbye to her sisters, who never spoke to the three of them, hesitant as they were to make acquaintance with blasphemers.

Instead, Kyr, Vyktas, and Atlan busied themselves with packing up the camp and readying the horses. They were standing at the edge of the wood when Two-Trees emerged on a massive beast, larger than their horses, and with great horns thicker around than Kyr's arm. They were adorned with beads and bone fetishes, inscribed with archaic symbols.

She'd never seen anything like it. 'What the *Six* is that?'

Vyktas had a horrified expression on his face. 'That's the biggest goat I've ever seen.'

'Not a goat. A bucca,' Two-Trees said, smiling and patting its neck. 'They're our herd animals. Most people, I hear, have never seen one. They're quite reclusive beings. Isn't that right Old Tom?'

The creature must've stood twenty hands tall, with a slight curl to his white coat and eyes that were yellow like a cat's. Old Tom huffed impatiently as they stood around staring at him.

It was Atlan's turn to be bewildered. 'Old . . . Tom?'

Two-Trees simply nodded, and added, 'He likes mulberries, if you see any.'

33

MOTHRIL

MOTHRIL AWOKE SUDDENLY, his head lolling against the stone wall of the Whispess's room. He raised a hand in front of his squinting eyes.

Some mornings, it was like he forgot all over again what the sun felt like. He got to his feet, still in the alcove of the door, and looked over to see Oria sleeping peacefully in her bed, her hair flung over the pillows, awash in the golden light of morning, and the blanket slowly rising and falling with her breath.

I have to tell her. But how?

It wasn't about whether she'd forgive him, he knew he wasn't owed that. He just wanted to make sure she survived this place. Now that he had this tether inside him, now that he knew what she was. An Oracle. Not just Whispess, a title he'd never even heard any of the other clans use, but those divinely touched throughout history, able to discern the hidden truths of their world. Only, he had his suspicions about just how divinely touched she was. The way the weather changed during those rites, the details of her dreams, and what she'd said about the dagger he'd given her.

Then there was the way she looked at him sometimes. He

could tell she had questions. Suspicions about his past. But how could speak of any of it without telling her *how* he knew about it?

His fear wrestled with a certain sense of urgency. He saw in her the steadfast leader this world so desperately needed, one who would do anything for her people, disregard the self completely for them. She wasn't without flaw, and she knew that. She was able to accept that. She possessed a true sense of nobility, of duty and sacrifice for others. It was why she felt such deep shame that she had tried to escape her role in her clan, and it was, he knew, why he needed her to succeed at it before the next rite.

Slowly, he backed out of the room, closing the door behind him.

Lyra would be there soon to ready her for the day, not that there was much use in that given her father's newest decree. At least Lyra was someone she could rely on, more than him. Lyra wasn't keeping secrets. He nodded to her minutes later when she came up the stairs, then carried on to the guard's quarters, dreading the only time he had each day to himself.

As he walked, head bowed against the wind of an oncoming storm—earlier than usual in the day for bad Northern weather—his thoughts drifted, strangely, to his father. He hadn't thought about the man in years, but lately, like a wraith, he kept creeping into his mind. It didn't matter that it was his father who had slaughtered most of the Ronin clan, and that Mothril had begged him not to. As he grew older, he realized his presence at the raid made him just as guilty. By that age he could've overpowered his father, but he didn't.

'Lo, *strip them* lay gilt aye *silver,' came his father's rough voice, speaking an odd mixture of Borean Poet and the common tongue. 'We've got to clear the others off the road.' The ones they'd freshly killed, he meant.*

'Yes, sire,' Mothril answered. He knelt over the body, examining

it. A glint of metal caught his eye, a silver necklace with a small garnet pendant. He turned the head, blueish and stiff, to get a better look, and a swarm of flies flew out of the mouth. Mothril turned his head away, shutting his eyes tightly.

He felt his father's boot nudge him. 'You'll not turn away from death, scion.' His large palm gripped the back of his head, forcing him to look at the body. 'Not but a few flies.' Mothril reached down and ripped the necklace from the rotting woman's neck.

Later on, in the free order, Mora always told him how he appreciated his father. Told Mothril he was lucky to have a wise man to teach him the ways of the world. He couldn't say Mora was wrong, but he couldn't say he felt lucky, either. It was a double-edged sword.

Mothril bit his cheek, and a voice from one of the alcoves off the Elders' chamber caught his attention.

'We are concerned that the Whispess is taking on too much. Her visions haven't been fruitful as of late, and—'

'Is that what you think?'

It sounded like Elder Sybil and the Prime.

'My daughter is the key to holding our position in the North.'

He heard another voice sigh and say, 'Is this all really worth it? I would be remiss not to bring up the view of most of the Elders. We trust in your leadership, Prime, but it's becoming harder and harder to justify why we even moved to take the citadel in the first place.'

'This citadel is sacred ground to our people. The Erángal belongs here.' An edge of danger seeped into Edril Sil's soothing words, like a predator deciding whether to strike. 'I'm surprised to hear such sentiments from a longtime Elder like yourself.'

'I mean no offense, Prime. It's just . . .' They seemed to be considering their words carefully. 'We lived well in the surrounding wilds. We haven't needed the rites for centuries! Most Wiccars don't even remember them.'

'These are unprecedented times—the Far Clans are lost to us, there is talk of mages and magical happenings in the south of the continent, my daughter has constant visions of the Eradomin hunting her down! We need to maintain our domain over the Erángal now more than ever!'

'The rites will not protect us the way our knights can. It is time we devoted what we can to what has been proven to protect us time and again.'

Edril Sil's voice lowered. 'I value input from the Elders. I always have, in the Cailir clan and as Knight Commander before that—'

'That's another thing. There are whispers, Prime. People are concerned about how centralized the final word has become. Your daughter is the only remaining Wiccar of Cailir blood, and—'

'Well,' Edril Sil said, pausing for a moment. 'I'm going to give whoever these whisperers are the same advice I'm going to give you.' His words became cutting. 'Maybe you'll pass it on to them. I have never steered our people wrong. And I am no longer asking, but *commanding you*, to support my pursuit of Oria's visions.'

'We will always support the Whispess,' said Sybil. 'She is going to lead us one day, after all.'

A curt, dry laugh came from Edril Sil. 'Sybil, I hope you're not implying you look forward to a shift in power. If it were that Oria did not make it long enough to see her days as Prime, I, and I alone, am all we Wiccars have. If we want any chance to stand against the Sentinels *and* the Eradomin—and let me remind you, we *know* they are returning—if there is any hope of us wielding the Erángal, then I am our only salvation.'

Mothril shambled backward, nearly colliding with the wall

in an effort to be sure he wasn't seen. He clung to the shadows looming at the corners of the room.

A rush of thoughts came to him, pieces of things he had suspected over years, things his father had told him, but most of all, the Prime had all but confirmed the Whispess's life was in danger. Mothril knew a threat when he heard one, and his tone, so careless . . .

He couldn't ignore it. The memory of his father's last day came rushing back.

That accursed room in the tunnels stretched out before him as it always did, never-ending in its consuming depravity. Before him, a man who looked only a few years younger than him was tied to a chair. It'd been a fight getting him there, too. Mothril was still breathing hard as he secured the thumbscrew to his hand.

Once he did, he pulled up another chair in front of him and reclined. 'You know how this ends,' he began. 'I'm sure you've heard the stories. You know what I do.' The man began stammering, and Mothril put up a hand to silence him. 'See, you even know what you're going to tell me. It's only a matter of how many stubborn lies it's buried under.' He exhaled, leaning forward, dwarfing the man. 'I'm going to tell you exactly what I'm going to do to your body, and then I'm going to give you an opportunity to answer a question. If I don't like your answer, I will do to you what I said I would. You will scream, you will beg, you will swear to your clan Elders that you've told the truth. And then we will begin again.'

He continued. 'We will start with the thumbscrew. It's going to be very painful. Your joints will bleed, and break, until they are no longer . . . acceptable. Usually, we have to take a break then. You'll grow tired. But I'm getting ahead of myself.'

The man ground his jaw. 'A man paying respect to his ancestors gets accused of all manner of sacrilege!' He looked away nervously. 'I-I honor our Elders, the Fäendhmar. Hear me, Sarthura, so far from the light, I exalt you!'

Mothril's expression turned curious, almost amused. 'No one is listening, least of all her. I've never heard of one paying respect to his ancestors with lantern and shovel. Have you?'

He shook his head. '*I wasn't robbing no graves!'*

Mothril leaned across and, slowly, began to tighten the cold metal device. The man bit his lip at first, as if trying to hold in the sound, but the screams came soon enough. They always did.

'*Tell me why you were there,' Mothril said softly.*

'*What does it matter to you?' the man yelled.*

'*It doesn't. I've been asked to find out.' Mothril's hand went to the screws again.*

'*Please,' the man whispered, but Mothril ignored him, tightening them until blood seeped out between the man's fingers. He strained against his bonds. 'Wh-why?' he sobbed.*

Mothril shrugged. '*Someone important must want to know. Are you going to tell me now?'*

The man's eyes were watering, and he cried out again, softer this time. '*Alright! Alright, I'll tell you.' He looked hatefully up at him. 'I went there looking, but there wasn't even anything good worth taking! Please,' he begged again.*

Mothril sat back, listening as the words flowed out of him.

'*With them new edicts after the spate of recent robbings, we thought there must be treasure hidden in the mounds! But there wasn't nothing, even looked like most of the bodies were gone—'*

Mothril was about to ask who he meant by 'we,' when they were interrupted by loud pounding on the door.

'*Please,' the man said again, as Mothril stood and went to answer it.*

It was one of the healer's assistants. A man with short brown hair and a reddish tint to his beard. He had a grim look. His father had taken a turn. '*He's called for you,' he said. 'Says he has something important to tell you. I'm not sure how long he has.'*

Mothril left the sorry prisoner behind and followed him across the citadel to his father's rented room. As soon as he saw the figure *lying there, he knew. Too stiff.* He walked over to the head of the bed and put a hand on his forehead.

Numbness overtook him.

He breathed in deep, letting go of the memory as he thought back to the night before. *I knew that draught smelled off.* Mothril was no alchemist, but he knew that whatever that was, it wasn't jewel-dock for sleep.

His suspicions had been confirmed, but also, his hand had been forced. *I have to tell her. Even if she never wants to see me again. It doesn't matter. I don't matter.*

He looked around and, seeing no one, continued swiftly and silently to the guard's quarters. There, he packed up what little supplies he might need—a waterskin, bandages, salves, a tinderbox, and soap—from the meager offerings guards were given, and looked around the low-ceilinged, windowless room. His was the only bunk that didn't have family trinkets, letters, or personal effects. It would likely be the last time he ever saw it.

Well, good riddance.

34

KYR

'Blights?' Two-Trees asked. 'What do you mean?'

'The Spirits wove this world out of the essence of magic, you agree,' Atlan offered. Two-Trees nodded. 'Well, Saartho and I, and most in Yorenth, suspect these blights are essentially autonomous errors in this fabric. A misfolding of magic, if you will.'

They had stopped their horses just beyond the road, near the outpost. Two-Trees's expression was troubled.

'Like magic itself disobeying the Spirits?' she asked.

'It's possible,' Atlan replied.

They approached the once-distant fires now, with nothing around but their conversation to keep them company. Summer's last hold on the days was loosening to autumn, and a breeze rustled the tall grasses, threatening to scatter flame and ash.

'How did I not know a threat was so close to our nullah? I have not felt any such disturbance in my communion.'

Kyr knew from Atlan's expression he was debating what to say next. 'Some of my mother's council in Yorenth believe rogue mages are causing them. Until now, I never believed there was anyone else but myself,' he glanced at Kyr, 'and her, who could affect our world in such a way. But now we've seen what you can do. Is there any chance . . .' Kyr couldn't believe what he was asking after she'd nearly killed them with a *tree*.

'You think my sisters and I are causing this? Our relationship with the nullah, the forest?'

'Well, I think it's worth considering. I mean, if the tree reacted to what you were feeling earlier, like you said, who's to say other elements of the Spirits would not?'

'Isn't that just Spiritsinging?' Vyktas asked as they grew closer. A wall of heat radiated from the area, even so long after the fire started.

'No,' Two-Trees answered quickly. 'We do not impose our will. We interpret, communicate. The nullah defends, it would never act without reason.'

'There are different ways to access magic, Vyktas,' said Kyr. 'It's like Sylas said. There are those who can tap into a given well of magic, like Two-Trees and their nullah. Others, like Atlan and I, are direct conduits.'

'You're saying I could learn to harness magic?' Vyktas asked. 'Where do these other sources come from?'

'I don't know,' Kyr replied. 'Add it to the list of questions we'll have to try to get answers to in Bellgard.'

The fires were a more gruesome sight than Kyr had been expecting. It wasn't simply eternal fire, like she'd thought when they'd spoken of the blights back in Yorenth. The fire's source was burning bodies. Dead soldiers, Sun's Own and another uniform she didn't recognize, perfectly preserved in flame, as if it were amber.

It was one thing to imagine their pain upon death, and another to see it in their faces as she passed them by. She'd expected them to be burned, their faces fused to their helms—

which would've been horrific enough—but instead she could still see them through each ocularium, their faces masks of pain and horror.

She swallowed and looked away. 'What livery is this?'

'Noblegard,' Atlan answered.

'I see why you think Bellgard will have a mutual interest in providing you access to its Archives,' said Two-Trees grimly.

These were no natural deaths. Even before she believed in magic's existence, it would've been undeniable what this was. *Surely a report must've reached Queen Attiqah.*

'It's worse than I thought,' said Atlan, squinting out at the sight. He walked on, passing each body slowly, kneeling down by some despite the immense heat. Kyr turned to where Two-Trees and Vyktas stood.

'Don't you want to go pay your respects?' Kyr asked.

Vyktas gave her an annoyed look then stepped forward, though hesitantly. He walked up to the first group of Sun's Own and when he turned back his face was so anguished that Kyr regretted her words. He looked out at his brother, then hurried back to them.

'Mother only mentioned this to me in passing. It's—it's so much worse than she said. They look like they can still feel the flames.'

Kyr grimaced. Atlan was a few hundred yards away now, standing over the body of a Sun's Own. He'd been there for a long time.

'Does he know these poor souls?' Two-Trees asked.

'All of them,' Vyktas answered.

Atlan startled suddenly. He yelled something, but at that distance his voice was faint. Kyr ran toward him, with Vyktas and Two-Trees following closely behind. 'What?' she called out.

'She's alive! They're—they're all alive!' he shouted. His voice was unlike she'd ever heard it—a mangled, broken sound. 'Afsa's breathing. Look!'

They reached him and Kyr looked at the body he'd been standing over, watching. A woman. Short brown hair, a tattoo peeking out of her uniform. Though it was difficult to get close enough to tell, Kyr could see her chest beneath half-melted breastplate slowly rise and fall. Her face was frozen in pain, but her flesh was unburnt, just like the rest.

'How is this possible?' Vyktas breathed.

'These blights seem to be of the matter of our world, and yet they don't behave that way,' said Two-Trees. She put a hand on Atlan's shoulder. 'I am sorry about your friends.'

'We have to do something for them,' Vyktas urged.

'No,' Atlan said quietly. His answer surprised Kyr, and Vyktas too, it seemed, judging by the incredulity on his face. 'Kyr and I could try to mend the blights somehow. I wouldn't know the first thing to try, but . . . I was able to do it once, in a village near the Middevale overtaken by fog, but it's always unpredictable. I won't put the only route between Bellgard and Yorenth at risk trying.'

'But they're still alive!'

'Because of some anomaly, but these people died a long time ago, Vyktas! I don't expect you to understand. Look at their faces. The faces of people who burned to death. What if I'm able to mend the blight, and the fire begins to burn true, whatever's preventing their flesh from burning no longer protecting them? What if they still feel like they're burning to death, even after they've been saved? I want nothing more than to deliver them from this, or at the very least, to try to ease their pain, but we don't know what we're dealing with here, what kind of magic, what kind of corruption.'

Kyr would've tried if he'd asked her, but after what happened at the counting house, she understood his position. She reached out and clapped a hand on his back. 'Come on. I think we can say the fires on the Western Road are magical in nature. If we can learn more about the blights, about the abilities of past Spiritsingers, maybe we can come back and help these people.'

Atlan didn't answer her. They walked silently back to the horses.

35

ORIA

WITHOUT HER BOOKS TO occupy her time, Oria found herself sitting by the windows on the far side of her chambers more and more, looking out at the rugged landscape.

She thought often of what she had seen in the citadel gardens that first day she and Mothril had walked the grounds. It must've been a trick her mind was playing on her, but in that moment, the fox, woven of branches and leaves with puffs of cloud for the white fur of its ears, looked so real. If it was a vision, it certainly wasn't like any she'd ever had before.

A waking vision, then?

Though she hated to admit it, even to herself, she felt increasingly distrustful of her father these days. Where once she would've immediately gone to him for answers and comfort, now she avoided him. Locking her up in this place had been the ultimate, final betrayal.

She shifted in the uncomfortable wooden chair and sharp pain exploded through her spine and hips. She hissed, frozen in place as she waited for it to pass, then gently tried to change position. It was no use. She eased out of the chair, and the pain dissipated. She didn't want to go back to bed, so if she was to stay standing, then she at least wanted something to do.

She walked across the room, passing the bookcase's shadow on the floor, and grabbed Mothril's knife and her cane from beside her bed, then retreated back to the windows. She'd practiced throwing the knife one other time since Mothril showed her how to use it, and she found the repetition steadied her.

With one hand on the crown of her cane, she held the knife out in front of her, gripping it firmly. Her body relaxed as Mothril's words came to her. She eyed the distance to the bookcase's edge, calculated the distance, then drew back and released in one fluid motion.

Thunk.

She was getting better. Oria pried the knife from the wood, and a small piece chipped off. The knife had gone in deeper than before.

She resumed her position, her practice taking on an almost meditative quality, as long-held emotions welled up within her, and she let them go with each throw.

Thunk.

Again.

Thunk.

Hurried footsteps sounded outside her door, heavier than Lyra's and moving with purpose. She put down the knife, noting how the shadows had given way to dusk, and turned to face the door just as Mothril opened it and stepped inside.

'Whispess, I need to speak with you.'

That's a first. Does that mean he's beginning to trust me?

'What is it?' she asked.

Still catching her breath herself, she took in his form, his own deep breaths and wild eyes.

'Can he see ahead?' His voice was ragged.

'What?' she asked.

'Edril Sil, can he see ahead?' He was ... frantic.

'No,' she blurted, surprised by the emotion behind his question.

He shook his head, steadied himself. 'Listen, you have to come with me. I overheard your father and the Elders speaking in his halls. There's no plan for your ascension, and I don't believe there ever was. Your father—he sees you as a conduit for your visions. He would have you remain here until he gets what he wants. Oria, I can't explain how I know this. Not here. The thing he wants is going to destroy you. I don't think he knows how to do it yet, but he's getting closer. Your injuries . . .'

His face was a mask, as always, but his eyes had a desperation to them that scared her.

Her head spun. 'What? Mothril—'

'I heard it myself, Whispess.'

It can't be. 'I don't understand. What exactly did you hear?'

'Sybil and another Elder were asking after you. They're worried about you. But he dismissed their concerns, saying your visions were of greater importance. There's danger here, Oria. I can't fully explain my reasoning to you right now, but I will, I promise. I need you to trust me.'

Oria took two steps and slackened against her bedpost. She knew Mothril would not react this way without good reason.

'I—it's not that I don't think about leaving.' She took a deep breath, considering her words. 'You know I do. More often than I'd like to admit. Especially at night. But what about the clan? They're not all like my father. You said it yourself, Elder Sybil was asking after me.'

Oria steadied herself, continuing. 'Do you know why it is so hard for me to leave? I lived in the war camps with my father as a child. I slept in warm furs while other children's bellies were bloated from starvation. One day, I fell into an Eradomin trap in the woods and cut my leg, badly. I was taken immediately to the healers. A knight bled out waiting while they stitched me up, and he did so willingly. And on, and on.

Countless situations like this throughout my life! They've sacrificed for *me*.'

Mothril shook his head, frustration bracketing his mouth. 'The ritual your father is trying to do would invalidate all of that! You're here now, that knight isn't. Let his sacrifice mean something!'

His voice softened. 'I knew your mother, Felith, you know. I see in you what a great leader could be. Who she should've been. Remember when I said what you can do is something rulers would search the world for? I think you're an Oracle.'

Her eyes met his. 'An Oracle? What do you mean?'

'You're a powerful seer, able to see ahead, yes, but I think, even part the veil between worlds. I've seen your pragmatism, your dedication to others, how you consider all sides of things, never putting yourself first. The reason you won't leave is precisely why we need you!' He looked back toward the door. She barely heard what he said under his breath next. 'I need you ...'

It sent a rush through her, like ice water sluicing through her veins.

'I know you think I'm keeping secrets. You're right, I am, and I'll tell you all I know, but not here.' Oria sat there, frozen, and Mothril's face grew sympathetic. 'Come with me. Oria, that draught he's been giving you, it's not a sleeping draught. I don't know what it is, but—'

She lifted her head to him suddenly. 'What?'

'I don't think you should take it anymore.'

'Lyra gives that to me,' she said plainly.

'She does?' He considered her words. 'Hm. Well, that's good. I was worried they might be making you sick, weakening you somehow.'

She shook her head. 'I'll ask her, but Mothril,' Oria said, her voice lowering almost to a conspiratorial whisper, 'we can't just leave!'

When Mothril opened his mouth to protest, she spoke again as tears began to well. 'I know I can't stay here, I know. But I won't abandon my people to my father's whims. Pass a message to Sybil for me. We must come up with a plan, learn who we can trust and who we can't.'

He pulled a chair beside her bed, and it creaked as he leaned on it. He rocked back and forth on his feet, clearly anxious to act, but straightened, nodding and taking a deep breath. 'Alright. But we leave as soon as we're able.'

He sat down beside her.

Oria waited for the weight of all Mothril had revealed to settle on her, but paradoxically, she felt lighter. Instead of shock, she wondered instead if long hidden intuitions were being confirmed.

Beside her, Mothril straightened his legs, his eyes fluttering closed, and began breathing rhythmically. She watched the chainmail which fell over the bulk of him swell with an inhale, his throat dipping with the movement. He paused, holding the breath in, then slowly released it.

'What are you doing?' Oria asked.

'Hm? Oh, just something my father taught me. A kind of meditation.'

Oria nodded, letting him continue. She sat on the bed and, once he'd closed his eyes again, observed him more obviously. Mothril remained an enigma to her, but there was a steadfastness, a promise of safety about him.

Somehow, despite the uncertainty of what lay head, she felt hope.

36

KYR

KYR KNEW they were getting closer to Bellgard as thick forests began to overtake the desolate lands surrounding Yorenth.

They made camp along a small stream, from which they could still see the Wravellian Sea in the far distance, and the ruins of an old city built into the cliffs bordering the Outlands. Crumbling stone and tarnished brass, the old fortress sat forgotten. She'd pointed it out to Atlan, and he'd said he had never seen the place on any of the countless maps he studied in childhood.

He asked Two-Trees about it. 'What was that place we passed?'

'My foremothers called it Kharupan. I've never been, but some of my sisters used to search for minerals there. These were found there,' she said, indicating to the beads in her hair. 'It used to be a famed city, with technology fueled by magic. The Kharupani people even crossed the sea to trade with people. The city was destroyed in the last Yawning.'

'Yawning?'

Two-Trees scoffed. 'What history do they teach Yoren princes?'

Kyr giggled, Atlan scowled. 'I suppose just what we'd need to rule our people and conquer our living neighbors, and nothing more.'

'That doesn't seem like much of an education to me.'

'That's becoming clearer to me every day,' he said with a sigh.

'You must've learned of the cataclysm that heralded the Second Age?' Two-Trees asked, more insistent.

'Of course,' said Atlan.

'Well, the Yawning was said to be a rending of worlds that brought it about. My foremothers know stories of beings that came here from other planes of existence. It's said they destroyed the city, and all of their innovation and advancement along with it.'

'You never learned about this?' Kyr asked.

Atlan shook his head briefly, turning back to Two-Trees. 'What kind of beings?'

'We don't know. My sisters said there are depictions of many-eyed creatures all over Kharupan—sigils, maps, old books left behind—but the script is illegible. Perhaps it's some kind of lost dialect or proto-language.'

'Fascinating,' Atlan muttered. 'To think all of this is within the purview of my family's realm, and I know so little. Yorenth's nobility seemed to think themselves the pinnacle of knowledge. How in the dark they are.'

'It's amazing how your world is changed as a traveler,' Kyr said. 'There's a whole wide world out there, and it's full of secrets, little king.'

Atlan made a grunt of acknowledgement, looking out at the landscape as it passed. 'I always knew that, in a way. I mean, I got out more than Vyktas did.' She turned toward Vyktas, who looked in awe of the natural beauty. 'Maybe you're surprised to learn that even a royal has limits to his education. Fighting, statecraft, the history of the kingdom itself—those were the most important things.'

'I guess it surprises me a little, what with all those books you've got up in that castle. I may not know the Sayings and Histories, but I learned a lot from Sylas.'

'You spent a lot of time with him, I take it?' Atlan asked.

'Most of my life. Much of it in Yorenth, but I traveled many places with him too. Bellgard, once, when I was young, but also Quormanth, Telhav, Greenflower, and even the Shattered Isles.'

'The Shattered Isles? I'd like to hear about that,' said Atlan, intrigued.

'Lots and lots of fish, and the best juniper berry ale you've ever had. I got so drunk on it that . . .' Kyr gave a wily smile. 'Anyway, Vasha and Sylas had to practically carry me back to the inn.'

She continued. 'My favorite place was Quormanth, though. I'm not allowed to go back, sadly. I'm still wanted by the castle guard there for'—she cleared her throat—'impropriety.'

'*Impropriety?*'

She glanced over one shoulder to see Atlan with his brows raised.

'It's a long story. Anyway, they have the best food there— there's this cheese that's probably the best thing I've ever tasted. It's sheep's milk, but they ferment it with barrelspider eggs.'

'Hold on, hold on,' Atlan laughed. 'You can't just *not* tell me why you're wanted in Quormanth. And what in Solq's name is a barrelspider?'

'Who knows? But if you run across any merchants selling their eggs, do let me know, eh?' Kyr shrugged. 'Anyway, as far as Quormanth goes, I was caught in a, er, compromising position with the duchess.'

Atlan burst into laughter. 'Duchess Othdia?'

Kyr looked coyly back at him. 'The very same.'

'I can see why you would take the risk. She *is* beautiful.'

Kyr smirked, recalling a particularly pleasant memory. One that involved a dish of cherries and several hair ribbons. 'That she is.'

'And a distant relative of Vyktas's father, if you can believe it.'

Kyr squinted at the back of Vyktas's head, repulsion rippling across her features. 'Hm. I don't see the resemblance.'

Atlan's laughter was low and resonant against her back.

'Anyway, what about you? You must've got up to some dastardly deeds in your time. Break any hearts as prince?'

'No, I'm afraid not,' Atlan replied vaguely.

Kyr sensed she'd made some kind of misstep and tried to fix it the way she always did, with lightheartedness. 'Oh, come on,' she nudged.

'I said no,' he snapped.

Kyr straightened, surprised to find a sore spot. 'Alright.'

She fiddled with the reins, focusing on the passing pines.

Atlan exhaled sharply through his nose, relenting. 'Shit,' he muttered. 'Kyr, I didn't mean to be short with you. There are things in my past that I . . .' He sighed.

Kyr glanced behind her. She could tell by his expression, the set of his shoulders, that he was wrestling with something. 'I understand,' she offered.

She remembered his words to her the night they'd gone drinking with Vyktas. It felt so long ago now. 'You don't have to talk about it, but when you want to, I'll be here.'

His reply came, his voice low, grateful. 'Thanks, Kyr.'

37

THE LOST ONE

EACH MOMENT of lucidity was a relief and a torment.

'Aerith,' they whispered. Nothing. They tried their Borean Poet name. 'Athlaya!'

Peering over the edge of their prison, they searched the skies. *Has a storm taken them? Pushed them far off course? Lost to me. They are lost!*

They would not give up their vigil. 'Carry my starlings back to me,' they pleaded. They had known the Spirit who made the wind beneath their starlings' wings once. All in white, as if he belonged to the skies himself. Now he was silent. Gone, like her mother. And Crescian, too—the dice no longer weighted by his meddling hand.

Gone, but not dead. At least they could take solace in that. That they had done what they set out to.

Riparus would be safe. She always was. She embodied patience, she could wait forever in some forgotten corner of her domain. An underground river, a tidal pool at the edge of the world. Tellurn, too, must've retreated to his solitary Greenwoods.

Solq, the first to fall, was somewhere his light could not permeate. *Trapped, but alive.*

They felt the clarity of their mind, their vision, dimming. 'No,' they whispered. 'I must keep watch!' But it was no use. Shadows came upon them.

38

ATLAN

ONE MORE NIGHT and they would be in Bellgard. The second largest Sentinel city, and the closest one to Yorenth, it had become a center of knowledge the way Yorenth was the center of martial mastery.

As dusk fell, Atlan could see the braziers along the cliffside in the mountain watchtowers descending along its walls. He thought of the fires back at the outpost and clenched his jaw.

Their camp emanated a similar ruby glow, with Two-Trees tending the fire and Kyr preparing a stew from mushrooms and wild greens they'd managed to forage earlier in the day.

'This is going to be good,' Kyr said, grinning as she chopped up mushrooms the size of her hand.

'Do you ever stop thinking about food?' Vyktas asked, picking at his nails with a small knife. It was a gift from their mother, with a gilded handle inlaid with a small, jeweled sun.

Kyr stopped what she was doing and looked pointedly at him, smiling. 'No.'

Atlan couldn't believe how much his understanding of Singers, magic, and his own brother had changed in only a few days since their journey began. He'd gone from thinking he was alone in his experience with magic, to meeting two people who could understand in only a short time.

Kyr and Two-Trees had made him realize his understanding of magic and its place in the world was a myopic one, and his brother showed him that that extended to his family as well.

'Here,' Two-Trees said, passing him a piece of bread. He blinked away his thoughts and took it from her.

The flatbread was more than a little stale by this point in their journey, but he didn't mind. He was thankful the journey had gone as well as it had. He tore off a piece and bit into it.

'You know, I've never had someone use magic against me before. The feeling is awful,' he said, turning to Two-Trees.

'Happy to have been your first,' she said, laughing. 'I have spent much time practicing. Honing my connection to the land. My sisters and I, and all Followers of Their Return, believe we are joined to this world the moment we are born into it—we learn the languages of rivers and grasses, but we know their names from birth.'

'That's not what my magic feels like,' Kyr added, sitting across the fire from them. 'It gets rip-roaring hot in my chest and then . . . it just happens, whether I want it to or not.'

Two-Trees took the estimation of her with her eyes. 'If you're new to communion with the Spirits, that makes sense. Spiritsingers, I'm told, have patrons. Perhaps you have one of the more unpredictable ones as yours.'

Kyr nodded. 'Crescian.'

Two-Trees raised her brows.

'Patrons?' Vyktas questioned.

Atlan leaned forward, poking at the fire with a stick. 'Spiritsingers of the First Age often had certain attunements to the matter they could manipulate. Sylas told Kyr hers is Crescian, just like our family's is Solq.'

Vyktas scoffed. 'So it's like being a god's favorite?'

'I guess you could put it that way,' Atlan replied.

'Spirits, it's like toting a broken mirror or some other bad luck charm around with us,' said Vyktas, nudging the Knave. She playfully shoved him back.

Atlan chuckled. 'The Spirits were creators, shapers, but also guardians. They had physical presence across the realm before they slowly began to disappear, and magic began to dry up along with them. Not that it was very common to begin with. The divination that our mother and other rulers employ today seems to be the only magic that holds any bearing. Saartho always said that that art, imbuing card and die, was granted by Crescian. Though now I wonder if what the diviners can do is more like what Sylas mentioned,' he said, looking to Kyr. 'With the loss of so much history of magic, we can do little to understand why.'

'Wild magic,' he continued, eyeing Two-Trees, 'is said to be Tellurn's domain. Light and flame, Solq, rivers and rain, Riparus, then there's the wind'—realizing he'd been rambling, he coughed and went back to kindling the fire—'and so on.'

'They may have disappeared,' Two-Trees added, 'but they are not gone.'

With a mouthful of bread, he nodded his agreement. 'Do you know of the Lost One? Only ever mentioned in Northern manuscripts written in Borean Poet, some think it's just another name for Calligone. But there are others who speak of a seventh Spirit.'

'I've never heard of the Lost One. Do you mean Maren?'

His brows furrowed. 'Maren?'

'There are inscriptions about her all over Kharupan. I first heard about her from my family's stories. A mage of the First Age, apparently she protected the Kharupani citadel from enemies for millennia. I'm told she would shroud the entire city in a reflective ash, making it appear as though there was nothing there at all. When she was lost, so was the city.'

Atlan cocked his head. *Maren . . . the name's definitely not familiar.*

'That's an interesting story, but I've never heard of anything like that in my studies. Sometimes it feels like we have but the fragments of a much larger story. Like burnt pieces of a tapestry. We're trying to piece it together, but I worry there are things we'll never know.'

Two-Trees nodded. 'I know the feeling.'

His eyes connected with hers. 'Do you?' he asked softly, more rhetorical than a true question.

She nodded, and soon they fell into a companionable silence. Atlan lay back on the soft ground of the scrubby forest, studying Two-Trees from an angle where she would not notice him.

Her expression always looked so serene to him, and he wondered if she truly felt that way, or if there was more emotion under the surface. As her eyelids fluttered closed, his gaze traveled down her cheeks taking notice of the small freckles there and a birthmark. He found himself wondering about her sisters, her family.

A cold zephyr drifted off the sea, though it was quite some distance from them. It made them all huddle closer to the fire. Across from him, Kyr and Vyktas traded barbs.

They were more similar than he thought, and it made him have a greater appreciation for his brother.

How had he missed his wit and humor all these years?

They had been pitted against each other for so long. Somewhere amongst the chaos of his younger years, he missed the part where his brother had grown into someone he could admire. Someone like the man he'd gotten to see on this trip—up before dawn, practicing the blade, helping set up camp, listening to Kyr's stories and laughing when he'd misunderstood something rather than reacting with anger like he always did under their mother's thumb.

Vyktas, he could see, was lighter now too. Freer.

Maybe, Atlan thought, *when we reach Bellgard*—when the two of them had a room of their own at an inn, he might finally be able to talk to him about all the things that felt too frightening to say up until now. Too painful to say out in the open.

That, and they could finally discuss what he knew about the council's plotting. Together, they could do something about his mother's fracturing sanity. As he drifted off to sleep, content for the first time in a long while, he was unmindful of the world turning outside of their fire's reach.

39

KYR

'What do you think it means?' Kyr asked.

They stood a short distance away from their thirsty horses, which were drinking eagerly from a small mountain brook that trickled down toward the distant sea. A ways downstream, Two-Trees bathed.

Atlan ran his palm over the first page of Saartho's translation of the Oracle of Yoren's notes. 'Some of it is familiar to me, other passages are a complete mystery. It's fascinating, isn't it? Something about looking down the long road of history like this. It feels like both an intrusion and a wonder.'

'Oh, will you two get on with it? There's got to be an appendix or something,' said Vyktas, biting his half-eaten apple between his teeth.

He wiped hands on his shirt, then snatched the book out of his brother's hands and flipped it open to one of the back pages.

'Vyktas—' Atlan growled.

Vyktas's voice was muffled through the apple. 'The Book of Primes? This is from the First Age! . . . And what's this?'

He took a bite and rifled through a couple more pages. 'Poetry, lovely. Bunch of drivel . . .' His brows furrowed as he read over a random page. 'There's even drawings of . . . ash motes? What's an ash mote?'

'Give it here,' said Atlan, snatching the book back.

The pages were thin and delicate as moth wings. Sure enough, there were pages and pages of text side by side with detailed drawings. Things Kyr had never seen nor heard of before.

'Ash motes . . . living manifestations of unliving matter? That sounds like the blights.' He turned the page. 'There's all kinds of them apparently.'

'What's that?' Kyr asked, looking over his shoulder. She pointed to a poem beside an illustration of a tower with massive, thorned plants growing around it.

'With ash as my sentry, to this end I am pledged . . .' Atlan read. 'This line in the Book of Primes indicates the presence of ash motes at the last known location of—'

'The Pentaculum,' Kyr finished, astonished. 'This must be the riddle Saartho mentioned!'

'Well, I'll let you know if I see any odd towers in the woods,' said Vyktas. 'Now, can we get going? I want to reach Bellgard before we're old and gray. I'm starting to get sick of all this dried meat.' He patted the saddle bag that contained what little food they had left.

'You can't tell me you don't find reading the words of an Oracle of the First Age at least a little bit interesting, Vyktas,' Atlan chided.

He rolled his eyes. 'Oh, it's *fascinating*. It'd be even more fascinating in a chair instead of on a log. A chair with cushions! And a good glass of wine!'

'You'll look back at this and laugh one day when you're king, sitting around in a war camp in the rain.'

'My reign will be a time of peace,' Vyktas said smugly.

Kyr laughed, and in moments, Atlan and Vyktas were breaking out into laughter too. She found she much preferred it to their arguments.

'Come on,' said Kyr. 'Before we go, what's the full poem, riddle, whatever you want to call it, say?'

Atlan grinned, then flipped the page. He read the words aloud.

> *You will not find me in glades of plenty*
> *To seek me is to come up empty*
> *An era cleaves onward, ten and then twenty*
> *A tower, a knavery, and legend's envy*
> *Forgotten as I am, I slumber at the edge*
> *With ash as my sentry, to this end I am pledged*

'A tower, a knavery, and legend's envy,' Kyr repeated.

'Does it mean something to you?' Atlan asked, tilting his head toward hers as they huddled over the book.

She shook her head. 'No, I don't think so. I've heard bard's tales of a relic kept in a tower, but it's supposedly a map carved into stone that will lead you to riches, I doubt it's related to the Pentaculum.'

'Now there's something I'd spend all this time searching for. Where do these bards say it is?' Vyktas asked.

Kyr snorted. 'Didn't take you for a treasure hunter. Don't you have enough riches?'

Vyktas narrowed his eyes.

'Besides, it's in the Outlands. And all alleged, of course.'

'Too bad,' Vyktas murmured.

'I've never been this close to the Outlands,' said Kyr, turning her head as if on instinct in the direction of those distant cliffs that haunted travelers and listeners of bard's tales alike.

Monsters lurked there, it was said, and those who got too close often simply disappeared into the thick clouds that rolled off of them.

'I heard there are giants in the clouds,' said Vyktas, clearly distracted by the same sorts of thoughts.

'Have you heard of the wraiths that will drag you into caves along the cliff faces?' Kyr asked, one eyebrow cocked.

'If you two are done telling children's tales, I've found something interesting,' Atlan said.

'I wouldn't be surprised if you found the whole Spirits-damned book interesting,' Vyktas muttered.

'Listen.' Atlan gave him a playful shove and held the book out before them. 'The Histories tell us only a fraction of what the Pentaculum can do. The scholar's first pursuit should be the recovery of this artifact. It is no doubt the pursuit of those in power, and power needs the tempering of knowledge. Sentinel legend says it was created to preserve the world's magic when the Kharupani mage Eadr burnt the great cities of the First Age with his powers stolen from Solq . . . betrayed by his own Singer.' As he spoke those last five words, Atlan's face grew mystified.

'I've had just as many boring princely lessons as you,' said Vyktas, 'and I've never heard of him.'

Atlan shook his head. 'I haven't either.'

'Think I knew a guy named Eadr who sold *great* quail on a stick,' Kyr said thoughtfully. 'But I doubt it's him.'

Atlan and Vyktas both broke into laughter again.

'Doesn't that sound like a Yoren name, though?' Vyktas questioned.

'It does,' Atlan agreed. 'And his patron was Solq. Wouldn't that make him related to us? But he was Kharupani? How strange.'

'Kharupan's not far from Yorenth,' Vyktas offered, and Atlan nodded, still studying the page.

'If only we could ask Saartho,' Kyr sighed.

'Mm,' Atlan agreed. He ran his large, weathered hand over

the page. 'But he seemed to think this would tell us all we needed to know.'

'Will you risk a meeting with Vizier Rumail?' Vyktas asked him. 'He is quite learned.'

'He is,' Atlan agreed, 'but he is also beholden to our mother.' He snapped the book shut. 'He may be helpful to us, but at the same time, I wonder if it is not best if as few people as possible know we are there.'

Vykas nodded. 'Maybe ask Two-Trees? She might know more about Kharupan.'

'Good idea,' Atlan said, and Vyktas smiled. 'We certainly have plenty of time to ponder it.'

Kyr and Vyktas looked on as he stowed the book in one of their saddlebags. 'Come on. We'd best try to make for the pass today.'

40

ORIA

LYRA RUSHED INTO THE ROOM, a whirlwind of emotion on her face. 'I spoke to Mothril and came as quickly as I could. What happened?'

Mothril was likely already on his way to the Elders' chambers now to deliver her message to Sybil.

Oria rose, making her way to the windows. Leaning her cane against them, she ran her hand over its smooth, carved handle. Each time she used it, she couldn't ignore the thought of how much it disgusted her father to see her using it. How he saw it as reason enough to confine her to her room, too much an object of pity to be looked upon by others. Her nostrils flared with anger. Her cane was no curse, and she would no longer be his victim.

'Mothril tells me my father and the Elders may be conspiring against me. Not outright, but it seems he overheard my father speaking with some of the Elder-knights. He has no plans for me to become Prime, Lyra, and the Elders support him.'

'*What?*'

Oria nodded. 'His only concerns are for my visions and

protecting the Erángal. It all seems so clear to me now.' She turned away again, and her eyes fell. 'I feel so foolish, Lyra.'

'I can't believe he would speak so cruelly . . . and so openly,' Lyra replied. Her eyes darted back and forth, assessing, as they often did when she was thinking quickly. 'What are you going to do?'

'We're leaving,' she answered simply, surprising even herself. 'We're going to make it this time. Mothril is going to help us.'

Lyra bit her lip. 'Oria, I've heard stories of things he's done.' Her voice lowered. 'Did you know he's known as 'the Prime's Shadow'? It's creepy. What makes you think we can trust him?'

'It's just a feeling I have. I'm learning I need to listen to that more.'

Lyra walked over, placing a hand on her shoulder. 'Oria, this could be a trap. What if he betrays us?'

Outside, a light rain began tapping against the windowpanes.

Oria crossed her arms. 'Believe me, I've thought about it. But I don't get that sense from him.'

'You're good at reading people,' Lyra agreed.

Oria looked at her out of her periphery, thinking about how to bring up what Mothril had said. 'By the way, you know those sleeping draughts you bring me?' Lyra nodded. 'I broke one, and it—it didn't smell like jewel-dock.'

'You could *smell* it?' she asked, laughing.

'Y-yes,' Oria said, only half-convincingly. *How* did *Mothril smell it?*

Lyra sighed. 'Well, that's because it's not jewel-dock. It's false merryfern, a less common ingredient but with similar effects. It grows near the falls.'

Oria nodded. 'Ah.' She wondered why Lyra had never mentioned it to her before, though it seemed a harmless enough explanation.

Satisfied, she continued. 'Regardless, I want to know who we can trust and who we can't. I'm not abandoning our people, Lyra. We will return, once we understand my father's intentions.'

She nodded, smiling softly. 'You don't have to tell me that, Oria. You will return a Prime.'

Oria looked away—her voice growing small but firm. 'If I am worthy.' She returned to the bed, and Lyra followed, sitting beside her. 'Mothril says I am an Oracle.'

'He did?' Lyra reached out and held Oria's hand.

'Last night he told me stories he'd heard about a learned Sentinel woman. They called her Oracle too. She saw things others didn't, like me, and knew much about the world. She could even call upon the Fäendhmar. He thinks my father may be trying to rend the veil between worlds, something he would need a seer for.'

'What?' Lyra gasped. Her voice lowered almost to a murmur. 'Is that possible?'

Oria shrugged. 'Mothril seems to think so. He is so peculiar. One moment, I feel we are so alike, and another, it's as if he is from another world entirely.' She sighed.

'I can sense the tension between you at times. You know, I tried to keep him from entering the clearing—'

'I'm glad he did,' Oria interrupted. 'If he hadn't, I may never have learned more about Eildroth, about the true nature of my father's interest in my dreams, and about all Mothril knows.'

Lyra nodded, but her face looked less sure. 'What else do you think he knows?'

'I'm not sure. He says he learned all he knows about the Eradomin from his time as a knight-errant, or from books, but ...' She paused, considering her words. 'One of his first nights as my guard, I offered him something to read and he couldn't have been less interested. So many things about him seem to contradict themselves. I know there is more to him than he lets on. He finally told me he is keeping secrets—he told me he would tell me the truth, but . . . I don't know.'

'When?' Lyra asked.

'After he overheard my father's conversation.'

Lyra nodded.

'All I have is trust.'

Lyra sat silently with her for a long time.

'It will be okay,' Lyra said, stroking Oria's hair.

She lay there and tried to believe her.

————

They were awoken sometime later by Mothril's return.

Oria rose with a start at the sound of her door opening. 'Were you able to speak with Sybil?'

Mothril frowned. 'No. Sybil has been with the Prime all evening. I waited, but they and several other Elder-knights are still meeting. I wasn't able to learn much, but from what I over-heard of the knights gathering at the gates, something has happened to the Far Clans. Something bad.'

'What?' Oria was stunned. 'Were the knights not able to find them on the road? My father said all was well!'

'I know nothing more,' he said regrettably.

Lyra, dumbfounded, was trying to make sense of all he was telling them as well. 'I should go down there. See what I can find out.' Oria looked at her and nodded.

'Whisp—Oria,' Mothril began, 'have you ever tried to look into past events?'

Oria could not hide her surprise. 'I am gifted when it comes to my family's sight, but the past?' She shook her head. 'No, I cannot do that. Can anyone?'

Mothril leaned against her bedpost. 'I would stake much on the likelihood that you can do a lot more than you think you can, Whispess. Do you remember the way skies opened during the rite? *You* called that storm. And when you calmed, the rain stopped.'

Oria looked at him curiously. She was remembering a fair spring day, nearly forgotten now to the obscurity of reminiscence. A peaceful afternoon with her mother. She'd been thirsty, so Oria cupped her hands and, wordlessly, they filled with freshwater to drink. Her mother, Felith, had seen it and chuckled. 'Ah, you've discovered a little trick, have you?' Oria had been only seven or eight then.

Mothril tried again. 'What you can do extends far beyond seeing ahead. The Oracle of Yoren—'

Oria felt the weight of so many thoughts collapsing in on her. 'Mothril, it's not possible.'

'You can,' he urged. 'You already have.' When she looked at him with doubt, he added, 'I know you don't remember the rite well, and would like to think about it even less . . . but some of what you said you saw could not be happening in the present. It must've happened in the past.'

'Like what?'

He hesitated, looking at Lyra, who was still lingering in the doorway. 'There are no Eradomin blood rituals still occurring.'

Oria's eyes widened. 'You know of their rituals?'

His eyes shifted between Oria and Lyra again. 'Yes. I witnessed one. But Whispess, the Eradomin are gone—'

Oria was filled with so many questions it frustrated her. She took a deep breath, clearing her mind. 'That may be, but what I saw—it didn't feel like the past.'

Mothril's face was unreadable.

She continued. 'Regardless, this isn't what we should be focusing on right now. We still need to speak with Sybil.'

Mothril nodded. 'Of course. I will find Sybil after tomorrow's meeting with the Elders. We know she's sympathetic to you, so I'm hopeful she'll be forthright.'

Oria's eyes fell. 'That's if my father has even let her in on all that he knows...'

'True,' he conceded. 'Still, it's our best opportunity. She is part of his inner circle. We just need to get an idea of what we're dealing with so we can be prepared.'

She figured she must've looked unsure because Lyra gave her a reassuring nod.

'Oh, I brought you this,' Mothril said. 'It's only a fraction of your old collection, but it's one I think may be useful.' He handed her a small, clothbound book.

A book of Eradomin poetry.

Oria looked up at him, then opened it to the first page, with Lyra taking a few curious steps back into the room.

'An epic?' She flipped through several pages. 'Fascinating. It mentions Eildroth too,' she added, trying to hide the trepidation and fear the name caused her.

'It's all in Borean Poet, so it may take some time to understand its true meaning,' added Lyra, leaning over her to study its pages for a moment. She headed back toward the door. 'Alright, I'm going, I swear.'

Oria smiled at her.

'I speak Borean Poet,' Mothril said abruptly. That made even Lyra pause at the threshold.

'*What*?' Oria cocked her head.

His gaze flickered down her face as he spoke. '*Laifdirge lay a-mona, sideren lay o-sylfhares.*'

Lyra raised her brows, then disappeared out into the hall.

'What does it mean?'

Mothril looked away, out the wall of windows. 'It's just a proverb.' He didn't explain further, not about the meaning of the proverb or how he knew a Northern dead language.

Another one of his mysteries, Oria supposed.

'Well, that will make this a lot easier,' she said with a grin. She put the book down. 'Thank you, Mothril. For everything.'

He cleared his throat. 'Think nothing of it, Whispess.'

'Oria, not Whispess. We're friends, aren't we?'

He nodded. 'Oria.'

She sat back against the headboard and opened the book, then looked up at him again and patted the space on the bed next to her. 'Won't you come be my translator? Maybe we'll learn something together.'

He looked from her to the bed, then slowly made his way around the footboard. When he reached the other side, he began pulling off pieces of his armor, letting them drop to the floor with heavy, hollow thuds.

The bed sunk under his weight, and she watched him as he neared her, reaching across to light the candle beside the bed from the wall torch. There was something heady to it—his tousled white hair, so close it almost brushed her face, the thick silence of crickets, her bed creaking. She braced herself for him to pull away, but instead, he nestled his bulk against her and looked down at the book in her hands. Oria smiled beneath the screen of her hair.

The night deepened as they read, and Oria felt the most at peace she had since before the citadel, curled up in her blankets underneath glittering stars. When one of them found something of note, they marked the passage so they could confer later.

Lyra was with her when she'd been struck by her first vision. They were gentler then, just vivid dreams at first, followed by waking memories that weren't hers, and finally, reveries that transported her to other places entirely. She thought of Lyra as she read and wondered what she'd done to deserve such a friendship. Then she looked through her periphery at Mothril, felt the slow rise and fall of his chest against her, and wondered how she'd gotten lucky enough to have a guard who didn't see her as something to be kept, but as herself.

Oria, the friend.

41

KYR

THE HORSE'S hooves smacked against the muddy, sodden ground. They'd left camp early, following the ridgeline up beyond the cliffs overlooking Bellgard at Kyr's suggestion. She hadn't traveled to Bellgard in years, but the one time she did, Sylas had them avoid the lower road to its gates. At the time, he'd said it was swarming with bandits. They weren't traveling with precious cargo this time, unless you counted the princes, she supposed, but none of them wanted to take the risk.

'We're far from Yorenth now,' said Vyktas, looking down over the misty valley below. 'I didn't know a place could be so green.'

Kyr nodded. 'Bellgard was built here because of the oasis. That, and the port is the first stop for ships from Saeria.'

'You've traveled a lot, Kyr,' Two-Trees said.

'More than most from the Sledge, that's for sure.' When Two-Trees cocked her head, Kyr added, 'The poor district of Yorenth.'

She wondered what Vasha would think if he could see her now, traveling the same road she'd taken with him and Sylas, only now with the royalty of Yorenth.

She found herself smiling affectionately. Even with their sad ending, she would always think of Vasha fondly and hope that she got to see him again someday. She reminisced on all the nights sitting across the card table from him, laughing. Fenrow was in those recollections, too, and even that couldn't dampen her mood. *Strange what a little time and distance does to memory.*

'What about you, Vyktas?' Two-Trees asked, pulling beside him.

Behind her, Atlan had been silent for most of the ride. She slowed their horse's pace, falling behind Old Tom and Vyktas's white mare, then glanced over her shoulder. 'You alright back there?'

'Fine. Why?'

'It's nothing, really,' she said, squinting off into the distance. 'Just wondering if you wanted to talk.'

'Oh, you mean about the other day?'

Kyr nodded. 'Are you embarrassed to tell me you've never been with a woman or something? You know, I could help you.'

'I've been with a woman,' he grunted.

'What is it, then? You get your heart broken?'

'It's not that,' he said, the tension in his voice rising.

'Listen, I won't press you, but you can talk to me. You know that, right?'

When he didn't answer, Kyr twisted in the saddle to see him ignoring her entirely, looking out at the forested mountains dominating the sky to their left.

They were rolling and scabrous with stone here, old as time itself. Among them, a sharp spine of rock, bristling with pines. It was probably a day's ride away.

'What are you looking at?' she asked.

'I think I see something.'

She stopped their horse and whistled ahead to the others. 'What is it?'

Following his gaze, she saw nothing but the endless verdant expanse. Ahead, Vyktas and Two-Trees stopped their mounts.

They felt it before they saw it.

The ground beneath them began to rumble, quaking as though a giant was stirring beneath their feet, deep within the earth. All was deathly silent, eerie for such boundless wilds.

Then high-pitched wailing cracks rang out, as the distant rocky spine splintered to pieces. A crash like a thunderclap startled the horses as birds fled the surrounding trees in droves.

Kyr looked just in time to see the ridge Atlan had been looking at *move*. A cloud of rubble erupted, sending sheets of thick dust billowing in their direction. Trees cracked and twisted apart, brushed aside as though they were only grass. She could only stare, mouth agape. Atlan cursed under his breath.

The mountain crest, alive, slithered behind another peak like the spine of some massive beast.

'What in the fucking Six was that?' Kyr cried out, a thrill and terror coursing through her in equal measure.

Two-Trees turned back, circling them. They could hear trees being ripped apart in the distance, the beast carving its path, though they could no longer see the monstrosity.

'It almost looks like a mountain wyvern but it's far too big, and . . .' Two-Trees's eyes assessed where the creature had gone —a massive gap where an entire range had been now lay bare, the forest on either side left in ruins.

'*And?*' Vyktas urged, fear and hysteria palpable in his voice.

'And they're not usually *made* of the mountain,' she added.

Kyr had felt more in awe than worried until she saw the look on Two-Trees's face as she said this.

The intense rumbling returned, and the horses staggered back.

'They're going to bolt,' said Atlan, voice low and determined.

Kyr nodded her agreement. 'Ride for the mouth of the pass!'

They set off at speed, the trees flying past in a blur of green. Kyr chanced a look behind her to see a flash of color that had to be Vyktas's yellow cloak.

She heard Two-Trees yell something indistinct, but everything was moving entirely too fast, even sound itself. Navigating the narrow mountain path at such speed, she knew, was flirting with death.

As she looked ahead, her periphery caught a massive black shape overtaking them. Not a shadow, but a mass of stone. They took a bend in the mountain path quickly, looking up to see the enormous wyvern-like creature diving over them through the air, its gaping maw filled with rows of jagged stone teeth.

It had white mist for eyes, its underbelly made of mountain shale, enforced with rocky, plated scales. Pine trees, dangling roots and all, clung to it desperately as it flew with remarkable grace through the air.

Kyr tucked her head down. 'Fuck, fuck, fuck!' she repeated, over and over, under her breath.

'Eloquent as ever,' Atlan murmured, crushing her beneath his weight as they ducked under a tree fallen from high up on the bank to their right.

It made Kyr laugh, steadying her. The wyvern came to land somewhere off to their left judging by a second powerful reverberation in the earth.

The trees passing by began to change from the jagged shapes of pines to tufted, scrubby lowland forests, and Kyr knew they were nearing the end of their descent.

'We're close now.'

'Where is it?' said Atlan, frantic.

They turned a sharp corner in the path and Kyr gasped. She nudged her elbow backward. 'Atlan! Look!'

He said nothing, just stared ahead into the abyss before

them. At its edges, it looked like one massive shadow, but it quickly overtook them, enveloping them in something akin to dusk itself. It had been just after midafternoon when they reached the peak.

Kyr and Atlan exchanged a glance. This was no natural nightfall.

Behind them, Vyktas cried out.

'Stop!' Atlan yelled, and Kyr pulled hard on the reins. Their horse skidded to a halt.

They circled around, but the darkness had closed around them completely. Nonetheless, Atlan was off the horse in an instant.

Kyr could only hear fragments of his frantic voice as he disappeared deeper into the gloom.

'Vyktas! Where are you?'

In mere moments, they had lost the path completely, and Kyr realized the darkness was falling from the sky, like rain or snow might.

Well, at least that's how Kyr expected snow to fall. She had never seen it except in paintings.

She cocked her head and reached out her hand, trying to catch one of the drifting particles. When she touched it, her hand lost color, as though these strange flecks could devour all light.

Their horse had run off some distance, so Kyr made her way up the steep bend on foot in the direction of faint voices. If not for the sound, she might've worried she wouldn't be able to find them again, that the darkness had swallowed them all up, that they were lost to the Outlands, but then the faint outline of Two-Trees kneeling over Vyktas came into view.

Atlan was by his head, examining the blood gushing from his forehead. Vyktas's horse stood off to the side, nostrils flared, pawing the dirt.

'Is he alright?' Kyr asked.

'I think so,' Atlan replied, taking a piece of cloth Two-Trees had ripped from her robe and pressing it to his temple.

'He fell from his horse,' Two-Trees added.

'Enough,' Vyktas snapped, recoiling from them and spitting the blood that had seeped into his mouth out onto the ground. 'I'm fine. I can take care of myself.'

He snatched the cloth from his brother and collapsed backward onto the hillock with a sigh.

'He needs to rest,' Two-Trees said, rising to her feet. 'And we should check on the horses.'

Kyr nodded and stood too, and after a moment of hesitation at his brother's side, Atlan followed.

'What *was* that thing?' Kyr asked as they walked.

'I don't know,' said Two-Trees. 'The wyverns that inhabit the Outlands are large, but not like that.'

'It had teeth made out of rock!' Kyr shook her head. 'And now this?' She gestured to the blackened sky around them, falling in sheets of streaming inky motes.

Atlan turned to her. 'These must be more blights. Spirits, it's even worse here.' He looked up, shielding his eyes. 'We've heard stories of nights that never lift in the Free North, the earth coming to life like that—it would make sense that it's spreading. This is on a grander scale than anything we've heard reports of, though. I wonder if Bellgard knows about this. We're not far from their front gate now.'

Kyr turned to Two-Trees. 'Have you noticed anything different with travelers on the road. Any stories?'

Two-Trees shook her head. 'No, other than an increase in the number of travelers straying to the nullah. It's why I was so quick to set upon you. Two days before you arrived, a group of bandits came through, threatening to burn the forest down if we didn't give them what they wanted.' When she saw both Kyr and Atlan's faces, she added, 'They were no match for my sisters and I. The nullah defends.'

Atlan glanced down at her, thick brows raised. 'Impressive.' He turned skyward again, clearly as amazed by the sight as Kyr was. 'I'd say this is most definitely a kind of blight, but it's worrisome that not only are they spreading, they're growing in magnitude...'

Two-Trees looked troubled. 'It would make sense, if the road here is plagued with these blights, why the Misguided would come to our nullah in greater numbers.'

Ahead of them, the horses had gathered, huddled against the darkness. Old Tom stood regally, not unlike the yew trees at his back, some distance away. Atlan quickly approached his gelding, looking the spooked animal over.

Kyr sighed, ambling up beside him. 'It's too bad no one is going to believe me. This would make a great story at parties.'

Atlan and Two-Trees both looked at her like she was a lunatic. 'I mean, who's going to believe that I saw a giant mountain wyvern as big as the mountain itself. Made from it, too! Oh, oh, *and* it chased me into another realm where it was eternal night? It's a fairytale!'

Atlan half-smiled, then sighed. 'I think we have much to do before we'll be telling stories of this day.'

'You truly mean to stop these blights? And you think the answers lie in Bellgard?' Two-Trees asked.

'We don't even know if it's possible to stop them,' Atlan began sheepishly. 'I think we'd settle for understanding them.'

Kyr nodded her agreement.

'I see,' Two-Trees said thoughtfully. 'Vyktas is going to need some time to recover. The horses, too. Besides, I doubt we'll be reaching Bellgard today in this . . .'—she gestured to the darkness all around them—'I don't know what to call this.'

'We'll have to find the road again.' Kyr squinted past them into the darkness. She couldn't see much beyond the clearing's edge. 'When we took that last turn, I was just trying to avoid hitting a tree.'

Two-Trees began tending to their mounts. She gestured at Vyktas with her chin. 'I'll stay with him. Make sure he heals up well. Why don't the two of you scout ahead and see if you can find the way off this mountain?'

She looked at Atlan and lowered her eyes. 'And I'm sorry. I said I'd make sure you got to Bellgard safely, but—'

Atlan stopped her with a hand on her shoulder. 'Please. You couldn't have known there would be a creature like that. Thank you for taking care of my brother.' Two-Trees smiled back at him. 'If we're not back in a few hours, stay at camp until this blight clears.'

Two-Trees nodded and retrieved some herbs from her pack. 'I'd better get a poultice on that.'

They parted ways, with Kyr and Atlan heading down the slope, completely off the path now. They had no river to follow, no light to guide their path, but Kyr figured as long as they were heading downhill they were moving toward Bellgard and the Lower Road.

'Does it seem like the night is growing thicker here?' Atlan asked. His voice didn't sound nervous, just curious.

Kyr nodded. 'You read my mind. It's not an absence of light, do you see?' She waved her hand in front of her, and it disappeared. 'It's almost as if it's . . . made of something solid.'

As they walked, even the air seemed to thin, like they were still on a high mountain peak. Kyr pulled her cloak tightly around her. Her breathing grew labored and the urge to cough came on suddenly. She slowed.

Beside her, Atlan was shielding his eyes. He too had pulled his cloak around to cover his mouth.

Kyr held up her sleeve to her face, but it didn't help much. 'The darkness is so thick here, I can hardly breathe,' she managed.

Atlan didn't answer.

They continued onward, and Kyr tried to focus on her footsteps. *One foot in front of the other.*

After several coughing fits, after which she wiped gobs of blackened phlegm on her sleeve, she discovered that if she tucked her face deep into her cloak's collar, she could breathe easier. With barely any sight, Kyr peeked out through her hood to watch her boots crunch fallen leaves beneath them.

The longer they walked, the more she grew concerned that they were losing the light, too.

She looked up again and realized she could no longer see Atlan beside her.

Six. 'Atlan?' she called.

'I'm here!'

Shit. His voice was farther away than she'd expected. Was he ahead of her, or had he fallen behind somehow?

'Follow my voice!' she called out. She looked around. Ahead of her, weak white light was beginning to break through, as though she were leaving a cave and entering out into a new world. 'I think it's clearing up!'

Kyr began running.

'What the . . .'

Atlan's voice called out again, sounding even farther away. 'Where did you go?'

'I think I've found something!' she shouted back.

There, in the lonely clearing, leagues away from any village, stood a solitary tower.

42

MOTHRIL

MOTHRIL WAITED outside the meeting of the Elders, deep in thought.

He knew he should be focusing on his task ahead, but thoughts of the night before plagued his mind. If there were other books like that in the citadel, then Edril Sil unquestionably knew more than he was letting on about the Eradomin.

He knew what ritual he was attempting.

Mothril and Oria had stayed up well past midnight translating as many lines of the poem as they could. It was a history of Eildroth's conquests in battle. It told of their aftermath, ancient rituals which used the lifeblood of mages, augurs, and wisefolk to augment the Eradomin's ability to traverse the planes.

Edril Sil was doing something similar—the flavor of sorcery was different, her blood the conduit, but the purpose was the same. Oria had told him then about the ritual she'd experienced in her vision. Eildroth had done that. To *her*. Mothril throttled the pommel of his sword.

He understood why Edril Sil didn't want Oria having those

books. A careful reading could very well uncover his machinations.

The last time he'd spent any time considering Eradomin sorcery, he had been explaining some of its finer points to Lady Felith, just after she and her knights were attacked. The attackers fled without identifying themselves, and she was concerned they had been Eradomin, but Mothril had seen the ritual way in which they ambushed their prey.

'Unnatural,' many called it.

Lady Felith's curiosity about the feared warriors was insatiable. Mothril thought she almost seemed eager to have an encounter with them.

Leaves swirled around them on a fitful wind. Eradomin had come through this area recently, but the men who lay dead at their feet were no wind-walkers. Ordinary, petty bandits. Mothril watched as blood seeped from the eye of the one he'd just killed.

'Ghot, scion.' Rathwil clapped a hand on his back.

He said nothing, looking into his father's brown eyes. He was almost as tall as him then and becoming just as fearful of a fighter.

A woman descended the hillock toward them. Her ashen hair whipped around in the wind, almost the color of pure sunlight itself. She wore similar light-colored robes, and while her knights wore veils, hers was pulled down around her neck.

'I'm told I have you to thank,' she said, piercing him with her ice-blue eyes. 'My name is Felith of-Cailir. I'm also told you've lost your free order. Perhaps I could convince you to treat with my family. We lost many in the last year. We could take you in.' Rathwil looked her over, assessing. 'My husband will want to thank you,' she added.

'Aye,' his father replied, and began picking what he could off the dead. Felith furrowed her brow, bewildered by the sight.

'I suppose if you've been surviving out here this long you likely pick up certain habits . . .' She turned to him. 'I thought we'd been set upon by Eradomin.'

Mothril shook his head. 'No, we would've been no match for them—'

'I know,' she said. 'It's said they have incredible agility.'

'We lost our clan in an attack by them. It's like they say. They appear on the wind, and before you can even react, they're upon you.'

'I'm sorry,' she said. 'That must've been difficult. I'm grateful you two survived. I don't know what I would've done without you this day.'

Mothril shifted on his feet. He didn't know what to say. If his father hadn't noticed the mark on their barding, they'd have probably treated them like any other traveler they came across and their bodies would be floating downstream from the river crossing within the afternoon.

She spoke again. 'The men tell me you're of-Arcandras? Is that one of the Far Clans? We Cailirs have been isolated so long I know little of how the other clans have fared, or the families they've spawned under each banner.'

Mothril nodded. 'Yes, that's right. We have heard little of your clan, I admit.'

'That's a first,' she said, laughing. 'Most clans have heard of the Cailirs. Although, we haven't been involved in clan politics for some time now.' She let loose a breath. 'Either way, I'm indebted to you.'

'You are no such thing, Lady.'

She smiled warmly at him. It was the sweetest expression he'd ever seen, purely welcoming and kind.

A shuffling sound of Elders rising from prayer, voices murmuring, drew him back to the present. One by one, the Elders filed out of the room, their beaded blue cloaks and veils rattling. In the pale morning light, he thought they looked like wraiths.

These cloaks are so different from what the Far Clans wore. He wondered if the Cailirs always kept such unique customs.

Still, he recognized Sybil as she walked by, for she was the only one who kept her silver swords on her back, even during prayer.

'Sybil.' He grabbed her wrist, trying to be as non-threatening as he could manage, feeling the veiled faces of the others turn toward him. 'I need to speak with you.'

Sybil quickly pulled her arm away, offended. 'What do you want, you traitorous cad?'

Well, this is going to be a harder conversation than anticipated.

His voice lowered to almost a whisper. 'It's about the Whispess.' Instantly, she seemed to soften at that, her entire body uncoiling. 'Please. Come with me.'

Sybil nodded to the others, who turned, though not without long glances in his direction, and continued on their way.

'This had better be important. You're pushing your luck with this clan as it is.' She followed him behind a stone pillar, giving them at least the illusion of privacy in the airy hall.

'I come on behalf of the Whispess.' He had to be careful now not to call her Oria—it was far too familiar.

'She knows she can come to me herself. Why would she send you?'

'Because she's not allowed out of her chambers.'

'*What?*' Her voice rasped with shock.

'Edril Sil has her confined to her rooms—'

'You'd do well to speak of *the Prime* with more respect,' she scolded.

Mothril exhaled his frustration. 'I know you have no reason to trust me, but I have no motivations other than seeing the Whispess safe.'

Sybil sighed, looking away. 'What is it that you want?'

The Cailirs, and in fact all Wiccars, very much valued their personal autonomy. They viewed it as part of their bond with the natural world and the Fäendhmar. Much like inhabiting fortresses, locked doors were anathema to them.

He chose his next words carefully. 'The Whispess despairs, cut off from her kin. She desires an audience with you, but even you would not be allowed past the guards the Prime has posted at the entrance to the family's chambers. That is why she sends me as emissary.'

She studied his face through her veil, weighing his intentions. 'You speak true?' Her voice wavered with concern.

'We believe the Whispess's life may be in danger. These rituals are clouding the Prime's ability to see clearly.' He lowered his voice. 'Her injuries, the rituals—there is dark magic at work.'

Sybil crossed her arms. 'Dark magic? How would a lowly Ronin boy know anything about that?'

Footsteps echoed at the other end of the hall and he paused, waiting for them to fade into the distance before continuing. 'I don't. I'm just the messenger. A messenger whom the Whispess trusts.'

Elder Sybil was silent, considering. Her tone was measured. 'What does the Whispess mean to do?'

Mothril let the words Oria had given him flow easily from his lips. 'She wishes to leave the citadel. Only temporarily. Once certain that the Whispess is no longer at risk, she and her closest supporters will seek council with the Prime.'

Sybil's body, which had been tensely coiled like a warrior ready to spring, seemed to relax a bit at that. 'I see, I see.' She began nodding. 'And where will the Whispess go to collect herself?'

Mothril studied the Elder-knight, assessing her intention behind the question. He thought she seemed genuinely sympathetic.

'The Whispess hasn't revealed that to me. Her need lies with ensuring that the way is clear. Can she entrust this to you? With discretion, of course.'

Sybil's veil bobbed in a nod. 'I'm glad to see your faith in the Whispess has grown.' There was a poised and knowing quality to her voice. 'Say no more. I well understand the quarrels between father and daughter. The Whispess can trust me.'

43

ATLAN

THEY STOOD at the base of the ancient sandstone tower and gazed up at it. Behind them and about at a distance of ten armspans, a wall of darkness surrounded the clearing.

'Do you really think this is it?' Kyr questioned, staring up in wonder.

Before he could answer, she loosed a gob of pitch-black spit into the grass, then unsheathed the sword at her side and began clearing away overgrown brush that wrapped around the tower like a sleeping wyvern.

'I don't know,' he called to her, 'but the inscription matches. It has to be, right?' Atlan ran a hand down the roughhewn stone. At his feet was a piece of crumbled mortar. He bent at the waist, picking it up, then tossed it beyond the bounds of the tower into the gloom.

The stone struck the nightfall's edge and disappeared completely, as if sunk beneath the surface of a midnight pool.

Kyr had made her way around the entirety of the structure now, and rejoined his side. 'Why else would there be a tower here? That poem from the Book of Primes . . . it's uncanny.'

The quiet, the emptiness of the clearing, it seemed a trick or a vision. Atlan had kept up a vigilant watch from the forest edge, but no wraiths, giants, or other monsters issued forth. Nothing lay in wait or lured them closer. It seemed otherwise to be an ordinary tower.

Kyr showed him to the burled, redwood door on the other side. Profoundly furrowed and covered in brambles, it was obvious not a soul had touched it in many years, perhaps even centuries. Atlan glanced at Kyr, who quickly returned a knowing look that she shared his sense of apprehension.

Atlan and Kyr surveyed the height of the tower. Far above, he could make out the edge of a weathered red tiled roof, and just below it, a chamber at the top that was open to the air.

Strange place to keep a mythic relic. The whole glade was unassuming yet otherworldly in its still beauty.

On the door there was no knob, nothing at all to suggest the door could even still be opened.

'How do we get in?' he wondered aloud.

'Better not be another damned spelled lock,' Kyr muttered. 'I haven't had great luck with those over the past months.'

Atlan leaned in, running the palm of his hand over the door. Nothing but mundane wood.

He walked around the side of the tower, studying it further. Each sandstone brick was roughened and worn—chiseled by hand. He ran his hand across each of them, too.

Somewhere, he heard a thud.

'Damn thing.'

'Kyr, are you kicking the door?' he called back.

'No!' she answered, rather suspiciously.

He chuckled, leaning against the tower. Where he placed his hand, the bricks shifted, suddenly falling inward with a jolt. Atlan startled backward, nearly sending himself to the ground.

'I think I've found something!' he yelled.

Kyr's footsteps came running, and he yanked the brick out of its slot. It fell to the ground with a thump.

'You broke the tower?' Kyr accused.

He looked over at her with a sarcastic eye. 'No, look,' he said, turning the massive piece of stone over and motioning her closer. 'It's engraved.'

'It's the key . . .' Kyr whispered.

Atlan turned it over in his hands, brushing it off.

'It's the same inscription from the Oracle's notes!' She pulled out the Oracle's notes from their pack and flipped to the page with the poem.

'Maybe we really should be praying to the Spirits more,' Atlan grumbled.

Kyr laughed, but it had an undone edge to it. 'What if it doesn't work?' she said, turning to him. Still, Atlan knew he and Kyr were much more concerned that it *would* work.

She held her hand to the warped wood, just as the translation described, and recited the matching passage from the Book of Primes, the same one they had wondered at only days earlier.

The door thrummed with an ancient power, clicking as it unlocked itself, and rasped open. Stale air rushed out of the chamber.

Kyr and Atlan exchanged a wary glance.

'Last chance to turn around and forget we ever saw a creepy, lone tower in the woods,' Kyr offered.

Atlan chuckled and put a hand on her shoulder as he walked past. They had come too far now to turn back without finding out what secrets this place was hiding.

He peered inside. It was a small square room, completely empty except for a looming sandstone staircase that wound upward. Oil torches lined the walls, but they had long since burned down to nothing and were covered in cobwebs.

Kyr wandered in behind him, her gaze pulled around the dim space. She ascended to a landing farther up, still straining to see. 'It looks like there's a door in the ceiling,' she called down to Atlan, who began bounding up the steps toward her.

'How has no one found this place?'

He was asking himself the same question.

The way they'd stumbled upon the tower—still panicked by the forest blight and fleeing the descending night—he wasn't sure they could really say they had even found it themselves. Instead, he had the distinct sense they had been drawn to it.

With this place not far from Yorenth, Bellgard, and Quormanth, and with his mother's penchant for conquering, it was hard to believe there was such a place anywhere that had been left undiscovered by either the Sun's Own or Sentinel forces.

Sure enough, however, they had already been here at least an hour and the entire forest surrounding the tower appeared totally deserted. He'd heard no sounds the entire time they scoured the clearing, nor any sign of civilization nearby.

There wasn't even any birdsong. As he thought of it, Atlan hoped that wasn't a harbinger of something worse to come, but he had to admit he felt oddly safe in this place.

They steadily climbed several flights of steps, reverent of the age-old energy that seemed to linger there. As they reached the top, they came to the door in the wooden ceiling Kyr had spotted from below.

The space was cramped and both Atlan and Kyr stooped under its low height. The hatch door was affixed with nothing but a simple iron latch and a carving of an eye.

An eye?

There had been several sketches of eyes on one of the pages in the Oracle's notes. He made a mental note to reexamine that section later.

Atlan unbolted the latch and drew a deep breath before giving the door a heave. Next to him, Kyr cringed as if waiting for something to happen.

Nothing.

Soft evening light streamed through the open hatch, illuminating patches of the stairwell. They waited another moment.

Kyr chewed on her lip. 'Alright, I can't take the suspense anymore.'

She poked her head through the door. Atlan could see the whites of her eyes grow from below where he stood.

'What is it?'

'Uh . . . th-there's someone . . . here . . .' she whispered, still staring straight ahead.

'What do you mean there's someone here?' Atlan yanked on her waist, and Kyr stifled a yelp as she was pulled back into the tower stairwell.

She glanced wildly back up at the hatch. 'I don't know. I think—I think they're sleeping.'

Thoughts raced through his head. 'That's not possible,' he whispered, trying to keep his voice quiet, but failing miserably. 'You saw the door. No one has gone in or out in ages. That latch was rusted shut! And we're in the middle of Spiritsdamned nowhere!'

Kyr shot him an exasperated look. 'See for yourself!'

Atlan braced his arms on the trapdoor and climbed through. This was an old bell tower, he realized, and the chamber they had seen from the ground was the belfry. A large, deeply tarnished bell hung impressively from the ceiling, but there was no rope, and the tongue of the bell was missing, either rusted out or removed.

Kyr clambered up after him, pointing frantically at what was unquestionably a sleeping figure.

'What do we do?' she whispered.

Atlan looked at his friend with wide eyes and shrugged, turning back to the person suddenly as they shifted on a makeshift bedroll of straw. The stranger let out a long breath and continued dozing soundly.

Atlan and Kyr froze, watching the sleeping figure for several minutes as they weighed their options. From what he could tell, they were well-muscled and had a strong, healthy build, so they must have a way to leave the tower to find food and water.

A hunter? That was his first thought.

A coil of long, braided red hair was peeking out over the worn burlap blanket the figure covered themself with. Atlan thought the ends of their hair looked as if it was cut crudely, like with a blade.

He hoped this stranger would be able to illuminate their current predicament, or at the very least, let them go peacefully on their way.

Red light crept across the shadowed belfry, and Atlan could see distant mountains from this vantage through the thinning darkness. It was the setting sun, he realized.

What time was it?

Kyr finally moved to approach the figure. Atlan took position on her right.

Suddenly the shadows around them began to dissolve and move, swirling magnetically to the sleeping figure, who turned over on the bedroll.

The figure's eyelids fluttered open, revealing cloudy white eyes.

44

KYR

'WHO ARE YOU?' Atlan commanded, staring back at the unblinking, unmoving stranger.

He was already in a fighting stance, one hand gripping the pommel of his sword as he watched them through whorls of shadow which clung to them like a swarm of bees.

'And what manner of power is that?' Kyr murmured.

Through the thickening shadows, the stranger moved to sit upright on their worn and dirtied bedroll.

They looked to be quite young, no older than early into their second decade. And those pale eyes, perhaps they were blind?

Kyr was surprised by the cherubic quality of their face, their full cheeks and calm, youthful expression. Their skin was near colorless, as if they were rarely exposed to light, and yet they looked strong. She now noticed the dagger at the stranger's waist, tucked amongst burlap rags and a long, light gray wool cloak with several moth-eaten holes in it.

'I'm sorry,' Atlan said carefully, drawing Kyr from her daze, 'we thought—' She glanced over at him, and saw that he was making similar assessments.

The stranger cut him off.

'You are here, interrupting my sleep, and you do not know who I am?' Their voice was lilting and hoarse, as if they did not speak often, as if they had nearly forgotten the act.

The shadows encircling them revealed more now, displaying almost a sentience. Kyr had the sense they were *obeying* the stranger's command.

She took a step closer and the darkness parted around her. At last, Kyr realized it was not shadow, nor nightfall they were beset by, but thick plumes of ash.

'You have the Book of Primes, I hope,' they said, clicking their tongue and giving them a pointed glance, though Kyr could not tell exactly who their eyes were looking at. 'You must, seeing as you got in.'

'We—'

Atlan gave Kyr a not-so-subtle nudge, likely wondering exactly why she was telling this mysterious stranger about the most important item they carried. Atlan anxiously cut in, 'How do you know about that? We seek the Pentaculum. Do you know of it? We were sent by Saartho Ulam of Yorenth to retrieve it.'

'I do not know of whom you speak,' they said, brows knitting together. Kyr forced her gaze away. She had never seen anyone like this person before—strong and yet soft, commanding and yet gentle.

'Surely you must know Yorenth, it's the largest sovereignty on the continent.' Their face took on an almost humorous expression, and they shook their head. 'You do not know of—'

'I do not enjoy being called 'it,' you know. I have a name.' They sighed. 'It seems my father did a better job concealing my existence than I thought.'

'I'm sorry, I don't follow. Your father is . . . ?' Kyr asked, confusion blooming on her face.

'Edril Sil. The Moth Prime, the Usurper Mage? You have heard of him, at least?'

Atlan's eyes widened. Kyr noticed, the expression so unusual for the prince, and asked, 'Who is he?'

The stranger shook their head and *tsk*ed disapprovingly.

Atlan looked at her. 'Remember what Saartho said? He leads the Wiccar clans in the Free North.'

'He's a puddle of Riparus' piss is what he is,' they went on. 'Locked me up in this tower and threw away the key. That's an ... expression. I think that's the term. Obviously, you know that there isn't a key to this tower, at least not the kind you are used to. I will be needing that book though. My sister is coming to get me. Yes, she is.' Their face broke into a distant smile as they looked up over the belfry's walls. 'Soon, starlings.'

'Edril Sil,' Kyr breathed, turning to him. 'I remember something in one of the books Saartho had me read before we left. It said his family created the Pentaculum and then hid it away so the Five Princes could not use its power for corruption in the First Age. You . . .' she looked toward the stranger. 'Are you—you're the Pentaculum?'

Atlan looked between them incredulously. 'That would mean they're nearly a thousand years old!'

Kyr shrugged and the stranger looked between them, vaguely amused.

Atlan shook his head. 'You said *he* locked you away here? That would make Edril Sil over a thousand years old too!'

And it would also mean that all the scholars' descriptions, all the rumors, every piece of knowledge that they had managed to dig up about the Pentaculum was wrong, all this time.

'The Pentaculum is . . . a person?' he breathed.

'Oh, indeed,' they said, still smiling faintly. 'It's a rather silly name though, isn't it? Let's go with . . . Penta. Less of a mouthful, too. I am certain I had a true name once, but I do not remember it.' They sighed. 'It matters not. You have reunited me with the Book of Primes. I will follow you now, as it must be.' Ash continued to flutter in the air around them. 'But first, we must wait for the arrival of my sister. She is coming to get me. Yes. She is. She must be right behind you. It's odd, I didn't foresee the two of you.'

'Your sister? Foresee?' said Kyr, the space between her eyebrows creasing. 'Listen, we've come a long way, and—'

'Yes, I saw it in my dream. She was me, and I was her.'

Kyr raised her brows. 'Right . . . listen, we don't have the Book of Primes, only the Oracle of Yoren's notes on it. The Book of Primes was lost in a fire, probably before I was even born.'

Ash exploded around them with a fury so drowning in its power, so overwhelming, that Kyr instantly inhaled a lungful and began coughing harshly.

'*Atlan*?' she choked.

She heard only a deep, hacking cough in response.

The darkness grew and grew, so thick the belfry disappeared around them, until Kyr felt she had been swept up in another realm entirely. A realm of pure darkness, in which the world as she knew it no longer existed. She wept and gasped and tried to shield her eyes. The darkness *burned*.

'Penta!' Atlan roared, but his plea was quickly drowned out. They were each becoming lost.

'Penta, *please!*' Kyr shouted. 'We'll—we'll take you to your sister!'

Then, as swiftly as it had overtaken them, the ash dissipated, and Kyr squinted to find Penta braced over the stone, breathing hard and fast.

'I-I'm sorry. I don't know what came over me.' Their eyes looked peculiarly less clouded to Kyr. 'The Book of Primes was lost? It's too late?'

The sadness lining their face struck Kyr's heart.

Penta was clearly strong, powerful and ancient, and yet

when Kyr saw their eyes in that moment, she only wanted to
care for them.

'Too late for what?'

'My father did it. He killed her.'

Atlan still stood frozen in shock and confusion beside her,
so Kyr went and knelt down by Penta. She held out her hand.
'Killed who?'

Penta placed their hand in Kyr's. 'My mother.'

45

ORIA

FROM THE WINDOWS of her room, Oria looked out upon the
entirety of her world—the distant teal waters, the pines
drooping and dripping with water from the storm the night
before, the rocky foothills and gray skies clotted with clouds.

Not my view for much longer, she hoped.

She frequently went back and forth with how she felt about
leaving. Escaping. Mostly she still felt overwhelmingly guilty
that she was not fulfilling her duties to the fullest. But during
the long, painful, and lonely nights she knew she was doing the
right thing. If she just had a little room to breathe, a little time
to recover, she could think clearer and be the seer her clan
needed.

I will return, she promised herself.

Her dreams and visions over the past month ran through
her mind. That curious waking vision of that strange forest
creature, the dreams that were like memories. She'd been a
prince in one of them, she was sure of it. It was there in how she
remembered the weight of a crown on her head, the confidence
with which she walked.

Then, in another, she'd been someone even more powerful

than a king. A mage, a skilled one. She was nimbler, an adept, and knew things beyond the scope and span of a normal life. Communing with magic, that's what felt so familiar. And in that dream, she knew whoever's eyes she was seeing through was reaching out to her somehow. Their connection had severed only moments after waking.

Oria breathed deeply in an attempt to calm her racing mind.

Another reason to be free of this place. She needed peace to sort through her memories, to figure out what they meant for her and the clan.

The door creaked open behind her. 'Oria?'

'Lyra,' she said softly, turning to face her oldest friend.

'Mothril is on his way back. I saw him talking to Sybil, and I think it went well.'

'Why does this feel like I'm sneaking around, going behind my father's back?'

Lyra crossed the room. Oria looked at her, her heart-shaped face and long, wild hair that framed it.

'Because you are,' Lyra answered simply. She matched Oria's worried look with one of sympathy. 'Because he's left you no choice. Whether you were Whispess or not, our future Prime or not, you are important, Oria. Not because of who you are or what you can do, but because you're you. My friend.'

Oria was surprised by the tears that began to well up in her eyes. To hear such a thing spoken aloud—she looked away.

Lyra went on, looking out across the citadel grounds. 'Do you remember that time we collected dandelion leaves for your mother, thinking we were helping with her alchemy?'

Oria giggled. 'I do. We mixed them with a bit of water from the falls and called them potions.'

'You swore up and down they would help with everything from unrequited love to warts!' Lyra let out a loud, hearty laugh that made Oria laugh too. Lyra tucked a loose strand of hair behind her ear. 'You were happy then.'

'I was.'

'I want that again for you.'

She smiled. 'I want that again for both of us.'

She gripped her cane, kneading its handle against the painful scar across her palm. A new one from the last rite.

'Lyra,' Oria started hesitantly. 'I've been thinking about the risk you're taking in helping me. Of course I want you to come with me, but what about what you want, your family?'

Lyra nodded. 'I've thought about it too. I've spoken to my siblings. It wasn't easy, but I think they understand. My banner will watch over them.' She paused, smiling at her. Oria thought there was a tinge of sadness behind the expression still. 'Oria, we've been together through every celebration, every hardship, every sleepless night—I don't intend to stop now. I want there to be life in you again, in this place.' She turned back to the windows. 'I want our people to be happy again. I want all of this, not just for us, but for the old oaks in the forest, the fish swimming beneath the falls, the dandelions! It's this *world* I care about, Oria. It's more than what I want. It's what I need to do.'

'For the dandelions,' Oria laughed.

Lyra smiled. 'For the dandelions.'

———

Oria awoke sometime later to loud knocking at her door. Outside, it was night. Startled, she peeled herself from her blankets and furs, trying to straighten her hair as she sat back against the pillows.

'Since when do you knock?' she called out to either Mothril or Lyra. Then the door opened, and her smile fell.

Standing in the vestibule was her father. She thought how

lucky it was that she'd fallen asleep reading the book Mothril had given her, and now it lay hidden under the covers. His dagger sat on one of the bookshelves, and she fought the frantic urge to glance at it so as not to draw his attention there.

'Oh, father,' she said, bowing her head. 'I'm sorry, I wasn't expecting you. Please, come in.'

He wore long, beaded robes with armored gauntlets and sabatons. It was clothing fit for a king headed to battle, not what he usually wore meeting with Elders, meditating, or playing a game of dice with his old order around the citadel. His face was set with stern lines, and his deep-set eyes glittered in the low light of her ever-gloomy, cramped chambers.

'Don't trouble yourself,' he offered, almost cautiously. She furrowed her brow and turned to face him fully. She wasn't used to this—seeing him unsure of himself. 'I came to see how you were faring.'

'Better than last week, but not as well as I'd like,' she answered carefully.

Slowly, as if not wanting to scare a frightened animal, he made his way to the edge of her bed and sat down on it. Oria searched her father's churning blue eyes, framed by long, auburn locks of hair. Just like hers.

She often found herself looking at her father for signs of shared ancestry. In this moment, it struck Oria for the first time why she always did. She was looking for signs of common humanity in her father. Something in the lines of his smile or the crooked bridge of his nose that told her he was kin. That he cared about her. That he cared about the world the same way she did.

'I know I've been hard on you lately. I've asked much of you—'

Oria crossed her arms. 'I'm alright, father.'

He quirked a brow, his dubiousness accenting genuine sadness and concern. 'Are you?'

'What's brought this on?' she asked, feeling awkward. 'I'm alright, truly.' As much as it pained her to lie to him, she didn't feel she was lying to the father she loved. If he was in there somewhere, she hadn't seen him in some time.

'I regret my actions at the last rite. Then to take away your books when you were only craving understanding—as all good rulers should, might I add.' His lips drew momentarily into a thin line. 'I acted in error.' She eyed him, unsure of his motivations behind saying all of this. 'I fear a wedge has been driven between us. I know it's not been the same since your mother died.'

'I don't want to talk about Mother.'

It wasn't just that she didn't feel like examining such painful memories with her father, she didn't want to think about them at all. She hated remembering the sound of her mother's breath catching in her weakened lungs, or the way she begged for water at the end.

Oria had seen the aftereffects of battle. She was a child, but she remembered the camps filled with the injured, potent with the metallic odor of blood and vomit. She saw the families crying out for their dead brothers and sisters, their daughters and sons. It was horrible, but in some ways, sickness scared her more than anything she'd seen when they were warring with other clans or Northerners. Oria fingered her own freshly removed stitches and tried to ignore the ache in her hips that made her bedridden some days.

Her father still hadn't said anything. He just looked out into the night beyond. 'I came to tell you how much you mean to me. I know I ask for a lot from you, often with little in return. You've sacrificed the life you were owed. That of a healthy, young girl. You've experienced pain the same as any soldier might. It's time I repaid your sacrifice, even if it's only a modicum of it.'

Oria watched as he rose and went to the door, then

returned with a large piece of metal. It looked like a birdcage. 'It's a brace,' he said. 'I had the healers take measurements for it the last time you were there.'

When? she wondered. She had no memory of it. Had she been asleep?

'It will help you to walk, and you can wear it under your clothing.' She sighed. She knew she needed more than just her cane to help her get around, especially given her plans, but her father's motivations for giving it to her bothered her. She knew well enough from his bitter glances that he hated seeing her struggle to walk at times and how slowly she moved.

You can wear it under your clothing. It was a way of making her pain invisible.

Against how she felt, she smiled. 'Thank you, father.'

'I'll have one of the healers show Lyra how to help you put it on. Though that isn't the only reason I came.'

'Oh?'

'I've been thinking about the books you had.'

'Father—'

'Let me finish, Oria, please.' The words came out almost as a stutter, with emotion behind it her father rarely let show. 'I've been thinking. It's not fair to you how I've kept you in the dark. I thought I was protecting the sanctity of your visions.' He paused. 'I still think that. But you're my daughter, my only blood, and a better daughter than I could've ever hoped for.'

She couldn't help herself—a genuine smile crossed her face. 'It's time I bring you into the fold,' he continued. 'You're the one experiencing these visions firsthand, you should have the knowledge to help you understand them. Ask me what you want to know.'

Her expression faded to a look of poorly masked disbelief. She hadn't expected this.

'You mean this?'

He smiled warmly. 'Of course.'

She tried to imagine what that would be like, working with her father, instead of in secret against his wishes, and waited for the guilt to come now that Mothril had told her of his true plans.

Unexpectedly, the guilt never came.

Her father was too late.

Too many times, she had suffered without him, and now she trusted in Mothril and Lyra more than she ever could in him.

But that didn't mean she wouldn't use this as an opportunity to learn more about the inner workings of her father's reign.

She did not hesitate.

'We are all worried the Eradomin will return to this plane. I know they are skilled fighters, but are you so worried we cannot best them?'

He nodded, letting out a relieved breath. 'You were young when the war happened. They had long been our neighbors. We traded with them, practiced different religions peaceably, even intermarried once.' When she raised her brows, his lips spread in a smile. 'Long ago.'

How long ago? She had never heard of such a thing. Wiccars were long-lived, but her father was not *that* old.

As if he could read her mind, he added. 'Or so the stories go.'

'Regardless,' he continued, 'they turned on us. We still do not know why. They slaughtered Wiccars by the thousands. I think the bloodshed, those hard winter nights in the forests without our food stores or any supplies, they hardened me. They hardened all of us and,' he emphasized, 'it's why I sought the stability of this fortress for our people. That and your mother and her scouts had retrieved the Erángal. We needed a place to protect it.'

'Didn't you worry about changing our way of life

completely? We never lived in one place before.'

'Of course,' he said, more emphatically than she'd expected. 'But we needed the protection more than we needed our old way of life. It took some getting used to. Many of the Far Clans left rather than live this way. I fractured us, but I also had no doubt I was doing the right thing.'

He continued. 'When you become Prime, you'll need to make those choices too.' Now she let the shock show completely on her face. Her father laughed. 'Did you not think I was preparing you for the role? Of course I am, Oria.'

A nervous tension gripped her chest in a vise. Could she believe everything Mothril had told her? *Should* she? What if he had been mistaken in what he overheard?

'Anyway, occupying an old Eradomin fortress only angered them more. They were hurting by then, though. We'd mostly driven them from the area, and only occasionally came across rogue bands of fighters . . .' He scoffed. 'By Sarthura, they're all damned good at fighting, though, the brutes. At first, we thought we had killed many of them. It was later that Melsze and I discovered they were traveling between planes.'

She knew this about the Eradomin—everyone did, of course—but now she only wanted to know more. 'Why is it— *how* is it possible for them to do such a thing? Why can no one else?'

'Well, they'll tell you it's part of their religion. They follow only one of the Fäendhmar. Sarthura, we call her. Others call her Calligone. If I knew how to answer your second question, well, I'd be a Fäendhmar myself.' He waved a hand. 'According to them, she's imbued them with the power to lift the shroud between realms. They have these elaborate rituals of meditation which allow them to briefly reach a plane outside their body, and then . . . transmogrify themselves. It's why they move so quickly in combat.' His head dipped in a slight nod. 'Why we call them wind-walkers. It's a bit of a misnomer, we should call them shroud-walkers or veil-renders.'

This was more than her father had ever explained before. The questions that rose up within her were insatiable.

'Why are you telling me all of this?'

'It's as I told you,' he said casually. 'You're a Cailir. You deserve to know.'

She nodded. 'How did you discover that they were doing this—this traveling between planes?'

He seemed to be expecting her question. 'Melsze and I saw it happen, one day when we were out checking the watchtowers in the mountains. We thought it was just another small group of them wandering the wilderness. They hadn't spotted us, far below in the valley as they were. You can trap them, you know?' His eye took on a mischievous glint. 'They need a river crossing to travel. Anyway, they mounted their horses and took off at speed toward the river. We were curious about where they were headed, so we stayed and watched them. About ten feet from the water, they began to disintegrate, and then they disappeared completely.'

She must've had a dumbfounded expression on her face because he nodded. 'I saw it myself, Oria. Melsze was with me, along with Elder Rin, may she rest in the Longwilds.'

'Did I ever meet Elder Rin?'

He shook his head. 'No, she was before your time, I think. One of the best knights the Wiccars have ever seen. Damned good at dice, too.'

Something about hearing her father reminisce fondly about his days as an Elder-knight seemed so at odds with how imperious he'd become. 'So, you three discovered their secret?'

'We did. It gave us a greater understanding as to why they had begun to vanish, but it also meant that they weren't dead. It meant we had no idea of their numbers. The last time I met with their Abbot, he made it quite clear that they would never give up trying to see us destroyed.'

'Where did Mother retrieve the Erángal from?'

It was a change in subject, but Oria had the sense it was connected somehow to her father's worry about the Eradomin.

'Ah,' he smirked. 'I knew this question would come sooner or later.' His face took on a far-off look. 'Your mother was so uniquely determined, so special in so many ways. She had read about the Erángal, a relic from the First Age that contained hidden knowledge from kingdoms and rulers past. Of course, she couldn't let the idea of its existence go. She thought it would give us an edge against the Eradomin. Imagine my surprise the day she returned with it, saying it was in some dusty old crypt, or shrine or something, somewhere in the mountains.'

Oria mulled over all he was telling her. 'You don't have any theories as to why the Eradomin attacked us?'

'The greatest mystery of all. I have many theories, and I'm certain about none of them.' He gave her a tired smile. 'Perhaps their goddess prophesied something that required them to attack us, or maybe they simply grew tired of sharing their domain? I wish I knew. It would put my mind at ease about much.'

'So, *this,*' she said, gesturing widely with her hands, '*all of this,* is to defend against a civilization that hasn't been seen in years, that we were successfully defending ourselves against already?'

'We thought we were, but now we can't be sure.' He clicked his tongue. 'Oria, you may have witnessed some of the aftermath, but you did not see the slaughter the Eradomin are capable of in battle.'

Despite how her feelings had begun to change as of late, her father's words were still capable of making her ashamed, and she looked away. 'I know.'

'The Erángal has revealed things to me that I still cannot put into words. I do not know what it all means. The crux of it is this—if they were to return, it would be our end. That much is obvious. Old Era, named for the Eradomin, used to be an empire stretching across the entire continent. I know you like your books of poetry, but had you picked up some of those boring atlases in the library, you would see its former boundaries on the old maps. When I last spoke to Abbot Dymorra— admittedly, he was no longer any kind of leader by then, old and weathered as he was—he not only said as much with words, but he told me to go to the Erángal. Somehow, he knew we had it. I did as he said . . . I cannot begin to describe to you what I saw.'

He rose from the bed and began to pace before her. As she watched him, Oria wondered when the last time he had come to visit her here was. She was so used to seeing him addressing the Elders or telling war stories, but here in her room, he was just an ordinary man.

'Villages burnt completely to ash—it rained down so thick you couldn't breathe. War, pestilence, a world destroyed. It wasn't just our people, either. This is what lies ahead for us. I don't know how to stop it.'

Oria could hardly contain her disbelief. She hadn't expected her father to be honest with her, to actually want to involve her in the details of caring for their people, but it seemed he was. Not only that, but he was also telling her things he alone knew.

Could this be the truth?

'I see. This is a lot to take in.'

'I understand,' said her father, looking satisfied. 'I want to start involving you more in my decisions. It's only right after all you've done for us. I'm sure you feel overwhelmed with questions, and I intend to answer them as best I can moving forward.'

Oria did feel overwhelmed. She had also never felt more torn. 'I appreciate your candor, father.'

He nodded, then stood, and turned his back to her. 'I have one more thing to ask of you, my little Fäen. I am sorry. The knights we sent to scout the pilgrimage route found the Far Clans' camp, but they never returned. We don't know where they have gone.'

Oria's brow furrowed. 'They're missing?'

He turned back around, his eyes cast downward. 'I fear the worst. You know I wouldn't ask this of you if it weren't dire.'

Oria sighed, focusing on the flickering torchlight. 'Another rite?' she guessed. 'When?'

'Tomorrow.'

She nodded. Her father, clearly satisfied, must've thought he'd played her perfectly.

There would be no rite.

Oria waited for a sense of fear to assail her, but instead found only calm determination in its place.

46

ATLAN

KYR DROVE her elbow into Atlan's side as he looked back at the strange new addition to their traveling party.

'You're staring,' she whispered harshly.

Atlan whispered back, his voice growing more frantic with each passing word, 'Oh, *I'm* sorry for staring at the *ancient relic* in *human form* standing behind us who just told us they're a *thousand* years old, waiting for their mysterious sister they *saw in a dream* to come get them! Oh, and their father murdered their mother, so that's what we have to go on when it comes to their family! They guided us through blighted darkness with no apparent concern or difficulty whatsoever. Nothing strange or suspicious about it at all. *Nope.*'

Kyr chuckled. 'You have a point.'

In all directions, the green tunnel of woodland surrounded them. Penta strolled behind them at a short distance, the hood of their cloak hanging down over their face. Red braids fell from it as they looked down, deftly carving an apple with that blunted, old knife of theirs.

Atlan and Kyr had tried to glean more details about Penta's ominous mention of their parentage, but they were unable to remember much. They claimed that their mother was once a very powerful witch, and that Penta's father, ever the opportunist, wanted control of her power. Penta had tried to protect her but had ended up locked away in the lonely tower. The events that preceded that, though, they had no knowledge of.

'Between you and Penta,' Kyr had told him, 'I'm glad for once to have no parents.'

Now, Kyr rolled her eyes at him. 'I don't know how much to believe about any of that—clearly *something* magical in nature is going on with them. Living out there, the ash, of course we have no idea what we're dealing with. But *who* we're dealing with, at least as of right now, seems to be a lost soul looking for the only family they have left. We're right to help them.'

Penta had promised to come with them for safe passage to the North. They'd offered to take them to the old fortress, Castle Forlorn, that Edril Sil and his clan lived in, but Penta had been adamant they did not want to go there.

'I know, I know. I just worry.'

'You think too much, is what it is,' Kyr said, laughing.

'An understatement,' he muttered. 'I'm sorry if I've been distant these past few days—'

'Don't worry about it.' Kyr waved a hand. 'I can hardly even remember that after all we've been through.' She let the silence between them unfold, as if sensing that there was more he wanted to say. She *was* good at reading him.

He looked at her out of his periphery. 'Kyr, I-I have these . . . thoughts,' he began. Kyr's brow wrinkled. 'I—Spirits, why do I even say anything—I haven't been with a woman in a while, not because the offer hasn't been there,' he assured her, much to her amusement, 'but because it's . . . hard for me. I can't stop them from happening.'

'Is something wrong with your . . .' She glanced downward. 'You know.'

'*Kyr*,' he groaned.

'What?' she asked innocently.

'No, it's—it's like a . . . mental thing.'

Kyr opened her mouth to speak when they heard that uncanny, hoarse voice from behind them. 'What are you two talking about?'

'Nothing,' Atlan answered quickly before Kyr could make some remark.

She had one ready anyway. 'We were just discussing the different species of . . . snakes in this part of the continent.'

Atlan narrowed his eyes at her.

'Oh,' said Penta. 'Ghastly creatures.' Kyr smiled, nodding. 'I'm not too familiar with these lands, coming from the North.'

'Your father still lives there. How? I didn't know the Wiccars were so long-lived.'

'Some have lived for many years,' Penta said, nodding in agreement. Then their face shifted to an odd, puzzled expression. 'But . . . no, I can't remember. If he is still alive, it's unnatural, I promise you that.'

Atlan furrowed his brow. 'How is that possible? Alchemy?'

Penta's still-clouded eyes searched his face. 'I can't remember. I'm sorry.'

'You say your sister is coming for you. How do you know she isn't still with your father in the North? That—' Atlan swallowed. 'That nothing has happened to her?'

Penta nodded, an easy, absentminded look on their face. 'Ah, that I do know. I have a . . . friend, like me, in a way. Even older, actually. My mother saw my sister in a dream long ago, and she promised us she would look after her. She has—I can feel it in my bones, you see.' As they said this, they tapped on their prominent cheekbone.

'Alright, but *how* do you know it?' Atlan pressed.

'It's as I said. I can feel it,' they repeated, as if it were a common, obvious experience.

'Right,' Atlan said, unconvinced.

On foot, they neared the place where they had left Two-Trees and Vyktas. They found their bedrolls hidden in the brush, a common tactic for travelers but not one that was really necessary this far out from civilization. They hadn't seen a soul in days, and Atlan thought it odd how empty the world seemed out here.

They found the two of them by a nearby creek, sitting on its banks. Two-Trees sat on a rock in just a thin, thigh-length tunic. A beam of sunlight was streaming through the canopy and illuminating her form. For a mage, she looked surprisingly strong.

'Hey! You two!' Kyr called, grinning and racing down the bank. Atlan looked away quickly.

'You're back!' came Two-Trees's voice. 'We were starting to get worried.' Vyktas was wading in the water and splashed at Kyr as she drew near.

'Dastard!' Kyr yelped, recoiling from the water. 'What do you mean?'

'It's been two days at least,' said Vyktas. 'Hard to tell though, before the blight cleared.'

Atlan approached, and Two-Trees turned to him. 'As you can see, your brother is doing better.'

'Two *days*?' Kyr echoed.

He flashed a smile at Two-Trees. 'Thank you. I didn't realize we were traveling with such an accomplished healer.'

'It was really nothing.' Her smile was warm and knowing, as if amused by how little he knew about magic and healing. He had traveled, yes, but the world he largely inhabited, the world of Yorenth and its reaches, felt so insignificant now.

He took off his worn shoes and waded across the water to her. 'No need to be modest. It's very impressive.'

She looked at him askance as he sat beside her. 'You are really the most learned magician where you live?'

She was teasing him, he knew, and it made him smile. 'What if I told you I was the *only* magician?'

'Actually, that would explain much. Who is this?' she said, eyeing the new member of their company who had appeared from beyond the thick brush. Her face was cautious but not unfriendly.

'This is Penta,' said Kyr, smiling. 'We found them in a magic tower in the middle of nowhere.'

Vyktas whirled around to face where Penta stood on the other bank, watching the four of them. 'You're kidding,' Vyktas said flatly.

'Wish I was,' Kyr answered.

'*From the book?*' Vyktas said again, looking between Kyr and his brother. Atlan raised his brows, surprised his brother connected the name to the Oracle's notes so quickly. 'This journey grows increasingly cursed by the day!' He stumbled out of the creek bed and gripped Penta's arm—startled as they were. 'Well, Penta, it's nice to meet you.'

Penta looked at Vyktas shyly. 'I thank you for allowing me to travel with you. For not attacking a stranger, as many would. I need to find my sister.'

'Sister? The mystery deepens,' Vyktas said jadedly under his breath.

'I'm Two-Trees.' She stood and lifted a hand to cover the sun from her brow. 'You can call me Two-Trees or Teleri, if you'd like.'

'Teleri?' Atlan asked.

She looked at him and nodded. 'It's my given name, but we sisters don't use those often.'

'Why didn't you tell me?'

She shrugged. 'You never asked.'

Atlan felt a rush of embarrassment flush his face. He'd been so concerned with learning about the Pentaculum, getting away from his mother, and his and Kyr's magic, that he'd neglected getting to know the very people he'd been traveling with. He looked over at Vyktas, who was laughing with Kyr and Penta.

'So, where do you think your sister is?' Vyktas asked Penta. Atlan didn't know why, but he was surprised again by the interest his brother showed.

'I do not know. She was the one who was supposed to find me, not you,' they said, looking at Atlan and Kyr. 'Though I am just glad to be found. At the moment, I would ask nothing more than a place to rest my head.'

'We head to Bellgard then?' Kyr asked.

Penta nodded. 'Yes, I would like much to see how your cities have changed.'

The gates of Bellgard loomed large above them as they descended the rocky path along its outer walls. They'd left their mounts at the stable in the upper field and made their way to the city on foot, except for Old Tom, who had refused to go beyond the treeline.

Two-Trees, unwilling to enter the city, stayed with them, sleeping in the hayloft above the nearby barn. They tried heartily to convince her to come, but she refused. Atlan couldn't help but admire her strict adherence to her vow.

An old, rumpled blue flag fluttered in the wind high on the tower spire. On it was the city's emblem, an owl. Atlan noticed Kyr staring up at it and nudged her.

'You alright?'

'Fine.' She smiled at him.

He hadn't realized just how close to Bellgard they were, but with Penta's uncanny guidance they were able to find their way out of the forest and back on the road. They'd claimed not to have any familiarity with this land, but they made up for it with a seemingly innate knowledge of direction and tracking. When

Kyr asked Penta how they knew the way, they simply said they could see the whole forest. He'd never seen Vyktas so befuddled.

He turned to Vyktas now. 'So, is this the adventure you bargained for?'

'All that and more,' his brother answered with a smirk. 'I know I've been a burden to you on this trip, and in the past, but . . . *thank you* for bringing me, Brother.' Vyktas flung an arm over his shoulder.

Atlan felt a swell of something unfamiliar within. He gave his brother a sideways glance and smiled. 'Ah, I might've been a little hard on you. You turned out alright.' Vyktas grinned back, and Atlan shifted, pulling him into a playful headlock. Vyktas twisted out of his grip and gave him a rude gesture, but both of them were smiling. Happy.

They passed under the gates along the cobblestone streets. It was different from Yorenth, but it still felt familiar to be out of the wilderness and back in a city. Instead of limestone, it was built from field stones with wooden supports. Instead of sweltering glass forges, shops of all kinds lined the streets, with the upper floors serving as homes.

They passed a bookshop, a butchery, tailors, launderers, and even an apothecary all together on the same street. Children laughed and played in the streets and Atlan watched as a nearby vendor gave them pieces of wrapped candy that in Yorenth they might've been accused of stealing.

He thought about how life in Bellgard, with less wealth than Yorenth but a much greater emphasis on knowledge and education, seemed so much more well-off when it came to the daily life of its citizens.

They passed no beggars, no one down at the docks looking to make a quick mark stealing, no one sick and out on the street. He'd always thought of Yorenth as successful, no other dominion could boast such yields or success in trade, and nowhere else had a trained army like theirs. In every measure, they had the most power, but was power all?

Power didn't feed or find homes for ap Sands like Kyr. Power did nothing to ensure the elderly didn't have to do hard labor in the sand mines until their dying breath, if they even made it that long. It did nothing on its own.

In truth, it was a grand show, for the gratification only of a paranoid monarch, cheered on by those who were taught it was the only way they could get a leg up on others.

As the five of them made their way deeper into the city under the bright, pleasant afternoon sun, Atlan continued his ruminations. He loved his brothers and sisters in the Sun's Own still—the work they did protecting Yorenth, keeping dangers at bay from the gates, he still felt a sense of honor about. But other times, particularly the work they did within the city itself, those they answered to, it felt like nothing more than a way to protect power for power's sake. To enforce the will of a few on the many.

'Are you thinking about home?' Vyktas said suddenly. Atlan hadn't realized his brother was still paying him any attention.

He eyed him. 'How did you know?'

'You get this faraway look. I can just tell. I miss it less than I thought I would.'

'Mm,' Atlan agreed. 'It wasn't all it was supposed to be, was it?' Vyktas looked at him with a sad smile and shook his head.

'The inn's up here, if memory serves,' Kyr called back.

They passed a courtyard with a small fountain and came upon a large wooden building, lit with the amber glow of lamplight. A raucous party was going on at the bar downstairs, but they were all so tired even Kyr didn't try to convince them to have a drink.

They paid for the last two rooms in the house for the night, using some marks they'd stashed in one of the saddlebags.

It was more expensive than they would've liked, owing to

the fact that the two rooms were connected by a larger common area, but well worth it. Kyr collapsed into a chair by the fireplace as soon as they got in the door.

'It's not where I'd choose to stay, but it is nice,' Penta said, looking oddly at the ceiling.

'And where would you choose to stay?' Atlan asked.

'Somewhere with a little less memory. It's like I can feel the presence of the people who've stayed here clogging up the room.'

He raised his brows and turned away. Penta didn't notice.

Kyr and Penta disappeared into the other room, and Atlan wondered what it was they talked about. Sometimes he remembered that the five of them really were strangers, placing a lot of trust in one another. It wasn't long before Kyr returned, demanding food, and then promptly nodded off, her snores across the common room.

'Care to explain more about where you've found our newest friend?' Vyktas asked.

'I already told you.'

'You expect me to believe, after growing up in a world we thought was without magic, that in just the past few weeks we've stumbled upon *three* other people who can wield it, or in some way have knowledge of it?'

'I don't expect you to believe anything—I hardly believe it myself—but it's the truth. I mean, stranger things *are* happening in our world, Vyktas. The blights? The unrest in the North? There is something at work that we don't understand. When the library in Yorenth was destroyed, we lost so much that could help us understand all of this.' He said that last part under his breath, almost bitterly.

Vyktas interrupted his rambling. 'I guess you and Kyr have your work cut out for you down in the Archives tomorrow then.'

Atlan sighed, sloughing off his armor. 'Well, I'll be going to see Vizier Rumail first, and joining them at the Archives after.'

Vyktas looked at him sidelong. 'You decided to? Are you sure that's a good idea?'

'No, but I think it's better to make him aware of the blights and to let him make an informed decision for his people, than to sneak around. Don't you?'

Vyktas nodded. 'You're right.'

Atlan continued. 'I'm curious to see what we will find. I'm sure Penta is anxious to understand more too. They know much about certain things, but they have also lost many memories. You should've seen the way they were looking at the houses, the water wheels, and the weaponry of the guards. They know little of our modern world.'

'How do you and Kyr know you didn't just pick up some lunatic living in the woods?'

'You didn't see the way they commanded the ash floating down from the sky, Vyktas. It was similar to what Teleri did in the forest, only more intense. There was no fire to be seen— they must have created it, and the ash . . . it *listened* to them. It wasn't like they were a conduit for it. More like, they were a *forebear.*'

'So, what, they're a Singer? From the First Age?'

Atlan shook his head. 'I don't think so.' He stared off. 'I think they're something greater still.'

47

KYR

KYR AWOKE SOMETIME LATER to a darkened sky beyond the curtains and the soft down bed in the room at the inn. She could feel eyes on her in the cramped room and rolled over.

Penta was perched on a chair in the corner, looking curiously over at her. There was a soft glow from a candelabra in the corner, but most of the room lay in shadow. To her left was a small shelf in one corner with a few odds and ends on it. A portrait of a woman in a collared gown hung on the wall by the door.

She rubbed at her eyes. 'Now, I could swear I fell asleep out there on the chair . . .'

'You did,' Penta answered matter-of-factly.

'Were you watching me sleep?'

'You looked peaceful. It's been so long that I've been around another without some strife or crisis coming along to ruin it.'

Kyr propped herself up on her elbows and took in Penta's image more fully. Their red hair was unbound, falling in blunt sections nearly to their waist. They had an angularity to their features she hadn't noticed before, but still a softness in the cheeks and lips. Their hands were thin and nimble, with freckles dotting them.

'I see. Penta, can we speak plainly?'

'Of course,' Penta answered.

'What *do* you remember of your life? You mentioned your father but . . . I don't understand how he's still alive. Are you sure you remember correctly about this Edril Sil?'

Penta stood abruptly and turned their back her, looking at the portrait. Beneath the linen of their shirt, Kyr could see muscles flexing as Penta released tension. 'Yes.' The solemn note in their voice was not lost on Kyr. 'Of that much, I am sure.'

She was about to ask them to elaborate when they spoke again. 'But I don't want to speak of him. I don't remember much, other than him locking me away. I remember my mother vaguely. Shadows of her. My sister, I never met, but I know she is alive. I can feel her.'

Kyr sat up. 'What does that feel like?'

She got the sense her question surprised Penta. 'No one ever asks how it feels.'

'You talk to others about all of this?'

'Only in dreams,' they replied. 'When my sister and I dream, we are connected. I see through her eyes and she through mine. It's not like I'm there with her, but more that . . . dreaming is a language all its own, and we both speak it.'

A smile ghosted across Kyr's lips. 'You make it sound beautiful.'

Penta nodded, still facing away from Kyr. 'It is. In truth, though, I am scared to meet her.'

Kyr leaned forward, resting her elbows on her knees. 'Well, that's understandable. Do you think she knows about you?'

'I don't know. I doubt my father ever speaks of me. Perhaps he has forgotten me. It was so long ago when he last came to visit, I think maybe he has forsaken me altogether.'

Kyr's head whipped toward them. 'What? He came to visit you? In the tower?'

Penta nodded. 'I think so. I would make these etchings in the wall when I was there, but I made a special symbol each time he came to visit. There were over five hundred marks since he last visited.'

'Five hundred days?'

'No.' Penta cast their eyes over their shoulder. 'Years.'

Kyr paused, taking in the enormity of what Penta had just said and uncertain what to say. 'What are you going to do when you see him again?'

'Oh, enough about him,' Penta said, brushing her off. 'Tell me of your life.'

'What's to tell?' said Kyr, lying back on the bed. 'I've been a picklock for as long as I can remember.'

'A . . . picklock?'

'A thief.'

'Somehow I can't picture you as a thief.'

'What, can't you see my roguish charm?'

Penta smiled, their face half-illuminated by flame. 'Oh, you definitely have charm.'

Kyr leaned up and cocked her head, smiling back, her eyes roving over Penta. The room was so quiet you could've heard the slightest creak from the floorboards, the gentle whipping sound of the candles burning tall and hot.

'Tell me more,' Penta pressed, still watching Kyr like a cat.

'Well, let's see. I lived for all that time with a notorious thief named Sylas. He was like a father to me. I never had family. They died when I was too young to remember. I was delivered to Yorenth by an old man—a shepherd I was told. He saved me from the desert. I was supposed to be placed in an orphanage, but I ran away. I didn't want to go with strangers.' Kyr shrugged. 'Sylas found me a year or so later, I reckon.'

'Where is Sylas now?'

Kyr huffed a laugh. 'Ah, that's the unfortunate bit. You see, my magic came in on a job. Worst possible timing. I—I collapsed a building. On accident, of course,' she said, raising her hands. 'I had no idea I was doing it. I still don't really understand.' She turned her hands inward, studying them. 'Anyway, the guild turned on me, just like that, after all those years together.'

She heard the soft sound of movement and looked up. Penta now stood directly in front of her. Drawn to them, Kyr rose to sitting. They held out their hand slowly as if they would brush it softly over Kyr's cheek. 'That must've been difficult.'

Kyr looked up into their eyes, gripped by the infinite quality of them. She'd caught it in glances over the past few days, the way they looked more than human sometimes. It unsettled Kyr, and at the same time, drew her like moth to flame.

'I was so scared,' she breathed.

Penta studied her. 'You don't strike me as someone who's scared of anything.'

Kyr raised her brows and smiled. 'You'd be surprised.'

She remembered that day at the counting house again. She replayed the day often in idle moments, always finding ways to distract herself before she got to the end of it. Before Grym's face could flash through her mind. She had been afraid that day. Truly afraid.

'What are you thinking about?' Penta asked, their eyes a little too knowing.

The flames in the corner of the room began to burn so bright Kyr thought they might catch. 'Penta, what's happening?'

Penta turned to look at the flames. 'Easy, Kyr. Your magic is chaos, isn't it?'

Kyr breathed. 'How do you know that?'

Penta only looked amused. 'It is as I said before. I can feel it. You call on the Fäendhmar when you're overwhelmed. It's what draws Drithas.'

Kyr's expression grew puzzled. 'The . . . what? Who's Drithas?'

'The Fäendhmar. The worldbeings. Drithas is chaos.'

'Is that like the Spirits?'

'The word could be a rough translation, I suppose.'

'You're talking about Crescian, Solq, Tellurn . . .' Kyr prodded.

'I do not know those names,' they responded, their brows wrinkling.

'What do you call them?'

A faraway look took over Penta's face. 'I-I do not remember all of their names. Why don't I know their names? Drithas and . . . ? Who are the others?' Penta's chest began to rise and fall in increasingly rapid breaths. They looked at Kyr, and their eyes widened. Where they had been fully clouded at first, now the true light brown color of them began peeking through. 'What did he do?'

Penta's voice was rasping and unsteady—*panicked*.

'Hey,' Kyr said softly. 'Looks like you're the one who needs to take it easy now. Come here,' she said, steering them toward the bed. 'Rest, breathe. It's a lot to take in. I know what that's like. I felt the same way when I learned I had magic.'

Penta looked at her with an almost startling intensity. Kyr continued talking about her life, hoping to calm them. 'I saw Sylas again, not too long ago. Just before we left on our journey to Bellgard, actually. He told me he knew I had magic, too. Told me he looks for those connected to Crescian, to chaos magic, for the guild. Said I was the strongest he'd ever come across.' Penta took a deep breath, nodding as they tried to listen. 'And,' Kyr added, 'he told me that he needed my help to find Crescian. That she was lost, or something like that. Isn't that strange?'

Penta's eyes searched hers. 'Lost? Yes. Fragmented. Hidden. He—he took pieces of my memory! Stored them in . . .'

'Easy, easy!' Kyr said, putting a hand on their back. 'I'm sorry, I didn't mean to—'

Penta's eyes darted back and forth, as if they were seeing something, or remembering something.

'Penta? What's happening?'

Penta ignored her, their eyes still seeming to study an image before them that did not exist. They blinked—once, twice—and when they looked at Kyr, she got the distinct sense that they had been returned to her.

'You went somewhere. Where?' Kyr asked softly.

They shook their head. 'You're very perceptive.' Pressing their lips together, Penta looked lost in thought. 'I visited the Lightbringer. What did you call him? Solq?' They blinked. 'I heard them calling him that. He toils in deep chasms, his gems the only way his light reaches us. He stores his power and bides his time until his return. My father always underestimates.'

Kyr blinked. 'I don't know what any of that means, but we're going to make sure he gets what's coming to him.'

Penta smiled. 'Stay with me?'

'I will. Here, lie down.' Kyr patted the bed next to her. 'You're safe with me.'

Penta lay cautiously next to her, relaxing as they talked, though their eyes remained vigilant, their body never fully uncoiling. Kyr kept repeating those words throughout the night, hoping they would get through.

You're safe with me.

They fell asleep like that, entwined on the edge of the bed. When Kyr woke again, it was to the gentle light of dawn.

She snuck out to wash up, closing the door with a soft click, and ran into Atlan in the hall.

'Morning, thief,' he said playfully.

Kyr snickered. 'Hey, thanks for moving me from the chair to our room last night, would've woken up with the *worst* crick in my neck.'

Atlan furrowed his brow, confused. 'I didn't move you.'

48

ORIA

Oria woke with a headache. The scar along her face ached. She rose slowly, remembering pieces of her conversation with her father. He had offered her everything she'd ever wanted—an understanding of her position, answers to her questions, and he seemed so reasonable about all of it, too. Just a month ago, she might've been fooled, coalesced and gone along with his desires, but now his honeyed words only increased her suspicions.

Lyra arrived first, and then Mothril a few moments later.

'Ready to go?' he asked.

Oria nodded. 'But first, I should tell you that my father came to visit last night. I'm worried.'

'What did he say?' Lyra pressed.

'He told me more about the Eradomin and why he's so afraid of them. It was like he suddenly wanted to answer all the questions I had. He claimed it was because he wants me to be Prime one day.' She looked to her guard. 'Mothril—'

'He's lying,' Mothril urged.

Oria looked at him intently. 'You're positive of what you overheard?'

Mothril nodded.

'I don't believe him either,' Lyra added. 'Remember the last time we did this, Oria. Remember his words. They were only intended to hurt you further.'

They echoed through her now. *I thought I raised a daughter who loved her people. Was I mistaken?*

She cast her eyes downward, wringing her hands. 'I remember.' Her hand wandered to the handle of her knife under the fabric of her skirts, letting its weight in her palm reassure her. 'It's strange though, isn't it? It's like he knows something has changed.'

'Very strange,' Lyra agreed. 'The way I see it, he knows he has gone too far. He knows he has asked too much of you. I don't think the Elders would agree with his treatment of you if they knew the truth, if they knew of all of your injuries and the restrictions he's placed on you.'

'I think that's likely, but why tell me so much? He even told me of what he saw in the Erángal.'

Mothril's eyes widened in recognition of something. 'He trespasses within the Erángal?' he asked. She'd never seen his face look shocked before.

'Well, I don't know how it works exactly, but it seems so. He said he saw a great calamity, the world burning. Everything he's doing, he says, is to try to stop it from coming to fruition.'

'What?' Lyra asked. She turned toward the windows of Oria's room, looking out over the citadel with contemplative eyes.

'This is much more dire than I first assumed,' said Mothril. His tone was even, but his eyes betrayed his spiraling thoughts.

Oria sighed. 'It's quite inconvenient timing. It would be useful to know more, but ...'

Mothril nodded once. 'Time runs short. Let's get you out of here.'

Lyra turned back to them. 'Alright, I'll ready the horses and meet you two once I'm sure no one is following. Oria, you've never tried to use magic beyond divination before. Are you sure—?'

'I can do this,' she assured her. 'The storm will give us the cover we need so the guards in the watchtowers can't spot us. With luck, they won't even give chase.'

'A chase means a fight. We're not equipped to outrun a hunt.' Mothril unsheathed his blade. The one Oria had wondered if he'd meant to use on her, a tool of her confinement. Instead, he would use it to set her free.

He eyed its edge and frowned. 'This Southern steel?' he asked to no one in particular.

'I think so,' Lyra answered. 'Why?'

'Brittle for robust use . . .' he muttered.

Lyra raised her brows.

Oria took a deep breath. 'I wish there were another way.' She stood before Mothril and looked up at him. 'I don't want anyone hurt.'

'There's no reason for them to offer any resistance,' he replied, sheathing the blade. 'Sybil is going to help us.'

Oria gave a nod, more resolute than she felt, and the trio set off.

Her fingers gently glided along the old, buckling stone wall, still carved with sigils of those who had lived and ruled here before the Fall, when her folk still lived in the hills and mountains, under the stars. She stood now on the precipice above the clearing, leaves of citrine floating past.

'Ready, my lady?' said a low voice at her ear.

A quiver ran across her skin at his words. She nodded.

Mothril hesitated a moment, then took the strip of linen, reaching his arms around her shoulders to fasten the blindfold.

She felt the brush of cold, scarred flesh on her cheek, and then her sight vanished.

She tried to call the rain.

Her feet recognized the stones she tread upon as they approached a fork in the path—one set leading down to the clearing, the other to the eastern gate. Hurrying toward the gate, her new metal brace dug into her skin painfully.

Mothril tightened his hold on her hand for just a heartbeat. He said so little, but she'd begun to recognize his movements had a meaning all their own. *I'm here,* it said.

Oria felt small drops on her skin at first. It wasn't coming fast enough. In a few moments the guards would come to see why she hadn't arrived. Her fear, though, that seemed to enliven the storm greatly.

Rain began falling faster. A small smile crept across her face. They were close now, so close to being clear of guards and out into the wilderness.

'Come on,' Mothril said, leading her farther down the path.

Her blindfold, now soaked, was slick to her eyelids, blackening her vision even more. The deprivation of her senses only served to intensify the storm, and Oria worried a vision might overtake her at any moment. She focused on Mothril's hand in hers, smooth like a river stone. The rainstorm grew and grew, becoming a downpour that soaked her clothes through, and blocked out all sound except their hurried footsteps.

Thunder cracked somewhere high above.

'Oria,' Mothril warned.

She nodded, taking a deep breath. They came around a bend in the path Oria knew from childhood. The gate lay just ahead, wedged in a narrow gap between two massive walls of rock that abutted the citadel and the lake on either end.

'Sybil?' Oria cried out, desperate to say her goodbyes to the one Elder who had helped her, who had listened.

Instantly, Mothril grabbed her around the waist, and she was jolted backward against him.

'Oria—' Muffled against her hair, his voice was ... *sad*.

'Let go of the Whispess,' Sybil said coolly.

Mothril's arm around her didn't move.

'*Sybil*?' She lowered the slickened blindfold. There, surrounding the eastern gate, were all of the Elder-knights of the Order of the Bear, along with the gate guards. 'Sybil, how could you?' she breathed, drowned out by the rainstorm.

'Oria!' Sybil yelled back. 'I spoke with your father. Your mind isn't well! He tells me the visions can cloud one's judgement, particularly when a seer is so close to a revelation. It must be confusing, keeping so many realities untangled. This is why it is more important than ever to keep faith in the Prime!'

Oria listened, horrified. Sybil was completely earnest. Sincere.

She felt tears come then—hot, angry tears of frustration. She hated the feeling, ever since she was a child, the familiarity and the feebleness of it.

Exasperated, Oria said, 'I am so tired of not being listened to. You will hear me! This isn't your decision to make. For the good of the clan, I *am* going, and you are going to let me through these gates!'

Behind her, she heard the metallic sound of a blade singing out of its scabbard. Her blood ran cold.

Sybil's face was impassive. 'Whispess, you do not command me. The Prime does.' She regarded Mothril coldly. 'Drawing your weapon is a threat that will not go unanswered.'

Oria took a deep breath, trying to ease the tension. 'Please, Sybil. I cannot go back.'

'You will,' Sybil said, with the force of a command. She whistled. Efja and another helmed knight advanced.

Instantly, Mothril was in front of her and in a fighting

stance. Oria didn't think she'd ever seen someone of his stature move so terrifyingly quickly.

Sybil scoffed. 'You think you can best me and a dozen of my knights?'

Mothril waited a handful of heartbeats before replying, simply, 'I do.'

Sybil, taken aback, laughed incredulously, but there was a hollow ring to it. His words had found their mark.

'Oria, put it back on,' he called back to her.

'What?'

He looked over his shoulder. 'The blindfold, Oria. Put it back on. It'll be a close thing, and I could really use the storm's shadows. And anyway, you won't want to see this.'

'*Mothril.*'

'Go on, Oria.' Rain streaked down his face. One who did not know Mothril might've mistook his expression in that moment for more of his usual stoicism, but Oria could see the mettle in it. 'I promise, after this, you will do the asking. Ask anything of me, of anyone, that you wish.'

With one last look at Sybil and her order, her vision went black once more.

Unseeing, each sound was amplified. She heard Mothril's form move away from her—jostling armor and footsteps. Above, the tempest churned violently, the wind thrashing hungrily at her.

The power of it made her nervous. It occurred to her, almost as an afterthought, that while she'd spent so much time wondering how she was going to call the storm, she hadn't thought how she was going to *stop* it.

Through the pelting rain, she heard a sudden clang of metal meeting. The fight had begun. Oria stumbled backward. Boots scuffled on the wet path somewhere ahead of her.

Mothril grunted. She knew it was him. With so much time

spent alone together, she had committed much of his voice to memory, even wordless utterances.

Amid the sounds of the fray, she could hear gurgling, choking. Something wet. *Blood*, she knew.

No! She couldn't lose him. *Not now, not like this. Not ever*, a smaller thought echoed.

'Mothril?' Oria screamed.

'No, my lady,' he rasped, his voice low and suddenly much closer than she realized.

Then he roared with a terrifying ferocity, sounding like he was moving away from her again. Another clash.

It was Sybil's voice that rang out clear through the storm next. 'Rew, Balodan, Drim!' She was commanding more knights to attack.

Footsteps hurried toward Oria and she braced herself, but they passed her by. She heard blades scything through the air. A man screamed, and then she heard a sword clatter to the ground. Somewhere, Mothril growled his frustration.

He sounded close to her and yet far away, all at once.

The knights began barking battle commands. 'Rew, take point. Flank him! I'll go high, you go—' He was cut off by a yelp of surprise, followed by a gasp. Another scream.

Two heartbeats.

More running and then, the sound of frantic parrying.

Sybil bellowed, 'That way! Look out!'

At the same time, another voice. 'Rew, look—! No!'

A soft keening, a hollow sound like a maul making contact with wood, and then that voice was silenced too.

More scraping and a blood-curdling scream followed, punctuated by several squelching sounds. She felt sick.

'It's alright,' Mothril said, suddenly by her side once more. He was warm and slick with sweat and rain and something slimier. She could feel his heart pounding in his chest like a wild rabbit's. The wind slowed, and the rain let up.

'Mothril of-Arcandras, release the Whispess!' Sybil called out again.

Mothril moved away and the awful fighting sounds resumed. She bent her will to the storm, to darkness, to shadows she somehow knew were enveloping the courtyard. The storm drowned out all light as she poured everything she had into the effort.

Thunder broke so loud in the sky Oria could tell they were in the eye of her storm.

A sudden choking sound, like someone's throat filling with blood, erupted close by. *Too close.*

She tried to calm herself, but the tears were coming again, burning her face. She hadn't wanted this . . .

There were other voices shouting now, in fear and astonishment, trying to reorganize the attack, in notes of clattering armor and steel.

Another howl rang out. Pained. Dying. She knew whose voice it was, too.

Sybil.

Oria could stand it no longer. She tore off her blindfold.

The storm had descended upon them, darkening the sky as though it were the underside of a lake. The Elder-knight lay on the ground only an armspan from her, a slash to her throat. Sybil's eyes regarded the courtyard lifelessly.

Her eyes found Mothril.

He was lumbering toward the gatehouse. One of the guards, a man with scarred lips, cowered against the wall there. Cornered. Mothril wrested a sword from a body as he passed, dragging it along.

'Drim, is it?' she heard him ask.

'Please,' said the man. 'I didn't mean nothing by what I said. I was only repeatin' rumors I heard about you! That's all!'

'I don't give a fuck what you said about me.' Without another word, Mothril plunged the sword into the man's chest.

Oria was too horrified to look anywhere else. The man sputtered, still breathing.

She heard Mothril curse. '*Feskjir*. Southern steel.' The sword was jammed in the man's ribs. With a quick jerk downward, Mothril snapped the blade. Holding the broken handle aloft, he brought the pommel down hard on the man's head. The sputtering stopped.

Oria looked away quickly, taking in the rest of the scene before her.

Efja lay dead nearby, along with several other knights. At a greater distance, another knight and gate guard had been struck several times in the head with a rock, which lay, coated in blood, on the ground. Other dead were scattered about, some with stab wounds, and others bludgeoned.

All in less than a few minutes.

Mothril looked like Death's own herald. His hair was soaked, his mouth bloodied. He had taken a few wounds that she could see, but was largely unharmed. The blood that streaked his hair and covered his armor was not his own, and the now gentle rain did little to wash it off.

Horse hooves echoed from around the bend in the path and they turned. Lyra pulled on the reins, coming to a sudden stop.

'I heard shouting, came as soon as I—' her voice broke off. She looked around, eyes widening. '*What . . . happened*?'

Passing one of the dead knights, Mothril picked up an unbroken longsword. He scabbarded it and came to stand by Oria's side. The two exchanged a glance, Mothril searching her eyes for understanding. As if seeking her approval for what he knew was a horrible act. Still in shock, she turned away.

'Sybil betrayed us.' Oria could barely choke out the words. 'Her order was waiting for us when we arrived.'

'Mothril, did you . . .' Lyra faltered. 'How?'

Oria didn't know what to say. Mothril hung his head, his

breathing slow and measured. Meditating. His eyes were unseeing, as if in a trance.

More shouting sounded from behind them on the ramparts. Oria whirled around. Mothril looked up and his eyes cleared. He gathered himself.

'Traitor!' her father bellowed. 'I knew you could not be trusted!'

Once again, Mothril readied himself to fight, resting his hand on the pommel of the sword.

Edril Sil caught the movement. 'Release my daughter at once!'

Just off to her left, Lyra slowly lowered herself from the horse.

'And *you*,' Edril Sil accused, looking at her. 'Not another step. I knew you had to be a part of this. You and your mother, you *poisoned* my daughter's mind!' He spat the words with such venom that Oria didn't register what he'd said at first.

Lyra's eyes darted to Oria, while not turning away from Edril Sil. 'Oria, there's something I have to tell you.'

'You have nothing to say to her!' her father roared.

Oria felt dizzy. 'Lyra?' she whispered.

'Oria, you have a sibling,' she urged.

'*Silence!*' Her father's knowing command only horrified her more.

She looked between him and Lyra. 'Father, what is she talking about?'

He loosed a breath, his voice curt with rage. 'How should I know?' The blatant lie sent Oria's fury over the edge.

'*What is she talking about?*' she bit out.

Lyra's gaze was on Edril Sil, but it was the way she was looking at him that confused Oria most of all. It was as if she *knew* him, approaching him as though he were a peer. 'If you don't tell her, I will.'

He nearly bared his teeth. 'You will do no such thing.'

If Lyra's behavior was confusing, then her father's reaction truly shocked her. His arms were stiff at his side, and his glare was unflinching. He seemed almost afraid of whatever it was Lyra had to say.

'And why not?' Lyra asked defiantly.

'Because there are crossbows trained on you as we speak.'

They looked up along the cliffs to see that more knights had crept along the forested rocks and surrounded them. By her count, there were at least five of them.

'Father, what is this?'

'They won't hurt you, my Fäen. Only those that would harm you.'

'Mothril and Lyra have never harmed me.' She'd said the words without thinking, but now that she had, she realized it was true. They were the only two people who had never hurt her. She didn't believe they ever would. Mothril had done terrible things, but since she'd known him, they had only been in service of her protection. True to his word, she was always safe in his presence.

'They're lying to you, my kin,' her father said, his voice and words suddenly smoothing out into that dulcet tone he always used with her. It wasn't caring, she realized.

It was patronizing.

Lyra handed Mothril the reins and stepped forward. 'Not another *step!*' her father shouted.

Oria watched her raise her hands, a movement of surrender. 'You should have planned for this eventuality, Edril Sil.' Oria's mouth nearly fell open at the casual tone with which she addressed her father. He looked so angry she could see his eyes bulging from the end of the path where they stood.

'What eventuality? The one that ends with you dead, just like your mother?'

'Father!' Oria gasped. He looked to her as if he had forgotten she was there.

'It's like I said, Oria,' he replied. 'There is still much you don't understand.'

She looked up at the guards on the cliffs, noticed how they held strong to their weapons, seemingly unhearing of the vile words her father spoke.

'Have you no concern over how my father treats kin?' She stared up at their strangely fixed gazes, and her father began to laugh.

'They will not say anything to you. They trust their Prime.'

Her features twisted with rage. 'What are you doing to them?'

'Have you been so corrupted against me already? Oria, if you think I'll trust you with any of this knowledge, you are deeply mistaken. There will be no bringing you into the fold now.'

Lyra moved closer. 'No, there will not. Because Oria will be free.'

'Not ... another ... step.'

'Oria will know the truth. She will know her mother, her—' Lyra's words were cut short by a bolt piercing her chest. She crumpled to the ground.

'Lyra!' Oria cried, stumbling as she tried to get to her. Mothril flinched, but his eyes stayed trained on Edril Sil and his guards.

She looked up at her father. '*Why*? How could you do this?' Her words came out in strangled notes.

Lyra dragged herself along the ground toward Oria.

'I told you. She has warped your mind—'

'*No*,' Lyra cut him off. Blood spilled from her lips in sickening gushes. She turned to her. 'The draughts ... Mothril, she needs greater darkflower to dream. Oria, go—go south. You will find what you seek there.' Another bolt hit her. Oria shook as she tried in vain to wipe the blood from her friend's mouth.

'It's okay,' she whispered. 'It's okay. I'll see you again, okay?'

Lyra reached out and ran a hand along her cheek. Already she was weak and too cold. 'Felith was not your mother, Oria,' she said, barely audible. Oria's eyes widened.

'Wh-what do you mean?'

'South.'

Oria nodded.

'I love you. Do good, Oria.'

She could only nod once more. She touched Lyra's face, still as it was.

'Get her up,' her father's voice ordered. 'And you're not to kill the traitor yet, he has things to answer for. I'm going to enjoy this.' Expressionless, he glanced at Oria once more before turning his back on her.

A distant rushing sound could be heard then, like water. Confused, Oria looked around to see a faint shimmering around Lyra's left hand. She stepped backward in a confused daze. The crashing sound grew louder.

'Oria,' Mothril said, coaxing her to him. With both of them still watching the path ahead where the sound was echoing from, he lifted her onto the horse.

Her father whirled around. 'No!' he bellowed. It was the most emotion she could ever recall hearing in her father's voice.

Mothril swung onto the horse behind her and thrust the reins into her hands. They sped through the gate. She looked down at the ground below their horse. Flashes of blood and clover.

They were both still soaked by the rain, and her hands slipped on the saddle's horn. He banded one arm around her waist, the full weight of his armored chest pressing into her from behind. They rode fast, not daring to slow down.

When Oria turned to look over her shoulder, she saw a massive wall of white-water flood through the citadel and come crashing out of the eastern gate.

49

MOTHRIL

THEY DIDN'T STOP RIDING until they reached the cairns at the mountain's peak. Though she hadn't said anything, Mothril could see from Oria's face that riding was growing difficult, especially with that new brace she wore. So, as dusk descended on them and Mothril scouted the area for any dangers, they made a small camp behind an outcropping of pines.

Mothril still didn't know what to make of the look Oria had given him after he'd slain those knights, and they'd spoken little since. Only what was necessary.

'A fire would be nice.'

'Not here. At least not at night. We're still too close to the citadel. And get out of that dress, you'll catch a cold.'

'Would you like any water?'

A nod.

Mothril rested slumped against the tree, facing toward the road, while Oria slept on a bed of moss in his furred cloak and her chemise. He wore his trousers and an only slightly damp tunic.

Morning came painfully slow, all blue light and cold mountain air. They were supposed to have two weeks of supplies for the journey to the port city of Greenflower in the Middevale, which despite still being in the North, was far enough south that no Wiccars traveled there, but Sybil's betrayal meant they'd left with nothing but the clothes on their backs and a sword he picked off one of the slain knights. He went off in search of breakfast.

His fingers worked familiarly at snares—nooses made from a dried long-grass that grew on the mountain's south face—that he would check again before they left. As he walked, he collected some mushrooms, the trumpet-shaped Piper's flute. That would have to do.

Oria awoke as he was getting the fire going. She looked at him with a soft sleepiness, but then the memories of all that had happened came rushing back to her, and her face grew serious.

'Did you sleep well?' he asked cautiously.

'I did,' came her soft reply. She paused. 'No dreams.'

'That's good, right?'

She nodded faintly. 'That smells delicious.'

Without another word, he handed her a skewer of roasted mushrooms and they ate, so hungry they licked the char off their fingers.

The crackling fire was the only sound between them for a long while. There was so much he wanted to say, but instead he waited for her to speak.

'It's so cold,' she said.

He wished she would say something about how she was feeling, about what had happened, but he'd settle for a remark about the weather.

'It gets cold earlier in the year up here.'

She said nothing.

'I've been here before and I know a hot spring nearby. I could take you. So you can warm up.'

Oria nodded. 'That sounds nice, thank you.'

They finished eating and Mothril tended to the horse. When he returned to her, he found her holding her brace.

'Much as I loathe the thing, it does help me balance when I ride. Would you mind?'

He brought it to her. 'May I?'

She nodded again, and he folded the cloak back to just below her hips, then reached underneath her dress, his hands working deftly. He didn't look at her as he secured it in placed, then slid his hands down her thigh, fastening the first buckle. There was something against her hip, the side of her leg.

His hand brushed over his dagger, strapped beneath her skirts, and paused. 'Good thinking.'

He cleared his throat, and bent her knee, tightening the strap there, the metal caging in her entire upper leg.

She made a sudden movement, almost like a spasm.

'Does this hurt you?' he asked, gesturing to one of the metal hinges near her knee.

'It just pinches sometimes.'

He examined it, then walked back to where he'd hung his gambeson and ripped a strip off the lining on the wrist with his teeth. 'Here.' He wrapped it around the hinge, providing some padding.

'Better,' she smiled. 'Thank you, Mothril. For your guardianship.' She sighed. 'I wish what happened at the gate hadn't needed to happen, but it . . . it did. I know now that my father, the Elders, they were never going to let me go. I'm thankful for all that you've done for me. Even that.'

'Thank me for anything but that,' he said, standing and extending a hand.

There was so much more she wanted to say. She bit her lip and placed her hand in his.

———

The greenery grew sparse and the cool, thin alpine air was crisp with the scent of pine.

'Is this the place?' Oria asked, peeking out from behind him as they slowed.

'It is.'

They had come to a long, narrow glen with bright green long-grass and low, rocky pools. Steam wafted off them, dissipating into the cooler mountain air. Mothril helped her down from the horse and she slipped off her leather boots, feeling the earth beneath her feet. The ground felt active here, warm and rumbling like a sleeping cat. She saw the water was bubbling slightly as she stepped closer.

'Let me guess, you found out about this place in the free order?'

'Mm. Too much time in the wilds.'

Oria crossed her arms and cocked her head. 'I thought you said you would answer whatever I asked of you when we left the citadel.'

He sighed. 'You're right. I did say that, didn't I?' He ran a hand down the trunk of a pine. 'Oria, I haven't been quite honest with you. Not because I haven't wanted to, but because if your father or the Elders knew the truth of who I am, I'd be hanging in the Cloakwood right now, and you would still be in your chambers. In danger.'

'Are you a wanted man? A brigand?'

Mothril laughed in that low, amused way of his. 'My lady, you already know I'm a brigand.'

Her gaze was piercing, but not angry, not accusatory. 'You are a Wiccar, though?' she asked. 'Speak true.'

Mothril thought the question had been gnawing at her for some time. Only now could she speak it.

'I'm going to get in the hot spring now,' Mothril answered, pushing himself off of the tree's trunk.

'What?' she asked, confused.

Mothril walked to the edge of the water. He began pulling his tunic over his head, wincing as the fabric whispered over his back, knowing. He threw it to the grass. When he heard Oria's gasp, he knew what she was seeing.

Stoneflesh scars.

His back was covered in them, deep gray and ridged, wrapping around from one shoulder down to his hip, where they crept around to the front of his torso.

He didn't say a word. He didn't dare turn.

He took off his trousers and got into the water, sinking beneath its placid surface. The quiet of the water rushed around his ears, and it soothed him. The nothingness of it. When he rose, shaking the water from his hair, only then did he turn to see Oria's face.

Her mouth was slightly open, her eyes blinking fast. 'You are . . .'

'Eradomin,' he answered. 'Yes.' He tried to hide the longing he felt—for his old life, rhapsody, his people, for her—from his face.

'But how? And why?' She took a clumsy step back, as if truly frightened *by* him for the first time.

A sinking feeling dug its claws in him. 'You're not in any danger,' he urged. 'Oria, I have no designs on you.'

'Answer my questions,' she replied stonily.

'Alright,' he said softly. 'I am one of the last Eradomin. Likely the last.'

Oria stood rooted to the spot. For once, he could not read the emotions on someone else's face, and it killed him.

'My father was leading an attack on the Ronin clan when we first came to this plane. I was young, and never told much about any of it or why we needed to fight, just that we needed to. I wanted to impress him. What boy doesn't want to impress their father? So, I came along. It was my first skirmish here in Old Era, a lowly ambush.' He huffed an ashamed laugh. 'We never used to do things like that, but we had become desperate. Our goddess, Sarthura, had abandoned us for this realm, this plane. There was something important she was doing here, and we were desperate to find her.'

'Sarthura, I know that name,' Oria said. 'My father mentioned it. Calligone.'

'Yes, that is what the people here call her. Sarthura comes from the Borean Poet language, I'm surprised your father referred to her as such.'

Oria's face tensed. 'You—you slaughtered that little girl.' Suddenly, she looked on the verge of tears.

He quickly shook his head, gripping the rock ledge. 'We did not. The clan did it to her themselves. Said they would show the others our brutality. She was already dead from a sickness when they decided to mutilate her.'

'You're lying,' she bit out. 'The Ronin would never do that.'

'No, Oria,' he said softly. 'Not the Ronin. The Cailirs. When they found her.'

She stilled.

'I vowed to you I would only tell you the truth once you were free of the citadel. I told you before I won't make a promise I can't keep. And I intend to keep this one, Oria. It may not seem like it, but honor still means something to me. I've reached the thirtieth rhapsody. More than that, I . . . I've grown to . . . to care for you. Oria.'

He looked away, having finally admitted it aloud. To her face, no less.

Oria's eyes darted toward him and away. He hoped that, completely defenseless before her, she could see that he was not a threat. *Not a monster. Never to you.*

'Why did you and your father come here?'

'The others we came with were all killed. My father and I the last men standing. I wanted to return, to leave this place, but my father insisted. He had plans, he said, to seek Sarthura out. Or at least, other Eradomin still living in Old Era. We joined in with the pilgrimage of the Far Clans, disguised ourselves as Ronin refugees, the only survivors. It was pure luck that it worked in our favor. As you know, the Ronin were incredibly reclusive. No one suspected we were not who we said we were.'

'And then?' she asked.

'We joined a free order with others who broke off from the pilgrimage, lived like that for a year or so, until they died.' He gave her a pointed look. 'Not by our hand.'

'And then you came upon my mother.'

Mothril nodded. 'Lady Felith, yes.'

Oria looked like she might slump to the ground. 'Is she not my mother?' He thought she might cry then.

'Whatever the truth, you have her kindness, and that counts for something. It was she who took us in. Another year out here and we'd probably have starved.'

'So that's why your father agreed to work as torturer and executioner?'

'Yes,' he sighed. 'A fate I tried to avoid. My father, though, he sought it out. Said it was perfect. No one questions the torturer. The executioner. It's bloody business, and no one wants to ask questions. He was right, they hardly even want to look at you.'

She looked down. 'What happened to your father? I vaguely recall seeing him once or twice around the citadel when I was very young. Then one day it seemed like he was just ... gone.'

Mothril nodded. 'He died of a sudden sickness. He sent a message to me to come see him, but by the time I got there, he was already dead.'

'I'm sorry.'

He shook his head. 'It's alright. It was no great loss.' They looked at each other for a long moment. 'Are you going to get in?'

'Not with you standing there staring at me!' she scoffed.

Mothril laughed and turned around, glad that the tension seemed to have eased. 'What about now?'

'It does look very warm.' He heard footsteps, the rippling sound of fabric, and then a soft splash. 'Very warm,' she confirmed with a sigh.

'Can I turn around now?'

'Fine, just . . . don't look too long at anything. My body is not exactly the most pleasant sight.'

'I disagree.' Mothril turned.

Oria unbound her hair which tumbled around her shoulders, hiding her face from view. 'Well, then imagine what I looked like before I had all these scars.'

'I like your scars. They tell the story of all that you've survived. Show others your strength. The strength to overcome is innately beautiful.'

Oria's face reddened slightly and she looked off into the distance. 'What's the thirtieth rhapsody?'

'Hm?' He was still staring at her.

'You said you'd reached the thirtieth rhapsody.'

'Oh,' he said, looking away again. 'The Eradomin meditate to reach different planes, a process called rhapsody. I have focused my energy well and been to many of them. It is a great honor bestowed on those favored by Sarthura.'

'What is that like?' she asked, leaning in conspiratorially. The pool was small enough that as they faced each other their legs intertwined slightly.

'I can't really explain it in words. It's sort of like . . . . transforming yourself into the music or frequencies that make up each world. It's very restorative. We often enter rhapsody instead of sleep.' She frowned slightly, and he spoke again. 'I'm sorry, it's not a very good answer.'

'No, no, it's fascinating. I wish I understood.' Oria's gaze fell to his chest. 'Which rhapsody does this plane occupy?'

'The eleventh,' he answered.

She nodded and looked out at the surrounding wilds for several minutes, seeming not to know what to say. 'You survived stoneflesh?'

'As a boy, yes.'

'Is it painful?'

'Very much.'

'Even now?'

'Sometimes.'

She nodded. 'I'm sorry. Did your father ever find what he was looking for?'

He looked off into the distance and, with a splash, lifted a hand to his chin. 'I don't think so. He settled into life in the clan soon enough, talked about it less, at least to me. But I know he kept up his search. And he always prayed to Sarthura.'

'She's the worldbeing of darkness, right? Shadows, veils . . .'

Mothril nodded, sinking back into the water. 'Indeed. Mysteries, the unknown, too.'

Oria snorted. 'Well, I certainly feel like she's been following me around then. There is so much I don't know.'

'We will find answers,' he assured her. *If you will have me.*

Oria sighed. Her eyes were filled with apprehension. 'Part of me is afraid of that, and the other part of me is afraid of what we *will* find.'

50

KYR

THE CITY of Bellgard was much quieter than Kyr remembered. In those younger days when last she'd visited, it had still seemed distinctly scholarly, orderly, but it had also felt more alive to her, more colorful. Perhaps it had been the novelty of it then, or the difference from her fast-paced life in Yorenth. Or maybe she was just getting old.

'I wonder what we will find. What history has been unspoiled, and what has been lost. The world is so different now,' Penta said as they walked.

The princes trailed behind them, giggling about something amongst themselves. Kyr smiled.

'I'm sure we'll find something,' she replied, 'but I'm doubtful it'll give us answers rather than just more questions, since that's how things seem to be going for us.'

'Questions can be answers in their own right,' Penta said in that cryptic way of theirs.

'Alright, this is where I leave you,' said Atlan, coming to a halt as they approached the market square two streets up from the inn. 'I'll meet up with you after I return from my meeting with Rumail.'

'Give him my regards,' Vyktas said with a wave.

'Good luck,' said Kyr.

With a nod, Atlan turned down the street opposite them, blending in with others going on their way. In the distance, the grand building that housed the Great Archives of Bellgard rose above the rest of the city. Kyr remembered its impressive exterior, but she would've never been able to go in such a place as a Knave. Sudden relief flowed through her that she could walk through the city without suspicion or guilt, without looking over her shoulder.

So, this is what it's like. Doing something honorable.

'What are you thinking about?' Penta asked her.

'How do you always know I'm thinking about something?' Kyr asked.

'You think very loudly,' they remarked.

Kyr huffed a laugh. 'Oh, just reminiscing on the last time I was here. Is it bringing back any memories for you?'

Penta's eyes traveled up to the steepled roofs, and they shook their head.

'Do you know anything else about your sister?' Vyktas asked as they walked beneath the shadow of the famed marble arches surrounding the Archives' courtyard.

Again Penta shook their head. 'I wish I did. You are prince of this land, would they have any records of Wiccar life here?'

Vyktas's face flushed slightly. 'I don't know.' He paused. 'You must not think me a very impressive prince.'

Penta looked him up and down. 'Hm.'

'Who's this friend of yours you asked to look after her?' Kyr interjected.

'I don't think I should say.'

'Why not?'

'Because he might hear me.'

'Who? Edril Sil?'

Penta nodded.

'He can . . . hear you?'

Kyr was beginning to wonder exactly who they were up against. She and Atlan hadn't really agreed to do more than deliver Penta to their sister in the North, or wherever she may be, if she was even still alive. But now that Kyr thought about it for more than a passing moment, she quite liked their merry little band, and secretly hoped they'd stay together somehow.

Penta looked around, and Kyr thought they really did look paranoid. 'He might be able to. He has before.'

'Like, when you were in the tower?' Kyr cocked an eyebrow.

'Yes, and before. I have memories of a strange mirror. Large and temperamental.' They looked skyward. 'My father wanted to keep me from it. I was looking for it, I remember, and he knew that somehow. He banished me before I could find it. I think he looks at me through it.'

'A mirror?' Kyr asked. 'Damn,' she cursed under her breath. 'I wish Atlan were here. There's something in the Oracle's notes about that. I'll have to look.'

'Did you bring it with you?' asked Penta.

Kyr turned. 'Vyktas?'

Vyktas looked at them sheepishly. 'Shit. I . . . may have forgotten them. I'm sorry! I was up late reading it, and I-I left it on the desk.' He held up his hands. 'In my defense, you all know so much about all of this, I have to catch up!'

Kyr sighed, shoving him toward the massive wooden doors. 'Come on, we'll just have to compare notes when we get back to the inn.'

If Kyr had thought the library in Yorenth's royal palace had been impressive, it paled in comparison to the massive, many-storied Archives of Bellgard.

'Welcome to the Archives,' said a librarian dressed in a plain brown robe, a piece of thick twine cinching it around her waist. Both her hair and eyes were the color of honey. 'My name is Klotho. If I can help you find anything, please let me know.'

'Thank you,' said Kyr, swaggering up to her. 'Actually, we were looking to see if you had any old records of the Wiccars, or anything regarding the Oracle of Yoren?'

'My,' said the librarian, glancing between them doubtfully. 'Those are quite unusual requests. Please, take a seat,' she said, offering them one of the tables by her desk, 'I'll be back shortly.'

'Kyr?' Vyktas sighed. 'You know, for a former thief, you are the least discreet person I've ever met.'

'Thank you,' she said, putting her hand on her chest and bowing her head.

He rolled his eyes and laughed. 'I'm going to go look around. You two'll stay here and promise not to get in any trouble?'

'Promise.' Kyr winked.

'That's not very convincing,' he muttered before walking off and leaving her and Penta alone.

Penta watched him go, then turned toward Kyr. Kyr studied Penta in turn, both of them not saying anything. She thought back to last night. If Atlan hadn't brought her to bed, then that meant Penta did, because Vyktas sure as shit wasn't strong enough. As she looked at them, she realized there was a strength in Penta's features that sang to her own vigor.

'You know, you never finished telling me about yourself,' Penta said, breaking the silence.

'Well, I told you about what happened,' Kyr said, almost a question.

'I want to know about *you*, Kyr.'

'I'm not too complicated.' She shrugged. 'Food is the way to my heart, I know lockpicking, daggers, and ale *really* well . . . I like birds, oh! And I wanted to be a bard when I was a kid, you know, paint my face, be in stage shows. Play the flute or something.'

Penta laughed, and Kyr smiled seeing a less serious expression on their face for once. 'You just made me remember something. I used to keep a falcon once, I think. When I was very young.'

'A falcon?' Kyr repeated, raising her eyebrows.

Footsteps interrupted their conversation as the librarian approached with a massive stack of books. 'Here you are!' Kyr couldn't help but smirk thinking about how this adventure all the way across the southern end of the continent just led to . . . more books. 'If you need any help, I'm quite curious to know what it is you're researching.'

'We're, uh, historians from the, uh, Middevale,' Kyr said awkwardly, her smile unconvincing.

The librarian nodded once. 'I see, well, I'll be right over there if you need anything.'

Kyr thanked her and took the first book off the stack. 'Well, we'd better get started,' she said, more to herself than anyone else.

Kyr gave the old atlas to Penta, hoping the names of landmarks might prompt them to remember their life in the North or past events they had been alive for. It was strange to think someone so soft-spoken and without airs was around a thousand years old, though she supposed they certainly were also wise enough at times for Kyr to believe it.

The book Kyr chose to read was far less scholarly, *Crucis' Book of Riddles*, written in the First Age by a scribe of the Descarian House of Old Era. They fell into a quiet monotony. One passage in particular caught her attention as she flipped through the pages with a slightly less analytical eye than maybe she should have.

Spirits let loose, essence unbound
Try to contain them, and Singers are crowned

Kyr blinked, looking over the page again. *Is this about the origins of Spiritsingers?*

'Hey, I think I found something,' Penta said, breaking her concentration before she could read further.

'Yeah?' said Kyr. She got up to look over Penta's shoulder.

'These boundaries of Old Era, I remember learning about them in my astronomy lessons. They were so *boring*.'

'*Astronomy?*' Kyr tilted her head. 'But still, maybe some of it was interesting? I'd rather be out in the world doing things, you know, getting my hands dirty. But the older I get the more I think it wouldn't have been so bad to have learned a bit more, had a bit more structure.'

Penta smiled up at her. 'I can imagine you needed a lot of structure.' Kyr chuckled. 'But listen, I remember learning that after a . . .'—their eyes roamed around the room as they searched for what they were trying to say—'calamity, a great calamity of some kind, the boundaries of Old Era were redrawn in accordance with a treaty agreed to between King Raviq and the usurper-mage, Eadr.'

'Eadr?' asked Kyr. 'His name comes up in the Oracle's notes as well, I think.'

'Damn him,' Penta sighed.

'Er . . . who?' Kyr asked.

'Vyktas! If only we had those notes here.'

'What did my brother do now?'

Kyr and Penta both turned, surprised to hear Atlan's voice. He stood behind them, a hand on the back of a chair.

'You should've been a Knave the way you sneak about!' Kyr kissed her teeth.

Atlan laughed.

'He left the Oracle's notes at the inn, so we're studying blind here,' said Kyr. 'Stayed up late reading them and forgot.'

'What an unusual display of diligence,' Atlan remarked.

'See? We're interesting people,' Kyr said, gesturing to Penta and herself. 'We're growing on him, I think.'

Atlan laughed. 'Let's hope you keep rubbing off on him, then. He's been entirely too pleasant this past week. I almost like having him around.'

'Did you speak to Vizier Rumail?' Kyr asked.

Atlan made his way around their chairs and sat across from them at the table. 'I did. He was none too pleased about the news I brought, nor that I've put him in a bit of an uncomfortable position if my mother were to discover that we're here, but he understood the reason for our visit and was relieved when I told him we will be leaving shortly.'

Kyr nodded. 'Did he believe you? About the blights, I mean.'

Atlan swayed his head from side to side. 'I think so. He knows what happened to his Noblegard at the outpost was no natural attack. He's a wise man, and without the delusions that plague my mother. He can see all of this for what it is—a significant change in the order of the world. He knows magic is part of that.'

'Good,' Kyr replied.

'So, what have you found?'

Penta repeated what they'd told Kyr and showed him the atlas.

'King Raviq?' Atlan asked. 'That was my great, great, great— I think—grandfather. What does it say about him? I didn't know anything this old survived the fires, the chaos—'

'You're a neighboring prince and you've never traveled to the Archives here?' Penta asked.

'I was a bit preoccupied trying to do anything I could to not study another text. All I cared about was dueling and licking my wounds.'

'Licking your . . . what?' said Penta.

He laughed. 'It's an idiom.'

'Ah.'

'Interesting. Eadr, remember that name, Kyr?' Atlan ran his finger over the text as he read. 'So, Raviq knew this man, and from the sound of it, he didn't like him very much. Eadr burned half the continent leading a rebellion and . . .' Atlan's voice trailed off before he spoke again. 'He was *against* the Spiritsingers for some reason.'

Penta sighed. 'I wish I could remember more.'

Kyr placed a hand on their back. 'Don't worry. We're going to get you answers.' When Atlan looked at her like she was crazy, she shrugged. 'I think we know that the blights have something to do with an imbalance in how the power of the Spirits flows through our world. Helping Penta remember can help us understand what happened in the First Age that led to what sounds like a similar cycle of imbalance and destruction now. It makes sense that something similar could happen again, and I'd bet that this Edril Sil character knows about it.'

'We can't just confront him,' said Atlan.

'Atlan's right,' Penta quickly agreed. 'My father is a cunning and ruthless man—more than you can expect, even if you plan for it. If you can accept your fate as Spiritsingers without knowing more, I'd urge you to consider anything else before getting involved with someone like him.'

Kyr sighed. 'He sounds like a delight.' She looked over at Atlan. 'Maybe we should introduce him to Attiqah. They could sort out their issues together and leave the rest of us alone.'

Atlan gave a mirthless laugh. 'Maybe.'

The sun dipped lower in the sky as they read, filling the room with golden, late afternoon sun. Outside, the faint sound of vendor carts and scholars going on their way filled the space with a soft sound that threatened to put her to sleep. She'd nearly drifted off when Penta gasped, startling her.

'This is it! A record of Edril Sil's daughter's birth.' Penta's eyes hungrily devoured the page. 'Born in the Winter of the Hare—the Whispess . . . Oria.'

Tears welled in their eyes like glass. 'Oria,' they repeated.

'Whispess?' Kyr asked.

'That's the title given to Cailir seers,' said Atlan. 'I remember it from my tutoring. The Cailir are an old Wiccar family.'

'Does it say where we can find her?'

The relief drained from Penta's face. 'No, there's only a record of her birth here. If she's still alive, I'm sure she is with him, wherever he is.' They indicated to a page of the atlas. 'This . . . Castle Forlorn.'

Atlan tried to disguise the look of shock that quickly fell over his face, but Kyr noticed. 'Is something wrong, Atlan? Do you know the place?'

'I fought there once,' he said. 'Bad memories.'

'That's where . . . ?' Kyr asked, remembering all he'd told her about the Battle of Kingdom's Fall. Atlan nodded. 'You don't have to go back,' she assured him.

He shook his head. 'No, I'm not leaving you two lunatics to go there alone. Besides, maybe it will be good for me to confront some memories.'

'You don't need to force yourself to do something just because it's difficult,' said Kyr. 'It's alright to let some sleeping dogs lie.'

'I appreciate you looking out for me, Kyr. Really. But I think it's time I stopped hiding away from things.'

Kyr nodded and looked between the two of them. In each of their eyes, she saw the same resigned look. They were both going back to the place they dreaded most. And Kyr would protect them.

51

ORIA

THE STARS WHEELED OVERHEAD like blazing chariots to light the dawn. Oria was awake, a cold sweat on her forehead, breaths shallow, not only because she'd had another dream, but because she'd awoken to feel Mothril's solid chest against her back, and it had gotten her thinking about things she ought not to be thinking about. She craved comfort desperately but did not think it hers to claim. She must've been cold in the night and huddled closer to him for warmth, and at some point, he'd slung an arm around her, and she'd had a bad dream and—

Oria took a deep breath. The dream she'd had wasn't helping either. She was in a macabre, dreary place that reminded her too much of home, looking for this mysterious sibling she'd only just learned of. It made sense. Almost every waking thought since Lyra had told her about them had been consumed with what they might look like, who they might be.

The stone walls were overgrown with moss and vines that snaked along it, as if they were trying to wrest it back down into the earth. This place was low to the ground, furtive and sunken. It felt forgotten in a similar way to the tower she'd seen in other dreams, leading Oria only to more questions. Why was it that she always sensed her sibling was in these lost, ancient places?

Oria shifted onto her back, and the movement cause Mothril to shift even closer, putting the weight of his chest on her.

'Shit,' she breathed. He was so warm. She glanced at his white hair spilling across his face, her collarbone, felt his breath along her jaw. There was something so strange about how comforting and safe she felt with a man who was, by many accounts, a villain.

At the hot springs, when she'd learned about his true nature, she hadn't known what to think. The realization she was in the middle of the woods with one of her greatest enemies, one of the Eradomin—people she'd felt, in turn, fear, hatred, and curiosity toward—rushed through her. But just as soon as the realization came, she was reminded he was still Mothril. Her Mothril.

When he looked at her with that steady expression of his, she saw only the knight she'd played the harp for, who'd protected her, laughed with her. Killed for her.

What would her clan, the Elder-knights, her father, be saying about her now? Would she be called a traitor, too? But how could the man who'd saved their Whispess's life be a traitor?

Though she didn't want to, slowly, carefully, she slipped from his grasp and looked down at him, watching his chest rise and fall in gentle breaths. She'd peeked out into the hall a fair number of times back in her chambers after the hours grew quiet, and she had never caught him sleeping. Nor looking so serene.

He'd always said he liked the wilds. They were similar in that way. Oria looked up at the sky through the tall pines, awash in that endless blue of the hour just before dawn. He moved again, slinging an arm across her hips this time. A smile not of her own doing crossed her face.

The light had been strangely similar in her dream. She walked along through endless dark hallways. The shadows stood out starker than the light. A voice was calling her, though softly. Around and around she went, traversing spiraling, old stone halls, looking for its source, but it only sounded farther away the more she searched. First it called her name, but as the dream went on, two words echoed over and over again.

'*Fire. Eternal.*'

Mothril stirred, and she realized she'd whispered the words aloud. In seconds, he had moved away from her. 'Sorry.'

'It's alright,' she said, smiling warmly. 'You must be freezing. Here, your tunic.' She started to remove it.

'No,' he said, 'keep it.'

She felt silly wearing it over her dress while he wore only trousers, his cloak thrown over them both as a makeshift blanket. In the low light, she studied his stoneflesh scars. The way they wrapped around his body, somehow built more like a bull than she'd even imagined.

She blushed when he noticed her staring. 'Sorry, I was just wondering . . . what was it like?'

'I was seven or eight, I don't really remember it well. The whole House had it.'

'House?' she asked, before realizing Mothril had had an entire life somewhere else. A whole world away.

'This is Old Era, hm? Well, where the Eradomin lived after everything that happened, we just called Era. We've always had six Houses. When I said my last name was of-Arcandras, it's true, sort of. I'm of the Arcandrian House.'

'Is your House your family?'

'In a way,' he nodded. 'Often you and your family are in the same House, but not always. It depends upon the stars you're

379

born under. I was born under an Arcandrian sky. The sky of the Artificer.'

'I see . . .' she said, taking it all in. 'Do you miss it?'

His gray eyes pierced her. 'Desperately.'

She reached for his hand, and Mothril visibly startled. 'I'm sorry,' she said quickly, and let go.

'It's alright, I wasn't expecting it.' His face was like stone.

Hesitantly, she reached back out and touched her fingers to the scarred flesh there. 'How did this happen?'

'Each House has a . . . like a knight commander of an order, who instructs us in rhapsody, so that we might become elite warrior-monks. I failed to perform one of the seven forms that make up each rhapsody in front of ours. As punishment, I was sent to meditate alone on the mountain near to our House's hearthstone. While on the mountain, I found a phoenix with its talons caught in a trap. I freed it, but'—he held his hands out in front of him—'as you can see, not without some difficulty.'

'You've seen a phoenix?'

He nodded. 'I have.'

'So, each plane is similar then? I mean, the creatures are the same?' she asked.

'They are. I suppose it makes sense, if they are reflections of the same,' he paused, 'worldbeings.'

'What do you call them?'

'We don't really have a word for it,' he shrugged. 'But I like that one. Goddess, too.'

She smiled. 'It's funny you mention a phoenix. I had another dream . . .'

Mothril straightened. 'You did?' He looked her over as if checking her for injuries.

'Don't worry,' she smiled. 'Since I've been with you, the dreams of the Eradomin attacking me seem to have stopped. Interesting, isn't it? Instead, in this one, I was being beckoned somewhere by this disembodied voice. There were ruins, sinking into a bog. I went inside them, and there was whispering everywhere. Fire. Eternal.'

'Fire . . . eternal,' he mused. 'I don't know what that could mean, but I do know of some ruins like that not far to the south, in the Middevale. In a bog, like you say.'

'You do?' she asked, brightening. 'It would make sense, the Middevale being the lowlands between the mountains in the North and the Yoren Mountains. It did look like a warmer clime.'

'I told you you would get your answers,' he said. 'That seems as good a place as any to begin our travels. What do you say?'

Oria's smile grew, and she nodded her agreement.

'Come, I'll take you to them.' He stood and held out a hand.

52

ATLAN

'COME ON, it's our last day in Bellgard, don't you want to do something fun?' Vyktas stood in his full regalia, clean from the washerwomen, in the sun streaming through the room at the inn's inlaid windows.

'You don't find reading fun? You sound just like Kyr,' he mused. He strapped his sword belt around his shoulders and smiled at him.

'Oh, come now,' said Vyktas. 'We could go to a gambling den, see a show. Go to a brothel.' He raised a brow at him.

'No. We have work to do.' He tucked the Oracle's notes into his cloak.

Vyktas frowned, sensing his playful brother had disappeared.

Another lifetime ago, Atlan might've been like him, but too many different experiences, and all the years between them . . .

Things that were lighthearted and meaningless for Vyktas held an entirely different significance to Atlan. He struggled against his thoughts, his ever-present memories, as always, but that only strengthened them.

The one he dreaded most came to him without warning.

'I'll make a man out of you yet,' said Taryq.

Atlan turned to face him. 'I can train with you?'

Finally, he thought. It's happening. *He couldn't help the grin that crossed his lips. He'd been looking for a way to redeem himself in Taryq's eyes since Kingdom's Fall, and as Captain of the Guard, his opinion was, perhaps, the only one left in Yorenth Atlan still valued.*

If his family wanted to abandon him, he would make his own.

Taryq was looking ahead as he readied the horses. 'Something like that,' *he murmured.*

They rode out into the desert, the sun setting as they left Yorenth behind, to a small camp of Sun's Own against the vastness. Three tents, some fluttering flags, pots and pans by the fire, and several bottles of liquor. He looked around at the faces of the others. Some of them he recognized, others he didn't. All, he knew, were elite members of the guard.

What had he been invited to? *he wondered.*

One of the knights he did recognize, Gharin, took a swig from the bottle. 'Taryq! Finally. Now the fun can begin.'

Atlan's eyes widened. He looked around more thoroughly. Not a sword in sight.

'And you brought the princeling!' *Even before Gharin grew close enough for Atlan to see his glazed eyes, he could tell he was deep in his cups.*

Another man he didn't know, but who apparently knew him, rose from the fire. 'I say the princeling gets first choice, eh?'

'First . . . choice?' *Surely, they weren't going to propose a duel when they were this drunk.*

'Alright, alright,' *Taryq said easily, a dark, sly look taking over his handsome face. Atlan's stomach churned at the sight of it.* 'You're eager tonight, Dess. I'd say give a man a chance to settle in first, maybe a round of cards, but you know what? I've had a long day. I'm looking to let off some steam.'

'The forge is hot, eh?' *Gharin replied.*

Taryq smirked. 'Atlan, why don't you go have a look in that tent? Hm?' He nodded toward the one set off from the others.

Atlan furrowed his brow in confusion. On instinct, his hand gripped the dagger at his waist as he inched closer to it.

Taryq's deep laugh resounded behind him. 'Look at him, he's afraid! Nothing to be afraid of, my boy, quite the opposite. Go on.'

Atlan glanced back at him, then approached the tent flaps. He swallowed, tilting his head to see in as he pulled them back. There, huddled against the far corner were two girls and two boys.

Around his age.

Bound and gagged.

At least one of them was crying.

He blinked. Looked back at Taryq.

'Go on,' Taryq prodded. 'Pick the one you like.'

'They're bound.'

Taryq rolled his eyes as if he'd said something exceedingly stupid. 'Atlan, you're focusing on the wrong thing. You said you wanted to be one of us. A warrior, the best of the Sun's Own. Well, the best of the Sun's Own have to cut loose and have a little fun once in a while, don't they?'

This was fun? Atlan felt like he was going to vomit at the sight of the four of them, and instantly it struck him that that was nothing compared to what they must be feeling. He stared back inside the tent.

'Atlan . . .' said Taryq, voice low and impatient.

'They don't want to be here,' Atlan said quietly. Mocking laughter resounded around him.

At his back, Gharin was closer than he'd realized. 'They came with six men for a bit of gold. They know why they're here.'

Taryq appeared at his side then too. 'Fine. Don't choose one—'

'No,' Atlan said desperately. He looked at the four of them. How could he choose?

Taryq tousled Atlan's hair. 'Well, except him, he's mine,' he said, pointing to one of them, a boy, with sun freckles and bronze hair.

*There was no reason to pick one over the others, no reason that
they deserved this, no reason for any of them to be here at all. None
of this was supposed to be happening.*

He grabbed the one nearest to him by the arm. She yelped.

*'Good boy!' Taryq called, patting him on the cheek as he passed.
He heard clinking bottles behind him.*

'You owe me fifty sunmarks,' someone said.

'Where are you going?' Gharin asked.

*'Oh, it's probably his first time! He's shy . . .' said Taryq with a
dismissive wave of his hand. 'Let him go behind the dunes.'*

*Atlan just looked down at the sand as he walked away, dragging
the girl along. There was a rocky outcrop not far from the camp and
he took her there, crouching beneath it and pulling her down
with him.*

*'What is your name?' he whispered, pulling the linen from her
mouth.*

'Zaphira.'

He placed a hand on his chest. 'Atlan.'

*Hesitantly, she reached for his belt, and he staggered backward.
Did she think he wanted that? After seeing her like that? A look
passed between them.*

*What followed in the dark was a memory-muddled blur as he
and the girl held tight to each other in their hiding place, listening to
the screams of the others and the howling of the men.*

The memory abruptly narrowed to nothing in his mind. He
couldn't think about what happened after. Even all these years
later he remembered each of their faces. The feel of Zaphira's
hair against his cheek as they stayed completely still for what
felt like hours. Many a night he would dwell in those dunes,
consider how the two of them should've felt lucky to be spared
the inhumanity roaring around them, if only for those hours.

He would return to his life, afraid of his mother's paramour,
afraid of the violence of intimacy, his own powerlessness—
singular things that deeply affected him, but that he could

nonetheless put away most days—and she and the others would return to a changed world, one in which the cruelty of men was not a vague possibility, but an eventuality.

———

'What must that be like, I wonder? Do you ever get lonely?'

Vyktas had been chatting with Klotho for the better part of the last hour. He leaned across the table now, his head in his hands, looking up at her.

Klotho ran a finger along the table's edge. 'I have plenty of stories to keep me company,' she said, smiling.

'But that's nothing like the world out there, is it?' he prattled on. Klotho frowned. 'We're stuck in here too. Kyr and Penta went to see after our horses. They're probably having a picnic lunch right now. Though, I can't complain too much. You're here.'

Atlan had to stop himself from laughing aloud at his brother's absurd flirting with the poor librarian.

Klotho laughed nervously. 'Well, that's very kind of you to say. We can't all be traveling historians.'

Apparently, Vyktas had seamlessly kept up Kyr's ridiculous story that they were historians from the Middevale.

'I wouldn't recommend such perilous work to just anyone,' he remarked. 'Why, just last week, we came face to face with a mountain wyvern on our travels!'

Klotho gasped.

'Oh, yes, we—'

Atlan elbowed him. 'Vyktas, look at this.' Both he and Klotho looked at him with disappointment at the intrusion on their conversation, though for different reasons.

'I'll let you get back to to your work, then,' she said.

Vyktas watched her go. She turned around once and he gave her a small wave.

He whirled on Atlan. '*What?*'

'If you're done with your dalliances, there's more about Edril Sil here.'

'I think this is a distraction, brother.' Atlan looked at him more closely. 'This whole thing with Penta, I mean, *think* about it. We have no idea who this person really is. You should stay focused on Yorenth. That's why I wanted to come with you, to see what we could do for our city, our people.'

'It's not that simple anymore,' said Atlan. 'Don't you see?'

Vyktas quirked a brow at him. 'Frankly, no. I think it is that simple. We do what we can to understand your power, the Knave's power, and how to protect Yorenth. Then we return to the council with this information. We can use it to treat with them, to force mother's hand to allow us a seat at the table. We can prevent her designs on Bellgard and whatever else she's planning.'

'She'll never listen to you. Haven't you learned that by now?'

'Maybe it's like that for you, but she listens to me plenty.'

Atlan clenched his jaw. 'Fine. Do what you want. I think there's more to this whole thing. Just—' He pointed to the page and read from it. '*These carvings depict Eadr leading his mages, disgraced followers of Solq, from the city of Yorenth to what would become Solq's resting place beneath . . . Kharupan.*'

Vyktas leaned in to look at the page. 'Resting place?'

'Klotho,' Atlan called. The librarian appeared from behind a nearby shelf, eavesdropping as he'd been expecting.

'Hm?' she said innocently.

'You archivists are trained as translators, yes?'

She nodded.

'What does this say?' He pointed to an inscription in the book from an old Eradomin carving.

She leaned in, chewing her lip, her hair falling over the page. 'This is old, very old. Where did you find this book?'

Atlan pointed vaguely in the direction. 'In the section on Northern Folklife.'

'I didn't even know we had something like this . . .'

'Klotho,' he prompted.

'Right. Yes. It tells the story of a great mage who traveled from ruler to ruler, dominion to dominion, offering his services as court diviner, promising glory to whomever would heed his advice. He had at his disposal a powerful artifact that gave him and his chosen ruler a distinct advantage over all the others.'

She paused, looking between them. 'Though it does not say what this is.' She continued. 'In return, he asked for small favors at first, but his demands grew greater with time. He came to the Eradomin first, but they were suspicious of his motivations and rejected his terms. Then, he went to King Raviq of Yorenth, who at first accepted his terms.' Atlan and Vyktas looked at each other. 'After a time of great prosperity, King Raviq grew disillusioned with the mage and threw him out. The carving is partially destroyed here. It looks like . . . a time of great strife followed until Solq could be freed.'

'Freed?' Atlan wondered aloud.

'Could the blights be Spirits trying to communicate?' asked Vyktas.

'Thank you, Klotho,' Atlan said hastily, closing the book. He could hardly wait until she was out of earshot. 'I think you're right, brother. It would make sense. Sylas told Kyr that Crescian was 'lost to him.' If the Spirits are being meddled with some-how, that could reasonably cause all kinds of errors with the expression of the matter they're responsible for!'

Vyktas sighed. 'It does make sense. As much as I hate to extend our sojourn into this madness we've gotten ourselves into, you may have a point. Let's see what Penta, Kyr, and Two-Trees have to say, but then promise me, Brother, after all this, we will discuss Yorenth, mother, and the council.'

Atlan nodded. 'I promise.'

53

ORIA

ANOTHER EARLY MORNING. This time, though, Oria was alone. They were no longer in the alpine forests and pine-dotted wetlands she was used to, but the thick deep woods that served as a barrier between the harshest of the Northern lands and the Middevale. Still, the air was warmer here, and though the canopy was many-layered, sunlight dappled where she lay.

Where was Mothril?

She rose, slipping his cloak around her as she circled their camp. There was no sign of him, the fire from last night gone cold. *The snares,* she remembered. Certain he was out checking them or otherwise foraging, as he often did before breakfast at each place they camped, she set off to look for him.

She no longer wondered at how little he slept. It turned out Eradomin did not need to often, if at all. A boon for her—they had made great time on their travels because Mothril often rode late into the night as she slept against him, waking occasionally to forests and mountains rolling past.

Her makeshift cane fashioned from a stick sunk into the earth as she walked along, her brace discarded back at camp. Before they came to the citadel, she had learned briefly to hunt and trap with her father. She knew vaguely what to look for and checked for spots Mothril might've set some. Sure enough, in the first place she looked, slightly obscured, was a simple rock trap. She smiled.

But still no Mothril.

She kept walking, thinking how easy it would be to get lost in this place. Not lost in a sense of losing one's way, but rather, to stay here, admiring its beauty forever. Nature, true nature, untouched by civilization, was a wonder unlike anything else. In nature, in this world of her own choosing, she wasn't the Whispess, nor Edril Sil's daughter. She wasn't trapped, hunted, or threatened. She was just Oria, existing. It cradled her, allowing her to be whoever she felt like in that moment. Whoever she needed to be, or to be nothing at all.

As if she'd willed it, she looked around and realized she'd strayed completely into the wilds, but she wasn't afraid. She felt at home.

Thwack.

The sound interrupted the landscape of the forest's characteristic sounds. It was coming from off to her right and she followed it.

Thwack.

The distinct sound of branches being cut, leafy refuse flying. She came to a ledge, looking down upon a small, flat glen.

She had found Mothril.

It took some time to understand what she was seeing. Mothril by the oak directly across from her one moment. Mothril with his sword held up by his brow at the other end of the glen the next, his sword striking the brush. It wasn't merely that he was moving quickly. He moved in flashes she almost couldn't catch.

In a sinuous movement, he arced toward the shadows and folded into them. He *became* them. Then, out of his own shadow, he appeared again elsewhere, as fluidly as air or water moved, in the shade of the tree just in front of her.

'How do you do that?' she marveled.

Though he didn't startle, he seemed surprised by her presence. 'Whispess. You're awake. And you found me.'

She looked at him in wonder, waiting for an explanation.

'This is how we Eradomin fight. It is why your father and your Elder-knights consider us so formidable. It is a minor form of veil-rending, of travel between planes.'

Oria smoothed her stunned expression. 'I see.' She tried to understand how something like that was possible. Was it only possible for the Eradomin, or could others—could anyone who followed Sarthura—learn too?

'Is that what you did to—?' The words came out of her without thought.

Mothril stilled. Planted his sword in the earth.

'Whispess, I—'

'Oria,' she corrected. 'Friends, remember?'

He hadn't looked like he was breathing hard at all practicing his forms, but now Oria noticed his chest, the mosaic of scars there, rising and falling rapidly.

'I-I hope you know—' he cursed under his breath, letting loose the braid his hair had been in. 'I didn't wish for that to happen. I know the knights must've been important to you, particularly Sybil. Eradomin are taught that we are each reflections of each other in rhapsody, so when someone falls in combat, it is also as if we have. Each person is like a note, a resonance. There is great honor in rejoining the harmonies, but there can also be great disharmony in our lives when we lose someone.' He looked up at her. 'You asked about my meditation. I do not only do it because it is restorative, but to remind myself of what I have done when I have taken a life. To reattune myself to the harmonies. It's not an act I seek out, Oria. I swear it. But it always seems to find me.'

'I didn't know,' she answered simply. Suddenly feeling foolish she'd brought it up, she looked at the tree beside her, feeling the urge to peel at its bark. She ran her fingers over it. 'I'm sorry.'

'You have nothing to be sorry for.' He looked at her from where he stood in the grass below her. In his eyes was a rare gravity, something she suspected he seldom let show. 'Remember whose actions led to this. The only one who should be sorry is Edril Sil.'

Slowly, Oria began lowering herself down on the ledge to the clearing. Mothril rushed over to lend her a hand, hesitantly extending it. She wondered if he thought she might not take it.

'You don't scare me, Mothril.' It was something she'd said to him once before, and she meant it still. She placed her hand in his, steadying herself against him as she stepped down. 'I know what it is to put on a mask and become something else.'

He nodded. 'Even with the destruction I've wrought . . . ?'

Yes, her thoughts urged. But as visions of bludgeoned knights, of Sybil, her throat slashed, forced their way into her mind, it was as if a mask of her own that had allowed her to face the carnage that day slipped. She didn't know what to say.

Mothril turned away from her, his palm grazing the pommel of his sword and then withdrawing as if burned.

'I shouldn't have asked you to deny it. And I wouldn't want you to. I deserve the guilt and shame of what I've done. It is but a poor payment in return.'

He knelt for a spell, bowing his head from the sun, then dropped his other knee. She waited for him to speak, but he only looked forward silently into the forest's edge. The scars on his back flexed, and she stepped closer. He was trembling.

No, not trembling. *Crying.*

Mothril was breaking before her in a way she didn't think he ever let anyone see. She wondered if he had ever unfettered himself in this way before at all.

'I thought Sybil understood.' His voice was a rasp.

She stood behind him now and put a gentle hand on his shoulder. 'I thought she did too.' He flinched, like it pained him to be touched.

She half-expected him to wipe his tears, stiffening as he apologized and told her to forget this rash moment. Instead, heavier sobs racked his body.

'I'm sorry, Oria,' he managed to get out. 'So—sorry.'

She leaned down, pulling him into her arms, and he tightened around her, even leaning into her touch as she ran her hand through his hair in soothing strokes.

Not pained, she realized. *Starving.*

She didn't know how long they stayed like that. Two more days of travel lay ahead of them to Greenflower, but as she stood there, she thought only of her warrior.

54

ATLAN

ATLAN AND VYKTAS caught up with Kyr and Penta just outside the city gates. It wasn't too difficult to find the two of them—they cut quite the pair, and they weren't exactly inconspicuous about their haggling with the stablemaster. They approached the two of them, Kyr standing close to the man, and Penta behind her, a faint look of amusement gracing their features.

'Just pay him!' Vyktas said, outraged.

'What kind of a game are you running?' Kyr accused.

'Hey, I know you,' said the stablemaster, a middle-aged man with a tattoo on his arm. He was pointing at Atlan. 'You're the prince! Prince Atlan! Of Yorenth!' He began looking around, trying to gather the attention of others nearby. 'Look at that! I'm being shortchanged by a prince!'

'No,' said Kyr, 'you're talking to me. And I'm no prince. We've only been here two nights!'

'That's not what my records say,' he said dismissively.

'Oh, forget it,' Atlan grumbled. He shoved a sack of marks at the man and began the short climb to the upper stables, to a small barn behind the yard.

'Teleri!' he shouted as he entered the stuffy room, thick with the smell of hay and sunlight streaming through various cracks and holes in the walls.

A head popped up out of the hay pile and Atlan couldn't help but laugh at the sight. 'There you are.'

She smiled lazily. 'I've had some really, *really* incredible naps up here.'

He smiled back. 'Come on, we're heading out.'

'Did you manage to find anything useful?' Two-Trees asked as they led the horses from the stables over to his brother and the others, Kyr still looking like she wanted to fight the stablemaster.

'Well—'

Kyr overheard them, muttering, 'More poetry.'

'Indeed,' Atlan said, pressing his lips together. 'But I haven't told you what Vyktas and I found today. Klotho translated something for us. It seems that in the First Age there were stories of the Spirits being trapped, or maybe even killed,' he said, his voice lowering, 'and I think it has something to do with our family's history. At least, something happened with Solq long ago. It's related to Kharupan and this mage, Eadr. This is all from an Eradomin inscription, too. Apparently, this Eadr went to the Eradomin as well. There's mention of an artifact. At first, I would've thought this would be the Pentaculum,' he said, glancing at Penta, 'but now . . .'

Penta gasped. 'The *mirror*! Mirror in the fortress!'

Kyr turned to them. 'The mirror?'

'Yes, that is the artifact you speak of. The one my father hides. It is not a mirror exactly, but that is the closest way I can describe it in your language.'

Kyr looked at them. Atlan saw wonder there on his friend's face. 'Are you remembering more?'

Penta shook their head. 'He kept it in a courtyard then,

when I was young. People would come from far and wide just for a chance to look upon it. For a chance to look upon the answers of the world.'

'Penta, is your father this—this usurper-mage?' Atlan asked. 'Eadr?'

'He has gone by many names, but I cannot remember them,' they answered.

'Why the Yoren name?' Vyktas asked.

They looked at both Atlan and Vyktas. 'I—I am not sure. Perhaps to blend in? He is the ultimate pretender. I would not be surprised if it was simply a disguise he took on.'

'You mentioned the Spirits being trapped,' Kyr said, looking at Atlan. 'I read something about that.' She paused for a moment, thoughtful. 'Spirits let loose, essence unbound . . . try to contain them, and Singers are crowned.'

'Try to contain them,' Atlan repeated. 'Who, or what, is containing them? Containing? Penta, can things be contained within this mirror? Beings, I mean?'

Penta shook their head. 'No, I-I don't think so.'

Two-Trees who had been watching this exchange in silence, folded her hands together, looking at each of them. 'This is grave news, indeed. Don't you see? The Spirits face great peril, Spiritsingers are returning. This portends a second cataclysm when we've hardly recovered from the first one. The nullah may remain safe, but I worry for the Misguided that will flee their homes in droves.'

'It hasn't come to that yet,' said Vyktas. 'All this over something my brother read in a book? We don't even know who wrote it! What if they were some crackpot?'

'No,' said Atlan. 'But we are right to be concerned over burning bodies on the road, the living mountain we all saw, the unpredictability of magic, the instability in Yorenth, the unrest in the North. No, I don't think we're being unreasonable at all.'

With little more said on the subject, the five of them set off from Bellgard in anxious trepidation. Anxious to return to the road, anxious to uncover more about the mystery of the Spirits, and of Penta's past.

Castle Forlorn lay far to the east, past Yorenth, and farther north, through the Middevale. It would take nearly a week to reach by horseback if they moved quickly. Filled with the newfound importance of their journey, day's rides got longer, their travel more efficient, though their questions still weighed heavy on them.

For Atlan at least, though, Bellgard had been a respite sorely needed, a safe place for them to catch their breath after all that had befallen them on the way here. They decided this time to take the lowland route—highwaymen were preferable to stone dragons.

It had given him some perspective of his own, too. Despite the dangers of the wilds, he felt a loosening in his chest the farther out they rode—he and Teleri on Old Tom and Vyktas and Kyr on their horse, bickering incessantly. Penta rode alone on his gelding, spending most of their time looking off into the distance as if watching for something.

Atlan's breath came easier, and his muscles relaxed in the saddle. He realized he did not like the city as much as he thought. Looking up at the open sky, he breathed in the solitude of it. This, and a few good friends around him was all he needed.

They came to a well for travelers later in the day. An old, stone one limned with moss and algae. Atlan wondered if Eadr had ever passed it by on his pilgrimage—or was it a war march? Who was the mysterious mage? Was he simply a conduit, or another like Penta, mysterious and powerful?

His mind raced with the possibilities. He and Kyr were Spiritsingers, of that much he was sure. Their emotions called on the matter of the world, shaping it, changing the outcome of things. He tended toward fire, Solq's gift, and she toward the chaos of Crescian. But Penta, and Teleri, for that matter . . .

Teleri's magic seemed limited to her nullah, as if it was the connection to the land that was important. When Kyr came running to him that night that Sylas found her, she told him of what he mentioned, that there were those, like him, that could tap into a source of magic at the right time and place, with certain practice, and certain things aligned. He suspected that was what Teleri was capable of.

Penta was the biggest unknown of all. They were clearly unnatural—their age, their parentage, the way they summoned power, commanded ash and darkness. He hoped they were right to trust them.

Vyktas and Kyr rode up beside them. 'Settle something for us.'

Atlan rolled his eyes. 'What?'

'Have you noticed those little blackbirds following us?'

'Starlings,' Kyr cut in.

'Yes, starlings,' Vyktas agreed. 'Did you know starlings can be taught to mimic your voice? I've half a mind to bring one home as a pet, but Kyr thinks me cruel. I think it would be hilarious to teach it to bother Taryq all the time. I'd take good care of it, too! Give it all the fruit and peanuts it wants.'

'You shouldn't cage a bird,' Kyr snapped. 'It's not right, y'know, with the ways of the world.'

'I really think we have other things—'

Ahead of them, Penta turned sharply left, circling back toward them. They only made it a quarter of the way before they stopped their horse abruptly.

Penta stared behind and into the distance, as if watching something play out among the clouds. A chill clattered down Atlan's spine at the sight of it.

Suddenly, what looked like cataracts grew and then dissipated like clouds passing over their eye. 'Starlings,' they whispered. Then, louder, 'Starlings . . . yellow castle . . . mirror in the fortress!'

'Kyr, I think we broke your new friend,' Vyktas said under his breath.

Kyr quickly dismounted and ran to them.

'Penta?' she asked, reaching for them. The gelding began pacing and Kyr lurched forward, trying to calm the nervous animal.

'The Erángal!' Penta screamed. 'He sees me!'

Kyr was back by Penta's side in an instant. 'Penta, you're safe. He's not here,' she said softly, stroking her thumb across the back of their hand. 'But I am. I'm here.'

Penta blinked. 'Kyr?'

'Just me.'

Penta brought their other hand to Kyr's, as if it could anchor them to her. Their breaths slowed, but their voice still held a weary edge.

'The Erángal—that is the artifact, the mirror, that he possesses. When he uses it, he knows the answers to what he seeks. He knows I have left my tower. It must anger him greatly. He will try to figure out how.' They were trembling. 'I remembered something else, too. The starlings. My mother sends them. She is not yet dead!'

Atlan and Teleri had already begun drawing closer, but now Vyktas rushed forward, anxious to hear more.

'Your mother?' Kyr studied their face. 'You're remembering? Where is she?'

Penta nodded, but by their troubled look, Atlan sensed this was not a good thing. 'I know what the starlings mean now. He continues his foul work. Those poor people—they may be gone completely. Dead or disappeared to another plane, I am not sure . . .' Penta's eyes darted back and forth as they spoke.

'Who?' Kyr asked.

'Wiccar nomads.'

'You're remembering.' This time, they were words of awe.

'My sister thinks herself a Wiccar, but she is not. My father,' they gave a rueful laugh, 'the *pretender*.' Penta looked at each of them. 'I know not where she is, but my mother, *our* mother, is Calligone. Sarthura.'

55

ORIA

'WHAT IS THIS PLACE?' Oria asked, as they approached the crest of a hill and looked out on gray ruins sinking into the mire of a peat bog.

Since she had left the citadel, but especially over the past days as they rode to the ruins, she hadn't been able to stop thinking about the new world that had opened up to her. A sibling. A mother she didn't know. Other planes. Unknown magic.

She stared at the ruins, then closed her eyes and imagined her dream. The place looked right.

'Hm. Prophetic dreams of a place where murderers and thieves sleep—' She looked at Mothril, wide-eyed. 'Don't worry. The road here's been abandoned for a long time, but it used to be quite the den of debauchery for unsavory characters, myself included. One night, one of your Far Clan absconders, Sorril of-Iais, told us all that the place had been used for Wiccar rituals long ago. Said his grandmother remembered it.'

'Strange. I've never heard of it.'

The ground grew soft, so they left their horse and continued on foot. When the ground got too uneven, Mothril carried her. They reached the small arch opening into the stone and peered in. Mothril called out, but only his echoing voice answered. They were alone.

'Does this look like it?'

'It does,' she said, running her hand along the wall. 'But I don't hear anything.'

'Has a voice ever spoken to you before, dreamwalking or otherwise?'

'In dreams, many times.'

'Do you think it was this sibling of yours?'

She nodded, still looking around the dark space. 'Must be. They're awfully enigmatic, whoever they are.' She stared down the long hall beyond the vestibule. 'Well, only one way to find out where this goes, I suppose.' She hiked up her dress, took Mothril's hand, and stepped inside. Immediately, she was hit with a foul smell of decay. So terrible was it, that it made her hesitate.

Behind her, Mothril covered his mouth and nose. 'Shit. Whispess, something's died in here.'

'I didn't smell death in my dream,' she said, her voice muffled by her sleeve.

He looked down at her. 'Do you want me to go in ahead?'

Oria shook her head. 'No, I need to do this.'

Inside the ruin's husk, the dim halls had a cramped, claustrophobic and yet boundless, eternal feeling, like she might make a wrong turn and be lost forever in its narrow passageways. She walked slowly, examining the old walls, the ruins reminding Oria of a dead tree. Outside, the structure was old and crumbling but standing well enough—barely containing a rot within.

Just like in her dream, the corridor began to curve around like a spiral, delving deeper into the earth. From the outside, it looked like a small barrow, almost in the shape of snail's shell, but inside, it was labyrinthian.

There must be magic at work here, Oria thought.

In her dream a voice had spoken to her, but now there was only cold silence. She didn't know which she preferred.

At the end of the winding halls, they came to a stone archway with a door of metal bars, like a cage. On it, there were six symbols engraved: a spiral, a crescent, lines moving outward from a center point, interlocking circles, and two that were unique. One looked like an eye bisected by lines, the other an eye that had been blacked out.

Something about the last symbol drew her, how she'd been venerated and cursed for being a seer, an Oracle. She brushed her hand over it and felt a jolt.

With a gasp, she stumbled backward, bumping into Mothril.

'What is it?' he asked, steadying her.

'I don't know . . .'

Mothril put his hand to the same place Oria had. 'Did you see something?'

'No, it was a strange feeling in my hand.' Oria looked from him back to the door and hesitantly lifted her hand to it again. She pressed her fingertips lightly to another seal, this time to the spiral on the left.

Nothing.

She touched the blacked-out eye again. 'Ah!' she gasped and pulled her hand away. 'It's this one symbol in particular, for some reason.'

'The unseeing eye,' he said. 'Sarthura.'

She whirled around. 'You recognize it? Why didn't you say so?'

'I didn't, but it matches up with our symbols of lore. The unseeing eye is often a symbol of Sarthura's presence.'

She tried to remember all that her father had said now about Sarthura, but he really only mentioned her in passing. It bothered her that she kept coming up in their search for her sibling, and she desperately wanted Mothril to have the answers she knew he must still seek as an Eradomin.

'It hurts me to touch it. Why?'

He tilted his head, studying the door. 'This door is elaborate. Maybe it's a passkey of some kind.'

'A passkey?'

'Maybe you know of the Eradomin blood magic present in the tunnels below the citadel? I'm sure you've heard rumors about it.'

She pushed thoughts of their rituals from her mind. 'Not much, I admit. What is it?'

He looked surprised. 'It's all over the tunnel walls below the citadel. Our people use blood as a key. This place doesn't look Eradomin to me, but perhaps it's worth a try.'

When Oria hesitated, Mothril said, 'I'll do it. I don't mind, can hardly feel the flesh on my palms anymore.' He pulled his sword from his belt, and before she could say anything, slid it across his palm. Red blood seeped out from a line, thin as parchment, across his skin.

'Mothril!' she gasped.

He held his palm to the symbol and immediately pulled it back with a hiss. 'Goddess, it burns.' He paused, looking curiously at his palm. 'Been years since I've had any feeling in my hands.'

'Maybe you're on to something,' Oria said. She did the same, slicing her hand, and held her hand to the symbol.

In the unlit room, deep underground, the door glowed to life. She looked at Mothril, illuminated by the curious blue light. For the first time, it occurred to her that they were potentially toying with dangerous magic.

The metal door began to click loudly, as pieces of it began to move of their own accord. It was an elaborate thing to watch, the metal folding in on itself and hinging to completely fall away into the stone walls at its sides.

'I can't believe it,' Oria said. 'It worked!'

Mothril looked less than thrilled. 'Be careful. I get a bad feeling in this place.'

'Shouldn't have shown me how to unlock it, then,' Oria teased.

He huffed a laugh. 'Perhaps I should've held my tongue.' They walked into the small chamber ahead of them and looked down the hall. 'The decay is stronger here. We should tread carefully.'

The hallway ahead was increasingly confined, so much so that it gave Oria a sense of anxiety just to breathe as she stepped into it. She couldn't imagine how Mothril must've felt. After that long, breathless squeeze, they came to a larger chamber.

'Whatever the purpose of these ruins, I can't help but feel that it's been abandoned for a reason,' she said, her voice low and assessing as she looked around. The ceiling stood high above them, cavernous in its height. At the far end stood a stone dais with an old stone altar. Unadorned, there were no offerings, carvings, or other ornamentation one might expect to be at a resting place or shrine. Cautiously, Oria approached.

The altar had a thick slab atop it, etched with the same symbols that had been on the gate. One was more prominent than the others, though. It made her stomach drop. The unseeing eye. As she walked around the slab, Mothril bumped its edge, his armor grinding against the stone.

The surface of the altar *moved*.

'Did you see that?' she asked. 'What is this?'

'I don't know,' Mothril replied, looking just as rapt by this place as she was.

Oria pressed her weight against the slab, but it didn't budge. 'Can you try to lift it?'

Mothril looked at her for a moment, as though trying to decide if it was worth arguing over whether or not it was a good idea, then braced his hands on either side of one edge. 'Stand back.'

She stepped away, and heaved his weight against it, moving the stone edge until it was hanging over the side of the altar. Another shove, and it fell to the side with a crash that echoed throughout the chamber. It wasn't an altar, but a large stone box with a lid.

A vault.

The putrid stench they'd smelled traces of poured out of it. Oria backed away, clutching at her nose and mouth. But not before she caught a glimpse of thin, red hair around a skull.

At first, fearing this was her lost sibling, she gasped and felt her eyes begin to burn with tears, but it was unmistakable who it was. She would recognize him anywhere.

Wrapped loosely in a white shroud, the body's arms and legs were desiccated, the chest vivisected to expose a perfectly preserved heart.

'Oria—' Mothril sounded just as shocked as she felt.

He quickly crossed the chamber to where she stood, one hand at his sword belt as always, the other pulling his tunic over his nose to try to abate the terrible smell.

Time slowed and reset, as a sense of unreality overtook her.

'No! This can't be!'

In the vault lay her father's half-decayed body. Far too decomposed to have been dead from Lyra's flood.

'*What is this?*' she said, her horrified eyes roaming over the sight before her. His skin was white and dry, puckered with death. He had no eyes and no lips, but still she recognized him. Her father. Dead.

'This is impossible,' she said again. 'He's—the citadel . . .' She tried to make sense of what she knew to be true, and what was staring her in the face. 'Who *is* he?' she finally asked.

Finally, she let Mothril pull her away and out of the chamber. 'We shouldn't be here,' he said quickly, hustling her through the narrow passageway.

'Clearly, I'm supposed to be here. My blood let us in! That was—that was . . .' She couldn't make herself say it.

'Yes,' Mothril whispered.

'*Why?* What the *fuck* is this place?' she yelled. Mothril didn't need to answer, because they both knew what this was.

The tomb of her very much alive father.

56

ATLAN

YORENTH FINALLY ROSE in the sun-dazed distance. The Lower Road had turned out to be mostly deserted, and he and Kyr had cursed themselves for their error in judgment on the way there. They'd passed one caravan going between Yorenth and Bellgard, a group of very friendly glassworkers and silk traders traveling together.

Smart of them, he thought.

'We're weary, and we've one bottle of wine left,' said a man with a kind face and a long black beard streaked with gray. He produced a clay bottle from a crate on their wagon. 'Care to share it with us? We'd be interested to hear the conditions of the road ahead.'

'You don't have to ask me twice,' said Kyr.

They settled in, the caravanners on the back of their wagon and the five of them in the clover-dotted grass, beside an old stone cairn serving as a signpost, just beside the road.

He told them his name was Eft, and they warned him and the other caravanners not to take the mountain pass. Of course, Kyr took great joy in telling their harrowing story, even adding quite a few flourishes, though Atlan didn't think it needed any.

'A mountain wyvern . . .' one man breathed.

'It's like my cousin says,' Eft added. 'He lives in the Middevale. Says he's seen the forest come alive.' He gestured wildly with his hands as he spoke. 'The creatures are all wrong up there.' He turned to the woman seated next to him and swatted her arm. 'You didn't believe me! Listen to these folk!'

'Please, you can't believe anything Airan says,' the woman replied, doubt sharpening her rounded features.

'What did your cousin see?' Two-Trees asked, passing the bottle to Kyr.

'Oh, what didn't he see! Little creatures made of sod harassing the vegetables. Way out in the fields, he thought he saw a golden stag, but as he got closer, it was made of straw! And one of his haybales was missing. He said the thing galloped off straight into the woods.' Eft shook his head. 'Airan might be a little barmy, but he's no liar.'

'The Greenwoods too?' Penta mumbled.

Eft looked at Penta in the same way everyone except Kyr seemed look at them. A little curious, mostly afraid. 'Er, you folk know about these strange happenings?'

Atlan exchanged a glance with his brother. 'We're studying them, actually. Trying to find out why they're happening.'

He nodded. 'Well, I wish you the best of luck. Times are hard enough as it is in the Realm without all of this going on.' He sighed, muttering his next words. 'Not just for us travelers either. Those poor soldiers . . .'

'Soldiers?'

'The outpost,' said Eft. 'It's a terrible sight.'

'Ah.' Atlan hung his head. 'It is—'

'I don't know what Queen Attiqah does sitting up in that grand castle day in and day out, but it does little for the rest of us. The tithe increases each year, yet our lives only get harder.'

Atlan leaned forward, nodding, but Vyktas took the words right out of his mouth. 'It's not right.' He glanced at Atlan, as if looking for reassurance, then continued anyway. 'But I don't think the plight of everyday people is much on anyone's mind up in that grand castle.' Atlan raised a brow. 'I have an intuition, though, that if more of the royal family and councilors knew what was going on, if they met with their subjects, things would change.'

'How can they not know?' Eft asked.

Vyktas looked down.

'All we can do is keep heart. Change can come faster than you expect,' said Atlan.

'I'll drink to that,' said the woman next to Eft, lifting the nearly empty wine bottle.

Vyktas smiled. 'Take care on your journey. May it be a safe one.'

'You as well,' Eft replied.

Since then, the second half of their journey had been mostly quiet, but not because the mood had turned sour. Atlan thought it had more to do with Penta's revelation. *Finding out you're traveling with a demigod will do that*, he supposed.

He'd caught Vyktas and Two-Trees both staring at Penta with no small amount of awe on more than one occasion.

The child of Calligone. The child of *Edril Sil*.

What kind of a match is that? he thought. Then, *how does that work?*

He shook his head as if to clear the thoughts and questions away, but they were relentless.

What will this sister of Penta's be like? What if she is not what Penta is expecting? What if she has been influenced or corrupted by this Edril Sil?

Then there was all they'd learned of Edril Sil's manipulations of the Wiccars. As far as his princely education was concerned, and for that matter, what the rest of the world believed to be true, Edril Sil was born a Wiccar. Though, now that he thought about it, it was strange that he didn't seem to have a clan name or other relatives, and had taken the name of his wife, Felith of-Cailir. He vaguely recalled learning of her death some years ago.

How much did Felith know?

There were too many questions invading his mind for him to notice what was in front of him. Had he been, he would've realized they were coming around a familiar bend in the cliffs. He would've noticed that Teleri had grown solemn, that Vyktas and Kyr were bracing themselves for what they were about to see. The flaming bodies of that inextinguishable blight out in the Barrens.

Kyr spoke then. 'You know the blights we told you about?' she said to Penta. 'We're about to come upon one of them.'

The road was grimly quiet, the ground scorched and signpost burned away to nothing. The bodies, still smoldering, remained preserved in flame. They had entered a hallowed ground, devoid of life but eerily full of the power life was fabricated from. Eft's muttered words came back to him then. What had they thought when they'd seen the outpost fires in the distance? Was his mother doing anything to allay their people's fears?

He clenched his jaw. *Likely not.*

Penta stopped their horse and dismounted.

'Must we really stop?' Vyktas asked.

They began walking amongst the bodies, their face a mixture of so much emotion Atlan couldn't make out one in particular. 'I see a form in shadow. Wielding fire.'

His brother turned to him. 'Just once, I would love to get something out of them that's a little less cryptic.' Atlan could see that his brother was trying his best to maintain a stoic face, but he knew the gruesome sight before them bothered him deeply.

Penta gazed at Vyktas. 'Alright, then. I see a scared boy, trying to impress his brother. On a horse.'

Kyr grinned. 'Good one.'

Vyktas raised his brows, a small laugh escaping him. 'Look at that, Penta's got a sense of humor!'

'Come on, Vyktas,' said Atlan, 'Let's give the horses a rest, hm?'

The brothers moved into the sparse shade with Two-Trees, delighting in Old Tom's spitting despite their grim surroundings.

'See? Even he wants to get going,' Vyktas said.

'Are you comparing yourself to a goat?' Atlan smirked.

Vyktas's answer was cut short by his wandering eyes. They were following Penta, who had dropped to the ground.

'Here!' they called. 'He's here!'

'Who?' Vyktas called back.

'Solq, he—he's trapped here. I can feel him.' Vyktas started forward, and Atlan and Two-Trees followed. 'That's why the flames can't be extinguished!'

'What are you talking about? I don't see anyone, certainly not a Spirit!' said Vyktas.

'You wouldn't see him—' Penta shot him a glance. 'But, no, he is beneath us.'

'Are you telling us there's a Spirit trapped under the earth here?' Kyr asked.

'Yes,' they answered simply.

Under the earth? This piqued Atlan's interest, and he began walking toward them.

He only made it two steps before a crossbow bolt whizzed by his ear and plinked off the hard ground somewhere behind him.

Old Tom and the horses spooked.

'What the Six was that?' Kyr cried out. Scrambling, the five of them got down behind some scrub brush next to a burned tree. 'Can you see anyone?' she asked.

'No,' Atlan replied, scanning the horizon.

'There,' said Vyktas, pointing to a cave in the cliffside. The Outlands. 'There's someone in that cave.'

Kyr said Atlan's thoughts aloud as they looked around at the empty landscape. 'Just once I'd like us to have a bit of good luck. Is that so much to ask?'

Two-Trees was looking off to their right. 'There's more of them over there.'

Sure enough, in the distance stood three figures in white cloaks. They had wide-brimmed metal helmets, and thin white fabric that hung over top of it, concealing their faces. Each was armed with a sword.

'Who are you?' shouted one voice. The accent wasn't Sentinel—not even the unique rolling sounds of the long-isolated Telhavi.

'Travelers,' Vyktas called back quickly.

'What do travelers want with burning corpses?'

'Northern accents,' Penta whispered.

Vyktas raised his eyebrows. Clearing his throat, he angled his head back toward the men. 'We were seeing if they had anything to take,' he lied. Atlan had never seen his brother so confident before. He did well under duress, better than Atlan had expected him to. Face down in the dirt, he smiled proudly.

'Have you seen sufficiently?' asked the voice. Atlan didn't like the menacing edge to it.

'I'd say we have,' yelled Vyktas. 'Let us on our way.'

Looking up through the dry grass, Atlan could see the men advancing on them. 'We'll let you on your way. But first we intend to find out the reason you're meddling in an area infected with magic.'

'Infected?' Vyktas said under his breath. 'Strange choice of words.'

'And how do they know about that?' Atlan whispered.

Vyktas shifted a bit, peering over the brush. 'I don't know anything about magic,' said Vyktas. 'I've told you the truth.'

'Perhaps, but one of you does. I can smell it on you.'

'Smell it?' Vyktas scoffed.

'Told you,' Two-Trees whispered. She fidgeted beside him. 'You four go, I'll tell the nullah to shield you. We are near enough that I think it will hear my call.'

Atlan's head snapped to face her. '*No*. You're coming with us. Besides, there's not a lot here for you to draw from.'

We're hiding behind some damned dried brush and a dead tree, he thought.

'What do you propose, then?' Two-Trees asked.

Atlan glanced up at the knights and breathed deep, loosening his jaw. 'We go together. Kyr, your magic is unstable, so you'd best not call on it here. With the blight present, we don't know what might happen.' He looked down the line. 'Penta, can you shroud us? Teleri and I will try to shield everyone as best we can. Vyktas, you stay in the middle. We just need to make it to the treeline beyond the road. That should be close enough to the nullah that we will be safe.'

'That's enough whispering!' yelled another voice.

Atlan nodded. Penta closed their eyes.

The clouds above grew gray as ordinary storm clouds at first, and then darker still. Burning bark peeled from the tree nearby, disintegrating into ash that swirled around them in an opaque cloud. A squall expanded from it, cloaking them in deep, flowing shade.

'Stop at once!' commanded one of the other knights. He could hear the others coughing—a good sign.

They took off running. Bolts flew, and Atlan could hear the knight's footsteps behind them. He tried his best to scatter them within Penta's ash storm, but he could not make himself focus. If anything happened—

'Spiritsingers!' one yelled.

How do they know what we are? Who are these people?

Another bolt ricocheted off a rock in the path. As he looked down, he noticed roots began growing through the parched earth. The nullah was trying to reach them.

Time slowed. They had put more distance between them and the knights, but still the archers in the caves rained bolts down upon them. The trees became a rapidly advancing blur ahead of them. Two-Trees's forest-given magic was ensnaring the way behind them now, building a wall of roots. Another bolt.

Atlan heard a grunt.

Behind him, someone fell. Atlan chanced a look over his shoulder to see two figures slumped over in the darkness. He doubled back. The whistling sound of bolts wouldn't let him stop and focus for even a moment. He got between his brother and Two-Trees, who were helping one another along, and rushed them forward, trying to reach out to Solq, to anything. His fear made him dangerous, he knew that, but he had to do something.

He went somewhere deep within himself.

Solq, am I on the right path now?

A crumbling sound answered him, like rock falling away from a surface. Worried he had caused a rockslide, he chanced a look toward the cliffs. He couldn't see much through the howling ash that pressed in around them, but what he could see looked stable. Then he looked over his shoulder.

A fissure was forming in the earth, at least as tall as him across, and growing in length. Burning flame and vapor erupted forth from it. Intense heat. Bright, flaring orange light. He hesitated a moment too long.

A stinging pain pierced his arm. It was familiar—somewhere deep inside him he registered what it was, but he couldn't acknowledge it. Not right now. The darkness grew and grew. He kept moving, able to focus only on putting distance behind him.

The breach will hold them, he assured himself.

They were almost to the forest's edge now. They must be. Atlan heard the welcome crunch of sticks and leaves underfoot and nearly collapsed. He could barely see his hand in front of him.

'Kyr,' he called, looking around for her. 'Tell Penta to ease up!'

He, Vyktas, and Two-Trees buckled to the ground, landing in a heap against the tree trunk, crushing the soft, green grass of the knoll beneath their weight.

'I'm sorry,' said Two-Trees. The panic in her usually calm voice struck fear in him.

'It's alright,' he breathed. 'We made it.'

Time moved along with the thumping of his heart. He looked from Two-Trees's face, filled with such pain, to Vyktas's oddly pale one. The shadows dissipated. Sunlight beamed down upon them.

It felt too harsh.

He saw it, then. What worried Teleri so.

'Atlan—' Vyktas laughed harshly. 'I'm having trouble moving my legs.'

Hastily, Atlan unbuckled Vyktas's armor, pulling it away piece by piece. As he lifted the breastplate from him, he saw the puncture wound more clearly. Vyktas's gambeson was already soaked through with blood.

'It's alright, you're alright. Teleri, I need rags. Water.' He looked around. Teleri shifted, but she wasn't moving.

'Tel—!' He froze, remembering they didn't have their packs, their saddlebags. They had nothing.

He put pressure on the wound, just like he'd done so many times, for so many soldiers, but the blood kept coming. It seeped through his fingers, hot and sticky.

Atlan gritted his teeth. He looked down at his unfamiliar hands, covered in his brother's red blood, outside of his body, where it didn't belong.

Vyktas looked up at him, sweating and shuddering in his arms like a foal. 'It's colder here, isn't it?'

Atlan took note of movement at the edge of his vision, but all he could see was his brother's face. His cape was pulled from him, and Teleri appeared at his side a moment later. She threw it over Vyktas, helping Atlan to apply more pressure to the wound.

'You're alright,' Atlan whispered.

Gold fabric turned red.

'No!' The shakiness of his own voice embarrassed him. 'You're alright!'

Those strange red hands began to shake violently. He looked at his brother's face—the serene expression on it all wrong.

'You don't have to stay with me,' Vyktas said quietly.

Atlan blinked. 'Wh—? I'm not leaving you. You're going to be fine.'

'You can't stay here. They're still out there.' Vyktas's eyes flicked from the forest's edge to his face. 'Haven't I caused you . . . enough strife . . . on this journey?' He shifted uncomfortably, his breathing more labored than it had been mere seconds ago.

Atlan laughed, but it was a cold, hollow sound. The first tear burned a line down his cheek. 'Not so much strife. Somewhere along the way, I guess I came to love you,' he joked.

'I have always loved you,' Vyktas replied. Blood seeped out of his mouth with the effort, staining his lips bright red.

Atlan brought his cape to his mouth and wiped it away. *That's better.*

Vyktas saw the blood then, seeming to notice it for the first time. 'Atlan?' he asked. His breathing picked up, and more cursed red spilled from him. Atlan bowed his head to his brother's. 'Atlan, I don't want to die.'

Atlan shook his head. 'You're not going to die. I'm here. I'm

going to make it better, m-make it alright. I'll make it alright.'
The once golden cape was wet and too heavy now. 'It's alright.'

His brother didn't answer.

He reared back, looking at him. 'No. No, no, no, no! Vyktas?'
He shook him, still making sure to apply pressure. 'Come on!
Wake up!' He shook him again, but Vyktas wouldn't
answer him.

Atlan grabbed his chin, staining it red. 'Shit.' He frantically
tried to wipe it off, but it only smeared it farther across his jaw.
'*No*,' he whimpered.

He fell over him, holding him close. In his ear, he whispered, 'I'll tell Mother you died just like her boy, like a Solorien.
I'll tell them all how beautiful you were going to be.'

Time was all forgotten to him, as he knelt over his brother's
body in the grass.

57

ORIA

ORIA STARED down at the corpse before her. She felt malign sorcery pouring off of it in waves, singing to a memory deep within her. Her thoughts swam. What did this mean for the Wiccars? Who *was* her father?

Somehow, she'd convinced Mothril to return to the chamber and study it—to learn everything they could about what her father was doing there.

'Oria?' Mothril asked softly.

When she looked at him, her face crumpled. 'Was he ever real at all?'

'I don't know,' he said, the hard lines of his face softening. 'I've never seen anything like this before.'

'Like this?' she asked, studying his every feature for some kind of understanding of what was before them. 'Tell me everything you know.'

'Necromancy.' He drew a gauntleted finger down the stone. 'This is powerful necromancy.'

Oria knew even before he spoke those words that they had found something they were never supposed to see. Now she made sure to commit every detail of the chamber to memory. She wondered how far underground they were, or even if they were someplace outside of the natural world altogether.

Large and round, the chamber was mostly empty, with nothing but some collapsed, broken stone in one corner and the vault at its end. The ceilings were high, with gaps in the rock to let the merest of pale white light filter through.

Mothril's Eradomin eyes had adjusted quickly, and he was studying the walls of the chamber. Symbols like those on the door were engraved on them. All of them, she realized. If they held magic within them, perhaps they acted like some kind of sigil.

'You said that the Eradomin use blood as a key. Is this an Eradomin tomb? Why does that body look like Father? And why is it here?' Saying it aloud felt ridiculous.

'No, I don't know what this place is, and I don't recognize these symbols, except for the unseeing eye. It does seem to work on the same principles as our blood magic, though.' Mothril knelt down and looked at the floor, which was also covered in whorls of symbols. 'We were right to be suspicious of your father. Oria, I wanted to let you ask your questions of me, but there are many things I've been meaning to tell you as well.'

She turned to look at him, her face growing serious. 'What do you mean?'

'I told you there were things I knew weren't safe to say within the walls of the citadel. The rites your father is attempting, I recognize them. This isn't an Eradomin tomb, but I think your father is using what he has learned—somehow—of Eradomin magic and twisting it, using necromancy to alter his natural life.' He paused. 'Your father knows much more than we realized, and I'd wager he's much older, too.'

A bolt of fear went through her. 'Do you think he knows we're here?'

'It's possible,' Mothril said gravely. 'Come. There's no need to stay down here any longer.'

She nodded.

Oria didn't dare speak again until they were free of the cramped darkness and out into sunlight's warm relief.

She was only in her twenty-seventh winter. If he was as old as this all made him seem, how could he really be her father? Did this foul magic make her life possible? She thought of her mother, of Felith, then. Was she a Wiccar? Was Oria? Or was she someone else entirely, not a Cailir, not a Wiccar, but someone she didn't even know?

'I can't believe all those nights my father and I spent out here . . . all this time . . .' Mothril's voice trailed off, echoing off the stone.

'You said you know of the rites. What do you think my father aims to do?' she questioned.

Mothril exhaled, leaning against a stone pillar. Oria sat beside him on a large field stone. 'I believe he aims to open this world to others, to let something in, or to slip into another world and extend his reach even further. I know not why.'

Oria's face was rigid. 'Is that how Eradomin do it? With blood? The rituals I've seen in my dreams?'

He had been looking at her throughout their conversation, but his eyes fluttered away as he heard those words. 'Yes,' he said hesitantly. 'I am sorry you witnessed that. They are intense, and usually only done among those of us who are closely bonded. You should not have been there, should not have been hurt. It is why I thought you may be seeing into the past.'

Oria flushed slightly, thinking about the dream now. 'You have done these rituals?'

'Yes.'

If Oria was embarrassed a moment ago, it was nothing compared to how she felt now. She looked away, trying not to think of Mothril in Eildroth's place. His smooth hands on her neck, digging into her hips, seated in his lap. His tongue rolling against her throat, the underside of her jaw. His hand wresting a fistful of her hair.

Who had he done such a ritual with?

'Oria,' Mothril said. She blinked, looking up at him. 'Are you alright?'

'Yes,' she said, laughing awkwardly. 'Sorry, I was just thinking.' She paused. 'Do you think it's possible to break the spell here? With my blood? I mean, is that how it works?'

Mothril raised his brows, looking surprised. 'I don't know if this is something to be messed with without knowledge of how it works. Who knows what far-reaching effects breaking such a spell could have? His life, his power, must be tethered to something.'

'What makes you think that?'

'Old Eradomin stories. Clearly, your father knows much more about the Eradomin than he's let on. You said he called Calligone by the name Sarthura? It almost seems as if he's deliberately trying to muddle the origins of stories and practices of Wiccar and Eradomin.'

'Maybe to hide what he's done here. He was never going to make me Prime. I think he is never planning on letting go of his power.' She paused, looking at the doorway to the ruins once more. 'But he's been Prime for years, and with the exception of warring with the Eradomin and the Battle of Kingdom's Fall, and he hasn't made any further grasps for power.'

'At least not ones anyone is aware of,' Mothril added. 'I told you, Oria, loyalty is a two-sided coin. It seems your father is depending on the loyalty of the Wiccars, of no one asking the right questions or reading too far into anything. Someone who has gone out of their way to perform necromancy as complicated as this is someone who is planning something.'

'I know,' Oria nodded. 'I've never felt so blind. Everything I thought I knew was all a—a fabrication. A world built around me that was never real. I don't know my parentage, I don't know if I'm even a Wiccar, and my entire life Wiccars have been taught that the Eradomin are our enemy, when it is we who have driven them from Old Era completely. I never saw any of this in my dreams. Are my dreams even to be trusted?'

'Of course you can still trust yourself,' Mothril said. He held out his hand. 'We're already learning more. You're on the right path. It doesn't surprise me that your visions were so clouded before. You couldn't safely dream in the citadel. I wouldn't be surprised if you now start to see and understand more.'

She took his hand and hoped he was right. The weight of their situation seemed to fall upon her all at once, and she leaned on him for support.

Mothril spoke again. 'You were led here for a reason, Oria.'

'Mm,' she agreed faintly. 'Though I feel no closer to understanding it all.' She paused. 'Is there no chance my father is possessed by some greater power? That someone is doing this to him?' It was a far-fetched question, but part of her still hoped her family wasn't as terribly ruined as it seemed.

'It's not impossible,' Mothril offered, 'but your blood unlocked the door. Someone in your family built this place and completed the ritual binding it to your blood.'

Fear wormed its way through her gut. 'We have to keep moving. And we have to consider the Erángal in all this, too. No one is safe until we understand what he has done, and what he plans to do.'

'It's got something to do with however he is able to maintain this power he clearly possesses, protecting or empowering him somehow.' Mothril looked out over the mossy green country. 'I didn't expect Lyra knew more than she was letting on. We're far enough south that we can start searching for greater darkflower now for your visions. They may give us some direction, if you're able.'

Oria nodded solemnly. 'Agreed. We heed Lyra's advice. I'll

do whatever it takes. I know I have to face my family, whatever dark magic is at work here.'

58

ATLAN

'WHAT HAPPENED?' came Kyr's fragile voice.

She and Penta appeared suddenly—Atlan knew not from where. They were breathless, as if they had been running. Kyr's face was strained, the cords in her neck visible. He was drenched in blood, leaning over his dead brother's body, with Two-Trees slumped beside them.

'Vyktas,' was all Teleri could get out. Hearing his name made him want to look at his face again. To will it into being warm, flushed, and reanimated.

'No,' Kyr whispered.

He heard footsteps and then felt a hand on his shoulder. He reached up and touched it with his own. His own voice was speaking, but it felt faraway. Quiet. 'I'll have to go back to Yorenth, Kyr.'

Kyr knelt beside him, her face inches from his. 'I'll come with you.'

'No.' He shook his head. Yorenth was a sobering ghost that settled over his shoulders. 'My mother will hold you responsible. She certainly knows by now that we weren't only studying the blights like we said we'd be.'

'I'm not leaving you, Atlan.'

I'm not leaving you. The same words he'd said to his brother. He would keep that last promise to him.

'No, I will go, after I see Teleri safely back to her home. You and Penta need to keep going. You need to find out how to stop these blights. You need to find our path as Spiritsingers. Those men, they knew what we were. Kyr, I need you to find out who those bastards were.' For the first time, he looked at Kyr. He could feel that his eyes were tired and reddened from crying, but he didn't remember doing so. 'Do this for me, Kyr.'

There was no hesitation from his friend. Kyr pulled him into an embrace. 'Of course. I will send word to you when we reach the Middevale, and again when we get to Castle Forlorn.' She pulled away and held his face in her hands. 'We will see each other again.'

He nodded. 'Of course we will, thief. If you and Penta require any aid, at any time, I will come as soon as I get word.'

Bless her, but she didn't cry, even though he could tell she wanted to. 'I look forward to it, little king.'

———

Atlan took in the rest of the journey only in fragments. He remembered words of his conversation with Teleri, some of the scenery they passed. Mostly, he spent the hours staring at the mass on the back of her steed, wrapped in the only white cloth they had—robes Penta bought in Bellgard to replace their old, worn clothes.

At some point, Teleri had convinced him that she was coming along with him all the way to Yorenth. He reminded her that she did not enter cities, but she told him a few Misguided would not stop her from coming with him. He didn't have the energy to protest.

Often, they rode in silence, but it wasn't uncomfortable.

Only a few times did he palpably sense Teleri's pain. Her guilt. If what happened was anyone's fault, it was his for allowing his brother to come with him into danger. He knew from the start he would've been safer in Yorenth. Instead, Atlan relived the memories he had with his brother on the journey over and over again in his mind.

When Yorenth came into view as they passed through the crossroads, Atlan removed his armor, but a weight still pressed upon him. He lay his blood-soaked cape across the back of his horse, but that didn't help either.

At the gates, panic began to dig its claws up his throat, his thoughts swirling with dread. His face, his outward appearance, however, remained calm. If his mother wanted to destroy him for the death of his brother, he thought he just might let her.

The Sun's Own posted at the gatehouse took one look at him and straightened.

'Prince Atlan! You've returned!' The guard looked relieved, and it only made Atlan angry somehow. He realized then how much he resented this place. He passed by without a word.

Teleri trotted up beside him. 'Are you alright?' When he looked at her blankly, she added, 'You look even worse than you did before we got here.'

'This place, it does something to me. It makes me into someone I hate.'

She nodded in wordless acknowledgement, her face somber.

Normally he would have stabled his horse just inside the city walls, but with Vyktas's body to carry up to the palace, he rode on, turning left along the canal and up the steep road toward the castle town. He could feel curious eyes on him and Teleri, not helped by her riding a bucca.

'Home is not a happy place then, I take it?' she asked gently.

'No.'

'Atlan—'

'We don't have to talk about it.' He felt himself going numb from the ice in his veins. He knew he wasn't being fair to her, but he was drowning. He couldn't talk about any of this. The words existed in his head, but when he tried to make them come out of his mouth, they got stuck.

'No, we don't,' she said. 'But one day, you're going to need to.'

He turned to look at her and met those steady brown eyes. Usually, he was met with scoffs or resentment, both of which felt more expected, more deserved to him than kindness.

'Why? Why do you care?' he asked her. 'Because I'm a Spiritsinger? Because I'm fairly certain at this point that Solq got it all wrong. I think he was looking for—' He stopped short of saying his brother's name.

'The Spirits do not err in their choices,' she said simply. 'The path of your heart burns bright, so the Spirits temper it for what comes. They bind our paths so that now the nullah would know you.'

Atlan was too numb to take in her words fully, but it eased his mind greatly to know that he had a companion.

They rode on, coming to the long steps up to the palace. Those accursed steps. There was a crowd following them now, their whispers a low buzz at their backs. Atlan was surprised Old Tom had come this far, and that he wasn't startled by the mayhem of the city as Atlan had been expecting. Rather, the bucca seemed delighted by all of the flags, vegetable stands, and other refuse and greedily eyed any potential fare they passed.

The guard at the gate stopped him. 'Prince Atlan! Queen Attiqah will be wanting to see you immediately.'

'Mhm,' he grunted. The guard stepped forward, reaching for the shroud.

'Get back!' Atlan roared. The guard startled.

'I'm sorry, my Prince!' The man lowered his head.

'Atlan,' said Teleri, in a voice that was both a comfort to him and conveyed her disappointment in his quick temper.

He lowered himself from his horse. 'I've got it,' he said, lifting Vyktas's body from Old Tom's back and carrying him in his arms. 'You don't need to come in. It's probably better if you didn't.'

'Is that what you want?' Teleri asked.

He didn't answer, because he couldn't tell her he didn't want her by his side. It was simply not true. He began the long walk up the steps with his brother in his arms.

Six. His body was so heavy. Atlan focused on the stairs.

Teleri followed quietly behind him. He could see her out of the corner of his eye, looking at the useless majesty of this place.

It must disgust her, he thought. Such grandeur, all for one family. A family who didn't even really know each other all that well.

Someone must've gone ahead of them, because his mother was already waiting for him in the throne room. Mercifully, it was just her, and she hadn't decided to call any advisors or guards to watch whatever torment she had planned for him.

As soon as he entered the room, her eyes, which never missed anything, went straight to what was in his arms, and she knew.

She knew but she wouldn't accept it. 'Where is Vyktas?' she questioned.

'Mother,' he said, his voice already breaking. 'I'm sorry. I tried to look after him—'

She pierced him with her icy stare. 'You *tried* to look after him?'

Here it comes, his body whispered to him.

To his horror, he heard Teleri's voice, instead of his mother's. 'He was killed by strange, cloaked knights on the Western Road.'

His mother looked as though she were noticing Teleri's presence for the first time. 'Who are you?'

'Teleri Two-Trees. I have been traveling with your sons.'

His mother said nothing to her. She looked back at Atlan. 'I'll never understand the company you keep, Atlan. Where's the thief? Don't tell me she died too.'

Atlan stared her down. 'And what company is that, Mother? We learned much about the blights, and *Kyr*,' he said, emphasizing her name, 'is traveling to the Middevale to look further into what we uncovered.' Conveniently, he left out any mention of Penta. They were the last person his mother needed to know about right now. After so long of her infecting every part of his life, allowing for no secrets between them, it felt good to keep something from her. 'I don't appreciate you insulting my friends.'

His mother looked everywhere but at the shrouded figure, ignored everything he said. 'My, Atlan. This little adventure of yours has gone much worse than I even expected. You lost the magician, the only upper hand Yorenth had in our plans against Bellgard. You clearly have done little to stop the blights, otherwise you would've told me about that first to soften the worse of what you've done. You murdered my son.'

'*Murdered* him?' Teleri almost yelled.

It startled his mother, but she didn't back down. 'Yes. What else would you call luring someone to their death?'

Atlan's head ached with wrath.

Teleri stepped forward. 'Your son did everything he could to protect his brother. He brought his body home to you, despite the danger of traveling through the Barrens!'

'I will not be spoken to like this!' Queen Attiqah rasped, gripping the throne tightly.

'Mother, *please*. Let us bury Vyktas and give him the honor he deserves. We can discuss whatever you wish after.'

For a moment, that seemed to soothe his mother's outrage.

When she looked at the body again, she was jarred momentarily, and he could see the delicate mask she wore fracture.

'Do you know what it has been like here without you?' his mother asked quietly. She began picking at her nails. 'The council plots against me. Sol Rywin has them believing I am unfit to rule!' A shrill bark of laughter escaped her. 'Every day I prayed to the Spirits for you and Vyktas to return.'

Atlan did note the suspicious lack of councilors about.

'If my sons are here, they will not depose me. They cannot go against me *and* my heirs.'

Attiqah stood and walked across the atrium to where Vyktas's body lay. As she lowered herself, her skirts pooled around her. She was so small. Fragile looking.

How can such immense force be contained within something so breakable? Atlan thought as he looked at her.

She said something, low and hoarse, but he couldn't make it out. Then, she did something he wasn't sure his mother was capable of before now. She began to cry, her body wracked by short gasps at first, before they turned to loud wails.

Atlan knelt too, but he could not cry in front of his mother. The door to the council chambers opened, and Taryq walked in.

He froze.

'Attiqah?' he said.

His mother turned and Taryq, seeing what they were kneeling over, came running. 'My son!' he gasped, crashing to his knees. 'Oh, my son!'

For the briefest of flashes, Atlan saw his brother in Taryq's features. He nearly did cry then.

Taryq pulled back the shroud, revealing Vyktas's bloated face. He bent down to kiss him, and Atlan had to look away.

'I will stay here for Vyktas's last rites,' Atlan began.

His mother looked up at him through tearful eyes. 'Atlan, you are Crown Prince! You have responsibilities!'

Taryq, consumed with his grief, didn't even look up.

Atlan stared down at them. 'I am prince of nothing. The Solorien dynasty ended with Vyktas. I suggest you do as your councilors recommend.'

He turned on his heels, the queen and Taryq stunned into silence, and walked out of the throne room, Teleri at his side.

59

MOTHRIL

As they traveled farther south toward the Middevale, Mothril wondered if leaving her father's tomb behind was a mistake. It didn't seem wise to linger there, but perhaps they could've learned something about the magic that permeated the ruins.

Their nights had been peaceful as of late. No visions pervaded them, and he no longer rose to hear Oria crying or gasping for breath.

Instead, he often awoke before her, watching her peaceful face, decorated as it was with scars, like lace. Wisps of red and ashen hair falling across her cheek. Sometimes, strands fell across his shoulder, and the sight was enough to render him statue-still and mute until she woke.

When she did, he would look away, pretend he was just waking up himself. It had been several days since he'd told her he'd cared for her, overshadowed, as it were, by all he had revealed about himself, and all they had learned about her.

There had been a few moments when she looked at him, when he thought maybe she cared for him too, beyond just who he was to her. A guard, a friend. He caught the way her gaze would linger on him when they bathed, and sometimes as they rode, she fell asleep against him. It was as much affection as he would allow himself.

He'd thought about saying something to her the night before, but thank Sarthura, he stopped himself. He could find her beautiful, charming—brave as any soldier—all he wanted, but he could never be who she deserved. Instead, he would settle for ensuring she was safe.

They sat now in a field, their horse beside them, eating a small lunch of apples they'd found by the road and some roasted rabbit that Mothril had caught on the mountain.

'I found some greater darkflower this morning,' she said.

'You did?' he asked, raising a brow as he turned to look at her.

'Just a few, growing along the river. Hopefully now a vision will be able to give us some direction.' She sighed. 'I wish Lyra were here.'

'I know, I do too. I feel as though you're being drawn to the Middevale, though. Like, even without her instruction, there's something about this place . . . it feels right, looking at you here.' She smiled at him, and he bit into one of the apples to make himself shut up. A bit mealy, but they needed their strength.

'Does it?' Her smile grew. 'I hope you're right. I'm beginning to feel like we're wandering aimlessly. Goddess, Fäendhmar, Spirits, if you're listening, I could really use a sign of some kind. Anything.' She bit off a piece of rabbit meat and Mothril couldn't help but laugh.

'What?' she asked.

'Nothing,' he said, a hint of a smile on his face.

She looked away. 'But I don't want to talk about all of this anymore.'

'What do you want to talk about?'

'I don't know. You.' He winced. 'Or this lovely field. The way the sun looks different this side of the mountains. Anything but what we're facing.'

'I doubt hearing stories from me is going to make you feel any better. I don't have many to tell that aren't grim.' He loosened his armor at his chest. 'This is the farthest south I've been too. There is something beautiful about how green everything is.'

'There is,' she said. 'There's so much more color in everything. But I do miss the trees of the Northern forests. They're so formidable, so ancient.'

'Mm,' he agreed.

They continued eating. Mothril felt her gaze. 'Surely, you have something you can tell me that isn't *so* grim?' she asked.

He stopped chewing. He really couldn't think of anything. His life was one solitary stain of loneliness and violence.

'Are you serious?' she asked, a disbelieving look on her face. 'Well, that just won't do. I'll have to think of something.'

'Something?'

'We'll make a memory. A good memory, of just the two of us. One for you to keep.'

'Those, I have plenty of,' he said, eyeing her.

'Then you don't need another one?' she asked, turning to face him.

'I'd never refuse a lady.'

Her lids lowered as she looked at him, first his eyes, and then lower. *Goddess.* If she was wanting him to kiss her, all she had to do was ask.

She leaned in closer, shifting her weight so that she nearly sat in his lap, but Mothril could not make himself move. *Sideren cruscia.* She smelled like damned milkweed and rose.

'I'm not sure you want to be making this kind of memory with me,' he said, almost a whisper. Her face was only a hair's breadth away now.

He could almost taste her lips, sweet from the apples. 'And why not?'

'Because if you do, it's not something I will be able to forget. You're a maiden, an Oracle, who will go on to rule someday. Someone respectable will want to marry you.' She cocked her head. 'They might not appreciate a scoundrel after their wife. A scoundrel who cannot forget. If this,' he said, gesturing between them, 'were to happen, then, my lady, there will be nothing to stop it from happening again. And again.'

She said nothing. Instead, she was still looking at his lips. His restraint coiled tight around him like a noose. He let it hang him.

'Come.' He pulled away. Stood. Offered her only his hand. 'There are better than dogs out there for you.'

60

KYR

THE STARS above the crossroads almost looked realistic. They were a near facsimile of the ones Kyr and Penta had fallen asleep under, but Kyr thought they twinkled a little strangely, a little too uniformly. Almost like someone was channeling chaos to create order, to make them shine as they thought they should.

She sat upright to find herself no longer at camp but in the middle of the crossroads they passed earlier that day. The whole scene was lit by firelight, but their campfire was gone too.

This is a dream. I'm dreaming.

The last thing she could remember, she and Penta had been talking about Vyktas, about those strange men who'd confronted them, and Penta's memories of their mother. The memories felt hazy and far away now, though. In this place, this world created in her mind, the desolate landscape of the Barrens and the long night felt never-ending.

She heard the plinking sound of a string instrument, slightly out-of-tune.

It was in a minor key. A dirge.

Kyr looked around, but the emptiness went on seemingly endlessly. She spun around in the crossroads to where the sign-post had been. Beside it was a boulder, and on it sat a person with fine, graying hair, their face half-masked. Their posture was casual, relaxed, and they played the old, well-loved instrument with ease.

'Who the Six are you?'

She wasn't sure she liked the look of them. They seemed altogether too comfortable intruding upon her dreams, and there was an eeriness about them that Kyr instantly disliked. She quickly got to her feet.

'That's no way to greet an old friend,' they chided. From their voice, Kyr could not tell if they were man, woman, or someone free of such constraints altogether.

'Old friend? I've never seen you before in my life!'

'Seen? No. Met? Well, no, not that either. I'm quite indisposed at the moment. But *known*? Absolutely, my dear.' They finally stopped plucking that unnerving song and propped the odd-looking instrument against the rock upon which they sat. 'I am sorry about your friend. Grym, was it?'

'Oh, for the *love of*—' Kyr threw her hands up in the air. She turned away to face the darkness that ebbed at the edges of the crossroads and found the stranger suddenly standing in front of her. She looked at them double. 'Are you? You're not—'

'Crescian,' they said, extending a hand. 'Charmed.'

Kyr looked at their outstretched palm in the flashes of orange light. 'You're a—you're—'

'Kyr,' they said, laughing. 'I'm surprised, I don't think I've ever seen you flustered.'

Kyr took in the Spirit's tall, slender form. 'How are you here? *Why* are you here?'

'There are *so many* questions, aren't there? Big ones, small ones. How am I here? Why am I not somewhere else? What is a group of ogres called? What is the exact weight of a Kharupani nightjar? What is Penta's sister doing right now?'

Kyr crossed her arms, staring at them impatiently.

'Not in a playful mood, are we?' Crescian sighed. 'A short lifespan will do that. Everything is *so* serious. Alright, fine. I grow tired, too, Kyr.' They looked off into the distance. 'Even now, as we speak, my heart wanes—the source of *your* magic wanes. You think us creators, that the world was made with some intelligent design. That we have a final say in this world. You think we are *saviors*.' They spat the last word.

Kyr cocked her head, her brows pulled together. 'What do you mean?'

'We are nothing of the sort. All of us sit at this calamity's table and it dismisses none. We can steward the healing of the damage already done, but the source is scaffolded by many ill-begotten magics. We cannot touch it. We cannot absolve you. We did not create this world, we simply *are*, Kyr. And something is killing us.'

'This is why we Spiritsingers are returning.' Crescian nodded. 'We want to help. Guide us.'

'I cannot say much more. I will be heard.'

'Why? Who will hear you?'

Kyr's question seemed to go unacknowledged. 'Your path is true, but we must gather allies for the inevitable. Stay alive, starling. Don't dwell.' The Spiritsinger's head turned. 'Sylas draws near. He has taught you everything I intended, Kyr. Do send him on his way.'

'Crescian, wait!' she yelled.

Kyr woke with a gasp, like rising from beneath water to the surface. It was still so dark and looked eerily like her dream. She scrambled back, looking around deliriously.

Only an ordinary campsite surrounded her, just as she and Penta had left it before they had fallen asleep. False dawn had yet to illuminate the horizon.

Sylas draws near.

Kyr looked at Penta as she crawled out of her bedroll, careful not to disturb them. The lines of their face eased and if Kyr could give them that peace for just a little bit longer, she wanted to.

The crossroads from her dream were just beyond the rocks and brush that obscured their low-lying campsite. Kyr scrambled up to it. At first, she squinted in the darkness, seeing nothing. It was, of course, not lit as her dream was.

'Inconvenient,' she muttered to herself.

The road stretched on for miles on either side of her.

'*Kyr*,' came a hushed, distant voice. In the silence of the desert, it sent a chill through her.

He was here.

'Are you following me?' she whispered back harshly, looking around.

Sylas appeared out of the dim a ways down the road, ambling toward her. *Was he limping?* It made him look older somehow. Frail.

'Sylas, what the fuck!' she said, her tone still hushed.

'I am glad I caught you, pup. Again, my lady leads me to Lady Kyr.' As he got closer, she realized he was having trouble walking.

'What happened to you?'

'Things are . . . not good in the Sledge, Kyr. Yorenth is in turmoil.'

'What do you mean?' she asked quickly. She could think only of Atlan and Two-Trees—they had to have made it there by now.

'I take it you know of Prince Vyktas's death?'

'More intimately than I'd like,' she said quietly.

He nodded, studying her. 'You journeyed with them.' She stared back at him, and was surprised to see that his clothes, his cloak, were stained and frayed. 'Well, with his death, Queen

Attiqah has gone completely mad. She does not care to have anything to do with her duties. Sol Rywin and some of the other council members had sought to depose her and take power themselves, but ...'

'But what?' she urged.

'The council members have been locked in the palace with her for days now. No one goes in or out. Decisions aren't being made. The city is entirely ungoverned. You might think it a good time for the guild, the lawlessness, but our enemies are many. Without Councilman Thay, they've decided now is the time to strike back for my years of offense.' He scoffed and bit his lip. 'And my lady, my lady leaves me defenseless to be set upon by Cyregoth's leg-breakers! Luckily, I can still manage a limp.' He smiled weakly, looking at her with a hopeful glimmer in his eye. She remembered the way they once looked so confident, similarly twinkling, in the candlelight of the trade union assembly all that time ago. 'Have you learned anything?'

Kyr considered her one-time guildmaster, always so self-assured, who seemed to her like the statue of a king—immovable, infallible, and outside of time—reduced to an old man walking along the side of the road at dawn. 'Crescian came to me in a dream.'

'A dream?' He pulled his brown cloak tightly around him. 'You saw her?'

Shit. She didn't know how to explain what she saw. Crescian wasn't some beautiful maiden like she'd been expecting from the way Sylas talked about her. 'I, er, yes. She said to tell you, uh, she will return . . . when the time is, uh, right. It sounded better than that when she said it, though. You know, more formal.'

Sylas clapped his hands together. 'Oh, this is good news! Thank you, Kyr! Thank you!'

'Don't mention it,' she said warily. 'What will you do now?'

He sighed. 'Yorenth's no good for me right now, and probably won't be for a while. It's been home for many years, but now I've overstayed my welcome. Think I'll continue on to Bellgard. Sail for a little while until my luck turns.'

'What of the guild? Is Vasha alright?'

'The guild's gone underground in Yorenth. I suspect Vasha and the rest are all on their way to other cities to see what work they can find by now. Our holdings are safe, but it's best we lie low for the time being.'

'So that's it? You've abandoned them, just like that?'

'I know we like to imagine ourselves a family,' he said, 'but it's a job, Kyr. Just a job. They'll find another.'

Kyr scowled, her lip curling almost involuntarily. She'd never had any illusions about them being a family, but brotherhood, knowing someone had your back—it was the only thing you could be sure of in the Knave's Keep. Without that, what good was any of it?

As she looked at Sylas now, she only felt sorry for him.

It all made sense to her. With Araman Thay's eyes on the Sledge, the guild was protected from those who would do it harm. Perhaps if Sylas could still tap into Crescian's power, he could've managed the onslaught of revenge against the guild. It was a perfect storm.

The guild gone. Atlan and Two-Trees locked within the palace.

Part of her wanted to ride straight into Yorenth and demand to see him, to make sure he was alright, but she knew Atlan was capable. He could handle himself.

She took a deep breath.

'Do me a favor, Sylas?'

'Hm?'

'Sail to Saeria or something. And next time Crescian leads you to me, or whatever, ignore it. I don't ever want to see you again.' Without even looking at him, Kyr turned and stalked off into the night, leaving him alone on the road.

61

ATLAN

ATLAN TOOK a deep breath and affixed his brother's golden cape to his pauldrons. It felt like a lifetime ago that he'd last worn this armor.

His mother had insisted he stay in the palace, but he had been hiding out in an inn in the dye district with Teleri instead. Somehow, she'd still managed to figure this out, and made a show of sending Sun's Own to guard the place day and night. He'd returned to his family's chambers only to dress in the regalia his brother's last rites deserved.

'I'm sorry again for my mother's behavior. I should've warned you.'

'Atlan,' she said, 'you cannot mend your mother's harms, and you don't have to. I'm here for you, not for any of this.' She gestured to the palace walls around them.

'Why?' he asked. 'Don't you wish to be back with your sisters?'

She smiled. 'I'm where I wish to be.'

He wanted her to elaborate, to ask her what she saw in him that made him a worthwhile companion for someone like her, but the door opened and a Sun's Own walked in.

'Prince Atlan,' said the woman, 'are you ready?'

He nodded and turned to take one more look at Teleri. 'You'll be off to the side, near the third column?'

She was standing in the sunlight from the window, setting her brown hair and skin aglow. Like a seraph from myth. 'I'll be right there.'

His armored footsteps echoed through the lonely halls as he followed the guard to the Solarum. These halls that felt so big to him for much of his life now felt somehow too small. And Kyr was right, all the tapestries and carvings were horribly gaudy.

He rounded the corner to see a familiar, stooped figure by the door. Saartho. His teacher's face was deeply furrowed with regret. Atlan had to look away.

His gentle voice echoed off the stone: 'I'm sorry, my boy.'

Atlan came to an abrupt stop. 'Please, Saartho.' He studied his sabatons with intensity, avoiding meeting his eyes.

His mentor nodded.

Atlan cleared his throat. 'We have much to discuss. I will find you after the rites.'

Saartho's smile was sad. 'Of course, Atlan. You need not feel you have duties to attend with me. All of that can wait. I merely came to make sure you were alright.'

His throat tightened, and he cleared it. 'Thank you.' He didn't know what else to say.

'It's still your path, Atlan.'

'I know.' The feeling in his throat turned to a choking sensation. Why did Saartho's words torment him so?

Saartho put a hand on his arm. 'No, you d—'

He shrugged it off. 'I have to go.'

It was a sweltering day for so late in the year, and he wiped the sweat from his brow as they crossed the sunlit square to Yorenth's sacred grounds. Atlan looked up at the sky, a bluebird day.

He'd have liked to show Kyr the Solarum, knowing she had likely never seen the inside of it. Great columns surrounded the massive open square, sunken into the ground like an amphitheater.

He heard the crowd before he saw it.

Sun's Own, nobles, and those who had the day off, or knew someone who could get them inside the Solarum, were all in attendance. It was a sea of faces and the brightly dyed fabrics the city was known for. He knew why he was there, to instill pride and confidence in his family line, the Crown, and to honor his brother, and yet when he saw the wooden pyre in the center of the square, he nearly turned on his heels and fled. His brother's body, now in a gold, embroidered shroud, rested atop it.

Queen Attiqah's eyes tracked Atlan from the far end of the square. She wore red, with a matching veil that hid her face. Still, he could feel her gaze. Atlan felt his palms begin to sweat. His breaths came in faster, shallow swells.

He looked to that promised third column.

Instantly, a sense of calm washed over him. Right where she said she would be, he kept sight of her as if she could keep him from getting swept away. In this endless throng of faces, he would focus only on one.

He swallowed thickly and proceeded to the center of the square. His mother had given her address and retreated to where she now sat, and he would be expected to offer a blessing. He had nothing to offer in the way of placation.

Instead, Atlan would do what he longed for. He would allow himself control over his path. He would ready the people gathered here for what was coming.

He didn't even look at the crowd. Only at his brother.

'I come to you today not with a blessing, but a warning. Prince Vyktas Solorien was not killed by roving marauders, but due to our willful ignorance of the magical blight which spreads across our land, bringing chaos and provoking fear.' Murmurs swept through the crowd. 'It is the fear that killed my brother. It is the fear that will continue to plague us if these blights are not contained. His death must not be in vain! If we value our faith in the Spirits, our might, and our humility to recognize when we have erred, we must take a stand! We must not live in fear of that which seeks to destroy us!'

Atlan looked pointedly at his mother then, who was already glaring at him from across the square.

'I know you all have heard the rumors.' His eyes swept across the expansive crowd. 'These are troubling times indeed. The fires of Solq's ruin burn brightly as we sit idle. I have no doubt that if he were here, Prince Vyktas would see us through this safely.'

A keeper, likely signaled by Attiqah or Taryq, tried to hurry him along by handing him a torch with which to light the pyre, but he waved the man away.

'I can offer you only this: Prince Vyktas showed me a vision for this Realm, a return to the ways of Solq, that will serve as a guiding light through the coming tempest!' He beat his fist against his chest. 'I intend to embrace this vision, and together,' he beat his chest again, 'we will overcome!'

Atlan focused his breathing, letting go of all of the tension that had built up in his chest since he'd walked through Yorenth's gates. In a great swell, his mind's eye turned outward. His skin felt like it was vibrating, like his power was a song that echoed through his very veins. He looked at Teleri and saw her give him the faintest of nods.

With his magic, Atlan lit the pyre all at once in a great eruption of flame. Some of the murmurs grew to shouts of confusion and horror, others began prostrating themselves and murmuring prayers to Solq. It was the first public display of greater magic any of them had ever seen.

The masses roared and cheered. He stood there for a few

more moments, regarding the Yoren people with a hand to his chest.

In that moment, a thought struck his mind like an arrow—he hadn't been *thinking* at all when he said those words. He'd just believed them. He expected the usual intrusions into his mind, nausea, guilt and shame, but—it had been remarkably easy to shrug on the mantle of a king.

He began striding toward the Solarum's entry, refusing to look back as his brother's body went up in smoke.

With each step, his confidence in his path forward grew. Whorls of color, people, faces, and voices blurred past, all talking about Solq and his chosen disciple. The reemergence of magic.

For once, Atlan's mind was quiet.

Returning to the dark palace was a balm to his senses, and as the doors shut behind him, he leaned against a cool limestone pillar and inhaled deeply.

Having done what he set out to do, he would return this garish costume and meet Teleri back in the dye district. Now that he was out of the public's view, he began loosening the straps of his armor. It was then that he realized he wasn't alone.

It took two guards to shut the doors. They *never* shut the doors. Atlan looked up.

'Hello, my boy.'

Taryq stood at the other end of entrance hall rug. In full armor. Holding Sun's Visage at his side.

'You're back early!' He sheathed it. 'It's put a little rumple in my plans, but no matter. It'll be far easier to get both you and your mother in the council chambers separately anyway.' He whistled, and two Sun's Own sprang forth, flanking Atlan.

Before he could react, the guards were upon him, and he felt his magic drain away as his wrists were pinioned with a strange cable.

'Taryq!' he roared.

Hadn't he been at the rites? Now that he thought about it, he couldn't remember seeing him there at all.

Taryq looked at him pityingly. 'You've grown to have quite the bark, but I know you, Atlan. And you have no bite.' His voice was mocking. 'That's bismuth, my boy. Your old friend. I had it made specifically for this occasion. Cost a fortune!' He stepped aside to give the guards room to lead him past.

Atlan looked at the eyes beneath the helms of the guards restraining him. 'Peria?' Her eyes looked straight ahead, unseeing. He looked to his right, and almost vomited. '*Wrasar?*'

Neither of them said anything, as though they hadn't even heard him.

Atlan could feel his fury growing.

'You think being prince, being a Solorien, has bought you the respect of the Sun's Own? Hardly.'

If he wanted any chance, he had to fight. Magic or not.

Atlan threw his weight against Peria's smaller form to unbalance her, then jammed his elbow into Wrasar's side. It seemed like he hardly felt the blow, but it was enough for Atlan to wrench free of his grip. He backed away.

'You idiots pinion a swordsman's hands in front?' Taryq barked.

Atlan spun around, kicking his legs out from under him. Wrasar slammed down on his back, the wind knocked out of him. That would give him a moment. His hands still tied in front, he crossed the room in seconds, picking up a poker from a brazier in the far corner by the window.

'What do you think you're going to do with that?'

Atlan's grin was feral. 'Bash your fucking head in, maybe.'

Taryq smirked humorlessly, drawing Sun's Visage once more. 'Wrasar, Peria, please do a better job restraining the prisoner this time.'

Blank-faced, Peria stepped closer and Atlan swung a

warning blow. She didn't react and kept advancing, something sluggish about her movements. He swung again, and the metal rod cracked against her skull. She went down instantly, blood pouring from her temple onto the floor.

'Oh, for Spirit's sake,' Taryq huffed.

Wrasar had risen from the floor and was standing still, silently regarding Atlan as he stood over Peria. He didn't even look down.

Outside, Atlan could hear distant voices as a flood of people poured out of the Solarum. His brother's rites had ended, which meant his mother would be on her way back. He prayed to whatever Spirits would listen that Teleri went back to the dye district.

Taryq drew his sword and adopted a fighting stance as Wrasar closed in. Atlan made to swing, but Wrasar closed the distance between them too quickly for it to be effective. Without thinking, he reached behind him and grabbed a handful of hot coals from the brazier, shoving them into Wrasar's face.

His friend screamed, thrashing backward and falling to the floor.

'Atlan?' he whimpered. The way he said was unnerving. Anguished. His voice sounded like his own again, like he didn't understand what was happening.

The heels of Taryq's boots clicked on the stone floor as he sauntered toward them. 'Unfortunate,' he pouted, looking down at Wrasar, who was still on his knees, clutching his face.

With a quick lateral swing, Taryq neatly parted Wrasar's head, as well as one of his arms, halfway between wrist and elbow, from his body. The greater part of his bulk sank to the ground, followed by two faint thuds.

A sickening silence fell over the room.

Earlier in the day he'd admired a rosebush with Teleri.

Mere minutes ago, he was giving a speech to his people. What moment had been the fulcrum when everything changed —went so wrong? Atlan stared blankly at Taryq, out of both disbelief and a fear of letting any emotion show.

Though it was difficult with Wrasar's blood dripping off Sun's Visage, Atlan concentrated on maintaining his defensive stance. Taryq could strike at any moment. Atlan watched the spreading pool of blood. No words came to him, fear trickling down his spine. Unspoken realizations choked out the air as they observed each other, Atlan breathing rapidly and Taryq with his calm smile.

Taryq lunged for him, but Atlan parried his blade with the poker. He applied pressure in the bind, forcing Atlan to side-step away from the corner. He moved quickly across the room.

Atlan didn't want to let him draw him in, but he saw no other choice. He could run, but the doors were locked, and he knew he could not get them open in time to avoid a stab to the back, which he did not think beneath a man like Taryq.

He had to disarm him somehow. Warn his mother. Get to Teleri.

Taryq circled him, his blade held out menacingly. 'Your mother will be back soon. I'd hate for her to see us like this. I was going to let her live out her days in the castle, but she might not be so forgiving once she sees her last surviving son bleeding out on the floor, a sword in my hand, and thinks *me* responsible! I'd hate to have to kill you both.'

Atlan was dumbfounded. 'This whole time you plotted to betray us?'

Taryq shrugged. 'I liked my life well enough, for a time. But you've seen her, Atlan. The woman's insane! She can't be allowed to rule the Realm any longer, and I'm clearly the next best option. I've been Captain of the Guard, I come from good stock, the nobles and the soldiers alike love me. My son *was* heir, you don't even want to be king, it all makes sense. Now you want to make this difficult?'

Atlan took stock of the situation and nearly laughed out loud. The man was holding a sword, poorly he might add, against a man armed only with a fire poker, to overthrow a queen, because she was 'insane.'

'Look at yourself!' he wanted to scream.

They stared at each other for a long moment. There was nothing left to say. He knew it was now or never.

Atlan lunged.

Sword and fire poker clashed, and Atlan kicked him backward, knocking him into the corner. He smiled defiantly and rushed in.

Taryq sidestepped at the last moment, avoiding his blow, and letting his sword fall to the side.

Atlan knew instantly that he had miscalculated.

He felt fingers dig into his scalp. Taryq grabbed hold of him and shoved him down, holding his face above the burning brazier.

'Do you remember this feeling?' he taunted. His arm curled around Atlan's neck so that his windpipe came to rest in the crook of Taryq's elbow.

The fire poker dropped from Atlan's hand as his focus narrowed to the flames and Taryq's voice.

'The last time we did this?'

'Zaphira,' Atlan whimpered.

'Yes,' Taryq said, voice smooth and taunting. The room disappeared completely. 'Zaphira, that was her name, wasn't it?'

Atlan felt the fire heating his skin. It was beginning to burn. Taryq wrenched him backward and began to apply pressure. 'You remember, Atlan, what happens when you try to be the hero?'

Atlan's eyes watered as his vision began to go black around the edges. His body went slack and Taryq released his grip ever

so slightly. Atlan's vision returned in a flood and Taryq asked,
'Atlan, did you hear me, boy? You remember, don't you?'

Atlan nodded feebly, and Taryq tightened his grip again.

'It's much easier not to be, isn't it?'

The blackness returned and it took him.

'Much easier indeed.'

62

KYR

KYR AND PENTA reached a small village north of Yorenth by nightfall. After riding for two days, they were exhausted.

All the while, Kyr thought of Atlan with every village, every tree, every moment that passed. Every cloud that drifted by overhead. She hadn't realized how painful leaving him was going to be. It was the second time she was leaving behind those she cared about, and she wasn't sure if she could do it again.

Penta was a great strength to her. They seemed to know just how Kyr was feeling. After her bizarre run-in with Sylas, Penta had known immediately that something was bothering her. They were still at camp, huddled together in their bedrolls against the chill.

'You have a troubled look,' Penta whispered.

'How do you do that?' Kyr asked.

'Do what?'

'My eyes are closed, and yet you say I have a troubled look. How do you know when something's bothering me like that?'

'I told you,' Penta answered simply. 'You think very loudly.'

'Yes, but what does that *mean*?'

Penta smirked. As close as they were, Kyr could count the freckles dotting their nose. 'Well, for one, you're very honest, Kyr. You don't pretend your emotions are anything but what they are. I like that about you. Beyond that, I don't know. Maybe because your emotions are so tied to your magic, and I am very good at sensing magic.'

Kyr nodded, rolling her eyes slightly. 'Well, you were right. I had a dream. At least, I think it was a dream. It felt corporeal somehow, though.'

Penta's eyebrows wrinkled. Kyr sensed she had alarmed them somehow. 'What do you mean?' they asked.

'Don't worry, it wasn't anything so serious. I dreamed of Crescian, er, well, at least, what I think of Crescian as, I suppose.'

'Drithas?' Penta gasped. 'You saw him?'

Kyr paused for a moment before remembering Crescian's Northern name. 'Yes.'

'What did he say?'

'Well, it was just a dream, Penta. But let's see . . . he's indisposed . . . his heart wanes . . . something about a table, and how we're all responsible for this world and one another. Oh, and I think he's disappointed in us or something. Also, he seems pretty disillusioned with my old guildmaster, Sylas, who thinks he's a woman.' Kyr let out an exasperated breath. 'I'm pretty confused about the whole thing, to tell you the truth.'

Penta, serious as they were, dissolved into a fit of giggling. It made Kyr laugh too.

'What?' Kyr asked.

'Nothing,' Penta said, still smiling. 'It sounds like a very illuminating dream. Clearly, Drithas means to warn us to be careful about what lies ahead. Did he say anything else?'

'To gather allies.'

Penta nodded, their smile fading. 'We'd best find my sister then.'

'Mm.'

'And does it matter to you?' Penta asked.

'What?' said Kyr.

'Crescian being male or female,' Penta prompted.

Kyr shrugged. 'Why would it matter?'

Each person they passed, Penta asked if they had seen their sister. They didn't have much to go on, just a vague description based on their shared father—red hair, possible blue or brown eyes—and a name, *Oria*, possibly of-Cailir. But Penta was head-strong. Nothing could deter them.

The village that stood before them now, a short ways down a sloping hill in a glade, stood where the arid, rocky lands of the Yoren Mountains gave way to the fertile mountain pass into the Middevale.

'I saw no village here on the map,' said Penta.

Kyr, less suspicious, said, 'I hope they have ale.'

Penta huffed a laugh. 'Of course you do.'

They approached cautiously, as they had since learned was always best to do. Kyr realized as they got closer that the buildings were all made of natural materials, like sticks and moss, many of them temporary. Small pens with fences woven from sticks held herd animals.

Kyr looked closer, and realized the sheep's fur was not hair, but a fluffy, almost vaporous thing. Just like a cloud.

'Is that . . . ?' She looked closer.

Penta looked with her, quirking a brow. 'Something is wrong with those sheep.'

'Right?' Kyr wondered.

They crept closer, still keeping to the outer edges of the fencing, and then Kyr understood. The animals themselves were made from leaves, cloud-stuff, and vines.

'What is this place?' she asked aloud.

As if in answer, a voice called from behind them. 'Can I help you?'

They turned around to see a woman in a long wool cloak. Her hair—tight black ringlets—was tucked back into a brown wool cap.

'Sorry,' said Kyr. 'We're travelers, on our way to the Middevale. We saw these sheep and, well, why do they look like that?'

The lady laughed heartily. 'Your guess is as good as ours. Maybe you can tell, we trade in wool.' She smiled and gestured to the sheep and then her cloak. 'One day, we got up in the morning and all of the sheep were like this. My father says the Spirits have blessed our flock, but since we can't use them for wool anymore, we've had to adjust to what we can trade for our crops alone.' She shrugged. 'Some blessing.'

'Huh,' said Kyr, turning to look back at the sheep. The more you watched them, the more it felt like a trick of the light. As they moved through the grasses, they almost felt like one with the surrounding landscape.

'They are cute though, aren't they?' asked the woman, approaching them cautiously.

Kyr nodded. 'Awfully.' She gave a broad smile. 'Would it be alright if we slept in the field tonight?'

The woman returned one of her own. 'Well, you don't have to settle for the field. We've got a spare room, and some food to go 'round for friendly travelers such as yourselves.'

'Thank you,' said Penta. 'We're glad to pay.'

The woman waved a hand. 'Help with supper and we'll call it even.'

Inside, the woman's cottage was warm and cozy. It had a dirt floor, earthen walls, and a thatched roof. Three small children played some sort of game involving marks and dice carved from nutshells, stopping to stare at Kyr and Penta with curious eyes as they entered.

Soft, warm green light came from lanterns filled with fireflies, something Kyr had never seen before. The wall was covered in various baubles—embroidery, plates and tankards and books on shelves, bundles of herbs and corn husk dolls. In another room off to the side, Kyr saw an elderly man sleeping in a rocking chair.

'Ro, Edda, Mora,' the woman called to them, 'we've got guests for supper, let's clean up this mess a bit, shall we?'

'Oh, don't worry on our account,' said Kyr.

'Nonsense,' said the woman. 'I made cabbage soup, and we've still got some bread and hard cheese from the cellar. I hope that'll be suitable for you.'

'More than,' Kyr reassured her.

The woman looked to Penta. 'What're your names?'

'I'm Penta,' they said awkwardly. Though they'd been away from the tower for some time, Penta's voice was still quiet and occasionally raspy, and Kyr wondered if they would ever grow used to using it.

'Kyr,' she said, extending a hand.

The woman clasped it in hers. 'It's dangerous now to travel, isn't it?' she asked curiously.

'Aye,' said Kyr. 'We wouldn't be doing it if it weren't necessary.'

'Oh?' the woman prodded. Kyr figured she probably didn't get a lot of travelers out this way. Not many people had a reason to cross through the Middevale.

Kyr decided to use the same excuse they'd given the archivist back in Bellgard. 'We're historians, from a scholarly society in the Middevale. We're returning from Bellgard and the Archives there.'

The woman clapped her hands together. 'How impressive! I hope for a fate so bright for these little ones someday,' she said, watching as the children darted past the table, playing another game.

Soon they sat down to a meal, joined by the children and father.

'You're quiet,' the one called Ro said, looking at Penta.

'I'm just not used to so much conversation,' they said, offering a small smile. 'So much time spent alone in libraries.'

'Why does your voice sound like that?' asked another.

'Hush, Edda,' their mother scolded.

'You know, we never got your name,' Kyr asked the woman.

'Oh, my!' the woman laughed, 'you're right. My name is Poeia.'

Kyr nodded, a piece of cabbage scalding her mouth. With how good the food tasted, she didn't care. 'So, if you don't mind me asking again about the sheep—' Kyr paused, gesturing to her head. 'A scholar's mind.'

Next to her, Penta bit into a piece of bread to stifle their laughter.

'Oh, go right ahead, though I'm not sure how helpful I'll be to you.'

'What day was it you said they'd changed?'

'It's been almost a month now,' Poeia replied. 'The night before it happened, we had an earthquake. My father always used to say there were leviathans living under the earth.' She threw her hands up and let them fall to the table. 'Never believed him until then. I was certain there would be all sorts of damage to the farm come morning, but the only thing different was the sheep.'

The old man, who had been silent up until then, turned toward them. 'It is true! You form bonds working in the mines, and I had such a bond once. Brim, was his name. He saw one of the leviathans, with his very own eyes! Down a freshly dug mineshaft, he did. Silver vein was completely bottomed out!'

'Hm. What did Brim say they looked like?' Kyr asked.

His glassy eyes connected with hers. 'Oh, they take all different forms,' he said. 'They can take the shape of anything you or I can see. I mean, everything in the sky above and the earth below. It's all connected.' He gave a nod.

'I see,' Kyr said. 'Have you and your family always lived here?'

'Oh, no,' she said. 'We traveled around quite a bit. Mostly around the Middevale, never straying too far north or south.'

'Well, you've settled in quite a beautiful place. I hope you're able to find a remedy for your sheep.'

They finished their meal, and Kyr washed the dishes for Poeia, telling her it was the least she could do. All the while, she thought about the old man's story, and wondered if it had to do with what Penta had said about Solq resting under the earth. To Kyr it sounded more like a fable to explain the Spirits to children, but maybe that miner really had seen something that day.

When they retired to their room, a small, enclosed terrace off the back of the house, she asked Penta about it.

'What did you make of that story at dinner?'

'The leviathans?' Penta asked. They let their cloak and trousers fall to the floor, so that they wore only their tunic. Kyr nodded.

They began carding their fingers through their long hair. 'I was thinking it reminded me of a story my mother used to tell me. It's the first thing I've been able to remember about her.' Casting a glance over their shoulder, they smiled. 'She would tell me to be careful with my magic, because if the wrong people knew about it, I would end up living below, with the leviathans.'

'Hm,' said Kyr. She didn't know what to make of that. 'Vaguely threatening. Can you remember anything else? Anything about what she looked like?'

Penta shook her head. 'I see red hair, or maybe blond, like yours, but lighter.' As they said it, they reached over and touched a strand of Kyr's hair. The gentleness of Penta's touch sent a shiver across her skin.

Kyr propped herself up on her elbow, letting Penta do as

they pleased for just a moment longer. She cleared her throat. 'Well, we best get some rest. We'll need it if we're going to continue moving at this speed tomorrow. And the day next.'

Penta smiled faintly, but nodded and blew out the candle.

In the dark, with only the crickets chirruping in the field, Kyr felt brave enough to do what she always thought about doing during the day. She turned on her side and pulled Penta in toward her, cradling their head under her jaw. Penta wrapped Kyr's arms around them, and Kyr fell asleep to the sweet smell of Penta's hair, like fresh rainfall, beside her.

63

KYR

THE MIDDEVALE WAS much greener than Kyr expected. Its brightness seemed to match a freedom she'd found most of the small villages in this part of the world to have. Folks who lived out here worked for themselves. It was often hard, back-breaking work, but it meant something. It offered something to the world, and the people out here could rely on one another.

They'd said goodbye to the shepherding family and set out early. According to the map they'd consulted in Bellgard, Greenflower lay just beyond the meadow they were approaching.

Glad as she was to be seeing Penta all the way to the Midde-vale safely, a part of her feared that once they figured out who they were, once they had their family back, their *real* family, they might send Kyr away. She pushed the thought from her mind as their horse started on a bridge across a wetland over-taken by reeds.

Penta, in front of her on the horse, looked over their shoul-der. 'What are you thinking about?'

Kyr let out a breathy laugh. 'Well, since you asked, I was

thinking about last night. About the blights. About that family. About falling asleep beside you.'

She could feel Penta's smirk, though they didn't turn to face her. 'I've been thinking the same.' They didn't specify.

Kyr bowed her head to Penta's. 'I've been thinking about it since Bellgard, actually. You know, I thanked Atlan for carrying me to bed. He looked at me like I had a third eye.'

Penta glanced back sheepishly. 'I'm sorry if I've been too bold. So many years alone has made me quite . . . eager.' Kyr tilted her head so that her lips were nearer to Penta's ear.

'Are you remembering something?'

'Yes,' Penta said. 'You've made me remember what it is to be part of something again. From the moment you decided to break into my tower, I was intrigued by you.' Kyr chuckled. 'Atlan, Teleri, Vyktas, they always looked at me with skepticism, and I don't blame them, but you, Kyr. You looked at me and saw *me*. I think this journey saved my life in more ways than one.'

'You getting all sentimental on me because we've reached the end of all this?'

Penta angled their head toward her. 'This is hardly the end, Kyr ap Sand.'

Kyr felt her heart kick in her chest. 'Right. The way things are going, I'll probably end up taking you all the way to the edge of the world.'

Penta laughed. 'Maybe. Kyr, I'd like to stay with you, even after I've found my sister, even after I've faced my past, whatever that may be. Whatever may come.'

Kyr leaned over Penta's shoulder. 'Far be it from me to deny you.'

———

Greenflower was charming. Full of crafters, artisans, and traders, there was something interesting to look at around every corner. If Kyr ever chose to settle down somewhere, she could see herself choosing a lively place like this.

They led their horse down the tree-lined main road, blossoms blooming in the fragrant night air. It was autumn now, but seeing this place, Kyr could've guessed how Greenflower got its name.

They'd asked around at the inn about a flame-haired Oria —no luck—and decided to rest there that night before the last leg of their journey north. The Northern Wilds were rumored to be the most dangerous part of the world they'd traversed yet, and Kyr was dreading it. She could deal with more loss, more pain, as long as it happened to her. She didn't fear that. What she feared was that something could happen to Penta. Another person in her life gone.

'This room's barely big enough for me, let alone the both of us,' Kyr grumbled as she stooped into the attic room. She nearly hit her head on the rafters and sighed. 'I'm going to need a drink.'

'I think it's cozy,' Penta mused.

'Of course you do. Can't imagine you upset with anything.'

Penta grinned. 'Well, you haven't seen me when I find out the bread is stale, then. Oh, or when the tea has gone cold.'

'A lot of these seem to pertain to food,' said Kyr.

'Or when my father locks me in a tower for nigh on a millennium.'

'You've got me there.'

Penta collapsed onto the bed, laughing. Kyr stood at the foot of it, looking down at them. The amber-colored lamps flickering away on either side of the door made Penta's hair gleam, their skin, the color of peaches, looked so soft. Kyr was lonelier than she realized, and Penta called to something in her.

'You're staring,' Penta said, their voice quiet and somewhat strained.

'You're beautiful.'

'Now, Kyr,' Penta warned. 'Keep talking like that and I might kiss you.'

'Like a rose in full bloom,' Kyr muttered, her eyes falling over Penta's body, lower and lower. Stopping. 'I wonder if you're as soft . . .'

Penta smirked and rose up on their arms, leaning back so that their face was only inches from Kyr's, who hadn't realized she'd been slowly leaning forward. They hovered there for only a moment, before Kyr leaned forward on the bed frame and lowered her head, her lips ghosting over Penta's.

The lamps glowed. Wood creaked.

She could feel Penta smile against her. Something in her unspooled, and Kyr placed her hand on the back of Penta's neck and brought their lips to hers. They tasted like sweet fire, and Kyr let herself burn. She crawled over the footboard and onto the mattress, settling over top of Penta. Her mind spun too quickly to think.

She ran her tongue along Penta's lips, opening their mouth and deepening the kiss, as Penta's hand snaked around Kyr's neck to grab a fistful of Kyr's hair.

Against everything that sang in her, Kyr pulled back. 'Are you sure you want this?'

'Kyr,' Penta panted. 'I haven't been touched for all these years. I more than want this, I—I need this. *Please.*'

Hearing them beg to be touched broke all of Kyr's restraint, not that she had much to begin with. Their clothes hastily and carelessly discarded on the floor, Kyr kissed a line down the column of Penta's throat and the soft flesh of their chest.

She breathed in deep, inhaling them, that warm and slightly smoky scent of leather, the rosemary soap they'd used that morning in the river, and a pleasant smell of sweat. Her knee rose to rub against that petal-soft flesh between Penta's thighs, making Penta gasp.

'Kyr,' they breathed.

'Tell me what you need.'

'I want you . . . to know how I taste,' Penta responded in a desperate whisper.

'I live to obey.' Kyr knelt back on her heels, lifting one of Penta's legs, and pressed her lips to the arch of their foot, the definition of their calf, their thigh, each spot softer still. She brushed a hand over the soft coils of hair between Penta's legs. 'Open for me,' she commanded.

Penta did so, and Kyr let her ravenous thirst take over to drink her fill. Her first taste was long and slow, savoring. She dipped a finger into the well of Penta's sex, flicking her finger, her tongue over that pearl of flesh, that touch she knew Penta so desperately craved. A soft cry tore from their lips, and Kyr relished the sound. She lingered there, letting Penta's desire kindle, before increasing her pace, plunging two fingers inside, curling them as she almost withdrew, again and again.

'*Kyr*,' Penta gasped.

'I love the sound of my name from your lips.'

Kyr kissed and teased them, and Penta's hips canted. The feel of their muscles tensing around Kyr's fingers was enough to drive her mad. The taste enough to intoxicate her. Another cry broke free, loud and animalistic, and Kyr pulled away slightly, mindful of her lover's sensitive flesh as they broke apart around her.

Penta clawed for her when she retreated even slightly. 'No, please, come to me.'

Kyr laughed softly, cupping their face in her hands and pressing kisses to their cheek and lips. 'Shh, the whole inn will hear you.'

'Let them,' Penta sighed. Kyr collapsed over top of Penta, burying her face in their neck, their limbs entangled. She couldn't stop herself from kissing them.

Heavy-lidded, their eyes fluttered open. 'I would hear what sounds you make,' they breathed.

She bit her lip, curling into a sly smile. 'Soon. We have all the rest of our time together,' Kyr said. 'Tonight was for you.'

Penta smirked, their cheeks flushed and lips swollen. The sight of it made Kyr want to do it all over again, but Penta sat up. 'Come on, then. Let's get you that drink you were promised.'

64

ORIA

IT WAS late at night when they arrived in the Middevale. Stars twinkled overhead, a peaceful sight after a lifetime of the stormy nights and bruised gray skies over the citadel.

They had been letting their horse rest when a passing merchant slowed to a stop on the road.

'Going into the village?' he asked, smiling. He'd seen Oria first.

'Oh,' she said, not expecting the question. 'Yes. But we've been riding for several days and our horse is quite tired. I'm not sure we'll make it by nightfall.'

'Nonsense,' said the man. 'Hitch your horse. You can ride in the back.'

Mothril appeared from the ditch where he'd been picking out the horse's hoof.

The man's eyes widened as his smile became brittle. 'Ah, didn't realize you had a, well, quite the big fellow with you. Heh.' He glanced nervously at Mothril's sword and Mothril crossed his arms.

'Is something wrong?' Oria asked.

'. . . Not at all!' The man was taking a closer look at her now, likely wondering about her association with one such as Mothril. 'Y-you can both ride along, if you like.'

Oria was still getting used to a life of traveling, of seeing new places and people each day. It was something she'd hoped for for herself when she thought she would be Prime one day, that she might travel and seek alliances—put an end this period of isolation her father had them under. She hadn't expected that it would happen so soon, or under such circumstances.

Her body strained under the demands of daily travel, but her mind felt more awake and alive than it had in many years.

'Are you awake?' Mothril asked, his body warm against her.

'Mm,' she answered.

His hand rested absentmindedly against her thigh, and Oria couldn't stop imagining the way his hands might feel on her skin. But he didn't want that. Or maybe he did, but he would not give it to her. She picked at the skin of her nail and looked away, the breeze cooling the flush of embarrassment blooming on her cheeks.

'We're almost to Greenflower,' the man shouted over his shoulder.

Wagon wheels groaning, Oria leaned in to Mothril's ear. 'I'll be glad for whatever's left at the inn and a pile of hay at this point.' Her legs ached, and she just wanted to rest.

'Mm. It's been a long day,' he agreed.

She shifted against the hard wooden bottom of the wagon, and Mothril pulled his hand away, unbuckling his gauntlets and pulling his glove off with his teeth.

'What are you doing?'

He reached down and placed his hand on her thigh, grazing just under her dress. Oria's eyes darted downward. 'May I?'

'Um, yes,' she said, still not understanding.

Slowly, he began running his hand up and down her thigh as they rode, kneading the muscle with the heel of his hand.

She couldn't help the sigh of relief that escaped her.

'Good?' he murmured.

'Yes, thank you.'

He nodded, resting his head against the boards at his back.

It wasn't long before they reached the small, quaint village, but Oria was quite a bit distracted. She understood she was some years younger than him, and the daughter of Edril Sil no less, but could he not see that she felt great affection for him? Wasn't that enough?

They thanked the man who seemed eager to be rid of them, then left their horse tied outside and entered the dimly lit inn, which was already closing down for the night. A scattering of oak tables across a wide-planked floor were still bedecked in the leavings from dinner, a few patrons still picking lazily while they finished their nightcaps. One man sat at the bar, obviously drunk, flirting with the barkeep who was trying to clean up and usher him home.

'Any rooms left?' Mothril asked. The woman startled momentarily as she looked up and saw Mothril's massive form, something which seemed a common occurrence for him.

'Plenty,' said the innkeeper, a stout woman with curly red hair and a rosy-cheeked face. 'Kitchen's closed but we've got some leftover bread, and barley soup. Oh, and there's tea if you'd like. I just put a pot on.'

'Sounds perfect,' Oria said, smiling. They took a seat in the corner of the inn, further observing the scene while the woman prepared their fare. Taking up the too-small corner, Mothril pulled out a long-stemmed pipe and packed it with amberleaf. He puffed it to a glowing cherry on the beeswax candle and blew a thick ring of smoke in her direction.

Oria looked at him, agape. 'Where did you get that? My father says that's terrible for you!'

Mothril raised an eyebrow, smoke billowing around him. 'You understand the irony of that, right?'

Oria shrugged. 'He's done much research on the body.'

'He's a necromancer,' Mothril said flatly, smoke curling out of his nose.

Oria picked at the wood grain of the table. 'Well, the thing about necro—' Her words were cut off by the barkeep arriving with a steaming pot of monkroot tea, two bowls of soup, brown crusty bread, and a wedge of crumbly blue cheese.

'Hope the bread's not too stale,' said the woman apologetically.

'Looks lovely,' Oria said, smiling. Mothril had already dipped it into his soup and taken a bite.

The woman nodded, turning to go, but Oria touched her arm, getting her attention. She lowered her voice. 'I meant to ask, do you know of any cunning-folk nearby?' Mothril raised his brows, clearly surprised at her bold question, and curious as to the meaning of it. 'We're looking to learn about ley lines in the area. You know, sources of magical power.' The woman's eyes widened. Oria let her expression turn sheepish. 'It's said there's a special mushroom that grows along them.' Her eyes darted quickly to Mothril. 'To help with . . . *fertility*,' she whispered.

Mothril coughed and almost spit out his soup.

The woman's face brightened, relaxing into a smile as she glanced between the two of them. 'Oh, how wonderful! Well, I don't know of anyone such as that in these parts, but I do know that there are ley lines to the north. A lot of them intersect around some old Wiccar ruins, but I can't recommend you go there.' Her eyes grew serious, her smile falling. 'Years and years back, when my grandmother ran this inn, a powerful sorcerer came through the village.' When she saw the look of fabricated shock on Oria's face, she began nodding. 'Mhm. Plenty will tell you mages have gone extinct, especially Sentinel nonbelievers, but we Northerners know cunning-folk are alive and well. Out in the woods. Anywho, this sorcerer came to warn us not to go there. The ruins, I mean. The whole place is warded. Death magic.'

'Oh, my!' Oria exclaimed, still feigning surprise. 'Well, thank the Spirits you warned us, we'll be sure to stay away from there.'

The barkeep nodded. 'You two'll need your strength. Let me check and see if we've got any mutton left.' She winked, and turned on her heels, disappearing into the other room.

Mothril shook his head. 'If she comes back with that mutton, I'm eating all of it.'

A tinkling laugh escaped her, and she wrinkled her nose. 'Mutton is foul. It's all yours.' She took a sip of her tea. 'What do you make of the story about the sorcerer? There's no way that's unconnected to my father, right?'

He exhaled, looking thoughtful. 'Could be.'

The barkeep returned a few moments later with a plate of cold, roasted meat, smothered in a thick brown gravy with a few scattered root vegetables. The scent of onions and allspice wafted from it. 'You're in luck!'

'Oh, thank you,' Oria said, mustering as much gratitude in her tone as she could.

'Don't mention it.' The woman smiled, then whisked away again.

She slid the plate toward Mothril, who smiled smugly and began tearing into the meat with his hands.

Thuds sounded on the staircase.

'I'm telling you, we're too late. You distracted me!' said a woman with short blond hair, laughing as she bounded down the steps. Behind her, Oria caught a glimpse of long red hair and cheekbones she could've sworn were her father's. She couldn't help but stare, and the stranger's eyes met hers.

The blond woman followed their gaze, then looked back at her companion. 'Fucking Six, Penta, you two look just alike.'

Penta? She didn't recognize the name.

Penta continued to stare at her. 'Oria?' they said. Their voice was hoarse, almost with the quality of a whisper. Mothril turned. The stranger knew her name.

'Yes?' Oria asked, not knowing what else to say.

'Oh, shit,' said the blond woman, raising her brows expectantly, as if it were commonplace for serendipity to befall them in the night. 'Looks like you two have a lot to talk about.'

65

ATLAN

'LET US OUT!' Sol Rywin yelled, banging on the door. The rest of the council members had stopped trying hours ago, but Rywin had only worked himself into more of a frenzy.

'Oh, give it a rest,' came another voice. 'He's not coming back until he's finished with his coup.'

'If he's smart, when he comes back it'll be to hang us,' said Councilman Thay. Atlan looked at him, a handsome middle-aged man from one of the wealthiest families in Yorenth.

How did Taryq possibly think he was going to get away with this?

'Don't say that!' Rywin snapped. 'Let us out!' He resumed banging on the door.

Atlan took in his surroundings—a banquet room, never used, that was part of the old, original palace. There was a long table in the center with chairs that were occupied by men and women who, until a couple of days ago, were the most important in Yorenth.

An ornate mirror hung on one wall, old family portraits on the others. There was a wooden cabinet against one wall containing plates and silverware. Among other family heirlooms that had been all but discarded here. Likely because his mother thought them ugly. It was one of the only rooms in the palace that wasn't open to the air. It didn't even have any windows. The acrid stench of urine and human waste had become nearly unbearable after the first day.

He wondered where his mother was. He had expected Taryq to throw her in here with them, too, but he never did. *Had she agreed to some terms of his?* Where was Osimar?

And where was Teleri?

Safe, hopefully.

He adjusted his position against the wall. The first day, the shackles had made him feel like his skin was crawling. The second day, he awoke with a headache that had grown in severity over the following hours. Just like he'd done in the dungeons, he lay in the corner and shut his eyes, imagining things far away from this place.

Kyr and Penta on horseback, somewhere in the Middevale.

Teleri safe at home in the forest, having put all of this behind her.

Vyktas, unbloodied, smiling in the grass.

66

ORIA

ORIA STARED at the person in front of her.

Penta.

Her lost sibling.

'It's you,' Penta said, equally confused. Their eyes had in them a wild desperation that both frightened Oria and made her want to cry. 'You're here.'

'Are you alright?' The blond woman next to her had a tattoo on her hand, which she had placed on Penta's shoulder.

Penta looked at her with a distinct fondness. 'I'm fine, Kyr.'

Kyr nodded, glancing at their food. She turned to the barkeep, who was looking at them curiously. 'Hey, you told me there was no mutton left when we first got here!'

The woman's face reddened. 'Well,' she scoffed, 'I was saving it for the stew tomorrow, but *they* asked very nicely!' She added dismissively, 'They needed it.'

Kyr's face darkened. 'What, I don't look like I need it?'

Mothril cut in then, his mouth still full. 'I'll share.' He swallowed. 'Let's let the two of them talk, hm?'

Kyr grinned. 'Good man.'

Then they were alone, the two of them, in the dimly lit

barroom, Kyr and Mothril having retreated upstairs with the bulk of the pantry in tow. Outside, the world was silent, a bright crescent moon the only witness to their reunion.

'I've been looking for you,' Oria said. It was all she could think to say, really. She couldn't understand how fate could conspire to bring her sibling to her so shortly after learning they existed. But there was no mistaking it. They looked like mirror images of one another in so many ways, and despite how much it unnerved her, there was no denying her father's features on Penta's face.

'So have I.'

Without another word, Oria reached out and cradled Penta's cold, slender hand in her own. 'I dreamt about you,' she said.

'So did I,' Penta replied, their eyes sparkling in the candlelight. They scrutinized her face, as if committing it to memory.

'But I don't understand,' Oria began. 'He never spoke of you.'

A tear fell from Penta's eye, and they hastily wiped it away. 'I think he'd rather have forgotten my existence altogether.'

'*Why*?' Oria asked. There was so much she wanted to know.

'You must know some things about our father which perhaps he has kept concealed from you. The first being just that. He is secretive by nature. Even now, there is much I can't remember about my life because of wards he's placed around my memory. I have spent centuries unraveling these wards, but have only scratched the surface.'

'Centuries?' Oria asked.

'I see,' Penta replied, casting their eyes downward. 'Perhaps this is the second thing you must know about our father. He has been a deceiver throughout time, throughout realms. You and I are pieces on his chessboard. I seek knowledge of his other pieces, and so he hides me from you. From the world.'

'So it's true then?' she wondered aloud. She recounted her

and Mothril's journey as they sipped their monkroot tea, the candles burning down around them. Penta was particularly interested when she told them of the ruins, and the gossip she'd heard from the barkeep earlier that night.

'I must see this place. Study these wards. They may yield further understanding of the sorcery that holds my own memories at bay.' Penta began nodding, already deep in thought. They blinked. 'Sorry, I am getting ahead of myself. I am relieved to see you, more than you know. I thought we might be too late. After all, so much time has passed. I thought you might have already become a tool of his destruction.'

Oria's laugh was hollow. 'It's funny you say that. Only a couple of weeks earlier that might've been true.'

'What do you mean?'

'I only recently escaped from the Eradomin citadel he occupies. I've lived there most of my life. As a seer.' She looked up and studied Penta's face, trying to judge their reaction. They nodded. 'He had me undergo these rituals.' Penta's face hardened at that. 'It's how I got my scars, and this,' she said, hiking up her dress to reveal the brace on her leg. 'Each time I underwent one of these rituals, I came out of my visions with more injuries. They quickly worsened beyond the scope of the healers.' She paused. 'One time, I swear I saw you. You feel so familiar.'

'I was in a tower,' Penta coaxed.

'Yes!' Oria could hardly contain her astonishment.

Penta nodded. 'He may have been checking in on me through you.'

'Really? He always wanted to know if I'd dreamt of the Eradomin. Do you know of them?'

'Mm, I know them.' For the first time, Penta looked hesitant. 'Oria, do you know who your mother is?'

'Again, I thought I knew much until recently. I was raised by a woman named Felith of-Cailir, until she passed away several years ago.' Penta drew in a sharp breath. 'I thought her my mother, but when I escaped the citadel, my . . . my friend, Lyra, she revealed to me some things.' Oria shook her head. 'It's a long story, but apparently, Felith is not my mother, either. I don't know who or what to believe.'

'Lyra of-Rowan?' Penta asked. 'She lives?'

Oria's heart sank thinking of her friend. 'Unfortunately not. Edril Sil had her killed. As I was escaping.' She paused. 'You know Lyra? How?'

'Damn it all,' Penta cursed. 'I'm sorry for your losses. They are losses to me as well. I am glad to hear you got the chance to know them, at least. They did their duties to the fullest and shall be rewarded in rebirth.' Oria's brows knit at the cryptic statement. 'I asked Felith to look after you, before . . . before—' She sighed. 'I don't remember. Before I left. Lyra is *Felith's* daughter.'

Oria gaped. 'What? Then they are—' She shook her head. 'I am as a child to all of you!'

Penta shook their head slightly, smiling. 'Wisdom doesn't necessarily increase with age.' Their smile fell. 'There's one more thing I have to tell you, Oria. Have you heard tales of Sarthura?'

Oria nodded, bewildered. 'How do you do that?'

'Do what?' Penta asked, sipping their tea.

'It's like you already know all the things that have been plaguing my mind. Yes, I know of Sarthura. Edril Sil seems to have a particular fascination with her. And when Mothril and I went to those ruins, he thought a symbol of hers was etched all over them. The unseeing eye, he called it.'

'Your companion is Eradomin, is he not? I sense it in him.'

Oria couldn't help herself and began to laugh. 'How could you possibly know that? I only learned of that after we escaped. He'd been hiding amongst the Wiccar clans for decades!'

Penta nodded. 'Does he not have his own House?'

'He did, once. Arcandrian. He believes himself to be the last of the Eradomin.'

Now it was Penta who looked shocked. 'Truly? The North belonged to the Eradomin in my time.'

'Edril Sil wages war on them too,' said Oria.

Penta shook their head. 'Anything to destroy Sarthura's last hold on this world.'

'What do you mean?' Oria pressed.

'Sarthura so loved the Eradomin,' Penta said softly.

She cocked her head. 'Penta, how do you know all of this?'

'Because I knew our mother. I loved her.'

'Our . . . mother?'

'Sarthura,' they said plainly. 'Calligone.'

Oria sat back in her chair, stunned. The silence in the room fell upon them like a weight.

'I know it's a lot to take in,' Penta said gently.

'But Sarthura is a—a—' She was at a loss for words.

'Yes,' said Penta. 'A Spirit.'

'What does that make us?'

'I don't know,' Penta said, smiling.

Something in Oria broke first. She smiled, before an uncontrollable bout of laughter escaped her at how preposterous it all seemed. This made Penta laugh too. Then Oria leaned forward, dipping some of her hair into the tea, and it only made them laugh harder.

'Oh,' Oria breathed, wiping the tears that had welled in her eyes. 'I'm glad I found you. It is such a relief to have these answers, even if they are completely absurd.' She laughed again.

Penta squeezed her hand. 'A great relief.'

They looked at each other. 'I look like him, don't I?' Oria asked.

'No,' said Penta. 'You look like my sister. You are nothing like him.'

Oria looked down at the table. When she didn't say anything, Penta spoke again, more urgently. 'Whatever he plans, we will put a stop to it. You're not alone in this anymore, Oria. I know his cruelty too. That you know where his body is can work to our advantage. The necromancy that our father practices is ancient and very powerful, but our knowing about it is something he won't be expecting. There may be a way to intercept the magic at work somehow.'

'I had the same thought but didn't want to linger there. Do you ever feel like he can see you, even when he's not there?' Oria asked.

'All the time.' Penta paused, still holding her hand. There was such conviction in their eyes. 'We will end this madness. I promise you that.'

67

KYR

By this point in her life, Kyr had had many strange encounters due to chance, but this one had to be one of the most extraordinary. What were the odds that a roadside tavern in Greenflower, which they'd decided to stop at because their horse needed a rest, would be the same one Penta's sister would walk into, mere hours later? At that moment, that turn of the mark, she believed in the Spirits, in Crescian, wholeheartedly.

Kyr sat in awkward silence with Oria's unnerving companion for a time, watching him gnaw off the ends of the sheep bones and suck out the marrow. He didn't seem to notice her.

She'd eaten her fill, but something was missing. 'No Spirits-damned ale in this whole place,' she grumbled. 'What kind of establishment is this?'

Across from her, Mothril chuckled through another bite of potatoes. Finally, someone who could eat as much as her. She appreciated that.

Seemingly out of nowhere, he produced a long and elegant hornwood pipe. Faint etching lined its stem. He set it down, sliding it across the table toward her, and then produced a small, sweet-smelling pouch.

Kyr's lips curled into a smile, her hand going to her chest. 'Amberleaf. A man after my own heart.' She picked up the pouch and inhaled—leather, molasses, and vanilla.

Mothril continued eating as Kyr stoked the bowl. She began happily blowing rings. It satisfied her, for a time, but as the lamps in the room began to burn low and Kyr felt the relaxing properties of the amberleaf, she wanted ale even more.

Mothril finished the rest of the food and now gestured for the pipe, leaning back against the wall of Kyr and Penta's cramped room. He took a long draw and issued forth a giant cloud of smoke.

'You've got a bellows in your chest, my big friend,' said Kyr.

Mothril smiled.

Kyr sighed. 'There's got to be some ale in this place.' She looked around. 'You know, I think we passed a storage closet on the way up.'

He quirked a brow at her and took another long pull, blowing more smoke rings. 'Alright. You've turned my mind toward ale,' he said casually. 'I'll follow you.'

Kyr nodded once and stood, impressed with Penta's sister's choice of companion. 'To yonder closet!' she said, and pranced out of the room.

In a cloud of smoke, Mothril trailed closely behind Kyr, down the narrow hallway glowing deep yellow with candle-light. Inlaid within the wall's mahogany wainscoting was a simple shelved closet.

Kyr knelt down, digging through brooms, bottles, and boxes of things, before grabbing one bottle in particular. It was corked, with wax covering the neck. She produced it, holding it up to the light.

'I think this is in storage from some feast day or something.'

She dusted off the label and read it. 'Mouseblossom brandy?' She looked inquisitively at Mothril.

He shrugged. 'Seems as good as any brandy.'

Kyr beamed. 'Let's see if you drink as well as you eat.'

He grabbed the bottle from her. *'Swealges selas I direr lay nemor.'*

She blinked at him. 'What?'

'An Eradomin toast,' he mused. 'It translates roughly to . . . we will drink over the bodies of our foes.'

'Fuck yeah,' Kyr whispered.

Mothril tore off the wax with his teeth and, lacking another way to open it, Kyr used the tip of her dagger to work the cork back into the bottle.

She took a swig from it, grimacing against its overly sweet, almost spoiled flavor. 'Let's drink over the bodies of whoever we run into together, eh?'

Mothril bowed his head to Kyr, looming over her in the small hallway. 'To stories well begun.'

68

MOTHRIL

MOTHRIL AWOKE BLEARY-EYED, his leg draped over the arm of an overstuffed chair in an unfamiliar room. He wasn't sure how he had gotten there, but the ache in his back betrayed that it had been a true sleep, something he hadn't done in a while. He had forgotten how stiff it made him.

He tried to recall the night before, but the last thing he remembered was Kyr balancing on a footstool, repeating back to him that phrase he'd said in Borean Poet, albeit very poorly. He laughed and shook his head.

As he rose from the chair, he looked over the room to see Oria fast asleep in the bed. She must've been up very late talking to Penta, seeing as he didn't even recall her returning to the room. Quietly, he made his way to the door, shutting it behind him.

The tavern was dead so early in the morning, but there was a small offering of fruit, bread, and tea left out. He grabbed an apple for himself and a smattering of things for Oria, and was about to head back upstairs when he saw Penta sitting alone in the far corner of the room. They yawned, rubbing their temples. A mug of tea sat out before them.

Mothril set down the food, regarding the Whispess's sibling and nodding respectfully.

'*Ghottarn, lay Arcandrian,*' Penta said.

Hearing Borean Poet from someone else's mouth left him dumbfounded. '*Eskenowen*? How?'

'Ah,' they said, looking a bit embarrassed. 'I thought you and Oria might've spoken. Perhaps you were in the same state as my Kyr.' They smiled.

Mothril gave a crooked grin. 'I'm afraid so.'

'I wish she could tell you on her own, but when you've lived for as long as I have, you find yourself worrying a lot about time. Even when you've had far too much of it. *Aye thaer a-enowen.*'

'*Sept!*' The question came out more demanding than he'd meant. He cleared his throat. 'Er, sorry—'

'No need for apologies. I understand how it is to crave understanding after so long alone.' He couldn't take his eyes off them. 'Our mother taught me Borean Poet, Mothril.'

'I take it this was not Felith of-Cailir.'

'No, it was not.'

'*Ken?*'

'*En-mathir waes Sarthura,*' they said, pronouncing the name the old way.

Mothril looked around blankly, taking their words in. He sat down across from them. For once, he could not leash the emotion, the disbelief and desperation, on his face. '*Say monar?*'

This whole time? Sarthura's own daughter . . .

'I do not know for certain,' Penta said. 'But I feel her. The Night still falls.'

'*Nocta rendscir.*'

'*Es-moram aye temeren Oria?*'

He nodded, feeling a sudden swell of emotion in his chest he couldn't identify. Penta smiled, as if they knew.

He never wanted to talk so much in his entire life. '*A-moram. Thaer fennor ken Sarthura?*'

'I-I tried to free her with the Book of Primes, but I was unsuccessful. That's all I know. And the Book of Primes has since been destroyed. I am sorry, I wish I had another answer for you.'

He nodded, expecting as much.

'She tells me you saved her from the citadel.'

Mothril looked up. 'She saved herself. I merely guarded the way.'

Penta nodded. 'Then I am eternally grateful to you. *Laifdirge lay a-mona.*'

'*Lay a-mona o-sylfhares.*'

He smiled at their words. He'd said a similar version once, too. For someone beloved, rather than a friend.

Blood of my blood, of my heart, whose drumbeat I will follow into the night.

————

'We set off for the ruins, then?' Kyr asked, still looking a little worse for wear.

The four of them stood by the small stables outside the inn, a soft autumn breeze blowing the smell of apples and hay across the countryside.

Mothril nodded. 'We should keep moving.' He turned to Oria. 'As you say, we should learn what we can from the sigils, the magic present there, before confronting him. We're not yet ready.'

He and Kyr set to saddling the horses.

Penta agreed. 'We cannot underestimate him.'

Oria's face was grave. 'I worry that this dark magic he attempts, these rituals, are tied to something much greater. Penta, you mentioned your travels with Kyr—'

'Oh, we have theories,' Kyr cut in. 'In Bellgard, we found several old texts about a mage from long ago that warred with rulers and Spirits. There were other stories of the Spirits being trapped or held by some kind of magic. Penta has had similar dreams and visions, too.'

Penta nodded. 'I believe that mage was Edril Sil, before the cataclysm that brought about the Second Age. Perhaps these things are even related. But my memories are shrouded, another of his deceits. I suspect whatever magic he uses to keep my memories from me, he uses to meddle in matters of the Spirits. Another reason to examine these wards.'

'Hopefully if we can free the Spirits, that will put an end to these blights,' said Kyr.

'Blights?' Oria asked.

'Where do I start?' Kyr replied, and began counting on her fingers. 'There's the one with the eternal flame that doesn't consume what it burns, the one where darkness fell from the sky, the cloud sheep, and the fucking mountain that turned into a wyvern before our very eyes.' Mothril raised an eyebrow at that. 'Those are just the ones that I've seen personally. But my friend, Atlan, who might be King of Yorenth by now, has seen many more. He had been traveling with us but had to, er, turn back . . . unexpectedly.' She looked down.

'You know Prince Atlan Solorien?' Oria asked. 'I've never met him, but I've heard talk of him in my father's meetings with the Elders. It is rumored he's a powerful mage.'

Kyr smiled. 'That's him.'

Oria looked away thoughtfully, then turned back to her. 'Did you say 'cloud sheep'?'

'Mm,' said Penta. 'We saw them in the Middevale, just before we got to Greenflower. They were rather adorable.'

Oria's brow furrowed. 'Mothril,' she said, turning to him.

'Hm?' It was more of a grunt than anything else as he adjusted his gauntlets.

'That day I saw that fox, I didn't want to tell you what I really saw for fear you would think me a lunatic. It moved like one, but it was made of leaves, twigs, berries, and the like.'

He recalled that day in the greenhouse. She looked so flummoxed, he knew she had seen something strange. It all made sense now.

'The Greenwoods again,' Penta murmured.

'So, the blights have made it that far north?' said Kyr. She glanced at Penta and, seeing their worried expression, added, 'That's not good. Not good at all.'

Mothril helped Oria into the saddle. 'Fascinating . . . that must be what I saw! What a relief. I thought I was going mad.'

'Madness might be a more welcome malady,' Penta replied warily.

With that, the others mounted their horses and spurred themselves down the road. Soon, they grew silent, the horses' hooves beating a steady rhythm, as they each became consumed with their own thoughts of what was to come.

69

KYR

WITH MOTHRIL'S experience tracking in the Northern woods, it took only the better part of a day to return to the ruins where Edril Sil's body lay. The ruins were smaller than she'd imagined, just a couple of fallen slabs of stone sinking into the earth, with a circle of a few standing stones like columns, and more stones lying across the top. The place looked ancient, like it no longer belonged in this world.

As they got closer, it became harder to traverse the sodden ground. Rain began falling.

'There's something wrong about this place,' said Kyr. It gave her a sickening feeling of restlessness—the hair on the back of her neck standing on end. 'Are you sure no one else knows about this place?'

'No,' Oria answered, her voice grave. 'We must tread carefully.'

They reached the ruins' entryway, which looked more like a cave, or a hole in the ground, than anything else. 'What possessed you two to go into a place like this?' Kyr muttered.

'I was looking for Penta,' Oria shrugged. 'I would look anywhere for them.'

Penta reached out and grabbed Oria's hand, and Oria smiled. Kyr couldn't help but smile, too. She liked seeing Penta happy. Mothril, who'd been silent as a ghost since they'd arrived, also looked upon them fondly.

Inside, the ruins were dizzyingly complex. What looked like a small structure sinking into the ground from the outside, was actually an intricate hive of hallways, tunnels, and collapsed rooms. After some time traversing the darkened halls, with Mothril leading the way, they reached a small archway.

'This is the gate we found that I unlocked with my blood,' Oria said, holding out her palm and showing them the cut across it that was now healing. Penta walked past them and studied the walls. 'The gate was made of interlocking metal and had six symbols.' Oria drew a few of them in the dirt so they could see what they'd looked like.

Kyr cocked her head. 'Six, huh? Are those symbols for each of the Spirits?' She looked at Oria. 'I'm told you call them Fäendhmar up here?'

'It very well could be,' Oria said. Mothril nodded his agreement.

'It's just that this one,' Kyr said, pointing to the spiral, 'could represent Aerith or Riparus. You know, something flowing, like air, or water. This one looks like an eye with bands of light, so maybe that's Solq, and this one was in the Oracle's notes. About you, Penta. So perhaps it signifies your family, or your mother,' she mused. 'That's exactly what the drawings looked like. A darkened eye.'

'It makes sense,' said Penta, running a hand down Kyr's back. Kyr smiled at them.

'Oracle? Notes?' Mothril asked.

'Yes,' said Kyr. 'The Oracle of Yoren. Her notes—really a collection of historical accounts, riddles, and old maps—led us to Penta.'

Mothril rubbed his chin. 'Hm.'

'Another strange coincidence,' said Oria. 'Before we left the citadel, Mothril told me he suspected I was an Oracle.'

'Really?' Kyr raised her brows.

'I believe Edril Sil knows this too. He seems to be using techniques of Eradomin magic, but twisting them into something corrupt. Eradomin rituals often use the blood of Oracles, seers. The more powerful, the better. I believe that is what he was doing during the ceremonies.' He looked at Oria, who crossed her arms.

'For what purpose?' Kyr asked.

'It depends on the aim of the ritual.'

Penta nodded. 'Yes, I have heard of this practice.'

'You have?' Oria asked. 'There is so much I wish to talk to you about. To all of you,' she said, looking at each of them.

Penta smiled. 'Soon.'

She turned back toward the door. 'When I touched my blood to the one representing Sarthura, that's when the door opened.'

Penta clenched their jaw. 'So, our father must've warded it to our family's blood, but I'll bet he never suspected we would be free, or alive, to find this place.'

'Bastard,' said Kyr.

Oria, who stood beside Kyr, laid her head on her shoulder. Kyr hesitated a moment, and then threw an arm around her.

Penta's face softened when they saw. 'Well, he'll be answering to us soon enough.'

They passed through a sickeningly narrow shaft, so deep into the ruins it felt like crawling into the center of the world, before the way opened up into a wide room.

Some kind of sanctum?

Oria stopped short. 'It's just there,' she said, pointing to a slab across from them on a small dais. Penta glanced at her, and Oria nodded.

'Penta, you don't have to look,' Kyr offered.

'No,' said Penta. 'I want to see this. I want proof that he's not invulnerable. He can be stopped.' Their eyes gleamed with fury in the dim. 'He can be dead.'

Kyr could understand that.

Determined, Penta crossed the room, and Kyr followed close behind. She wasn't particularly keen on seeing for herself, but something within her made her approach the slab. She wanted to be someone Penta could lean on.

She watched as Penta peered inside.

'Oria?' Penta asked. 'There's nothing here.'

'What?' Oria said. It came out as a whimper. 'What do you mean?'

She started across the room when shrill screaming rent the silence. The cacophony of cries was at once high-pitched and a low, painful moaning. Skyward, and far, far below the earth. Several voices, coming from somewhere beyond the chamber where they all stood.

'What the Six was th—'

She saw it then, before the question could fully leave her mouth. A figure began to manifest in shadow in the far corner of the room, opposite the dais where Penta stood. The smell of brimstone and decay suddenly permeated the room. Kyr thought to cry out for Penta, but could not find her voice.

Something was very, very wrong.

At first, the thing was just a mass of inky sorcery, bleak and swirling. Then, piece by piece, it became a man. Pale, with deep red hair, just like his children. His eyes were dark and glittering like an animal's, vicious in their intensity. He wore mage's robes woven from the dim itself, and glinting fetishes knotted in his hair. His pointed helmet, more like a flat, brimmed hat made of metal, was horrifyingly similar to those worn by the men who killed Vyktas. His lips curled into a treacherous smile that sent a cold chill of fear through Kyr's body. Nothing had ever made her feel like that before.

In that moment, Kyr thought she had never truly known before what it was to fear.

'My progeny, together again!' he said. His voice was all wrong, a sickening collection of other voices that were not his own. Were they of those disguises he wore while he pretended to be someone else, as his body lay here rotting? Did they belong to those whose lives he had taken?

Penta looked frantically from the vault to their father, seemingly flesh and blood, standing before them. Kyr knew what Penta must be thinking, now that they were trapped here with Edril Sil, and without the body they'd planned to study to understand his machinations.

Their chance to study this foul sorcery, come and gone.

Their element of surprise against him, wasted.

'And I see you've brought some guests to our reunion. I'm sorry to say that they won't be leaving this chamber alive with the knowledge that you've undoubtedly shared with them.'

'There will be no such violence from you,' Penta bit out. Dressed in dark red robes, Penta looked ready for violence.

'Oh? Isn't that what you planned for when you came here?' he asked. 'Were you not planning to use my vessel's power to kill me, your own father? What an ugly act.'

'A father would not lock his child away, nor let her die for his own gain! *That* is an ugly act.'

'A father must do what needs to be done when it comes to unruly children.'

'I'd hardly call protecting our mother from you unruly,' Penta spat.

'Your mother did not need your protection. She was plenty powerful, and mischievous enough, for the both of you. I suppose that's where you get it from. In the end, that was her undoing as well.'

'Why?' Oria asked. Her voice was quiet, and there was a note of fear, but it was nonetheless striking in its fortitude.

Edril Sil whirled around. 'My dear Oria,' he tutted. 'Your question has so many implications. If you're wondering why I never told you about *this* one,' he said, casting a glance at Penta, 'it's because your lost sibling here is more dangerous than you know. I'm grateful to you for bringing back to me what I've lost. Penta should not be let out again.'

Penta lunged for him and was flung back, seemingly by nothing but faintly shimmering air, like heat rippling the distance on a summer's day. Their body hit the stone like a doll before they sat up, wiping blood from their lip.

'See what I mean?' he said.

Kyr looked on in horror.

He continued. 'Perhaps you're wondering about your mother.' He looked at Mothril. 'I see you've brought your immovable guard. He'll be fascinated to know this too, I'm sure. Lady Felith never was your mother, as you've figured out. She was Lyra's. And before you ask, no, I am not Lyra's father. I took them in, and in exchange, they played a part, and they played it well. For a time. I'm learning that was another cruel trick of your mother's, however, and unfortunately, they both became disagreeable in the end. Such a shame that Lyra's worthless heroics cost me that fortress.' Kyr looked at Mothril as he spoke, saw his fist clenched in white-knuckled fury around the hilt of his blade.

Edril Sil looked impassively down at Penta as they got to their feet. 'Don't let that give you a glimmer of hope that your mother is alive. No,' he cooed. 'I find it so *disappointing* that no one can simply be content with our arrangement. Your mother grew tired of what we had *agreed* upon, and that wouldn't do.'

He turned to Oria. 'She died right where you spent your whole life. In the citadel. Why else do you think the clouds never lift, the fog never dissipates, and nights are so long? Of course, when she died, I didn't realize it would upset the balance of this plane's natural world like this. It grows worse by the day.'

He is responsible for the blights? Kyr wondered.

'Don't listen to him, Oria,' Penta yelled. 'Hope is not lost!'

He laughed at that. 'Hope. You know, for one who carries so much of me, I certainly don't recognize you some of the time.'

Penta's head whipped to where he stood. 'What's that supposed to mean?'

He raised a hand. 'Not yet. We're getting ahead of ourselves. I'm not done telling your sister about who she is. It's the least I owe her for bringing you back to me.'

'I did no such thing!' Oria protested.

'Are you and your friends not all here, now, because of you?' he asked. As he said this, he looked each one of them in the eyes. Kyr froze when he looked at her.

'Oria,' Penta called, 'he's going to tell you who he believes our mother is. He's going to tell you she was not strong enough, or clever enough. That she was unworthy. He's lying. She was all those things and more. I remember, I see—I see her!'

'Silence!' Edril Sil screeched. The bravery in Penta's words emboldened Kyr, rage kindling within her with every one of Edril Sil's mocking words. She watched him. His jaw ticked, and his eyes went wide with anger. For someone so ancient, his lack of control over himself both surprised and terrified her.

'You see only what your mother allows, in the pieces of her she left behind. She was, after all, lady of darkness and veils, night and shrouds, mystery, and the unknown. Can she really be known at all?'

'Our mother is *not* gone,' Oria breathed. But it wasn't Oria that caught Kyr's eye, it was Mothril. His face, always stoic, crumpled.

'Oh?' said Edril Sil. 'Enlighten me.'

'Penta and I carry a piece of her with us, and you can *never* take that away.'

A cold wind seized the chamber, whistling through the

crevices at its apex. The wind carried a whisper. A voice that each of them heard.

'My Fäen . . . you walk my shadowed path . . . fear the Deceiver not . . .'

Penta spun around. Mothril closed his eyes.

'A pathetic trick,' he scoffed.

'I told you,' Oria said.

'Lies! Sarthura cannot be here, no matter how much you wish it to be true. I made certain of that.'

'How do you know her true name?' Mothril snarled.

'I have seen Era,' Edril Sil said, smirking. 'I would return and personally see the end of your vile people if the way were not permanently veiled to me. Her last foul attempt at evading me. She truly *loved* the Eradomin.' He said the last part as if it disgusted him. 'I knew I had not rooted you all out. Even after I killed your sorry leader, Dymorra.'

Mothril let out a breath and staggered back against the wall. Edril Sil took the moment to strike. The shadows in the room shifted, overtaking him, swallowing him up. Mothril tried to move, turning his body and managing to lift his sword arm, but he became enwebbed.

'Mothril!' Oria screamed.

In moments, he was absorbed into them, seemingly gone from the world. Disintegrated into darkness. Lost.

Edril Sil breathed deep. 'Of course, there are so many bene-fits to this newfound power your mother gave to me when she forsook this world and left it for the taking. Your Eradomin warrior could be quite injurious to me if given the chance. Perhaps I shall find a way to return to Era, and then he and the rest of his kin can build me a new fortress.'

'Why tell me all of this?' Oria asked. Tears began to stream down her cheeks.

'Because, my Fäen, much as I wish it were different, you will not leave this chamber alive either. I really did enjoy our time together.'

Oria looked like she was going to be sick. Penta looked exhausted.

In mere moments, he crossed the room to Oria. 'This will only hurt for a moment.' Oria clawed at him, but he wrenched her arms to his chest and pulled her into a tight grasp. His hands began to shimmer.

Kyr saw a flash of red as Penta ran for him. They leapt, grabbing ahold of his shoulders, and bit him.

'Insolent child!' he yelled, turning to clutch at their hair.

Kyr felt panic rising within her. When she turned around, Penta was shielding a dark, sickening magic that swirled around them, threatening in its desperate hunger for them. Their flesh began to scar under the corrosive, sorcerous onslaught. Unnatural shadows crept about the room.

Kyr stepped forward and felt a sudden wetness. Water was seeping into her boots. She realized then that water was spilling across the floor and into the chamber through the walls, being drawn from the stone. She turned to Oria, who stood frightened against the wall. Kyr could see her right hand had that same shimmer.

She's drawing the water to us?

She turned back to Penta, still locked in a battle with their father.

'I see what you've done!' Penta screamed. 'Your power does not work on me!'

Edril Sil roared in anger and frustration. 'You think you can kill me?' he boomed. Locked in a stalemate of magic, he circled them. 'There is something you do not know. Something you will never remember, because I kept this little bit of knowledge to myself.'

'If you're trying to scare me, it won't work. You are nothing to me!' Penta taunted.

The chamber continued flooding with water.

'You and I are twin souls,' he said with a smirk. 'A bit of magic performed at your birth. Have you ever wondered why we are so evenly matched? Have you ever looked in the mirror and cursed my features? A part of me lives in you, and not just because I am your father. You see, I cannot die unless you do.'

'No,' Kyr whispered.

'You lie!' Penta sobbed. Outside, Kyr could hear thunder crack. His magic smelled of a sickening rot, and Kyr thought briefly of Two-Trees. It seemed to be seeking out Penta's power specifically, making the air itself inhospitable to it.

The water was up to Kyr's knees now. Edril Sil noticed it too. 'Oria, you have to stop now. You're flooding the chamber.' He sounded more disappointed than anything. 'This is what I get for letting you spend so much time with a daughter of Riparus.'

The distraction gave Penta what they needed. The stagnant water transformed, cascading and arcing toward him, enveloping him completely. Penta was going to try to drown him. They circled around the chamber behind him.

Oria was making her way across the chamber too, using her magic in tandem with Penta's. Kyr considered calling hers—she could feel it within her chest, trying to match some resonance that was just beyond her understanding, but each time it arose within her, Grym's crushed body flashed through her mind. She would never forgive herself if she did something like that to Penta or Oria, even if it meant ridding this world of a great evil. She couldn't take that risk. Even in a cold and terrible world, selfish as it might be, Kyr would rather have the people she loved.

Edril Sil clawed for Penta, coughing and sputtering as the water flooded in around him in the vestibule at the far end of the chamber. Kyr didn't understand it, but somehow he wrested control of the water from Penta and Oria and sent it crashing back down into the chamber. Oria went flying toward the wall with a sickening crack.

Kyr rushed toward her.

'No!' Penta roared. 'How could you? Haven't you taken enough from me?'

The sounds of their battle, crashing stone and rushing water, resumed as Kyr quickly checked Oria over for injuries. She was unconscious, but still breathing. Beside her, a strange looking dagger lay on the stone. The metal was odd, lightweight, with a dark gray tint and intricate engravings.

Kyr grabbed it. *I will protect my friends.*

She thought about Grym then. The counting house guards. The soldiers at the outpost. Vyktas. All the times when she did nothing.

Creeping closer, she tightened her grip on the blade's hilt and kept to Edril Sil's shadows. Going unnoticed came naturally to her.

Penta began to wail, a sound that was so inhuman Kyr set her jaw, advancing faster. All around Penta, the world began to blink out, darkness taking hold. Kyr could see only their red hair whipping about in the maelstrom. She felt a warm buzzing in her chest.

'No,' she whispered gently. '*Not yet.*' Still, she allowed the sensation to kindle.

But it wasn't her magic that set the chamber alight.

Kyr gasped.

Edril Sil heard, and his focus turned to her.

'And just who do you think you are?' he growled.

Dagger at the ready, she lunged for him.

'I'm Kyr ap fucking Sand!'

THE END

EPILOGUE
PENTA

THE FLAMES WERE SO GREAT, so devouring in their heat, they swallowed everything until all that was left was black shadow. Penta blinked, trying to understand the feeling and movement of their eyes. Nothing. All was smoke and ash.

'Oria! Kyr!'

They were met by silence.

'I can't see,' Penta cried. 'I can't see!'

There was a horrible burning smell. Were they still underground, in that accursed chamber? Had it become their tomb instead?

Fingertips crawling along stone. Feeling for ridges. Just like in the tower. Thousands of little ridges.

Their father's words echoed in their head. '*I cannot die unless you do.*'

Penta felt like crying. But their eyes ...

They could only focus on the fire. Burning, burning, burning. Instead of tears, their nose ran, and it stung their skin.

'Kyr!' they cried out again, but their throat was sore and tired.

Had none of them made it? Were they the last one left? *Again*?

How long would it be before they died here, with not even starlings to count?

ACKNOWLEDGMENTS

This book would not exist without community. The author would like to thank their charming husband for his endless love and support; the online reader and author communities; Holly, for the kind of friendship that makes all the difference; Rachel D., Heather, Sophie, and Aly, for reading and giving feedback on a truly atrocious first draft; Lindsey, Myanna, Rachel L., and Rowan, for the laughs, commiseration, and guidance; their brother, for staying up late into the night helping them build their author website and newsletter; and many more wonderful, fantasy-loving folks met along the way.

ABOUT THE AUTHOR

JULIA GREENSHAW hails from the Green Mountains of Vermont. When not writing, they can usually be found caring for their menagerie of animals, gardening, swimming in rivers, or hunting for mushrooms. *Knave of Sands* is their first novel.

For more:
https://www.juliagreenshawbooks.com/

www.ingramcontent.com/pod-product-compliance
Lightning Source LLC
Chambersburg PA
CBHW010518100726
47903CB00011B/2797